What Reviewers Are Saying

Holly & Ivey

"Perfectly sweet Christmas romance!"

Santa Dear

"an uplifting story that will give you the
holiday spirit
any time of the year"

Stand-In Mom

"a runaway good read"

"rich in emotional detail"

Romantic Times Book Reviews (4 1/2 Stars)
"charming romance"

The Marriage Solution

"a sweet story of love and parentin

For my husband, always.

With many thanks to my friends, without whom this book wouldn't be one-tenth as good: Lynn Cahoon, Carol Carson, Regan Loyd, and Pam Trader, and to Shawntelle Madison for her guidance.

Cover design by The Killion Group, Inc.

ISBN: 098860175
ISBN13: 978-0-9886017-4-1

The
WEDDING
RESCUE

Love in
LITTLE TREE
BOOK ONE

MEGAN KELLY

CHAPTER ONE

Lexi Marshall's pager beeped just as she pulled up to the ranch house on the Rocking W. She and their dad had split the morning rounds. The ranchers around Little Tree, Montana, respected that the vets' daughter/sister was getting married. No one would contact them except for emergencies.

The readout summoned her to the Rocking W.

Marco's foal, she thought, as she acknowledged the call.

Doris Gleason, Jack's housekeeper, stuck her head out of the front door into the June heat and dust. The woman had run the household for the past dozen years since Mr. and Mrs. Walker's deaths. Lexi's sister, Grace, didn't care two figs for housework, but she had definite ideas of her own. Watching which woman came out as alpha might be fun.

"Why, Lexi, what are you doing here this morning?"

Lexi climbed out of her truck, the rusty door creaking shut behind her. Grace's landscape of the Rocking W made a lovely wedding gift for the groom, but Lexi didn't understand the rush for him to have it. Still, she wasn't likely to argue with her sister, today of all days, and added it to her list of errands. She lifted out the painting. "Grace wanted Jack to have this gift, and she didn't want to fuss with it after the wedding."

Doris shook her head gently, so as not to disturb the curlers in her unnaturally dark red hair, and stepped back to allow Lexi inside. "You can leave it in the sitting room, unless you're supposed to watch him unwrap it."

"Don't know if I'll have time for that. I just got a page. Is Bella foaling?"

A frown drew lines between Doris's eyebrows as she glanced toward the barn. "They've been down there since about five this morning. You know how anxious Jack is about one. Is there trouble?"

"We weren't expecting any, but I'll have someone call you when we know."

Lexi grabbed her bag from the truck and rushed across the dry brown dirt. There would be a foaling kit in the barn, but it never hurt to be prepared.

Several men grouped around the stall near the birthing box, a large walled area that offered privacy and a sterile space. Bars along the top walls gave humans a view without disturbing the mare. The men stood back and kept their voices low, but the room didn't thrum with tension. This wasn't their first foal on the ranch. Nature ruled on the Rocking W, and this birth would happen with as little human interference as possible. Which made a call all the more notable.

She located Jack Walker and his younger brother, Clint, near the rails, taking a peek. Her brother-in-law-to-be wore tension across his broad shoulders. Clint, at twenty-five, stood as tall as Jack, and just as uneasy.

Jack's favorite horse, six-year-old Marco, had been gelded the past July after he was found to have a low sperm count, with weak mobility. However, within a few days after the procedure, the horse impregnated Bella with some remaining sperm. Jack had laughed with pride at his incorrigible steed.

"Hey, Lexi," Clint said.

Jack turned with eyebrows raised. "That was fast. We just called."

"Miz Lexi."

She nodded toward the cowhand who spoke as others turned to acknowledge her. She waved hellos at the other men. "Hi, George."

"Didn't expect to see you today, what with the wedding and all." George Brooks tipped off his hat, showing sweat-matted dark curls. He reminded her of Hoss on the old TV show, "Bonanza." Big, gentle, and sweet, but fully able to do the tough jobs.

Lexi wanted to hug him, much as she would a child, and ease his mind. She gave him a smile instead. "Pregnant ladies don't pay much attention to calendars."

She turned to another ranch hand, glad to see Rob Reynolds. "I'm going to need to wash up."

The gray-haired cowboy gestured toward the corner. He had watched her tag along with her father from toddlerhood. "Soap, paper towels, and water are over here, Doc Lexi."

She smiled her thanks and went to clean up.

"No need for that," Jack insisted.

"If I have to step in, I want to be ready."

"Let's call your dad again," Jack said. "You're supposed to be helping Grace today."

Lexi shot him a sour look, but instead of defending her position as a fully qualified, though *female* vet, she stepped up to the rail. Bella sprawled out on a sufficient layer of bedding, her tail was wrapped, and no obstacles were on the floor. A pile of towels sat ready. The scent of Ivory soap indicated Bella had been washed. The sac was out with one foot visible. Lexi nodded in approval. "How's our girl?"

"I was about to ask you the same about Grace." Jack tipped his head toward the stall. "Bella stopped pushing as soon as the foreleg appeared. She's been resting too long."

Lexi checked the breeding log, noting the time labor

started, then inspected Bella. The mare rested, breathing normal, no sweats. Hay stuck to her sides and back, indicating she'd been rolling. "She looks good. And Grace is fine, too. Already worrying about details." She ran a finger across the page again. "When did her water break?"

"Grace's?" Clint flashed a grin, his California tan smoother than his brother's hard-earned rancher-brown. Both men had dark blond hair, though Jack's was a little more like wheat, whereas Clint's tended toward platinum. Model-handsome, Jack would sell more Western wear, his rugged frame fit and muscular. Clint had the lean strength of a rock climber, despite growing up herding cattle on the Rocking W.

She aimed a playful glare at Clint. "Grace is no broodmare."

Jack, hours from becoming her brother-in-law, slanted her a look, an indication he heard her message loud and clear. "It broke twenty-seven minutes ago. It should have come by now. Bella's a few weeks early. Maybe the foal's not strong enough."

"Bella's not early for her first and not if it's a filly." Lexi watched for a reaction in and saw none. She assumed he'd hoped for a colt, for another Marco, but perhaps he didn't care. He hadn't wanted a sonogram just to determine the sex, and Bella hadn't required one for health issues.

"It's a miracle foal," he said, referring to Marco's having

been gelded. "I don't want to waste time if we should help. How long can you stay?"

She blinked. This wasn't a social visit. "I'll be here as long as Bellissima takes to deliver."

Ranchers were used to delivering foals and calves. Jack and the men had weathered some rocky births. The last foaling she'd attended here with her father had been a stillbirth, and the mare had been put down after complications. Jack had administered the injection himself.

"Grace won't like it," Clint predicted.

"Grace doesn't need me for the time being. She's getting her hair done."

Jack's gaze traveled to Lexi's hair pulled back in its customary ponytail, strands of yellow falling in her face. She shrugged. Neither of them would mistake her for a fashion model or a famous artist like her sister.

His hair looked rumpled, and she supposed he'd come to the barn straight from bed. His blue chambray work shirt had more than a few wrinkles and smudges, perhaps pulled on from the day before. Excitement and fatigue mingled behind his green eyes.

"She's pushing again," Clint said, and they turned to see Bellissima straining in the hay.

Everyone in the barn tensed, waiting to see if the birth

would resume normally. Lexi ran her gaze over the mare and was reassured by the clear focus of the mare.

"Good girl, Bella," she whispered to comfort the men. "Let's get that foal born before it's time to take the wedding pictures—or else *Grace* is going to have a cow."

Clint smothered his laugh with a hand over his mouth while Jack merely raised an eyebrow at her. "Grace would understand if I'm late for photos, as long as I make it for the wedding. Which I will."

But he glanced at the clock on the wall. Just before nine a.m.

"We have about seven hours to see this through. Plenty of time. She's picking up the pace." If Bella didn't tire out again and her foal presented properly, as it appeared to be doing, Lexi wouldn't need to assist. Nevertheless, she checked the stall for a pair of shoulder-length obstetrical sleeves. If the other foot and the nose appeared with the next few thrusts, Bella would edge closer to the home stretch.

"I checked earlier," Jack said, "and the foal is in position."

With a huff from the horse, more of the sac appeared, looking like a white balloon half full of water. Bella grunted with the next contraction and the other foot slid out. Two of the men peered in then withdrew. Huffing and grunting, the mare rocked the nose into view, then lay back.

"I hate this part." George appeared a little gray in the jowls. "Do you mind if I step outside, boss? I can't finish up barn chores till she delivers anyway."

"Go ahead."

They watched Bella's contractions for a few minutes. The mare kicked and rolled onto her back.

Clint frowned and looked at Jack. "Is she getting the foal in position?"

Jack shrugged. "Maybe I was wrong before."

"It's not usually unknown," she said, "but it doesn't indicate a problem. Sometimes a first-time mom is just seeking comfort from the pain, and trying to get that alien inside her to wiggle out."

Clint smiled. "Annabeth is inside so you don't have to put it quite so simply."

"Should someone go get her?" Lexi thought of the little six-year-old tomboy. "I'm sure Anna will want to see the foal born. And help you name it."

"Let's make sure everything goes smoothly first," Jack said.

She couldn't fault him for protecting his daughter. The child would have to learn the realities of ranch life, but perhaps not with the wedding festivities today.

Another heave and grunt from Bella brought forth the head.

Jack grasped the bars, strain shadowing his face.

"She's doing fine." Lexi hated to jinx the procedure by saying it aloud, but Jack needed reassurance. Maybe humor would help. "Were you this nervous when Anna was born?"

He jolted back, releasing the bars as though his hands had caught fire. "What?"

She laughed. "I don't remember you this anxious in the past."

Then she recalled that both the mare and colt had died last time and wished she'd kept her mouth shut. "Bella and Marco's foal will be a fighter. And if it's not, I'm here."

His short nod didn't indicate any confidence in her abilities.

Bella gave a huge snorting sigh after the next contraction and rested.

And rested.

Lexi watched the clock. Judged the mare's strength. Made her decision. "I'm going in to check on her."

She wasn't surprised to find Jack on her heels.

He proved a well-trained assistant, staying out of her way, and doing as she asked when he was needed. "I hate to pull the foal out," Jack commented. "Do you think she needs our help?"

Lexi massaged the horse and encouraged her in soothing tones. "Let's give her a few more minutes to do it herself."

"Where did you learn midwife massage?"

"New technique."

"I think it's working. She's not as tense."

"She also knows we're right here." Lexi swept a long stroke down Bella's neck.

Bella roused and delivered the foal's shoulders and eventually the hind quarters with minimal assistance from the humans.

The foal didn't raise its head or kick its leg to break the sac. Lexi pierced it and cleared the nostrils then stepped back to see if the mare would approach and lick her newborn clean. When Bella's maternal instinct kicked in, a thrill of relief ran through Lexi. "She's a natural."

Jack grinned. "It's a colt."

They slid out of the stall and watched as the newborn struggled to stand, urged on by his mother. Lexi kept an eye on the dangling cord and sac until Bella reclined once again on the hay.

After seven minutes of rocking and error, the colt brought his front feet into the correct position. One leg remained trapped under him.

"Come on, little guy," Clint muttered under his breath.

"Be patient," Jack replied in quiet tones. "I don't remember *you* walking a few minutes after you were born."

"But I'm a Walker now."

Everyone groaned. Now that the tension of birth was over, they could joke. As soon as the foal stood, they'd return to their chores. Some of the men had already been out with the cattle and would hear the news later. Good news, Lexi hoped, crossing her fingers as she eyed the colt.

He positioned his front legs and pushed up. Wobbled on the three legs and fell. If an animal could look confused, this one did. Lexi smiled. No matter how many times she witnessed a foal's first steps, it always tickled her. Such scrawny legs had to lift and hold up almost one hundred pounds of horse.

"He's determined," Jack said as the colt tried again, standing this time with his muscles trembling.

"We should call him Crusty," Clint said, "for sheer grit."

Lexi stifled a laugh. "Your uncle wouldn't appreciate the reason, though he might be touched that you named Marco's only foal after him."

"I didn't agree to that," Jack put in.

"You're right," Clint said. "We shouldn't hang such a cussed name on such a young horse. Let's see…Christopher Walker. C.W.? Seaweed?" He shook his head. "No. Christopher…Columbus?"

Jack nodded, watching the colt. "I can see that. An adventurer. We'll see if he has any personality traits that support such a name."

"Annabeth will want to call him Stripe," Clint said, referring to the thin white strip down its face.

"Or Socks." Jack nodded to the white markings on the colt's legs. "Which is why she doesn't get to name him, either."

"You'll name him?" Lexi asked.

Jack cocked his head. "I thought I'd let Grace name him. Her first Rocking W horse, born on our wedding day."

"Awww," Clint teased him.

Jack butted his shoulder into his brother. Lexi packed up her bag. "She'll appreciate that, Jack. As long as you don't mind if he's called Van Gogh or Rembrandt."

Clint laughed. "If he's fast, we'll call him Can Go. Or Van Gogh Can Go."

"I don't need your input." Jack knelt beside her. "Let me take that to your truck for you."

"I'm perfectly capable—"

"I know you are, Lexi. I'm not doubting your abilities, just being polite."

"Sorry." She stepped back and followed him out.

"Why were you here so quickly?" Jack asked. "I don't think you said."

"Oh, I forgot to tell you. I delivered a gift from Grace. It's in your foyer."

Jack scowled at her battered vehicle as he tossed her bag

into her pickup bed, wondering how the rusty truck didn't break down and strand her. Not a good idea in the isolated hills of eastern Montana, no matter the weather, which he'd told her countless times. But did she listen to sense? Hell, no.

She always took exception to his concern, twisting it around to him not liking female vets. Jack didn't object to a woman seeing to his animals. He didn't object—much—to the men being distracted by her. But something about Lexi got to him like a rash of poison oak.

"You need to tell Marco he's a father," Lexi said with a smile.

"I hope the colt's as good a ranch horse as his sire." Out on the range, the horse acted as an extension of Jack, anticipating his commands. Other horses responded; Marco read his mind. "Do you think the doc will be out to check on the colt tomorrow?"

Lexi's lips tightened. Which was a shame, given they were as full and pink as Grace's. Not that he paid much attention to Lexi's lips.

For Pete's sakes. Lexi reminded him of his fiancée. He didn't like it. The twin sisters were as different as a daisy and an orchid, and yet, he had a strong reaction every time he saw Lexi. She put his nerves on edge, and always had.

"I only meant to save you the trip, Lexi. You know I hate

this excuse for a truck."

Lexi shot him a skeptical glance. If she had any of Grace's charm, she didn't waste it on him.

It wasn't as though he'd ever burned daylight while contemplating Lexi's charms. Sure, once upon a time, he'd acknowledged how she looked good dancing at Kerr's Grill, her peachy dress swinging around her knees and a smile lighting her face, making him consider asking for a dance. And sure, maybe once or twice, he'd envisioned taking her to a movie in the next town over, and putting his arm around her in a dark theater, then claiming a kiss or two on the way home.

He hadn't acted on those impulses, thank the Lord. That would have made things awkward when Grace returned home from Australia, looking like every man's dreams—like Jack's dreams, anyway. Grace embodied everything feminine and soft and sweet. She would fit into his life here on the ranch, do her paintings, and raise Annabeth, along with whatever little ones they had together.

Grace wouldn't go tearing across the country in a battered truck to save a critter, or go head-to-head with an ornery bull or a cussed old rancher. And she'd never ride off on horseback by herself, like his wife, Sarabeth, and get herself killed in the back country.

Lexi was a different matter. She and her sister only shared

their good looks.

"How's Grace?" he asked, for something neutral to say.

Lexi smiled, her blue eyes like the sky on a cloudless day. "I told you, she's fine. She's so calm, it makes *me* nervous. I keep waiting for an attack of cold feet or at least some doubts, but she's eerily contained."

Jack's chest swelled with satisfaction. "Why wouldn't she be? She knows I'll take care of her."

"I didn't mean to imply otherwise. I just expect a bride to be nervous, no matter who the groom is."

Placated, Jack nodded. "Your sister knows what she wants. I'm lucky she chose me."

Lexi moved her bag to the toolbox and snapped it shut. "I'll see if Dad can check in tomorrow."

Jack put a hand on her arm. "If he's busy, you could come. Just borrow the doc's truck."

Lexi pivoted sharply past him toward the truck door, her yellow ponytail swishing across her shoulders, sassy and dismissive at the same time.

"Lexi."

She didn't stop, just climbed into the cab. The idea of her in that rattletrap gave him indigestion. After the wedding today, when they'd officially become family, he'd talk her into working in the doc's office where she'd be safe caring for small pets.

Puppies and kittens would give her a nice break from horns and testicles.

"I'll see you later," she said. "In whatever vehicle I see fit to drive."

"Lexi!"

Her once-blue rusty pickup didn't slow, even though he knew Lexi heard him holler her name. How they'd get along as in-laws he couldn't imagine. Sparks flew when they got together, most likely because they brought out the worst traits in one another.

They would make one hell of a family. Good thing they had Grace to keep the peace.

Lexi stared at the beautiful wedding dress her twin sister held toward her. Lovely satin shimmered and beckoned, and pearls gleamed in the light of the church's dressing room. Their mother's veil lay on top, luring her closer with its lace and pearls.

"Go ahead," Grace said. "Try it on."

Lexi shook her head in denial of the gown's promises. "I know what I'd look like. I've seen you in it."

"It's not just how it looks. A wedding dress *feels* different than any ordinary gown you've ever worn." Grace arched a brow. "Although no one would say you wear many dresses, let alone gowns."

A grin crossed Lexi's face. Grace traveled the world painting, gaining renown for her outdoor scenes and use of color and texture. Lexi's work as a vet kept her happy with her life in eastern Montana. As the crow flew, Little Tree lay three hours northeast of Billings, but it felt like a world away from everywhere.

"There's no time," Lexi protested.

Grace grabbed her purse and pulled out the watch Jack had given her for an engagement present. He'd hoped to curb Grace's lack of regard for schedules. She glanced at it, sobered for a moment, then turned to Lexi. "There's just enough time. Besides, if we run late, they'll wait for the bride, right? Come on, sis, share this moment with me."

Lexi capitulated, thankful to remove the goldenrod bridesmaid dress that made her look like a sickening weed. She could deny Grace very little, and if she were honest, the white dress tempted her. Lexi wasn't anywhere near to finding someone to build a life with, and she wouldn't choose an elaborate, fairy tale gown when the time came. Something with straighter lines and quiet elegance appealed to her more than Grace's outrageous miles of puff and extravagance. But, she justified as Grace fastened the thirty satin-covered buttons up the back, who could resist trying on this fantasy dress?

"Don't turn to the mirror yet," Grace instructed. "I want you to get the full effect with Mom's veil."

When Lexi married, she would also incorporate the veil in her ensemble. Their mom had died in a car accident when the girls were twelve, leaving them to the loving care of their dad. Today brought back that grief, that emptiness, those wishes for their mom's support and approval. Both girls missed her keenly on special occasions, and this one had been particularly hard. Lexi had tried to fill that gap for her sister throughout their lives and especially during the wedding preparations, but no one could.

Grace turned her to the mirror. Lexi's breath caught in her chest. She'd seen Grace in the dress, and yet, it did feel different. Lexi looked like a bride, in a beautiful dream. Still not to her taste but oh, so gorgeous.

Behind her in the mirror, Grace's eyes glistened with tears. "You'll make a beautiful bride."

"Someday, I hope," Lexi said. "I want the happiness you have with Jack."

Grace's grip tightened on her shoulders. "I'm not going to marry him."

Lexi froze in shock. Had she misheard? Her sister's blue eyes shone full of cold sanity. "What? That's not funny." But neither woman smiled. "Don't be ridiculous, Grace. The church is full. Jack's waiting for you to walk down the aisle."

"I can't."

Lexi's heart raced with alarm. "It's just cold feet. You're nervous, that's it. But Jack loves you, and you love him. Everything will be fine."

"I do care for him, Lexi. Too much to marry him."

"What does that mean?" Lexi stared at her sister's reflection, stunned. Her twin appeared rational and calm, despite her declaration. Lexi, on the other hand, could barely draw breath to form words.

"Exactly what I said. I'm not going to do it." Grace turned away and yanked on the sundress she'd worn to the church. Lexi took off the veil and let it fall to the sofa. She had to talk some sense into her sister. Guests were seated. The wedding music played. How long did she have to get into her own dress and button Grace into this one?

Panicked, Lexi grabbed Grace's elbow and spun her sister back around. She fixed her twin with a smile. *Be calm.* "This is just nerves talking."

"No, it's not. Jack's a great guy, but I can't be married to him." Grace glanced around the floor. "Where are my sandals?"

Lexi spotted Grace's flats and kicked them behind the couch. While Grace searched, Lexi would somehow convince her to change her mind. Or she'd run for help.

"I'll have to wear these." Grace gestured to her white satin heels.

"Stop it, Grace. Don't do something you'll regret."

Grace set her hands on her hips. "Now, are you going to help me get out of here or not?"

"I'm not. Because you've lost your mind. You took the wedding photos this afternoon." Lexi flung her arm out, gesturing toward the door. "There are already pictures of you as the happy couple."

"Then you'll just have to explain it to everyone."

Lexi's jaw dropped with astonishment. Her insides turned hollow and cold. She'd bailed Grace out of enough scrapes in their twenty-five years to recognize the dread inside her. Grace, the impulsive one, fully expected her to do this. "You're crazy. No way am I going out there and breaking his heart."

"Be sure to explain it just right," Grace said, "otherwise the Rocking W will use that new veterinarian in Cat Creek. Jack won't be able to face Dad if you screw it up and embarrass him."

"If *I* embarrass him?"

"You and Dad can't afford to lose the business, now that a younger vet started up his practice."

"Jack doesn't trust anyone except Dad with his animals. He even doubts me half the time." A proud man, he wouldn't take kindly to being made to look a fool, either. Her stomach cramped with doubt. He wouldn't want to see her—an exact copy of Grace—again after this.

Scenarios raced through her mind, none of them good. She took a calming breath.

"You can fix it, Lexi. You always do." Grace cupped the wristwatch in her palm before extending it. "Give this back to him, okay? It was his mom's."

"No."

Grace huffed out a breath. "Look, Lexi, it's better that he's a little hurt now than get stuck with a wife who doesn't want to be married. I can't be tied down on his family's ranch forever."

Why hadn't Grace chosen a second bridesmaid? Maybe someone else could talk sense into her sister.

She glanced at the door for help. Who could she call? Their dad? Cousin Rachel, who'd acted as a big sister to them both? Not that anyone could talk Grace out of something she'd set her mind to doing.

Lexi's stomach churned. Poor Jack. He'd be so humiliated, as well as hurt. And angry. Despite their frequent butting of heads, Lexi would never wish this on him.

"Grace, don't do this," she begged, even as Grace forced the watch onto Lexi's wrist. "Think of Jack, out there waiting, with all his family and friends watching. And yours. You can't leave him at the altar. This is just too melodramatic."

And so like you.

Tears formed in Grace's eyes. "Do you want me to be miserable just to keep Jack's feelings from being hurt?"

Lexi shook her head, contrite. "Of course not. If I really thought you didn't want to marry him, I'd stand behind you one hundred percent. You know I would. I always have."

Grace grabbed Lexi's hands with her freezing ones. "Then stand behind me now."

"You're just stressed, Grace. Marriage is a big change, especially as you'll be a stepmother, too. I know you love Jack. If you don't go out there and marry him, you'll regret it later."

"I can't." Grace's fingers covered her mouth. "I'm sorry."

"Help me out of this dress." Lexi twisted to inspect the buttons then looked to her sister when she didn't move. "Give me a hand here."

Grace shook her head and retreated toward the door, which opened directly to the parking lot.

"What are you doing? Grace? Help me out of it."

"I'm sorry."

The light bulb flashed on. Lexi went cold with shock. "You stuck me in this dress on purpose?"

"You were attracted to him before I returned to town. If I hadn't come home and ruined things, you'd probably be the one marrying him today."

"Never mind what I might have felt or not felt." Lexi ignored the heat of embarrassment washing over her body. "Jack barely even likes me. The point is, you did come back, and he wants to spend his life with you."

Grace shook her head. "I proposed to him."

The bombshell poleaxed Lexi. All other thoughts vanished. "You did?"

"To save his ranch. Crusty yelled at Jack and threatened to give the ranch to Jack's cousin, who has sons to work the land." Grace shook her head. "Crusty wanted boys to inherit and discounted any claim Annabeth might have, even though she's Jack's daughter. You know how old-fashioned Crusty is about 'women's roles.' "

Lexi nodded, well-acquainted with the man who had earned his nickname many times over. He resembled the Old Prospector from *Toy Story 2,* but without a lighter side.

"He promised to keep Jack on as manager," Grace continued, "like he is now. But Jack could never hope to inherit. Crusty accused Jack of still grieving for his wife and said how he, Crusty, couldn't wait forever for him to have a male heir. So I said we were getting married."

"Grace!"

"I know, I know." She groaned. "I didn't think. I just re-acted."

As usual.

"But I didn't want Jack to lose out on inheriting his family's ranch one day. He's given his life to the Rocking W. He looked so miserable, so unnerved."

"What did Jack say?" Listening to the story was akin to watching a tornado approach. Lexi stood rooted, expecting disaster, but unable to glance away.

"Jack is too much of a gentleman to call me a liar, so he agreed. When we were alone later, I apologized for being impulsive, and he called our getting married a good idea."

"A good idea?" Talk about damned with faint praise.

Grace shrugged. "He's not exactly a sweet talker."

Lexi sighed. "Okay, look. I'm sure you've dreamed of a fairy tale proposal all your life and this fell short. Way short. But you've got the prince from the story, Grace. Can't you just be happy with that?"

"No. No, I'm sorry. I can't." With that, Grace rushed out of the room into the twilight.

Leaving Lexi with the monumental job of informing the groom he'd been jilted.

CHAPTER TWO

How could she do it? What would she say?

Lexi gazed at the door. What fool had designated the bride's dressing area to a room with an outer exit? She watched, but it didn't re-open. Grace didn't return.

A high pitch of dismay shrilled through Lexi's head. Her knees buckled. She dropped onto the couch and picked up the veil. Fragile, transparent, delicate. Like Grace's feelings for Jack.

Lexi could picture Jack's face contorting with anguish, much as it had last year when her dad told him his mare would likely bleed to death after the stillbirth. Jack's green eyes had darkened, lines creased his tanned face, and his body slumped. After a split second, he'd straightened and set about doing what needed to be done, clenching his jaw and putting aside his emotions. In the adjacent stall, she doubted Jack knew she'd seen him falter.

That moment had softened her attitude toward him. She could more easily tolerate his constant second-guessing of her methods, knowing it stemmed from affection for his animals.

Staring hard at Grace's veil misted the recollection. No way did she want Jack to suffer again, but she couldn't do a thing about it now. Her sister had fled.

How could Lexi make telling him easier? Say it fast? Be discreet? Call him over to the parsonage and break it to him there? He'd still have to face the congregation, face his family, face his friends.

You can fix it, Lexi, Grace had said. *You always do.* Yes, Lexi had become very inventive while cleaning up Grace's messes, but this time her sister expected too much.

A burst of anger had her tugging at the dress, but she couldn't twist far enough to reach more than a few buttons at the neckline. How could Grace have put her in this position? It would have been hard enough to tell him there wouldn't be a wedding, that Grace had run off. Now she'd have to say it while appearing as the exact image of his bride.

Lexi had to come up with a solid plan, quickly. Familiar music sounded through the thin door. The next song would cue the bridesmaid—her—to enter the foyer. There went her explaining time. Any minute now, the bride should appear in the vestibule, ready to be escorted down the aisle.

A light rap came at the door before it opened to reveal Jack's daughter, Annabeth. She was reputedly the image of her mother, Sarabeth, but in Lexi's mind, "Anna" fit the small tomboy better.

A lively smile lit the six-year-old's face. "Miss Rachel said you're s'posed to be out by the church doors. Dad's going to be *sooo* mad. He doesn't like to be late or have to wait."

He'll like the reason for the delay even less.

"You look pretty." Anna reached out toward Grace's dress but didn't quite make contact. "I shouldn't touch it. I'll get it dirty."

"You look pretty, too, sweetie. Do you like your dress?" Lexi had to keep up the pretense. She couldn't let Anna tell him that Grace had left.

Anna twirled, her goldenrod skirt belling out at her knees. The dark yellow enhanced the girl's sunny nature. In the same color, Lexi had worried people would sneeze at her in the pollen-colored dress. Black sausage curls bounced around Anna's face, and her dark blue eyes lit with pleasure. "I love it. I'm going to wear this dress every day to school, and I'm going to keep it real clean so Doris doesn't get mad."

Lexi chuckled at the idea of Jack's housekeeper being angry with the sweet girl in front of her, although Lexi had heard of Anna's tendency to find trouble.

Anna tipped her head. "Have you got a cold?"

"No. Why?"

"You sound funny."

Anna expected the bride before her to sound like Grace, whose tone rang very slightly higher than Lexi's. "I'm fine, sweetie."

"Good. I don't want you to be too sick to marry Dad." She took Lexi's hand in both of hers, staring at the floor for a moment before locking her earnest gaze on Lexi's. "I don't remember my other mother. I'm glad we get to marry you."

Lexi froze, her throat closing with horror. A beat passed as she gazed at the girl. She'd never heard Anna refer to her mother before. Lexi felt the pain of her own mother's death rip through her as raw as though it had just happened. What had Grace done, leaving this child? Anna would be devastated at another loss.

The girl skipped to the door, then turned in the opening. "Are you coming, Mommy?"

Mommy? Lexi's breath formed a ball in her throat. What could she say that wouldn't have the girl in tears? "I'll be right there."

Lexi swallowed a bubble of hysteria as the door closed behind Anna. How could Grace have done this? Two hearts would break tonight.

Another knock sounded at the door. "Grace, Lexi," Rachel

called. "It's time."

"Coming." Lexi jammed on the veil and settled the lace over her face, though it offered scant protection. She took a deep breath and set her jaw for the task at hand. She'd rather extract sperm from a bull. Without gloves.

Lexi opened the door but blocked Rachel's view to the rest of the room. Rachel was a wild card who might not deem protecting Grace to be the most important factor here. Rachel's brisk, no-nonsense manner had always kept her and Grace on their toes. Even her light brown hair didn't dare to droop from its fashionable bun at her nape.

"You look like a princess." Rachel checked out the room. "Where's Lexi? It's almost time for her entry, but maybe she can calm down Uncle Kevin before she goes up the aisle. Your dad's yanking at his tie like it's a hangman's rope."

Lexi yearned for her dad or Rachel to help her through this, but common decency overruled her needs. She should tell Jack first. She owed him that, on the family's behalf.

"Lexi's not here. I need to talk to Jack." Lexi's knees shook hard enough to topple the Tower of Pisa. She attempted to keep her voice level, as it, too, shook with nerves.

"She's not here?" Rachel shoved the bouquet in Lexi's hand and wrapped her arm around Lexi's waist, herding her out the door. "Is she sick?"

"I'm afraid she's going to be. I need to talk to Jack. Now."

"It's too late for that. The ceremony's already started. We're just waiting for you. You can talk to Jack in a minute— when you say 'I do.'"

Lexi let herself be rushed across the lobby only because it brought her closer to her father, the one person she could rely on. His black hair was peppered with gray and showed the ruffles where he'd run his hand through it. He yanked on the hem of his black tuxedo jacket and hunched his broad shoulders at the unaccustomed restriction. His tie lay askew where nervous fingers had fiddled with it. The sure, steady demeanor that calmed animals had deserted him.

Her chest tightened with love and worry. He'd given her everything. Widowed at forty-one, he'd raised her and Grace on his own, from pre-teenagers to successful women. He'd devoted all his love and attention to them for fourteen years. Would Jack really turn to a different vet? The loss would have a mild impact on the business, but what if others in the county followed suit?

Anna's hand slid into hers, and Lexi found a smile for the girl. The girl about to lose her second mother.

Darn you, Grace. What a mess.

"You look fine," Rachel scolded him as he pulled at his tie again. She stepped away, talking to Anna about dropping petals.

He studied Lexi, and her heart pounded as she waited to be

unmasked.

"You look beautiful in your mother's veil. She'd be so proud of you." He squeezed her hand. "Where's your sister?"

Lexi straightened his tie again, needing to distract him. He'd always been her ally, and she really needed one now. "Dad, do you think I could talk to Jack real fast?"

Her dad frowned. "What's the matter?"

"I have something to tell him."

"Can't it wait?"

"Not really."

Her dad's mouth dropped open. "Are you... expecting?"

"A baby?" Lexi's surprised gasp drew gazes from the back pews. She groaned.

George Brooks stepped out of the corner of the foyer. What was Jack's ranch hand doing out here? She hadn't seen him there, which surprised her, given he stood as tall as Jack. His bulky muscles didn't exactly blend with the silk ficus tree bedecked with ribbons and doves from the corner where he'd emerged. On the other hand, she had a few things on her mind that overshadowed even someone so large.

"Miz Marshall," George said, touching his forelock as though he wore a hat, "we all wish you the best today."

"Thank you—" Lexi bit her tongue to keep from saying his name. Had Grace ever met the man? Thank goodness she wouldn't have to keep up this pretense for long. She'd never fool anyone.

"Is Miz Lexi okay? I didn't see her, and your cousin looked mighty concerned when the music started playing."

"She's fine. If you'll excuse me."

George shrank back behind the artificial tree. She regretted being short with the man who had been so kind when she came out to the Rocking W. But she had more dire matters on her hands than reassuring a near-stranger of her well-being. She couldn't let her father continue to worry that she—or Grace, rather—was pregnant. She leaned close and whispered, "Dad, no. Don't worry about a baby. Not happening."

Relief tinged his indulgent smile. "Not yet maybe, but it won't be long."

Rachel reappeared and tweaked the lace of the veil into smooth lines before fastening the buttons Lexi had opened at her neck when trying to escape the gown. She squeezed Lexi's cold hand with a smile. "See you inside."

Panic closed her throat. Could she get Jack out here first?

Her cousin bent and reminded Anna that flower girls don't skip down the aisle, and they both disappeared into the nave.

The last notes of the bridesmaid's processional trailed off without Lexi making an entrance. Rustling and muttering floated out from the church as the confused congregation whispered.

She didn't have time to explain anything.

"You never answered," her dad said. "Where's Lexi?"

"Sick."

His face creased with concern as his gaze shot over her shoulder to the dressing room. "You told that cowboy she was fine."

"I didn't think he needed to know."

"Should I go see about her?"

"She's not going to make it today." Lexi's feet felt encased in heavy work boots. Her conscience pinched her. All attention should be on the bride, yet he was concerned about her welfare. "Don't worry, it's not fatal. She feared she would faint or something, so she's not coming to the altar."

Lexi closed her eyes. Did that even make sense? Lying to her dad made her a horrible daughter, despite trying to protect Grace and Jack.

"But who will be your maid of honor?" Her dad's gaze strayed down the hall again.

"It's weird not having my twin by my side," she admitted with a bit of irony. "We've dreamed of this moment since we were four."

"I can't believe you're old enough to marry." He gazed at her, a little misty-eyed. "You look as radiant as your mother did on our wedding day. You're both such beautiful brides."

She widened her eyes to hold sentimental tears in check. Her mother would have known what to say to Grace.

"Dad—"

"Grace—"

They smiled. "You go," she said.

"This is the last moment when you're still my little girl. I have to say I'm proud of the woman you've become and the way you chase your dreams with such determination. People might think Lexi's my favorite because she's more like me. But you're just like your mother, so how could I prefer either of you over the other one? Never doubt that I love you. I love you both."

Lexi swallowed tears and stiffened her backbone. If she gave in to emotion, anxiety would have her blabbing the whole story. Would her dad still be proud of her and Grace for this? Wanting to tell Jack first started to seem like a stupid idea, but since it was her *only* idea, so she was going with it.

Her dad grinned at her. "Are you ready, my amazing girl?"

Lexi nodded as she accepted the time had come for Plan B. Since she hadn't figured out the A part and hadn't thought of a B yet, her brain went into overdrive.

Her dad would help her get down the aisle to Jack, and she would whisper a frantic plea for privacy. They could step outside where she'd break the news to him without witnesses. Once she explained why she hadn't told the truth, her dad would forgive her. Protecting Grace had always been her job.

As she and her dad rounded the door hiding them from view, the first deep notes of the fanfare for "The Wedding March" boomed, echoing in her chest. Her heart raced. People rose, blocking her view of the altar where Jack waited. Waited for Grace. Lexi swallowed the dread in her throat.

Her legs trembled, and from the corner of her eye, she noticed her father glance at her. From behind the veil, she turned up the wattage of her smile, just as Grace would do. Confident, poised, elegant Grace, who exemplified the very definition of her name. It had never been so hard to pretend to be her twin.

Family smiled. Friends smiled. Lexi smiled harder.

She took a deep breath for courage and nearly gagged. The fragrance of the yellow roses blended with the deeper scents of freesias and gardenias, clogging Lexi's breathing. Surely that explained her difficulty drawing in air when she spotted Jack.

His black tux emphasized the width of his shoulders and the tails showcased the muscled leanness of his waist. Yellow and red rays from the stained glass window behind him gleamed in his golden brown hair as the sun set. Compelling enough to be a model, no one would call Jack pretty. He was bold and strong and had a presence, whether in the saddle or in the barn caring for a newborn foal. Now his green eyes glowed with love as Lexi advanced toward him. She stumbled.

Her dad counter-balanced her misstep and shot her a surprised look. Grace had probably never stumbled, even when first learning to walk. It wouldn't be dignified.

Lexi only hoped she wouldn't fall on her face. She'd thought telling Jack would be the hard part, but walking down the aisle with all those people watching gave her the jitters.

Anna peeped around the people standing in the rows of pews. Her sweet face radiated happiness. Small fingers waggled a hello. Lexi relaxed a bit and gave her a genuine smile. She prayed Grace returned soon to be the mother this girl needed.

Lexi and her father reached the altar where Jack and his Clint waited. Her dad lifted the sides of the veil with his fingertips, as though afraid of tearing delicate memories. Lexi ducked as he flipped it over her head and smoothed it across her hair.

He jerked as though she'd jabbed him with a cattle prod. His brows crashed together; his gaze bore into hers. Heat flared in her face, even as ice coated her skin. His gaze flicked to Jack, then the doorway, and back to her before he leaned close. "Do you know what you're doing?" he whispered, incredulity clear in his tone.

Lexi registered Jack's start of surprise in her peripheral vision. Had he heard her father? Or had he recognized her as the wrong bride? Surely he'd stop the ceremony. People shifted in the pews. Beads of sweat coated her skin. When Jack didn't say anything, she exhaled shakily.

She eyed her father. What would he do? She nodded, trying to convey confidence with her expression. Confidence that she knew what she was doing. Confidence that she could explain the situation to Jack. Confidence that she didn't feel.

Jack relaxed, and Lexi let out a breath. He hadn't recognized her yet. Though maybe it would be better if he did.

"I just want you to be happy." Her dad kissed her cheek. "I love you, baby. Good luck."

She threw her arms around him and hugged him close, losing a few yellow rose petals as her bouquet thudded against his back. "It'll be okay. I can explain everything."

The congregation chuckled at what they must have regarded as an uncharacteristic show of nerves from Grace.

As her dad found his seat, Lexi turned toward Jack and took his outstretched hand. She leaned close to ask him to step outside with her. "Jack, we need to talk."

"Dearly beloved," the minister began, his somber tone booming over Lexi's words. She held on to Jack's hand, gripping it for courage.

"Jack," she mouthed quietly, widening her eyes to convey urgency.

"You look beautiful," Jack whispered.

She blinked. What a lovely way to calm his bride, but so not the point. Lamely, she replied, "You do, too."

Pastor Compton quailed her with a look, much as he had all her life. She clamped her mouth closed, frustrated.

Jack filled out his formal wear without appearing "fancified," as he'd objected to Grace. He stole Lexi's breath away, even though he didn't belong to her. She had no idea what she'd do with a man this overwhelmingly male.

A few wicked thoughts whisked through her mind, but she firmly banished them. She couldn't think of Jack that way, especially not in church. He would be her brother-by-marriage as soon as her crazy sister returned. Lusting after him would be awkward at best.

He smiled at her with such tender devotion tears welled in her eyes.

"Jack," she said through gritted teeth, trying not to move her mouth. The congregation didn't need to overhear. They'd learn the truth soon enough. No doubt, it would be up to her to tell them, she thought sourly.

The minister cleared his throat.

Lexi winced under his disapproving regard. But darn it all, she had a mission. "I have to tell you something. Now."

"Where's your sister?" Jack asked.

She blinked. *He knew?* It took her a second to realize "her sister" was herself, and he believed he'd asked Grace the question. He would have stopped the ceremony otherwise.

"Do you, Jackson Christopher," the minister intoned, "take this woman for your lawfully wedded wife, to love and to honor, in sickness and in health, forsaking all others, for all the days of your lives?"

What? How had they gotten to this part so quickly? Had Jack not heard her comment?

He reached over and cupped her cheek. "I absolutely do."

Longing struck her stomach with the force of a blacksmith's mallet, and she shuddered as he removed his hand. He frowned, and she gave a tiny shake of her head to indicate it was nothing. That she was all right.

But she felt far from all right. She needed to stop this.

"Do you, Audrey Grace, take this man for your lawfully wedded husband—"

Lexi gulped down the knot of hysteria in her throat as the minister continued the vow. When he paused, she choked out, "I have to—"

Jack jolted back and the crowd laughed.

"—Tell you something," she continued under cover of the congregation's murmuring.

Jack smiled and squeezed her hand. Giving her reassurance. This man was almost perfect. Granted, he wasn't a good listener, but his other qualities cancelled that out. Lexi just hoped he had a sense of humor and a tight control on his temper.

She held Jack's gaze, waiting for him to recognize her and stop the ceremony. Or recognize her and run after his true bride.

Or just recognize her.

He saw only what he expected, and it gave Lexi a chill. How could he not see her for herself? How could he not notice the differences? How could he continue to adore her with his eyes?

"I, Jack, take you, Grace, to be my wife and my partner."

She swallowed. Hard.

He continued, "I will honor our marriage and try to love you more each day than the day before. I will be faithful through good times and bad. I give you my hand and my devotion, from this day forward, for as long as we both shall live."

She thought she might faint. He recited his vows with such moving conviction. How could Grace have left a man who loved her this deeply? Or…wait. Did he mention love? She couldn't recall the exact words. Either way, Lexi glimpsed a side of Jack—a sweet, gentle, vulnerable side—she'd never seen.

And what part came next? Her vows? For a frightening moment, her mind blanked. She'd come up the aisle to save him embarrassment. Getting him aside to tell him quietly hadn't worked. She couldn't blurt out her identity so publicly. But she couldn't marry him either! That took sisterly devotion too far.

Maybe she'd pretend to be her sister and do what Grace had done—run. Glancing around, she spied an exit behind the altar. She wouldn't have to race through the congregation. Seeing no other alternative, Lexi searched for her dad, for support, and her gaze fell on Anna sitting by Rachel. The girl beamed—no other word for it—nearly bouncing on the pew, and waved again.

Oh, God. If she left now, everything would be in chaos. Who would soothe Anna? The girl would be distraught at losing another mother. Pain echoed in Lexi's chest as she thought of her own mom.

Would reciting the vows really matter? The license wasn't in Lexi's name so the marriage wouldn't count. When Jack understood the situation, he could explain things to Anna. In a quiet place, calmly. *Please let this be the right thing to do.*

Lexi fumbled through the traditional "to have and to hold" she'd seen in countless movies. Grace had memorized the more elaborate vows she'd written, but these would suffice. Jack's forehead creased in a frown.

"Nerves," she whispered.

He smiled and produced a gold band from his pocket.

A ring? Lexi's heart leapt in panic. She didn't have a ring for him. Then, remembering, she sighed in relief. Jack had decided against one for himself, not being a man who wore jewelry. Grace had teased him, but neither one wanted him losing a finger if the ring caught in ropes or equipment. Grace had promised to put hers back on if she removed it to paint.

Lexi pictured him leaning forward and asking the whereabouts of her engagement ring. The three carat marquis-cut diamond shone among the sapphires surrounding it—and currently rested on a hand heading off into the sunset.

"I give you this ring," Jack said instead, "as a symbol of my never-ending commitment."

He didn't mention love that time, she noticed, lending credence to Grace's assertion this was a convenient union rather than a love match.

But then, as he slid the band onto her finger, he held her gaze and raised her hand to his lips.

Her breath just plain stopped. Stopped. As though she'd yet to draw her first breath when emerging from the waters of life and wading onto land. Even if he was playing a part for the congregation, he was mesmerizing.

She couldn't *still* be attracted to him, could she? She'd shelved her interest when Grace returned from Australia last year and he'd fallen for her. Now Lexi's feelings seemed even more inappropriate. If anyone knew, they'd suspect she'd stepped into Grace's dress to trick him. No one would believe Grace had put her in the gown.

Going through with the ceremony had been an accident. Panic. Impulse. But she was never the impulsive one. She always cleaned up after Grace's reckless actions—though not usually in this drastic a manner.

"Then," the minister intoned, "with the giving and receiving of this ring and the exchanging of these vows, by the power vested in me by the state of Montana, I now pronounce you husband and wife. You may kiss the bride."

Jack lowered his head toward her. Lexi stood frozen, watching his approach with a fascinated horror. His warm lips met hers, and she closed her eyes, entranced by the tenderness of the moment. Her heart thrilled at the contact despite her distress. She returned his kiss, while her brain screamed a warning. But the feminine part of her melted a little while a handsome man pledged his love forever.

Although not to her. She pulled back, her gaze on his.

A tingle zipped through her. Surely it must be guilt because Jack looked so jubilant, and in a few minutes, she'd have to break his heart. Guilt because she'd had feelings for Jack before he fell for Grace. Guilt because a tiny rebellious voice urged her to delay telling him the truth until the morning. *One night,* it whispered with silky, dangerous temptation.

They walked down the aisle as people stood and applauded, Lexi moving along without thought, propelled along. Jack scooped up Anna in his other arm, a chuckle booming from deep in his chest. The minister followed them into the quiet dressing room—the initial scene of the disaster—and produced the wedding certificate. Clint and Rachel joined them as the congregation passed by on their way out. Lexi relaxed as she remembered the receiving line would form at the reception. Not only couldn't she face all those people right now, but she also needed an alone moment to tell Jack the truth.

The purity of the snow-white document mocked her integrity as Jack signed the certificate. Had she just *married* him? How was that possible? A flash blinded her, and she reeled back, not having noticed the photographer from Bozeman enter the room. Jack extended the pen toward her. A rattlesnake couldn't have been more threatening.

"You sign right here." Pastor Compton pointed to the appropriate line, as though uncertainty caused her hesitation.

Jack cocked his head as she stood unmoving.

It won't count. The license wasn't issued to her, Alexis Grace, but to Audrey Grace. Lexi took the pen, her lips trembling into a smile, and signed with her sister's customary signature, A. Grace Marshall.

"Yay!" Anna clapped her hands, breaking the tension and making everyone laugh. The camera flashed again, then twice more as Clint and Rachel signed as witnesses.

Rachel hugged her. "Congratulations, honey."

Lexi forced her frozen body to relax in the embrace.

Clint clapped Jack on the back. "Good job. Now, I'm taking advantage of tradition by kissing the bride. I figure it's unlikely you're going to let me do it later."

"You figure right." But Jack grinned at his younger brother with good-natured humor.

Clint embraced her then dipped her backward. Lexi gasped with surprise as the others laughed, followed by Jack's playful growl when Clint pressed his lips to hers. While it appeared amorous, Clint's gesture remained platonic. He swung her upright with a frown but then clapped a hand to his chest. "Damn, you're one lucky man, Jackson Walker."

Jack pulled Lexi to his side and slid a proprietary arm around her waist. "I know it."

She ducked her head, discomfited. The longer this charade continued, the harder it would be to tell him about Grace leaving. And now she had to explain this other problem of her accidentally marrying him.

Clint turned to Rachel. "Your turn?"

Rachel's lips twitched. "I've never heard of any custom where the witnesses kiss."

Clint's green eyes gleamed with wicked humor. "Every custom starts somewhere."

Rachel shook her head. "Tempting, but no."

"I'll kiss you, Uncle Clint," Anna said.

They laughed. No one noticed Lexi's smile seemed forced.

"Best offer I've had tonight." Clint swung the girl up into his arms, and she gave him a loud smooch on his cheek. He slid Anna back to her feet and winked at Rachel. "You had your chance."

Lexi fidgeted, the delay making her anxious. She needed to tell Jack the truth then locate Grace. And wring her neck. "We should go."

"Right," Jack said.

"Daddy, can I ride in the limo with you and Mommy?"

Time stood suspended as if in a Victorian tableau. *Mommy.* Lexi watched the others, gratified to see them as affected as she'd been in the dressing room.

Rachel recovered first. "Not this time, Annabeth. We'll get to the party faster than they will if we ride in my car."

"But I want to ride in the limo."

Jack brushed a gentle, if trembling, hand over his daughter's hair. "Not tonight, sugar cube. Tonight is for the bride and groom."

Lexi and Jack rushed outside into the twilight and climbed in the limousine. Jack helped her bunch her skirt inside the car, while Lexi tried to hide her goldenrod bridesmaid shoes. She didn't have time for questions now. They posed again for the photographer —how incredibly annoying he was becoming— and closed the door.

She turned to Jack, unable to hold back one more instant. Prolonging the pretense would be just plain wrong. "Jack, I have something to tell you."

CHAPTER THREE

Jack cupped his palm against her cheek, lust mixing with sentiment. "I've been lax about my husbandly duties already. I need to tell you something, too, honey. You take my breath away."

He placed his lips against hers in gentle worship, trying to express all the things his tongue tripped over saying. He'd seen the surprise in her eyes when he'd kissed her hand during the ceremony. It surprised him too, but when he'd seen her coming down the aisle, his heart had thundered so loud he could barely hear the organ music. For the first time, he'd been sure this marriage would work.

This woman was all he wanted, all he hoped for. He hadn't planned to marry this soon after Sarabeth's death, but when Grace returned from Australia, she'd knocked him sideways. The past three years alone had served as preparation for a new start.

Sensations swam through his head. He enjoyed their first private kiss as husband and wife, just for them instead of the cameras or the congregation. The poignancy surprised him. He wasn't a sappy guy, except maybe when it came to his daughter. He was a cattle rancher, after all. The softness of Grace's lips, and the sweet, hesitant way she trembled in his arms made him want to slow down and take his time. Gentle her like a skittish colt. He couldn't make sense of her sudden shyness, but it appealed to him on a basic level.

The limo swerved, and he jostled hard against her, her breasts pressing into him, kindling his lust. He gave a silent groan and devoured her, while wishing they could skip the reception, the cake, the dancing, the food. He only hungered for one thing, and she was in his arms.

She pulled back. "Wait," she panted. "Can we go somewhere else, not to the reception?"

A ray of pleasure exploded in his chest. "I was just thinking the same thing."

He kissed her again, sinking in, enjoying the lushness of this woman. His woman.

What had he done to deserve this much happiness? He'd won Sarabeth's love, and they'd had a healthy baby. Annabeth filled his life with joy. He thought his luck had been used up.

An elbow nudged him, and he gave his bride enough air to

say, "Where can we go?"

For a moment, he just gazed at her as the car passed the few town lights, alternately highlighting and shadowing her face. He was so damned fortunate to have found a woman like Grace.

"Only to talk. Not, you know, more." Her lids covered her eyes, and the tip of her tongue licked his kiss from her lips. "I'd rather not go to the hotel, but at least it would be private there."

Distracted by the sight of her tongue licking at anything, even the taste of him on her mouth, it took Jack a moment to focus. "As much as I like the idea—hell, love the idea—we have to go to the reception, honey. People are waiting."

"I have to tell you something first." She glanced toward the glass separating them from the driver, granting them scant privacy.

"Okay. What?"

She threw her hands up and huffed in a very un-Grace-like manner. She must really be ruffled. He frowned. What had happened to get her so riled? On second thought, she looked more in turmoil than angry. While he thanked God for that, he searched his memory for what might have gone wrong.

Then he understood—Lexi. A sharp pain in his chest stole his breath. Was Lexi hurt? Had she been kicked or trampled in that dangerous damned job of hers? She'd seemed fine for pictures that afternoon, but who knew what she'd gotten into since then. He swallowed. "Is this about Lexi missing the ceremony?"

She gasped and jolted back against the seat. She nodded.

Jack took her hand and pressed it to his chest. "I'm sorry, honey. I should have realized you'd be upset." He braced himself for bad news. "What's wrong with Lexi? It must be serious for her to have missed your wedding."

She winced.

His gut ached with worry. Lexi was a good, hard-working woman. He admired her gumption. Most of the ranch hands wouldn't stand their ground in an argument with him, while Lexi tended to go toe-to-toe for causes she believed in. Sparks would light in her blue eyes. That passion made her a great vet, and she'd be a good partner for some man someday. She hadn't shown any serious interest in any of the yahoos in town, at least not to his knowledge.

"Can we wait to talk until we get to the hotel room?" Grace asked.

Guilty of being caught thinking of another woman—maybe *especially* her—while sitting with his bride, he tapped the inner window and made the request of the driver. The man's stifled chuckle as the glass rose had heat rushing to Jack's face. He wasn't an animal who couldn't wait to have his bride to himself, for Pete's sake. For the first time, Jack appreciated Grace's insistence on hiring a limo and driver from Billings. Had the guy been a friend or neighbor, Jack wouldn't be able to live it down. "He thinks I'm going to jump you."

"I just need to talk," she repeated. "But my sister's not sick or hurt. There's another reason she wasn't there."

Jack nodded, relief easing the frantic rhythm of his heartbeat and bringing a return of logic. The doc had looked uncomfortable, but Jack put that down to the monkey suit. Doc would have been more ruffled if Lexi was seriously ill.

The two sisters were different in many respects, despite being identical in appearance. Grace rode well, with a natural, sensual seat, but she regarded horseflesh as dispassionately as her convertible. Lexi became a vet because she cared intensely for the welfare of all creatures.

"Thank you for waiting to hear," she said on a sigh.

Curious but patient, he hugged his bride to him, kissing the side of her head. Silky blond strands of her hair tickled his nose. A homey scent like white cake intrigued him, bringing to mind the ranch kitchen, of all things. It made his mouth water.

He wondered how anyone would know if they fit in a quickie at the hotel. He frowned. That wasn't at all romantic, but it fit his hunger level. Ever since she'd walked down the aisle toward him, his loins had ached with the need to have her.

Guilt hit him as he remembered Lexi. She might be in

trouble, and he could only think about getting his wife naked. Half-naked. Naked enough, he thought with a grin, which he quickly suppressed. Grace had enough on her mind, so much, in fact, she hadn't even remembered to bring her fancy designer purse. "Do you need to use my phone to call her?"

"No, not right now."

He sat back and stroked Grace's curled fist for the short ride, sending up a brief prayer of his own for Lexi's wellbeing. When the limo stopped, he helped Grace out, trying not to trample the huge skirt.

"Should I wait?" the driver asked, straight-faced.

Jack scowled. "Of course you should wait. She has to make an important phone call. Then we'll be back down. Twenty minutes."

He tried to appear as less of a horn-dog than he felt, hoping the man believed him. He didn't want gossip about his wife.

After a silent elevator ride, he shut the door to the honeymoon suite behind him, watching as his bride raced across the sitting room, dark yellow shoes flashing under the white skirt. He frowned. What had Grace so upset she'd wear mustard-colored shoes to her wedding?

Taking a deep breath, Lexi turned to face Jack and spied his and Grace's luggage sitting by the bedroom door. She couldn't delay any longer. Easier to blurt out the truth than struggle over how to phrase it. There wasn't a kind way to say this that would hurt him less. With a deep breath, she braced herself against the havoc about to be unleashed.

"I'm not Grace." She swallowed hard as his eyes narrowed. "I'm Lexi. Grace got cold feet."

His gaze went to the hem of her skirt.

Using euphemisms only confused matters. "Grace had a temporary bout of nerves. She didn't want to hurt you, Jack, you have to believe that. She just..." Lexi trailed off, lost for words. She just what? Went crazy?

"This isn't funny." The hoarseness of his tone told of his struggle. Hiding his pain? Confusion? Anger? "Why are you saying this, Grace?"

Lexi bowed her head, then realized she'd been twisting the gold wedding band on her finger. She should take it off, but would he accept it right now? Or would he hurl it against the wall? Crush it beneath his shined-up black boots? Lexi left it on for the moment to protect it. He'd want it when he calmed down, to give to Grace when she returned.

"No, it isn't funny," she agreed. "Grace didn't intend to hurt you. She wasn't thinking. I'm sure she'll be back."

"You're serious?" His gaze scoured her face and then swept over her body to return to her features. Her flesh burned as though she'd been washed with lye soap. "Oh, God, you are serious. You're really Lexi."

She nodded, keeping her chin up and her gaze on his.

"What was all that then?" He gestured toward the dark window behind her, obviously meaning the church and wedding.

"I tried to get you aside to tell you, and then it all happened so fast. My dad, Rachel, you—no one listened. Then the pastor got to the 'I do' part, and I didn't want you to be humiliated. I didn't want Anna hurt. I was put on the spot."

His jaw dropped. "So you *married* me?"

Lexi's face heated at the outrage and disbelief in his tone. She could well imagine the thoughts in his head. She stood in as an inadequate substitute for Grace with all her glamour. "No, it wasn't like that. I didn't want you to be embarrassed in front of everyone." She pleaded her helplessness with raised hands. "It's not like I had time to think about any of this. Grace had just left a few minutes before."

He glowered at her. "This is a hell of a thing to learn *after* the wedding."

"Jack." She tried for patience. "Grace will return, and this way, you won't have any awkward explaining to do. You can have a quiet civil ceremony, and no one will know. I'd be surprised if she wasn't back already, looking for you."

Okay, that might be stretching it. Grace would come to her senses and want to make amends, but no way would she show up at the reception to admit her error in public.

"That's why you married me?" He scrubbed a hand over his face. "An easy return for your sister?"

"Don't sound so skeptical."

"Did you trick me into marriage or not?"

She bit back her own sense of affront because he had a right to be angry. Not just angry at her for the switch, but at his runaway bride. It seemed she was Grace's stand-in today for more than just the ceremony. Lexi had to accept responsibility for her part in the fiasco, as well as guilt by association for Grace's part. But she had to set him straight on why she'd done it, and it wasn't to gain him as a husband. She nearly shuddered at the thought. "I didn't trick you."

"Really? Did you think I recognized you while I said my vows? That I knew it was you I pledged my ever-lasting love for?"

"Of course not." *Although you didn't actually pledge your love. And you couldn't tell your bride apart from her sister.* She swallowed back the words. This wasn't the time to accuse him of anything. She had misled him, and he'd only seen what he'd expected.

His gaze raked her again, undoubtedly noting the slight differences in her body versus Grace's. Ice flowed over her skin. She fell short of Grace's elegance, and she didn't need him to point it out. "Look, I didn't choose to do this. It was spur of the moment."

"Those decisions seem to run in your family. One sister makes a hasty decision *not* to marry me, and the other makes a hasty decision *to* marry me."

"I didn't *decide* to marry you." She ignored his raised eyebrows. Dammit, this was harder to explain since she'd gone through with the ceremony. "I tried to get you to come outside with me. Remember how I kept saying your name? Then the ceremony started, and I couldn't humiliate you right on the altar. I wanted to save Grace from embarrassment when she changes her mind and returns to town. Returns to you. I tried to save your daughter from being disillusioned. It got out of hand."

He snorted. "I'll say it got out of hand. Why are you dragging Annabeth into this fiasco?"

"Grace had me try on her dress, then she left. Anna came in to the dressing room, all excited about the wedding, and mentioned her mother. I could see the longing in her eyes, and I just couldn't..." Lexi let her arms drop against her sides. "Then she called me Mommy. What should I have done?"

His stance relaxed, as though the heat of his anger evaporated. "You could have told her who you really were."

"She would have starting crying and come running to you. Is that how you'd like to have found out Grace left? In front of everyone, with your little girl sobbing?"

"The alternative to being embarrassed is being married to you? That's the only thing you could think of to do?"

"I didn't plan it out in intricate steps, Jack. I couldn't get the stupid dress off by myself, but it was too late anyway. The entrance music had started playing."

Lexi wouldn't speak the ugly suspicion that Grace had timed her exit to the last second on purpose. That she'd had Lexi try on the wedding dress, trapping her at the church. Did Grace think Lexi would hide in the dressing room so no one would see her? Hide, so no one would question why she wore her sister's gown?

Jack walked to the window and stared out at the city lights. From the fifth floor penthouse, most of the small town and some of the surrounding countryside lay before him. Did he watch for Grace's miraculous return? A few street lights and those from open businesses shone bright against the black sky. Grace rushing back to him would make an incredibly dramatic sight.

"Anna called me Mommy," she said again to his back, trying to make him understand. "I couldn't tell her she didn't get to have a new mommy, after all. During the ceremony, I was looking for an escape route, and when I spotted her, she just radiated happiness. I acted like a coward when it came to breaking her heart, I admit it."

Lexi watched his body language, giving him time to overcome his initial anger. Their options ticked away as he stood. They needed to come up with a solution. Fast. Four hundred people waited at the reception. Her dad was there. She could call him to make an announcement. Pass this awful duty on to him.

But what would she have him say? Did they expose Grace's callous action, humiliate Jack, and hurt Anna? Wouldn't it be easier to wait Grace out and let her make amends to Jack in private? Grace and Jack could stay married. Lexi had stepped in as a temporary bride until the real bride got over her panic attack. Marriage by proxy, like in the old West.

"Thank you," he said, "for Annabeth's sake. But, dammit, Lexi, this is a major f— screw-up. We've got to sort out this tangle of lies."

"Jack, think about what will happen when Grace returns. If you tell everyone now, she'll be humiliated. People will think badly of her."

He snorted. "Yeah, that'd be a real shame."

"She put me in this dress for a reason. I think it means she's coming back, and she wanted to protect you from ridicule."

She ignored his hollow half-laugh. She could fix this. As angry as she was at her sister, Lexi needed to protect Grace's interests. "When Grace comes back, you can just go on as though she'd been the bride today."

His hand clenched against the glass, and he muttered something Lexi didn't ask him to repeat. Jack turned to her then, his eyes dry and face stark. "That's quite the fantasy. I didn't realize you were so naive. If Grace planned to marry me, she'd be here now. Do you honestly believe if she comes back, I'll want to marry her? Just kiss and make up?"

Jack shook his head. "Besides, you're forgetting the bigger question. What about our marriage? Yours and mine?"

Lexi stumbled back a step, horror tightening her chest, before she remembered the skirt. Tripping now would put the icing on her day. She could picture herself, flat on her back, with the skirt over her head, showing her fancy bridesmaid's underwear to Jack. "We're not really married."

"We spoke vows. We signed the license."

"No." She shook her head, stomach heavy with anxiety. "I mean, yes, we did, but it didn't count. It was just a show, to save face."

"Are you sure that's how the courts will see it? Did you jump on the Internet and do a search for the legalities before taking your sister's place?"

Annoyance flared at his sarcasm. "I didn't have time. I had to save your hide."

"Lexi, I admire you covering for your sister, as idiotic as

that turned out to be. But you've thoroughly screwed up our lives here."

You ungrateful jerk. She bit her tongue. "How would you like me to have handled it? Really, do tell me. Picture yourself at the altar and *no bride* comes up the aisle." She let that sink in for a moment, watching his eyes narrow. "The whispers, the shifting of the crowd, the stares. Maybe I should have left you to hang. Running away with Grace would have saved me from all the worry and hassle. I thought about it, but I didn't do that. *I* didn't abandon you."

"Okay, look, I appreciate that."

She planted her hands on her hips. "No, you don't. And I've said this until I'm blue in the face, but I didn't plan any of this! Do you think you're *that* irresistible? That I *wanted* to marry you?"

He walked over and tipped up her chin. Lines crinkled around his green eyes. "Uh-oh. Our first fight as a married couple."

Caught off-guard, she bit back a laugh. "We're not a married couple."

He released her. "I think we should find out about that, and the sooner, the better."

"It wasn't our marriage license, so it couldn't have been legal."

"Because you don't want it to be? Honey, life doesn't work that way."

Honey. His pet name for Grace. Regret pierced Lexi's chest. Just a few hours ago, he'd planned to spend his future with the woman he may have loved. Now he was probably worried he'd been saddled with an imitation. "Can't you just go to the ranch and wait for her?"

"I'm not that forgiving. And how long am I supposed to sit around waiting for my runaway bride?"

"Just give it the weekend," Lexi said.

He snorted. "You actually think she'll come back."

Grace had come to regret her impulses countless times in the past. She'd slink back into town, expecting to be forgiven. It had worked for her every time. "Yes, I know it."

One eyebrow hitched. "And you think I'll take her back?"

She looked at him squarely, familiar with this harder side of Jack. He'd been her opponent regarding animal care, in the barn and on the range. She knew how he thought and what swayed him. Romantic Jack was a stranger. Adversarial Jack she knew well, and knew he responded to logic.

She ticked off the points on her fingers. "One, you loved her enough to pro— to agree to marry her. Two, you know what she's like, so, three, you know she'll come to her senses."

Lexi could have listed a hundred times Grace had bailed

before, but making Grace sound flighty wouldn't help her case. "You're hurt and you're angry," she added, "but four, you know you belong with Grace."

Jack paced away to the window again. After a moment, he said, "I'm not agreeing to take her back or even listen to her explanations. But what if it takes longer than the weekend for her to 'come to her senses,' as you put it?"

"She'll be back within a week."

He turned. "So you intend to stay at the ranch, pretending to be my wife, for a week?"

Her eyes went wide as surprise stole over her. "Why would I do that?"

"You married me—or went through the motions," he added when she made to object, "to save me and Grace from embarrassment. You want her to step into the role of my wife when she comes back. If she comes back. But how do we explain her absence in the meantime?"

Lexi stared, her mind caught in a mini dust storm. How could she have missed this complication?

"Lex, I appreciate that you thought, in your own big-hearted but misguided way, that you were saving me from being humiliated and protecting Annabeth."

She narrowed her eyes. He made "misguided" sound synonymous with "stupid." He'd added "big-hearted" to salve her feelings.

"However," Jack continued, "you and your sister have just royally complicated my life."

Stunned at his lack of gratitude, she could barely keep from screeching. She aimed for an icy, "I beg your pardon?"

"I could have survived being embarrassed. It wouldn't have been my favorite memory, but it would have been a hell of a lot better than..." He trailed off, hunching his shoulders.

"Being married to me?" She clenched her teeth. "Is that what you're not adding?"

"No. Well, yes. Dammit." He glared. "I don't want to hurt your feelings, Lexi. You're a nice girl."

A nice girl. She'd bet he didn't think of her twin sister as a girl. Nor, at this moment, did he probably think of Grace as very nice, either.

"But since you did marry me," he went on, "we have to figure out if it's legal and how much trouble you're in."

She flattened a hand against her chest. "Me? I didn't do anything wrong."

"You signed a legal document with your sister's signature."

"It's my name, too. I signed 'A. Grace.' That's not my usual signature, but it is mine to use. Audrey Grace and Alexis Grace, after our mom. I did nothing wrong." She mounted a reasonable defense but doubted her babbling hid her panic. Could she get into legal trouble for this? Her knee-jerk instinct to cover Grace's backside would be her downfall.

"It might be fraud anyway," he said. "You knew you weren't the person issued the license. You knew I wasn't aware of who you were. I need to get my lawyer on this. Until we learn some answers, we should hide you at the ranch and let everyone think I married Grace."

Jack was protecting her?

Surprised by the realization, she just stared. She could barely catch her breath as her view of the day tilted one-eighty. She hadn't imagined that participating in the ceremony could be considered illegal. She'd just been caught up in the moment and said "I do" instead of "no way." For the first time in her life, she had acted on impulse.

And look where that had gotten her. She'd wind up in an orange jumpsuit in the county jail. Or shackled to Jack. She couldn't decide which she dreaded more.

While grappling with the idea, she thought of practicalities. "I can't pretend to be Grace for a couple of days."

"You've done a credible job up till now. Although since you made me look like an idiot, I ought to toss you out on your rear."

Lexi began to see why Grace fled. "I did no such thing."

"I just got hood-winked. One sister refusing to marry me is

embarrassing enough. But for me to stand up at the altar and not know who I married?" Jack shook his head.

Lexi took a deep breath. "I'll stay at the ranch until we get this figured out or for one week at the most. But it won't take that long. I'm sure Grace will come back tomorrow, and you two will iron it out."

Jack smirked. "I think you love her a lot more than I ever could have."

"You're just angry."

"Damn right." He exhaled, and his body relaxed, but she could see the effort it took him. "What do you plan to do if she doesn't come back?"

"If it turns out to be a legal marriage, we'll get an annulment."

He quirked an eyebrow. "An annulment? After living together for an entire week?"

She grinned. "Well, *there's* grounds for you."

A chuckle escaped him. "I can't believe I'm laughing about this. You're far nicer than Grace deserves."

"You and Grace will laugh about it together someday."

He grunted his disbelief. "Want to go to the reception and pretend to be married? We should get some food, and I could definitely use a drink."

Lexi's stomach sank with dismay. "God, no. I couldn't pull

off pretending to be Grace. I'm not anything like her."

Jack smiled. "You're identical twins."

"I don't even have the right shoes." She lifted her hem to expose the goldenrod pumps.

"Ah. Those make sense now."

"Nothing about this makes sense, let alone going to the reception. I could never fool everyone. I don't want to fool *any*one. That's not why I did this."

"Settle down, honey." He came nearer and stroked his hands down her arms. Over and over. Gentling her like a colt wearing its first saddle blanket.

Lexi stared at the black studs on his shirt-front. Shivers coursed through her. She didn't want to be this aware of him, of his size or strength or his suddenly enticing male scent. "Don't do that."

"Don't do what?"

Make me notice you as a man. "Don't call me honey. That's your nickname for Grace."

His hands dropped away. "Honey, right now you *are* Grace."

If she were Grace, they'd be truly married—and they'd be having sex. She snipped off that line of thinking as quickly as turning a stallion into a gelding. "I can't go to the reception."

"You can't go home. People will see you."

She frowned. "So?"

"How do you, as Lexi, explain your absence from your sister's wedding?"

"Oh."

He stepped back. "I guess we'll have to go to the ranch. We need to figure out a story to cover your absence, one that sounds plausible for when you return as Lexi."

"I'll call my dad and have him tell everyone that a good-looking drifter swept me off my feet, and we're having a wild week in Vegas."

He smiled. "No one would believe that."

Her jaw tensed as she turned away. Couldn't some good-looking man want her? Or didn't Jack think she knew how to have a wild week of sex? Was she that dull? She put on a bright tone. "I'll worry about that when I'm Lexi again."

"At the ranch, we'll only have to fool Clint and Crusty, and Clint will be leaving soon."

She glowered at the mention of his uncle, the rightful ranch-owner, and the one who'd prompted Grace's proposal in the first place. She'd encountered the man when tending the Rocking W's animals. Short and bow-legged with a white beard and mustache, he cussed more than he spoke, and grunted more often than he cussed. She wasn't sure she could fool his eagle eye, and she didn't want to endure his wrath when he found out.

Jack had also forgotten the ranch hands, most of whom knew her well enough as a vet. "I can only pass for Grace at a distance or for a few minutes, so I'll have to stay clear of the men."

"They won't expect Grace to be out much."

He had a point there. "Crusty won't be fooled for long, and what about Anna?"

"She thought you were Grace earlier. She won't suspect anything."

Lexi had her doubts. Anna had been raised by men on a ranch and acted more like a short adult than a child. "How long is Clint staying?"

"This is his last day. He's got to drive back to L.A. Tonight he and Crusty are watching Annabeth." Jack scowled. "Dammit. We can't go to the ranch."

She tilted her head in question.

"We just got married," he said slowly, as though talking to a dimwit. "It's our honeymoon."

Her eyes widened. "That won't work."

"Don't look so panicked, Lexi. I'm not likely to claim my husbandly rights." He smirked. "Despite you trapping me."

Both wounded and relieved, she tried to smile. "I just *rescued* you, remember? And don't worry, I never thought you'd want to...do that with me."

He grinned. "Are you blushing? You can't even say the words? You, who can extract bull sperm or determine when a mare is in heat and ready to be covered, all without even blinking, has to resort to saying *do that?"*

He rocked back on his heels, chuckling.

Lexi was not as amused. Her body flamed as though she stood in the summer sun. "We're not talking about animals."

"We're talking about you and me having sex."

"No, we definitely are not."

He laughed so hard he had to put a hand to his stomach. "Not talking about it or not having sex?"

Was the idea of bedding her that amusing? She didn't intend to make love with him, but a girl had her pride. "Both. Neither."

"Okay, honey, don't get in such a snit." He still chuckled.

"And don't call me honey."

The reminder of Grace sobered him. "We could stay here."

Lexi narrowed her eyes, sure he meant it as a joke.

He shrugged. "We can't go to the reception. We can't go to the ranch. We can't go to your house."

She couldn't come up with an alternative. "I guess you're right."

"Welcome to the honeymoon suite, Mrs. Walker."

CHAPTER FOUR

Rachel fielded yet another question from a reception guest regarding the whereabouts of the happy couple. She hoped and prayed they were happy and not off fighting somewhere. No reports had come in regarding an accident, thank God. And the moment she confirmed Grace was safe, she'd wring her neck.

She'd tried to evade the wedding guests with all their questions. Now, she supposed she should step up and help out her family again, as she had at the wedding by signing as witness in Lexi's absence. And where the heck was Lexi?

Uncle Kevin had disappeared a few minutes earlier into the corridor to take a phone call. His ladyfriend, Iris, hovered at his side, holding his arm, so Rachel had indicated she'd wait in the restaurant with the guests. Hopefully, it would be Grace calling to say she and Jack were a block away and racing toward the restaurant. A message from Lexi reassuring them of her safety would be just as welcome.

"Anything?" Clint asked.

"No." She regarded the best man and decided the title suited him. She'd never gone for the blond god look, but in his case, she could make an exception. Since first seeing him, she'd wanted to run her hands over his broad chest and muscled arms. To watch fire spark in those mirror-like green eyes. To taste his lips and kiss that strong square jaw.

He couldn't be more than twenty-two or so, and her eight years of extra life experience yawned between them. She'd built a career while he'd still been getting his feet wet. Or, more to the point, she'd loved and lost, where he was still flinging wild oats around.

"Damn it all."

His comment jolted her from her reverie. "What?"

"Where are they? This isn't like Jack. He's usually dependable. Boring, actually."

Rachel smirked. "I'm afraid Grace has been a bad influence then. She's anything but dependable. Or boring."

"Excuse me." A waiter from the catering company out of Billings stood at Rachel's side, making her regret hiding out so close to the side door.

"What can we do for you?" Clint asked.

Surprise flared in Rachel as he took control. She usually shouldered the responsibility. As for his use of "we," uniting them as a team, she had to admit she appreciated someone helping her.

The waiter cleared his throat. "I wondered when you'd like us to serve dinner, sir. The appetizer course has circulated, and your guests are seating themselves. If you'd prefer to wait, we can continue the hors d'oeuvres, of course."

Clint glanced at Rachel, who gave an inward scream but smiled. She was only four years older than the twins, not their mother. But she shrugged, knowing Uncle Kevin couldn't handle this right now. "We'll start the dinner portion. These people have earned it for their patience. Are you serving coffee with the meal?"

"Yes, ma'am."

Usually she wouldn't have noticed being called "ma'am"— she lived in the West, after all, where manners were still the norm—but she didn't need their age difference pointed out to Clint. Could her third graders address her as such? Sure. The waiter? Sure. The man she wanted to drag into a dark closet? Surely not.

She wouldn't act on that fantasy. She had family obligations. "Can you have your staff suggest the coffee a little more strongly? I'm afraid the guests might head out soon if the bride and groom don't show."

"Yes, ma'am. I'll get my staff right on it and start serving.

Thank you."

"Thanks," Clint echoed to her as the man hurried away. "I wasn't sure what to do. It doesn't seem right to serve the wedding dinner without Jack and Grace."

Rachel shrugged. "The guests are here and the food is ready. The badly behaving couple can eat when they get here. After they've apologized and explained where the heck they've been."

"Maybe they're celebrating their marriage." His eyes gleamed with humor.

"They could have waited."

"Oh, sweetheart." Clint shook his head, a smile flirting with his lips. "If that's what you think, you haven't been made love to properly."

Her stomach clenched with desire while hot shivers raced under her skin. Did he always come on to strangers or had he picked up on her interest? Arching an eyebrow as though he were a precocious eight-year-old in her classroom, she tried to hide her reaction to the deeper tone he'd used to tease her. A bedroom voice. "Is that right?"

"That's so right." He ran a finger down her arm, leaving a trail of goosebumps from elbow to wrist. "A Walker man knows how to please a woman."

Rachel gulped, wondering when he'd moved so close. Her

body ignited to match the heat radiating from him. Tilting her head, she offered her lips, hoping he could interpret her intention without more guidance. She dropped her gaze to his mouth then looked into his eyes again. Judging by the darkened green and his more rapid breathing, he'd gotten her hint. She put a hand on his chest and lowered her voice. "That sounds promising."

"I can promise you an unforgettable night." His mouth closed on hers, those lips firm and tasting of red wine. Dark and mysterious, smooth but with an undertone, he enticed her to discover more facets. She opened to him, her arms making their way around his neck as he lifted her up and into his embrace. His tongue teased her, stroked, retreated. She floated on his scent and taste, her toes barely touching the floor.

The floor of the restaurant, in full view of half the guests.

Rachel broke back, gasping for air. He pressed his body against her, igniting sparks of desire in her core. She nearly panted with need.

A quick glance around assured her no one paid them any mind. At least, no one stared right now. She'd take that as good enough. "How old are you?"

He blinked with obvious surprise, no doubt expecting her to say anything else. Perhaps something about how great a kisser he was or how turned on she was. Both true statements.

"I'm twenty-five. Why?"

Phew. Only five years' difference. At least no one could accuse her of robbing the cradle. "Shouldn't we be taking care of the guests?"

"They have drinks." He kissed the corner of her mouth. "They're about to have dinner." He feathered his lips across her cheek. "There's nothing we can do for them."

"We should look for Grace and Jack. Or Lexi."

"You've called. I've called. Doc Marshall called." He traced her bottom lip with a finger. "No one's answering. They don't want to be found."

"It seems we should be doing something helpful."

"Short of knocking on the door to the honeymoon suite and dragging them out of bed like Victorian prigs, I don't see what more we can do."

"They're being irresponsible."

Clint brought his lips against hers again. "Let's be irresponsible, too."

The words whispered across her skin, causing as many shivers as his delicious kisses. She should say no. She should be practical.

A pinging sounded behind her, and she turned, taking a moment to recognize someone tapping on glass. It took her a moment to locate the source. Uncle Kevin held a champagne flute and a fork. She stiffened. "He must have news."

Clint's hands cupped her shoulders as he stood behind her. "It must be good news, though. He wouldn't announce it like this otherwise."

She relaxed at the logical reassurance and let Clint pull her back against him. In her high heels, she could have rested her head on his shoulder but resisted. It was too soon to lean on him.

But not too soon to take him to bed? She hushed the nasty voice of conscience which stemmed from her prim upbringing. Longmont, Colorado, lay far to the south, and she didn't have to worry about what the kids' parents or school board might say. This qualified as a vacation. *What happens in Little Tree stays in Little Tree?* She smiled. Decision made. Given the opportunity, she'd take Clint to her uncle's house later.

The murmurs that arose when people recognized Uncle Kevin tapered off as he stood waiting. Tension grew in the room, and in her.

"Thank you all for coming," he said. "And thank you for your patience. I've just heard from...that naughty girl of mine."

The crowd laughed.

"She and Jack won't be joining us, but they urge you to enjoy dinner. Stay as long as you want, dance the night away in celebration. Just don't expect to see them anytime soon."

The guests applauded. He raised his glass. "To our hosts."

"To our hosts," the crowd echoed.

"To Jack and Grace," someone else toasted.

Glasses tipped, and the murmurs began again. As though cued to respond, the wait staff appeared with plates of steamy beef, mashed potatoes drowning in butter, and asparagus spears gleaming beside glazed carrots.

"Jack triumphed in the food war," Rachel said. "I know Grace wanted something more exotic. She ran ideas past me and Lexi for weeks."

"There's asparagus, though. Jack can't stand the stuff."

"He's never had it prepared by a *master*." She dropped her voice on the last word, hoping it came out seductively instead of making her sound like an idiot. "An experienced chef could have made his knees weak." Rachel winked as Clint's mouth fell open. Her words were mundane, so he must be reading her tone correctly. She turned and ran a hand down his tie, stopping where his lapels met. "It should be tender."

He gulped.

Rachel traced a finger across his mouth. "Warm."

He licked his lips.

"And buttered."

"You don't say?"

The raspy edge to his voice made her smile.

"Why don't you check with your uncle?" Clint suggested. "See if he needs you. I'll go get my car."

"Are you going someplace?"

He held her upper arms, and she balanced against him with her hands on his chest. His firm, muscled hardness made her smirk drop away.

"Come with me, Rachel."

"To bed?"

"Yep."

"Right now?"

"Yep."

She swallowed then gave in to what they both wanted. "I feel bad about leaving Uncle Kevin to handle all this alone."

"He's not alone. Mrs. Browning is supporting him."

Rachel didn't even glance over her shoulder to check. Iris had been at Uncle Kevin's side all night. A lonely woman or a special one? Rachel would have to find out.

Tomorrow.

"What do you say?" Clint asked. "Want to come to bed with me?"

"Yep."

Honeymoon suite? A shiver ran over Lexi at Jack's words.

"I'll order up some food." Jack's eyes closed and his complexion reddened.

She didn't think she'd ever seen him blush. "What's

wrong?"

"I have to let the driver go."

His unease made her laugh. "He'll think we're..."

"He thought we were going to, anyway."

"And you're wishing he were right." Lexi heard the words with utter mortification. "I mean, you wish Grace were here so you could have...been together."

"Been together?"

"Given our circumstances, we ought to avoid this topic."

"Think I'll jump you if you mention the word *sex?"*

She lifted her chin. "I don't think you'd jump me if I stripped naked and danced a hula."

A smile flashed before he sobered. "Sorry, Lexi. I seem to say the wrong things to you."

"Let's just drop it. Can you get me something light to eat, a salad maybe? I'm not super-hungry." She'd run Grace's errands during lunchtime and should be starving, but worry and drama had diminished her appetite. "I'll find linens for the couch while you're gone."

"As a gentleman, I should insist you have the bed. But..."

Lexi's heart lurched as a sweet, self-deprecating smile twisted his lips.

"I doubt you think I have any manners at all, after the way I've taken out my frustration on you tonight."

"Of course I think you're a gentleman, Jack." She smiled, holding his gaze with hers. "Otherwise, I wouldn't have cared about your feelings, and I would have run away with Grace. I'd never have gone into that church and rescued you otherwise."

She wheeled Grace's suitcase across the floor. The skirt got in the way, but she didn't want Jack to have to move—

The skirt. Lexi stopped half-way to the bedroom. She'd never get out of the wedding dress without help. Jack's help.

Lexi squared her shoulders. "Uh, actually, I'm relying on you to be a gentleman right now. I need a hand. Or, more accurately, two hands."

"Want me to lift that suitcase onto the stand for you?" He took a step toward her.

"No, I, uh, need you to unbutton my dress."

He stopped so fast he almost lost his balance.

Had she been watching this on a TV sitcom, she might have laughed. In a cartoon, Jack's eyes would have bobbed out of his head on springs. If her life took place on British TV, she could ring for her lady's maid. But this, unfortunately, was her new personal reality show, at least for today. In her judgment, it would receive a low rating for lack of humor.

"The dress has all these little buttons." She turned her back to him and looked over her shoulder, pulling her hair aside. "They're covered in fabric, which makes them harder to push through the holes. A moot point since I can't reach them, anyway."

She babbled, exposing her sudden tension. Like she'd be exposing herself to Jack in a minute. He'd just see her back, but still, she felt awkward undressing in front of her non-husband.

Jack crossed the space wordlessly. His fingers barely pressed against her as they drifted down her spine. The chill of the air conditioning tickled against her skin as the fabric parted. His warm breath and warmer fingers heightened the tingling sensation, and she had to suppress a shiver.

She held the front of the gown so it didn't droop with the weight of the sewn-on pearls. "Thank you. I think I can get out of it now."

"You're sure? There aren't many buttons left. I might as well finish the job."

"No, no." She stepped away, turning her nearly-naked back to the wall, feeling idiotic, trapping the bodice against her chest like a virgin in an old-time drama. "As you said, there are only a few buttons near the waist. But thanks."

He stared at her for a beat then cleared his throat. "I'll order the food while you change."

"That would be great. It won't take me a minute." She'd make sure of that.

"Take all the time you need. But Lexi?" His voice halted

her as she backed through the doorway of the bedroom.

"Yes?"

"Don't put that theory to the test. Because you're wrong."

"What theory?"

"The naked hula dance." He turned and left the suite.

Silence pulsed against her skin as his words registered.

Giggles bubbled in her throat before reality returned. Of course he liked her body; he'd nearly married her twin sister. Jack didn't desire *her*.

Which almost reassured Lexi as she viewed the garments Grace had packed. Layer after layer revealed lace and transparent lingerie meant to entice. Her heart pounded. She couldn't wear any of this in front of Jack. She wouldn't be far from naked, which would have been just fine for a bride's honeymoon night, but not for a sister-in-law.

On the bottom of the case, Lexi found a violet cotton and lace cami with matching twill shorts. She'd have to wear it again tomorrow when they went "home" to the Rocking W, but at least it would cover her for dinner. Lexi donned them and a satiny peach wrap to hide under. If he dared to say one word, she'd walk out, straight to the reception, and reclaim her identity. He could deal with his errant bride's escape alone.

"Grace, you owe me big this time." Lexi brushed the hairspray out of her hair with brisk strokes. She'd have liked a shower, but she wasn't sure how long Jack would be, and, all jokes aside, no way under the stars would she be naked—hula dancing or not—when he returned.

She put his mother's wristwatch in his overnight bag and exited the bathroom to see Jack had arrived with dinner.

The corner of his mouth quirked but he made no comment regarding her odd ensemble. "I tried to reach Dan Higgins, the Rocking W's lawyer, at home."

Lexi nodded. Given the size of the town, she knew Dan. "And? Am I free?"

Jack shrugged. "His wife answered. Dan left straight from the church to go fishing this weekend. He'll be back late tomorrow night, and in and out of cell range until then. You know how that is."

"Yeah." A day and a half at the least then, unless Grace returned. "So maybe we'll know by Monday morning."

"I hope so."

They finished their dinner in almost total silence, then she made up the couch. She fluffed the extra pillow, conscious of Jack's gaze boring into her, before turning to face him.

He eyed her then the couch. "We should have a game plan. An understanding of how things are going to work."

"I don't plan to trap you permanently into marriage. That's the last thing I'd want. No offense." She shrugged. "We've discussed most of this. Where should we say I am? Where Lexi is, I mean."

His head cocked to the side. "Your dad knows what you're doing, right? I remember his reaction to what I thought was Grace's cute panic attack at the altar."

"He didn't know until he lifted the veil. He'd seen me in the foyer, but I think—" She glanced at her hands. "I think he recalled my mom wearing the same veil and saw what he expected to. We've all been thinking about Mom this week."

Maybe that had influenced her when Anna had reached out to her. They all yearned for a mom.

"I'm glad the doc wasn't part of tricking—er, *rescuing* me," he amended at her glare. "You can update him that the pretense is going on longer than you'd thought. We'll keep it between us until we hear from the lawyer."

She stared at him. Did he think she lived in a vacuum? "What about everyone else? My friends? Men I might be seeing?"

He scowled. "I didn't realize you were dating anyone in particular. Who is it?"

Now she'd have to admit she didn't have a boyfriend to reassure. "I meant people in general. I *am* well-liked around here, in case you didn't realize it. Someone will miss me."

"We'll tell everyone you're sick. Food poisoning." He held

up a hand when she started to speak. "Right, never mind. People would come visit you. You want to try that wild week with a drifter story?"

It was the smirk that did it. Pushed her right over the edge of reason, which, given the events of the day, wasn't that far a drop. She'd already called her dad with that story, and it should be spreading throughout town by now.

She nodded and watched Jack go still.

"You don't seriously think anyone will believe that?"

"Why not?" Vanity and pride struggled for dominance.

"You'd never do it."

He sounded so sure. She narrowed her eyes to combat the sudden sting of tears. It wasn't as though she cared what he thought, but darn it. Did he think no guy would want her just because he didn't?

Jack shook his head. "No matter how you felt about it, you'd never leave your sister on her wedding day."

For a second, she was reassured. Pleased, even, that he believed a man would want to sweep her away. Then the first part of his comment registered.

No matter how I felt about it? About the wedding?

"You think I'm jealous of Grace? Oh, God, you do." She hooted with a bit of shock and zero humor. Did everyone believe that? The tomboy sister jealous of her identical, but somehow more-beautiful twin. How cliché. How pathetic. How untrue.

"I meant it as a compliment on how much you love your sister. You'd be there for her on the most important..."

She suppressed a mean-spirited smile. *Grace* had walked out on the most important day of her life. Lexi crossed her arms and waited him out, enjoying the color climbing his cheeks.

"Okay, look, I'm sorry you misunderstood me. We can't keep sniping at each other if this charade is going to work."

Darn it, he had a point. She dropped her belligerent stance. "Sorry. I'm just tired and keyed up. It's been a stressful day."

His mouth opened, then he must have thought better of his response. At the bedroom doorway, he turned back. "Lexi."

Hearing his serious tone, she braced herself.

"I know you stepped in to protect Grace, but you also did it to prevent Annabeth from being hurt. So, for that, thank you." He walked into the bedroom.

She stared at the closed door as the truth hit her. The truth she hadn't wanted to admit, hadn't wanted to face, which now burst into her heart like fireworks. The truth that revealed too much.

"I did it for you."

CHAPTER FIVE

"Clint's rental car is still here," Jack said, more to break the silence than to note his brother's presence, as he pulled up to the ranch house. Lexi had been awake and repacked before he rose at five. Despite the quality of their suite, he swore he heard her breathing in the other room all night long. He'd been restless himself. Half the night, he'd been tempted to throw off the sheet and call off the whole farce. Let people think what they damn well wanted about Grace leaving him at the altar. He wasn't taking her back anyway, provided she ever returned.

The other half of the time, he worried Lexi would decide she had no intention of going through with this. What if she had committed fraud while trying to save him embarrassment? How could he protect her if they weren't together? She'd done something extremely kind—if asinine—for him, and he couldn't let her be punished for it. Being yanked around by his own thoughts didn't allow for much rest.

Now here they were, staring at the ranch house, with barely a word spoken between them all morning. Their first test would be Crusty, Clint and Annabeth. If Lexi's charade couldn't fool them, there was no point in thinking she could fool anyone else.

He exited the car, his stomach in knots. Must be from skipping breakfast, as neither of them had had an appetite. Lexi stood beside the car before he could reach her door. He hid his scowl, but his displeasure deepened when she made to open the rear door. His mama had raised him with manners, and Lexi should know better. "I'll get your bag later."

"Right. We might as well see if I'm staying."

She had a valid point, but that wasn't what he'd meant. No woman he'd ever been with had to carry her own luggage. It bugged him that Lexi didn't expect better treatment from him.

On the wooden front porch with its fresh coat of white paint, he pushed open the door—and the obvious next action hit him. Lexi would probably hit him, too. "Brace yourself." He swung her into his arms. She sucked in a breath, her blue eyes wide on his.

With a grin, he buried his face in her neck, smelling that homey scent again as he nuzzled her. "Grace would expect it. So will Clint and Crusty. Even Annabeth knows this is the routine."

"Of course."

He stepped across the threshold. "Welcome home, Mrs. Walker."

Jack set Lexi on her feet just inside the front door and brushed a kiss across her cheek in case anyone in the house was watching.

"If that's the best he can do," Clint said, walking down the hall toward them, "you might as well run away with me right now."

Jack stiffened at his brother's joke, not amused at the idea of another bride leaving him.

Lexi put her small, strong hand on his forearm. "I think I'll keep him."

Clint punched Jack's shoulder. "You dog. Couldn't even come to the reception? I don't blame you with a lovely woman like this to distract you."

"You gonna stand in the doorway for the rest of yore married lives?" Crusty ambled into the living room, his limp putting a hitch in his gait. He refused to use his cane inside and lurched like a roller coaster car going uphill.

"Hello, Chris," Lexi said in her Grace-voice, just a little higher and faster than her natural one.

Crusty stared at her then pulled on his earlobe, head cocked. "Why are you calling me Chris all of a sudden?"

Lexi shot a glance at Jack before clearing her throat. "I

thought, now that I'm family, I should call you by your proper name."

"Well, don't. No one else does."

"I'm sorry. How are you feeling today?"

The old man scowled. "People are always asking me that, like they expect me to keel over any second. Maybe hoping I will. How're *you* doing after yore honeymoon night?"

"Where's Annabeth?" Jack asked to throw off his uncle. Crusty could take down a cantankerous bull without breaking stride, just with his own cussed orneriness.

"She stayed with a friend in town," Clint said. "Doris said it was okay."

Jack nodded as they entered the kitchen. The housekeeper knew Annabeth's friends well enough and knew the families with whom he would allow her to spend the night.

"Our girl was mighty disappointed," Clint added. "The reception wasn't quite the same without the happy couple."

Jack withstood his brother's inspection, as Clint rather obviously looked for signs they weren't a "happy couple" and that an argument had kept them from the party. Jack slapped on a wicked grin and hoped Lexi would forgive him. "We, um, got distracted."

Crusty, true to form, guffawed as he pulled a chair across the polished, hundred-fifty-year-old oak floor and sat at the table. Clint chuckled when Lexi blushed, but then she winked at him, just as Grace might have done, giving the impression of an equally lusty bride.

"Hey, I should get on the road." Clint turned to Lexi. "I have to leave soon if I'm going to visit those galleries we talked about. I made appointments to stop at two on my drive back."

She went still beside Jack. "That's great, Clint. Good luck."

Doubting she had any idea what Clint referred to, Jack asked, "What galleries?"

"Grace gave me some ideas of places that might show my photographs. Places she has contacts regarding her paintings. I'm dropping by a couple on my way to L.A." Clint shrugged, looking once again like Jack's awkward younger brother, all gangly limbs and suppressed energy. "It's worth a shot, you know, since I brought my portfolio with me."

"Just happened to have it, huh?" Relief at his departure flooded through Jack, along with regret that his brother had to leave so soon. He gave Clint a tight hug, not sure when he'd see him again. "Thanks for coming, little bro."

"Wouldn't have missed it." Clint, six foot two himself, clapped him on the back with a laugh. "I didn't have to do much serving as your best man as it turned out, but it was an honor."

"I'll return the favor someday."

"I'm in no hurry to give up my freedom." Clint touched his

forehead as though tipping his hat. "No offense, Grace."

Lexi kissed his cheek. "Have a safe trip."

Clint laughed and glanced at Crusty. "Well, now, I'm not leaving quite yet. I didn't stay around just to make sure you left the hotel, you know."

Crusty pushed to his feet, both hands on the sturdy oak table. He shuffled to the counter and retrieved a large brown envelope tucked behind the coffee maker. "I been waiting to give you this. Woulda done it last night in front of ever'body, but you couldn't bother to come to yore own damned party."

Jack shot him a warning glance, though he doubted it would do any good. Crusty would say what he wanted.

"Happy wedding day, boy. And you too, Grace." The older man extended the envelope. A smile split his white mustache apart from his close-shaved beard. Jack had never, not once, seen his uncle smile like that. His heart pounded against his ribs in warning. What was the old guy up to?

"Well, go on with you." Crusty gestured at Jack. "Open it."

Lexi frowned, but Clint and Crusty had grins as big as the state of Montana on their fool faces. If this were a box, Jack would know it contained a gag gift, and probably an improper one for his bride to see, at that. Certain it couldn't be anything good, he unwound the string from the back loops and pulled out some papers.

He couldn't believe the words before him.

"What is it?" Lexi asked at his side.

Clint whooped. "It's the deed to the ranch."

"Oh, my." Lexi breathed out the words.

Jack focused. She looked happy for him. But then, she didn't know the load of trouble that had just landed at their feet.

Crusty almost rocked heels to toes, he was so cock-proud of himself. "It's a done deal, all legal-like. I signed it over to the both of you together in honor of the occasion. So don't go getting divorced," he joked.

Or, at least, he thought he joked.

Jack stood unmoving while a thousand emotions collided inside him.

"To both of us?" Lexi's voice climbed higher with surprise and probably dismay. "Wow. Thank you, Crusty."

Jack watched her hug the old man, feeling disconnected, as though he knew neither of them. Crusty had just signed over the ranch. After all the years Jack's dad had been denied the pleasure of ownership, Jack couldn't quite believe it. Crusty's threat to disinherit him, the same threat that had made Grace propose, convinced Jack the old buzzard would hang on to the place until death. Even after the accident that had crippled him and confined him to only doing paperwork, Crusty had retained ownership. He'd hired a foreman until Jack finished college. The past six years running the ranch had filled Jack with pride as he worked toward his future, when he'd assumed he would inherit the ranch.

"Don't you got nothing to say, boy?"

Jack snapped back to the present to discover everyone staring at him.

"He's dazed," Lexi put in. "That's quite the wedding gift."

Jack cleared his throat. "Thanks, Crusty. This is..." *A nightmare.* "Damned nice of you."

If Grace had married him, this would be a joyful moment, fulfilling a lifelong dream. But Lexi had married him instead and complicated everything.

Crusty waved a hand. "I know, yore thinking I'm twenty-two years too late. That I shoulda done it back when I was forty and busted my legs. Given it to yore dad."

Shame poked at Jack. He should appreciate the old man's gesture, not begrudge what Crusty hadn't done years ago or worry about the future. "That's not what I was thinking, at all."

"You should be then," Crusty countered in his gruff voice. "You oughta be damned mad I didn't give yore dad his due. Barry ran this ranch for nine years, letting me, a cripple, claim ownership."

"As the older son, you were the owner, Crusty," Clint said. "Just like Jack is. Now that you've handed over the ranch, we're not going to say 'it's about time.' We're going to say thanks."

"Thanks," Jack echoed, glad his brother had his wits about him.

"I'm not about to see this land be sold off for *condominiums*." Crusty infused the last word with disdain as he eased down onto the chair. "I waited till you were settled again. Now you need to start having some boys to run the place after yore gone. So hang on to this filly, boy, and get her to breeding."

Clint rolled his eyes at Jack. "Only a dumbass would let loose of this pretty lady. And Jack may have been thrown on his head a time too often, but even he isn't that dim-witted."

"What about Annabeth?" Lexi put in. "She should be given the opportunity to choose whether she wants the ranch."

Crusty batted at the air as though to knock away her words. "Pshaw. Girls are good for some of the chores, I guess, but when it comes down to running a ranch, you need a man."

Lexi's jaw tightened. "I beg your pardon, Crusty, but I believe I could run a ranch just as well as any man."

Crusty and Clint laughed. Jack had to admit the notion of Grace doing such a thing would have made him chuckle, too. Lexi had obviously forgotten her role.

He put a hand on her shoulder. "Grace." He felt her start at the name. "No one doubts your tenacity, honey. It's just a good thing you'd rather have paint on your hands than cow dung."

Definitely not a subtle reminder, and she nodded her understanding, even though her jaw set. "Well, my sister could run this ranch if she wanted to."

Jack smiled. "I have no doubt about that."

"Where is Lexi, anyway?" Clint asked.

Lexi's eyes widened as she stared up at Jack, who froze. Crap. They shouldn't have mentioned Lexi.

"She never showed up?" Lexi asked with credible surprise. "I'm sure she was embarrassed to have missed the wedding."

"Doesn't the doc know where she is?" Jack asked. Lexi had given her dad the "wild week in Vegas" story to spread. The other man hadn't liked it but never said he would refuse to play along. Jack had to admire Kevin for not letting gossip spread about his daughters.

Jack shifted uncomfortably. Saving his own pride left Lexi open to gossip. Guilt pierced him so sharply he almost admitted the entire story right then. Only now there was the complication of this "gift." The Walker family had ranched this land for nearly one hundred and ninety years. Did having Grace's name on the deed jeopardize his continuing that tradition?

While the others discussed Lexi's possible whereabouts, a kernel of hope lit inside Jack. Was his marriage to Grace valid, given that Lexi had signed Grace's signature to the wedding license in her place? Could it be considered a marriage by proxy?

Was there even such a thing anymore?

If the marriage was valid, so was the deed, which meant he had really inherited the Rocking W. But if he divorced Grace, would he have to buy out her portion of the ranch? The Rocking W couldn't afford it. Their assets weren't liquid. They had land and cattle and history, not cash.

Jack rubbed his forehead. He'd have to get his lawyer on this, as well as looking into the legality of his marriage to Lexi. How had his life become so difficult?

"Is it too early in the day for champagne?" Clint asked.

Jack stared. He couldn't celebrate anything until he had more facts. "At nine in the morning?"

"If there's orange juice in the fridge," pseudo-Grace said in a perky voice, "we can have mimosas. The orange juice would make it breakfast-like, to comfort stuffy old Kangaroo Jack."

He pseudo-smiled back at her. Lexi teasing him while pretending to be Grace annoyed the hell out of him. But why? Because she mocked her sister? Because she used Grace's nickname for him? Because she called him stuffy?

"Would you get the champagne?" She winked at Clint. "Before the grown-ups overrule us?"

Jack watched as she sashayed her cute butt to the huge refrigerator. He'd have to tell her to tone down the sex kitten stuff. Since she wouldn't know where they were, he said, "I'll get the glasses."

"This is more like it," Crusty grumbled his approval.

"Does your housekeeper grow mint, by any chance?"

Clint fell over his feet to reach the refrigerator. "We had lamb earlier this week, and I think Doris put the leftover leaves in a bag in here. I almost made a salad with them."

"Salad," Crusty huffed in the same tone he'd used for *condominiums.*

Lexi mixed mimosas, adding sprigs of mint leaves no one cared much about. It amazed him how well she could imitate Grace, who wouldn't have considered the drinks complete until they were garnished.

Or was this just Lexi being Lexi? Jack didn't know much about her, having only spent time with her tending the animals. Of course, he'd seen her in town, nodded down the length of the feed store or waved across the dance floor at Kerr's Bar on a weekend. But he'd never seen her drink more than beer. Nor would he have described her as fussy—not that Grace was fussy for putting leaves in drinks.

Jack's head throbbed.

"To Crusty." He raised his glass and touched it to the others'. Crystal pinged out high notes of celebration. "Thank you for your generous gift."

After they drank, Clint raised his glass. "I gave this toast last night, although you didn't get to hear it. So once more, for the bride and groom. To Jack and Grace. May you live as long as you want to, and *want to*," he waggled his eyebrows, "as long as you live."

Lexi laughed without taking offense and clinked her flute against Clint's then Crusty's. Jack shook his head and did the same before tapping the rim of his glass against hers. He knew what was expected, what he would have said had this been Grace in the kitchen. He gazed into her sister's identical sky blue eyes. "Oh, I'll want to, believe me, as long as I live."

She blushed but held her smile as he leaned down to brush his lips against hers. Lexi tasted of the mimosa, citrusy with a sharp bite. He curbed a crazy impulse to take a nibble of her. Damn.

"Are you going to tell them your other news?" Clint asked Crusty.

Jack braced himself.

"I'm moving out, so's you can have the house to yoreselves."

"No!" Lexi covered her mouth as Clint and Crusty stared. "I mean, I don't want you to leave your home because of me. Really, Crusty, I'd feel just awful."

"I'm only going across the way," Crusty said with a scowl. "To the house Jack built you."

Jack closed his eyes with mortification while his uncle told Lexi of the idiotic indulgence. He'd look like a damn fool in her eyes. He'd built a house to make Grace feel more comfortable out here, but Grace hadn't wanted him enough to marry him.

"You built Gr—me—us a house?" Her eyes were wide and her face a little paler. She gripped a chair-back with fingers turned white.

"A romantic cottage so's you wouldn't have to put up with me. But as the owners of the ranch now, you should live in the main house."

"It made sense at the time," Jack countered his uncle, embarrassment crawling along his collar. "I thought we could use the privacy, and we have water enough here to support two homes. I didn't know the old coot planned to leave us the land."

The unspoken reminder of his ranch manager status echoed in the room.

"But even so," Clint said, eyeing Lexi, "it would be nice to have that extra privacy. I've heard newlyweds like to run around naked."

Crusty laughed with Clint while Jack frowned. When had his family become so coarse? Or was he just noticing their talk of breeding her, and "wanting to" have sex, and being naked because Lexi was the subject of the jokes?

Her cheeks couldn't get any pinker. "I wouldn't know,

never having been married before. And we have Anna here, too, so I doubt we'll be running around naked."

"Well, she can spend the night with me when you want to do that." Crusty chuckled. "'Course I'll know what yore doing while she's with me. But I can't move out right away. I've got some renovations to finish."

Jack stared at him. "You're renovating my house?"

"I'm renovating *my* house. Putting a bedroom on the first floor since I can't climb stairs. I doubt I'll use the upstairs at all, 'cept maybe when yore kids come for overnights."

Crusty and Clint laughed like mules—or their relatives. Jack ran a hand over Lexi's arm. "Sorry about this. About them."

"I'm used to it." Then she blinked, catching herself. Because while Lexi, the vet, might be accustomed to ribald humor, Grace, the city-girl artist wouldn't be. "I mean, I did grow up in a town full of cowboys."

"Still, you shouldn't have to deal with it in your own home."

"Speaking of which," Lexi turned to the man causing all these problems with his generosity, "I don't want you to go, Crusty. We'll continue the renovations since a first floor bedroom would be handy, but let's not talk about you leaving."

The men stared at her. Grace wouldn't have been so direct telling them what to do. She'd have made sweet suggestions, and they'd have fallen all over themselves to please her. Jack liked a woman to be soft, like Grace. Lexi tended to stand her ground and state her opinions. Mostly, it irritated him, but he had a grudging respect for her confidence.

"Hate to drink and run," Clint said, "but I'd like to take some photos on the way home. I have a location in Utah in mind for sunset, and it's a climb after I drive there. That means I need to leave now."

"It was so nice to spend time with you these last days." Lexi hugged Clint and kissed his cheek. "I'm pleased you could be here for Jack."

Clint cocked his head then looked at Jack, who held his gaze. Jack put his arm around Lexi's waist and pulled her close. "It meant the world to us, bro. Thanks."

Crusty rose to his feet. "Don't have to wait for a wedding to come home, you know, boy. It'll be a far stretch till the next one, since I don't have no plans to get hitched anytime soon."

Clint and Crusty shook hands before Clint pulled the old man into a one-armed hug.

"Get on with you now." Crusty's face turned ruddier under his scowl. "Yore wasting daylight."

"What am I thinking?" Clint slapped his hand on the counter, gaze darting between Jack and Lexi. "I should update you on Marco's foal. Let's go out to the barn and see him."

Jack felt Lexi stiffen at his side. Of course she'd be concerned with the colt's health. He tightened his grip on her waist, wondering why Clint would bring that up before he left. "Has something happened since this yesterday?"

"Nah," Clint said, gaze on Lexi. "I just thought you'd be interested."

She turned to Jack. "Go on and check it out. I'd like to get my bag unpacked. Maybe you could have someone take it to my...our room?"

That was more authentic, Jack thought with relief. Grace would expect to have her luggage carried up.

Of course, she also would have remembered they'd be sharing a room, but Jack gave Lexi points for effort.

"I'll have it sent up while I'm out in the barn with Clint."

"What the hell is going on?"

Jack swung around as his brother grabbed his arm. They'd barely cleared view of the house. He nodded his head toward the back of the barn and once there, propped his foot against the bottom rail of the fence, looking out over the corral. "What do you think is going on?"

"I think," Clint said, "you brought home the wrong bride."

Jack hid his surprise. He thought Lexi had done a credible acting job. "I brought home the woman who married me."

"Don't bullshit me, Jack. Is that Grace or not?"

He drew a deep breath and let it burst out, relieved to share the secret with Clint. "No, it's Lexi."

"I knew it."

Jack filled in the details as briefly as possible.

"Sonovabitch." Clint slapped his hat on his leg. "She married you?"

"Lexi didn't want me to be embarrassed. Said it was spur of the moment. Events sped along and carried her away."

"So she *married* you?"

Jack had to laugh. "That was my reaction, too, at first. But she meant well by it. She told me as soon as we left the church, the minute we had privacy."

"After you left church was a little late, if you ask me."

Jack hardened his expression so Clint would take him seriously. "I didn't ask you. Lexi acted impulsively, but you can't fault her intentions."

Clint grunted but didn't argue the point. "Is it legal?"

Jack shook his head. "I have no idea. The license isn't in her name, but the signature is legal for either woman. Maybe. And now there's Crusty's present."

Clint closed his eyes. "I'd forgotten about that."

"The ranch is in mine and Grace's names. Except Grace isn't Grace Walker. I can't lose the ranch, even to our cousins."

He rubbed his temple. "I've stepped in a pile of crap and I'm tracking it through the whole damned house."

"What can I do?"

Jack clapped his hand on his brother's shoulder. "Just having you here has helped. There's not much anyone can do until Dan Higgins gets me some answers."

"I wouldn't be too specific when you explain it to him. As a lawyer, he might have to turn in Lexi for breaking the law or something. He's an officer of the court. At least, that's how it works on TV."

"She didn't break the law."

"She signed a legal document that wasn't made out to her." Clint shrugged. "I don't know the ins and outs, but you should talk in hypotheticals until you get an answer."

"Maybe that's a good idea."

"Any clue where Grace might have gone? I could try to track her on my way home."

Jack's chest constricted. Clint shouldn't refer to anywhere other than the Rocking W as home. "No, but thanks for offering. I wouldn't know where to tell you to look."

Clint grunted. "Nothing is more important than keeping the ranch. Let's ask the bride you've got. Maybe she has an idea."

Jack stopped him with a hand on his arm. "Be nice to her, Clint. For the time being, she *is* my wife."

Clint shook his head. "You are one screwed up cowboy."

Don't I know it

CHAPTER SIX

Lexi felt the difference in the house the moment the brothers returned. The air recharged with electricity as though lightning powered the Walker men. Even her fingertips tingled.

She'd spent two minutes putting away Grace's "do me" lingerie and hanging the wedding dress. Grace had already brought her clothes over and filled the drawers and one closet. For thirty seconds, Lexi stared at the king-sized bed and for the next thirty, she talked herself into believing they'd find a way to make this work. There must be a bed somewhere in the house she could sneak off to after the others had gone to their rooms.

She called Grace's phone and been sent to voicemail. The rest of the brief time the men had been outside, she'd stared into space, trying to figure what to do next. She needed to get a ride into town to pick up some real clothes and her truck. They could say "Lexi" took Grace's convertible when she ran off to Vegas, so now she, as Grace, would "borrow" Lexi's pickup. What a muddle.

"Lexi."

She started at hearing her real name, stunned to see Jack and Clint at her bedroom door. "I guess you've told him."

"That was pretty gutsy," Clint said, "stepping in to marry my brother."

She sagged with relief. At least Jack hadn't made her out to be the villain. "I might have only made things worse."

Clint sat beside her while Jack closed the door. "You didn't know Crusty planned to sign over the ranch to your sister."

Lexi shut her eyes and inhaled a calming breath while revising her earlier judgment. The situation surpassed *muddle* straight into chaos.

Clint rubbed her arm, his bottle green eyes sympathetic. "We'll figure out something."

"No," Jack said, "*we'll* figure out something. You're heading back to California to work, and stopping to visit those galleries. Stick to the plan."

"Screw the plan," Clint said.

She put her hand on Clint's and squeezed it in gratitude. She couldn't wrap her hand around his muscular forearm. Clint's body was as strong and solid as Jack's. Blond highlights shot through his sandy brown hair, slightly lighter in color than his brother's. But in their deep love for the Rocking W, the men were as identical as she and Grace were in looks. "He's right. You can't mess up your life just because my sister and I have messed up Jack's."

Jack sat on the other side of her. The mattress sagged, with both men acting as bookends, holding her upright but boxing her in. "Lexi and I will straighten this out."

"Look," Clint said, "I'm going to be driving for a couple of days. I built in time on the return trip to stop and take photographs. I can use that time to hunt down Grace instead. I want to," he insisted as they both opened their mouths to object.

"If you're looking for her at someplace that's already on your way, that would be okay," Jack mumbled. "Thanks."

"Lexi, where do you think Grace went?"

She shrugged. "Vegas with a hot drifter?"

Jack smiled. "Those Marshall girls."

"What?" Clint asked. "I think I missed something."

"Doc Kevin was supposed to tell everyone Lexi ran off to Vegas for a wild week with a drifter."

"Lexi wouldn't do that," Clint said. "You'd never leave Grace hanging."

"Thanks, Clint," she said. "It seems my dad thought the same since he didn't tell that story at the reception."

"He doesn't want people to think badly of you," Jack said.

Lexi stood and leaned against the chest of drawers.

Fortunately, the heavy antique oak furniture could bear her weight. She needed a nap after having lain awake on the hotel couch listening to Jack breathe. How he'd slept, she had no idea. But then, she'd lain with guilt and remorse as sofa-partners.

"What about your cousin Rachel?" Clint asked out of the blue.

"What about her?"

He shrugged. "Just wondering if Grace might have gone there. I could, uh, stop by on my way home if you give me Rachel's address."

"It's worth a shot, I guess," Lexi said. "But Rachel was here, not at her place. You met her. She signed the marriage license with you as a witness."

"Oh, yeah, no. Right. I remember, uh, meeting her."

Lexi shared a puzzled glance with Jack. He shrugged. "Any other place you can think of, Lex?"

"I'll jot down some ideas, friends to call, old haunts of hers from before she left. But that was almost five years ago. Honestly, I have no idea what's in her mind right now."

"Not being found," Jack said, a grim twist to his mouth.

"I'm sorry," she said.

"You're not responsible for Grace's actions." Jack stood. "I'll get on the phone with my attorney tomorrow first thing. See if, had something hypothetical like this happened, what would be the consequences, if any. I have to figure out how to ask the status of the deed to the ranch if I hypothetically didn't marry Grace, just so neither of us gets in trouble for committing fraud."

"How would that be fraud for you?" Lexi asked.

"If I know you're not Grace and don't tell anyone, I'm abetting you in land fraud. Taking something that's Grace's. Or, on the bright side," he said as she groaned, "maybe the deed goes to me and my wife, whoever she might be."

"Couldn't we just ask Crusty to take Grace's name off?" Lexi asked.

Jack shook his head. "You heard him. He's got his heart set on male heirs. Signing the land to me was contingent on me being married so I can have sons."

"What a disaster." Lexi squeezed her eyes shut for a moment.

Jack patted her arm. "I won't let you get into trouble."

"I'll hit the road, I guess." Clint stood. "Head toward your cousin's, since you think that's a good idea."

Lexi didn't remember saying that, but it couldn't hurt to check. She and Grace knew where Rachel hid the extra house key. Grace would know the house stood empty. She'd be more apt to go to a hotel, but Grace hadn't foreseen making this road trip and didn't have luggage or money.

With luck, Jack's attorney would declare them not married.

No harm, no foul, as though they had taken part in a play. Or a bad dream. Lexi didn't want to have to endure an annulment, however quiet. It was bad enough she'd participated in the wedding. But then, what about the land?

"I'll help you get your gear to the car," Jack said to Clint.

The men deserved a moment alone. "I'll be down in a few minutes. Don't leave without saying goodbye."

Clint hugged her tight, her feet leaving the ground. A kiss smacked against her cheek. "That's my goodbye for Lexi. I'll give Grace a more proper one when you come downstairs."

She smiled as the guys left. Clint would have made a great brother-in-law. Still would, she reminded herself. For Grace.

A door slammed downstairs. The light thud of footsteps running up the stairs made Lexi's heart race. Anna was home. No matter what Jack said, Lexi felt sure the girl would discern the difference between her and Grace. The bedroom door stood open, leaving Lexi with little time to prepare.

"Hi!" Anna came to a dead stop in front of Lexi.

Why did she stop? Did she realize the woman sitting there wasn't the stepmother she expected to see? Lexi swallowed and took a breath to achieve that higher tone of Grace's. "Hi, yourself. How was your sleepover?"

"Good. But the reception party was boring. Where were you and Dad?"

Lexi inhaled unsteadily. So far, so good. "We decided not to go. After all the wedding craziness, getting ready for it, I mean, we needed to talk."

Anna nodded. "That's what Uncle Clint said. You two wanted to be alone together. But I wanted to be alone together *with you*."

That made Lexi smile. "We're here now. Have you seen your dad?"

"Yeah. He's outside. Uncle Clint's leaving so I hugged him goodbye."

"I'm sorry he couldn't stay longer."

Anna shrugged. "He never stays for long. It hurts him to be here."

"Why do you think that?"

"Uncle Crusty says it's 'cause Uncle Clint 'don't own the place and never will. Got to make a life for himself.' Dad says that Uncle Clint went as far away and to as different a place as he could." The girl scrunched up her face in concentration, looking like she'd eaten sour candy. "What's L.A. like that's so different from here?"

"It's a big city. Tall buildings. Lots of roads and cars."

"Tall buildings? Where do the horses live? And the cattle?"

"It's a big sprawling, uh, stretched-out place like the ranches around here, but it's full of people instead of cattle.

Everyone drives cars. Very few ride horses."

"That doesn't sound like a good place for Uncle Clint."

"Sometimes we can't choose where we work."

The girl broke out into a huge smile. "But you can. Isn't it great?"

"What do you mean?"

"Dad didn't...? Oh, never mind." Anna pressed her lips together and made a locking motion over them before grinning. "I have to change. Erin let me borrow her clothes so I didn't have to come home in my wedding dress."

Lexi smiled at the phrase. She'd come home in borrowed clothes, too. "You look very cute in those purple overalls, and your goldenrod shoes are certainly stunning with it. Bring Erin's clothes in here. I'll wash them and you can return them to your friend tomorrow at school."

Anna tipped her head to the side. "You're going to wash my clothes?"

"Yes."

"But Doris washes our clothes."

Lexi nodded, glad it was just Anna she'd fumbled in front of. Grace would have known what chores she'd have to do and who did the others. "That's because no one was here to help Doris before while the men worked the ranch. But I can't have her doing everything."

"Dad says the same thing. He only washes towels and sheets because Doris won't let him touch the clothes."

"That's probably wise. Still, I know how to wash clothes, and Doris won't mind." Lexi hoped she wouldn't, anyway. Doris wouldn't view Lexi doing a load of clothes as a threat to her place in the family. Hopefully, Grace would be back to deal with this in a day or so. The idea of Grace in a power struggle over laundry made Lexi grin.

"Hey, your dad and I have to go into town and get my truck. Well, Lexi's truck." She cleared her throat at yet another stumble. The girl would act as a buffer on the ride into town. "I'm going to use the truck for a couple of days. Do you want to ride along?"

"Okay." Anna went still, studying Lexi with an intentness that made her want to squirm. "Should I call you 'Mom' now? I don't think it would be right to call you Grace."

Not right? Lexi wondered if she'd slipped so often even a child hadn't been fooled. After a moment's panic, she controlled her expression.

"Erin calls her stepmom 'Mom,'" Anna continued. "I could do that, since you're a grownup. Dad says it's not polite to call adults by their first names."

Lexi slumped with relief. She'd dodged that one, but she needed to be more careful.

Anna yearned for a mother, and Lexi almost agreed to let the girl call her whatever she wanted. But when Grace returned, the two would forge their own relationship. Lexi couldn't sabotage that. If Grace had set it up so Anna would call her by her given name, then it should stay that way. "Why don't you stick to 'Grace' for a while. We don't have to make any hasty changes. For now, just go put on your own clothes."

The girl nodded and scuffed her feet along the carpet as she left, making her disappointment clear.

Guilt assailed Lexi. Anna needed a real mother, not a substitute, but Lexi couldn't let her get too close to fake-Grace.

In the meantime, Lexi had to go to town and fool whoever they encountered into thinking she was a happy bride.

It was going to be a long day.

Lexi just managed to catch Clint as he said goodbye to Crusty and Jack. She slipped him the few hastily written addresses and phone numbers of Grace's friends that she could remember, along with Rachel's. He pulled her aside and hugged her, whispering, "Jack photocopied the invitation list for me so I have everyone's addresses, but the phone numbers will help. I'll have to figure out what to say, though, especially without giving away that Grace rabbited."

"I should have thought of the invitation list."

"You just keep Jack from going crazy or spilling the beans to his lawyer. The man is too trusting. Jack, that is, not the lawyer."

"Dan Higgins is a good guy. He'll take care of Jack."

Clint tapped her nose. "And Jack will take care of you."

"I'll be fine. You make sure you keep those appointments with the art galleries, Clint. Don't waste too much time looking for Grace. She's already wrecked one Walker's life this weekend."

"Well, you're a Walker now, too."

Lexi shook her head. "Not really."

"Walkers take care of their family."

Jack came over and put his arm around her waist. She gave him a confused look until she spotted Crusty watching from the porch. Anna bounded outside in a powder blue shorts set and sneakers, providing another witness to be convinced.

"You have a safe trip," Jack said.

The men shook hands, Clint swung Anna in the air while she shrieked with laughter, then he tipped his hat to Lexi and took off. They stood watching his dust trail until Crusty gave a "harrumph" and went inside.

"Want to see the new colt?" Jack asked.

Lexi could have kissed him—er, shaken his hand really hard.

They stood outside the stall where Marco's Miracle had stayed overnight with Bella for observation. Lexi couldn't resist teasing Jack. She looked up at him and batted her eyes. "It's so pretty."

Jack stared for almost a whole minute before his face cleared, obviously catching on to her imitation of Grace. "Do you want to paint him? He's looking really healthy."

She bit back a pleased smile. "I'll tell Lexi. She'll be gratified you know she takes good care of your stock."

Jack gave her a wry glance.

Anna fast-walked down the aisle, having been taught not to run inside the barn and spook the horses. "Are we going to town now, Dad?"

He turned to Lexi. "Are we?"

"I want to borrow Lexi's truck," she said. "It's at the house. She ran errands yesterday, then Rachel picked her up to go to the church." Lexi navigated her way through the recounting, trying to keep the actions of all the women straight and use the right names. "I want to grab some clothes more appropriate to ranch life. I thought Anna might like to go with us."

"I see."

He probably did. Probably suspected Lexi didn't want to be alone with him. She shrugged.

He spoke reassuringly to the mare and foal, his tone so

soothing it made Lexi envious.

She almost laughed at herself. Jack didn't talk to her in a sweet tone? She was lucky he didn't sue her for marrying him.

Jack watched Lexi wander through the house she'd shared with her sister for the eight months Grace had been back in Little Tree. The three bedroom house made a nice investment for Lexi and gave Grace a room in which to paint. Now he took in the two loveseats, recovered in some sturdy tan fabric and mounded with colorful pillows, but still comfortable enough for his tall frame.

Had Grace been comfortable here? It looked like Lexi. Homey. Quiet. Small-town.

Annabeth trailed behind Lexi, chattering. Lexi approached Jack with a frown furrowing her brow.

"What's up?" he asked.

"I don't know. Nothing probably. It just feels... I don't know." She shook her head. "It's probably nothing."

Jack stood. He trusted her instincts. Maybe she'd found a clue to where Grace went. Mindful of Annabeth listening, he asked, "Is it because your sister isn't here?"

"No. Maybe." Lexi sighed. "Things feel mussed. Out of place."

"Do you think your sister stopped by here on her way out

of town?"

"She doesn't usually mess with my clothes, but it's possible. A lot of her stuff had gone to your place already so maybe she needed something to wear on her trip."

Jack glanced at Annabeth, relieved she hadn't caught Lexi's slip. They were supposed to be talking about Lexi's clothes, which weren't at the ranch. He examined the living room, dining area, and the part of the kitchen he could see from his place by the loveseat. Not having been here often, he didn't notice anything out of place.

Lexi gave a thin laugh. "Maybe I'm just paranoid. With so many changes lately, I've lost track of things."

He nodded but stepped into the kitchen to investigate. Thinking to search for a clue out by the truck, he pulled open the back door. It gave after a slight resistance. Gouges on the doorjamb made him look closer. Scratches gleamed around the knob.

"Lexi," he called, before remembering. Dammit. "Lexi might have done some home repair recently," he corrected for Annabeth's benefit. "Can you come look at this, Grace?"

"Sure, but I don't think she has." Lexi's smile held in place as she came near, but tight lines fanned from her eyes, betraying her worry. "What are you seeing?"

He gestured at the door.

She shook her head. "Neither of us did that."

His arched eyebrow asked if she thought someone had been in the house. Her nod confirmed his suspicion. "Did your sister have a key with her yesterday?"

"Yeah. On her key ring with the convertible's and a key to our dad's house."

Jack stiffened, alert for danger. If Grace had a key, someone else had tried to break in. *Had* broken in, if Lexi's sense of things out of place could be believed. And he did believe her. Two questions remained. Who did it and why? "Is anything missing?"

Lexi firmed her lips.

Is she hiding a smile? What could be funny about someone breaking into her home? She could have been hurt if she'd come home from the wedding last night.

The reminder of the wedding pulled him up as he understood the reason behind her amusement—the answer to his question. Grace was missing. He had to shake his head. "Maybe I should phrase that differently."

"Whatcha doing out here?" Annabeth asked from the kitchen, a few steps from the door.

"Just talking, sugar cube." He smiled at the replica of his wife—his first wife—while anxious to get her someplace safer. He didn't think the home invader hovered nearby, but suspecting someone had come here while the women were absent put him in defense mode. Had someone snuck in yesterday afternoon, knowing the Marshall sisters and most of their neighbors would be at the church? Or had he waited inside here for Lexi to return from the reception?

Jack had trouble believing anyone in Little Tree capable of malice against Lexi or Grace. Nevertheless, various ranches hired itinerant help who could have gotten a look at the women when in town. "I'll make the phone call." He didn't want to say "police" in front of Annabeth. "Don't touch anything else."

Lexi nodded before turning away. "I've gathered some clothes and boots."

Those more-suitable garments she'd mentioned. Remembering, Jack went still as the legal ramifications hit. "Uh, honey."

That brought her up short. She spun, and he could almost hear her choke on the reprimand not to call her that. "Yes?"

"Why don't you take Annabeth in to Lee's Freezes to get some ice cream while I make that call?"

"Yay!"

His daughter's smile lessened some of his tension.

Lexi frowned. "But it's my house."

"It's really Lexi's, right? *You* are just a guest."

Her mouth opened to no doubt protest—didn't she protest everything he said?—before she understood and nodded. She looked over at Annabeth. "Hey, Anna, would you run out and see if the keys are in the truck?"

"Sure." Annabeth skipped off.

"We're in a fix, aren't we?" she said. "I can't make a statement as Lexi without raising questions about where I was yesterday. And I can't claim to be Grace to the cops because that would be assuming a false identity. Maybe it's time to drop the charade and face the consequences. A break-in changes things."

"It does," Jack agreed. "But my main concern is keeping you out of trouble. You can't step forward as Lexi without raising the question of land fraud and identity fraud."

She rubbed her hands over her face.

He took advantage of her vulnerability to press home his point. "But we don't have to expose you yet. I'll say I came in to grab something for my wife and noticed the back door as I was leaving. I was making sure all the locks were secure. Dutiful husband and all that."

Jack tried to smile for her but not much would lessen their worry. "Leave the duffle of clothes and boots on the floor there. I'll let the police look through it as though I collected it."

Lexi looked away.

"What?"

"I have underwear and bras in here."

He grinned. "I can't wait to see them."

She narrowed her eyes. "Jackson Walker, you stay out of my stuff."

"I'll turn my head away and think of England."

"Very funny." She rubbed her neck. "Should we just give up the pretense? I can't let you get into trouble because of me."

"I won't. And I won't be lying. I did come to get my wife some things. I'll just leave out the part where you were here, too. And that I'm picking up your things instead of Grace's."

"This is getting too convoluted."

He stepped closer and took her hands in his. "Do you trust me, Lexi?"

"Of course, but this isn't about trust."

Pleasure filled him at her answer. "It's about keeping you safe. Before you come out of hiding, we need to know if you're guilty of anything illegal. We need to know if we're married, but even if you're not in trouble with the law, you can't stay here until we know what happened."

"I can stay with Dad."

Jack hesitated, reluctant to let her out of his sight until this mystery was resolved. "Maybe, once we know what we need to do about the wedding."

"Dad's house will be empty—Oh, my gosh." She smiled as her body relaxed. "Why didn't I think of this before? Rachel probably came over, looking for me when I didn't show at the wedding. She might have gone through my clothes to see if I'd packed a bag. Were my toiletries missing, that sort of thing. It's a thin possibility, but it makes more sense than someone breaking in."

"Do you think so? That would solve one of our problems."

"I can't see her jimmying a lock, but I'll call her and try to get some answers."

"Call from town. Or—" he continued in a rush as she looked ready to object once again, "at least from on the road. Because you need to get going. You don't want to have to answer questions from the police about where you were yesterday and have it on the record."

Convincing her took a few more minutes, but by the time Annabeth returned saying she couldn't find the keys and noting all the places in the truck she'd looked, Lexi had yielded to common sense.

"I even looked under the rug by the stick," Annabeth continued. "I climbed into the truck bed, but I didn't really think Aunt Lexi kept the keys back there. I just wanted to see if I could get inside by myself."

The stick. At the reminder, Jack laughed, drawing the females' attention. He held out his car keys. "You can take my car, honey, since you can't drive a manual."

"What do you mean? Oh." Lexi's body sagged. "Right."

She glanced at Annabeth. "The stick helps operate the truck. And I can't drive that kind of vehicle."

He grinned, despite her glare.

She blew out a breath, and he had to admire her for finding a smile for his daughter.

"It's an ice cream kind of day. Let's go, Anna."

"What about you, Dad?"

"I'll meet you at the grocery store. Wait for me in the parking lot, okay?"

"Sure." Annabeth headed toward the car.

"Are *you* sure," Lexi said, "this is the right thing to do?"

He shrugged. "I think it is. Let's go with that for now."

She nodded and climbed into his car. After adjusting the mirrors and seat, she backed out and both ladies waved when the car accelerated.

Jack called the police then checked Grace's room to be sure no one hid there.

How had it been less than a day that Lexi had turned his life upside down? In the last ... he did the calculations ... sixteen hours, he'd gotten married, then discovered another woman posed as his bride. He'd achieved his dream of inheriting the family ranch, only to have it held just out of reach by a technicality. Now he'd learned his maybe-wife couldn't return to her house, in the off-chance she didn't go to jail for committing fraud. One way or the other, he was stuck with her.

Red lights flashed outside as the police arrived. "And the hits just keep on coming."

The sheriff met him at the door. Carrying an extra few pounds didn't slow Tim Matson's instincts. Jack followed him into the house and related the truths he'd rehearsed.

"Any idea where Lexi went?" Matson's brown eyes arrowed in on Jack. "I heard she wasn't at the wedding. If someone broke in last night, it doesn't appear Lexi slept here or she would have reported it."

"Maybe she was the one who broke in?" Jack hoped Lexi would forgive him for making her sound witless, but at least breaking into her own place wasn't a crime. "Maybe she didn't have her keys on her."

Matson shook his head. "You ever met the gal?"

Jack took that as rhetorical.

The sheriff grinned like a teacher with a bright pupil. "I'd bet you a coffee at the diner that gal could have taken off a simple door knob. She'd have had the tools on her to do it, too. Hell, she probably knows how to jimmy a lock open with a paperclip."

Jack laughed along with the sheriff, who sounded proud of Lexi's supposed abilities rather than concerned she'd use her power for evil. Seemed Jack's possible-wife had hidden talents and hidden admirers. Hidden from him, at least.

What else didn't he know about Lexi?

CHAPTER SEVEN

"Don't look to your left," Lexi's fake husband muttered out of the side of his mouth, making her instinctively turn in that direction before reining in her reaction. She controlled her curiosity as she emerged from Jack's car to join him on the grocery store parking lot.

"What am I not looking at?" she asked in a whisper while pretending to look adoringly into his eyes.

"There's a cowboy staring at you." Jack's gaze stayed on hers. "I can't see his face under his hat. He's standing by that light pole, watching us."

Lexi cocked her head in question. They had far more important things to discuss. "So?"

"One, he's staring at you. Two, he's probably mistaken you for someone else." Jack's cryptic words were for Anna's benefit as she emerged from the backseat of the car. "Three, I don't like men staring at my wife."

"Oh, that." Lexi laid a hand on his forearm, feeling the heat from his skin and the soft brown hairs tingle against her palm. "You'll have to get used to it. We Marshall women draw attention."

"But you're a Walker woman now." He nuzzled her cheek.

"How many people are watching?" She figured witnesses nearby motivated him to pretend-kiss her.

"About five."

Five people could spread a lot of gossip in a short time. They would tell of the newlyweds unable to keep their hands off each other. It helped solidify her role as Grace and the cover for Lexi being out of town. The grocery store on the little main street would be the perfect place to hear the rumors circulating about Lexi's disappearance, but she wanted to know how Jack had dealt with the police.

"Are you guys going to do that a lot?" Anna asked from beside them.

"Yep," Jack answered.

The girl shook her head and started toward the store.

Jack shrugged and took Lexi's hand. "We're newlyweds, sugar cube. Honey, did you talk to your cousin?"

Lexi shot him a dark look and shook her head. "Rachel didn't answer her cell. I doubt she got up very early, so she's probably still driving. Longmont is about an eight hour drive, not including stops, so I'll check back with her later. My other call went to voicemail again."

His callused palm squeezed hers. She quickened her step to hide her awareness of him. Of his masculinity. Of his strength. And, darn it, of his good looks. He was supposed to be her brother-in-law. They had a history of barely getting along. She would never go all girly over holding hands in public, but it still made her itch between her shoulder blades. Pulling away would draw attention and not only from the onlookers. He'd realize it bothered her. She didn't need him speculating why.

"How'd it go with the police?" she whispered.

"Not a hitch." Jack tipped the brim of his hat toward several ladies.

Lexi recognized one of them as Maude Miller whose ranch she visited to oversee their new ranch manager castrating calves. Since she couldn't think of a situation where Grace would have met her, Lexi kept her nod of acknowledgment stiff and somewhat vague.

"Walker," a male voice hailed from across the asphalt.

She caught Anna's shoulder to stop her, and they turned to face the man approaching. Lexi gave an inward groan and put on her Grace-face. Darryl Peters was the biggest blowhard and flirt she'd ever had to deal with. In a country of cowboys, that said something. His slimy assertiveness made her uneasy. His father owned the feed store and his mother worked at the town's pharmacy, so it behooved Lexi to play nice.

Since she wasn't Lexi right now, however, she chose to remain aloof, as Grace would.

"Congratulations." Darryl shook hands with Jack while eyeing Lexi. "Didn't think we'd see you and the little woman out in public for a while. Heard you even skipped the reception."

His suggestive wink crawled along Lexi's flesh.

"Thanks. I know how lucky I am," Jack said.

"No honeymoon?"

"Jack's taking me to Australia this winter," Lexi said with credible disdain for the rough cowhand. He couldn't keep a job or a girlfriend. He currently lived with his parents and worked in the back of the feed store, away from the majority of the customers.

Darryl scoffed. "Putting off the *festivities* until it's convenient, Jack? That don't sound too romantic to me."

Lexi arched an eyebrow and stared him down in a manner second nature to Grace. "When it's winter here and the work slows, it's summer Down Under. Which makes a winter getaway a win-win."

Darryl spit some tobacco juice just off to the left of them. "Ain't that Lexi's truck? Clint stopped at the gas station this morning and told Hank that she left for Vegas with some guy."

Darryl's raw chuckle made her stomach flop. "Must say I'm surprised. She always comes across as a little stuck-up. No offense."

A muscle flexed in Jack's cheek. "I'm sure you don't mean to offend either my wife or my sister-in-law, Peters."

Jack paused while his rather obvious message sank in. Both women were his family now, and he meant to see they were respected as such. Lexi suppressed the warmth his claim generated. She hadn't considered how Grace's marriage to a Walker would change her own status in the townspeople's eyes.

"We're borrowing Lexi's truck while she uses Grace's car," Jack said.

Darryl grunted. "Maybe she'll be more fun once she's back."

"I doubt it." Lexi couldn't help herself. She felt dirty just standing this close to him. "A few days away doesn't change a person's character."

"Where's Aunt Lexi?" Anna asked.

Lexi almost jumped, startled by the child's presence. "She's taking a small vacation."

"A short one, we hope," Jack put in.

"Very short."

Darryl frowned. "Well, the timing is strange with your wedding and all, but then she's a strange girl."

Lexi pivoted to Jack. "I think I'll go to the feed store. There are a few things I need to get."

Darryl frowned. "What would a pretty lady like you need at our store?"

"Yes, Grace," Jack said. "What do we need there?"

Drat. In her eagerness to get away from Darryl, she'd forgotten her role. Again. "Lexi left a list."

"She left the list with you?" Darryl asked. "I was just there and saw your dad. You might catch him if you hurry. He won't want to have to make another trip to the store."

"I'll call him." Because, sure as shooting, she wasn't going to confront her father in public.

"Got to get this beer in the fridge." Darryl indicated the bag he carried. "Have Lexi call me when she gets back home, okay? Maybe she'll have had a change of heart."

"Yeah, I'll do that." Lexi watched the man saunter away. "When pigs fly."

"Did he make a pass at you sometime?" Jack asked, gaze on Darryl as well. "Or at your sister?"

"What's a pass?" Anna asked before Lexi could reply.

Lexi turned her toward the store and began walking again. "When a man is interested in getting to know a woman better, he does something or says something to let her know."

"Oh. Can I get a pickle from the barrel?"

"Sure." Jack matched his pace to theirs. "I notice you avoided that question."

"Darryl Peters is the least of our worries."

Jack scowled. "I'll take that as a yes. But you're right, we should stop and see your dad."

"I was thinking the same thing." Lexi paused, knowing he wouldn't like her next suggestion. They couldn't talk to her dad with Anna there. "I should go alone."

Jack shook his head before she finished speaking. "For the foreseeable future, we're a team."

"My dad already knows what's going on. What do we do about Anna overhearing?"

"We're going together."

Lexi sighed. Stubborn man. He always showed her this side: bossy, opinionated, and arrogant. They'd never had an easy relationship, and despite the past half-day's collaboration, it seemed they never would.

They hurried through the grocery store, buying very little and acting noticeably cheery. Once outside, Lexi switched the carton of ice cream into the thermal bag she carried in the truck and climbed behind the wheel of his car.

Pulling into her dad's driveway, Lexi experienced a pang of longing for home. Her dad lived in a two story gray-sided house with a large treatment room attached in the back. The office served for treating smaller animals, but most of his work involved calls to ranches and farms. She and Grace had grown up here, carefree. She missed this house.

She wanted to ask her dad about the horses she'd visited last week and the success of the feed he'd suggested for Carrie Moore's herd of cattle on parched land out west of town.

But Lexi couldn't inquire about that. Grace wouldn't have any knowledge of those things or be interested. Anna overhearing and, for some obscure reason, mentioning it to a friend or to Doris could spell trouble.

"You can come in," she said to Jack. "But after you've had your manly say or whatever, you should take the perishables home. Including Anna. I'll follow in the car."

He scowled.

"I know it's not what you want. But it's a compromise. Think you can do that?"

"Honey, marriage is all about compromise."

She grunted and swung open the screen door. "Don't call me honey."

Jack smiled at Lexi's back as she entered Kevin's house. He'd grown used to seeing her disgruntled over his decisions, but he'd never thought it particularly cute before. He put his hand on Annabeth's shoulder and steered her before him. "Come on, sugar cube. We're going visiting."

"Dad," Lexi called. "It's us. Uh, Grace and Jack, here with Anna."

"That ought to be warning enough," Jack muttered.

She shot him a sour look which turned to radiance as footsteps sounded.

He braced himself for the discussion to come. They wouldn't say much with Annabeth within earshot, but he needed to reassure the doc. Despite Grace's actions, and Lexi's for that matter, he and the doc should stay on friendly terms.

"Hi, Grandpa," Anna called out as Kevin Marshall descended the steps.

Jack stilled. *Grandpa?*

"Well, hey there, cutie." Kevin finished his way downstairs after a slight pause Annabeth wouldn't notice. "What are you people doing in town today?"

"We came to get Aunt Lexi's truck," Annabeth said, "but my...Grace can't drive it 'cause of the stick in the middle of the seats."

"I see." He gave Lexi a hard once-over before pulling her into his arms. Their embrace went on and on, giving Jack a moment to think.

He wasn't sure what he felt toward Grace at the moment or if he'd be able to forgive her. He'd been attracted enough to accept her hasty proposal. He had imagined their children running around with Annabeth, little golden cherubs with his dark-haired angel. He could envision Grace popping out of her art studio to watch the kids try to lasso calves.

He groaned at the image, distracted away from thoughts of Grace. He couldn't let Lexi know he'd been stupid enough to build a studio for Grace. He'd thought at the time he owed it to her for helping him save the ranch from his cousins.

"Me next." Annabeth held up her arms as though she were two-years-old.

Kevin laughed and swept her into his arms. She put her head on his shoulder. "I haven't held a little girl in a long time."

Lexi's smile wobbled. "Some things you never forget."

"We bought ice cream at the grocery store for Dad 'cause he didn't get any at Lee's Freezes," Annabeth said. "Do you want to come over to our house and have some too?"

"Sounds good, but I can't today. I'll check my appointment calendar." Kevin slid Annabeth to the floor. He stared hard at Jack. "How are things at the ranch?"

"They're fine, sir." Jack held out his hand. "I'm making sure of it."

The older man made him wait, hand out like a fool, while Kevin's narrowed gaze bore into him. A bead of sweat trickled down Jack's neck, but he refused to lower his hand. After a decade-long minute, Kevin grunted and shook hands. Jack surreptitiously blew out a relieved breath.

Lexi rolled her eyes. "Now that you've said hello and whatnot, why don't you get that ice cream home? We wouldn't want all the hot air in here to melt it."

Jack hid a smile.

"We're visiting," her father protested as though nothing had happened. "Why don't you put the ice cream in my freezer and sit a spell?"

"Jack has to get back. No rest for a rancher, as you know."

She implied "no rest for the wicked," but Jack ignored the unspoken accusation. He could have denounced her and her sister for frauds. He could have tried to take advantage of the situation. It wasn't everyday a man obtained a beautiful bride but didn't enjoy the benefits.

He gulped as the unbidden thought whacked him sideways. Lexi had been a beautiful bride, just as Grace would have been. What looked good on one looked good on the other, of course. Grace probably would have been as radiant. Although now that he remembered it, Lexi had been pale and trembly. She hadn't been radiant or certain of her actions, as he would expect his bride would be. But then, Lexi wasn't his bride, despite marrying him.

The headache tightened behind his temples.

"You're being treated all right?" Kevin asked.

"Yes, Dad. Of course."

Jack couldn't blame the doc for asking. If Annabeth were ever in a mess like this, God forbid, he'd do everything in his power to ensure her well-being. Some other man might have taken out his frustration and anger on Lexi.

Without Crusty's gift, it would have been better to have faced the humiliation of being jilted than being saddled with a bride he didn't want and who didn't want him. Although, without Crusty's gift, he could have quietly annulled the wedding, so perhaps he should stop blaming her for screwing things up.

He didn't blame Crusty, who had acted out of the goodness of his ancient moldy heart. Jack could only fall on his knees in gratitude to the old man for finally providing him with his heart's desire.

Grace, however, he still blamed. Last minute nerves, his ass. She'd behaved like a thoughtless child. He never would have suspected her capable of selfish behavior. Had he known her at all?

"Jack," Lexi's voice brought him from his musings. "Why don't you head on home with Anna. I'll be there shortly."

He looked at Kevin. "Are we good, Doc?"

"Are we?" her father countered. "I've got both my girls'

welfare to consider."

"Lexi acted in the manner she thought best at the time. I can't say I'm thrilled with what all happened yesterday afternoon, but the situation has become more complicated now."

"Is that possible?" Kevin asked.

Jack snorted a laugh. "Believe it or not, yes. My wife will fill you in on the details, but let's just say it concerns Crusty."

Kevin shook his head. "Should have known."

Jack glanced down at Annabeth. "Let's head out, sugar cube. We need to get the food home."

"Can't I stay and visit? I've never had a grandpa before."

Lexi squatted beside her. "Next time I come in to see my dad, I'll bring you. We can have dinner together."

"With my dad, too?"

Lexi glanced at Jack. They wouldn't be married long enough for him to worry about dinners with his father-in-law, but being left out of the arrangements didn't suit Jack at all.

Damn, Clint had hit the nail on the head. Jack was one screwed up cowboy.

"If he's available," Lexi said to Annabeth. "Between your rancher daddy and my vet daddy, it might be a while before everyone has a couple of spare hours at the same time."

"Okay. I'll see you at home then." She threw her arms around Lexi's neck in a hug that nearly toppled them both. A loud kiss landed on Lexi's cheek.

Lexi returned her kiss before rising.

Annabeth went to Kevin's side. "You're my grandpa now so you get a kiss goodbye, too."

"Glad to hear it." He leaned down to hug and kiss the girl. "You're a sweet one."

Jack offered his hand once again to Kevin, making sure to maintain eye contact, hoping the man would read all he couldn't say just then. He nodded at Lexi. "See you back at the ranch."

"Da-ad." Annabeth tugged on his hand. "You have to kiss her goodbye, too."

He smiled at his pint-sized dictator. "Are you sure?"

She nodded. "I've seen it on TV. All the happy families kiss hello and goodbye. Only the yelling ones don't."

"Well, we're not a yelling family." He shrugged an apology at Lexi and kissed her cheek.

Annabeth sighed. "Now we can go. Bye, Grandpa. Bye, Grace."

Her dad gave her a pointed look as they waved the Walkers out the door.

"That girl," he said, "is going to get her heart broken."

"Not if I can help it." Lexi shut the door and leaned back against it.

"And what about my girl?"

"Which one?"

"Let's start with you." He put his arm around her and hugged her close. Then he guided her into the kitchen, where they held all serious discussions.

"I'm okay, Dad."

"Good to know. Grace left a message on my office machine."

Relief buckled her knees. "Thank God. Where is she? When is she coming home?"

"She didn't say. Just that she was okay."

Lexi glowered. "Yeah, *she's* okay. She's not the one left to deal with all this." She sighed. "It's such a mess. Crusty deeded the land over to Jack and Grace Walker."

After a moment's surprise, her dad shook his head. "That old coot always had the worst timing."

"It would have been a lovely gift if Grace had stayed."

He grunted, his reluctance to give Crusty credit for kindness apparent.

"As it stands..." Lexi sighed. "There is no Audrey Grace Walker. Jack's checking to see what happens if he annuls the marriage or divorces her. Or me. One of us." She took a breath. "And his lawyer will have to check to see if I committed fraud by signing a legal document not issued to me."

Her dad paled, at least as much as his weathered tan

allowed, and sank onto a kitchen chair. "The marriage certificate. I didn't think of that."

Lexi pulled out another chair and turned it to face him before she sank down. "I didn't foresee any of this."

"I should have stopped you at the altar when I realized it was you."

"I thought I knew what I was doing. Saving Jack from being embarrassed. Giving Anna the wedding she dreamed of seeing, and a substitute mother until Grace returned." Lexi put a hand over her mouth. "What if she doesn't come back? But, then again, what if she does before Jack gets his answers?"

Her dad lowered his eyebrows in a censuring frown. "You don't think she'd take half his ranch, do you, girl? Surely you know your sister better than that."

Lexi ducked her head in shame but muttered, "I didn't think she'd run out on her wedding either."

"We need to get her back here to sign her half over to Jack. Then he can divorce her. Or you." Her dad chuckled.

Lexi's eyes widened. "What in the world could you find funny?"

"Jack doesn't even know which woman he's married to."

"Yeah," Lexi muttered. "I'm sure he finds that hilarious."

"As long as he knows he's not married to you, if you get my meaning."

She studied the tabletop, her face heating. The clock ticked away the seconds. She could talk to her dad about animals mating, sperm extraction, or insemination, but neither was comfortable when the animals were human. Less so if the human in question was in the family. She cleared her throat. "Jack and I had this discussion already. Neither of us wants *that*."

"Good." His face relaxed. "Now, do you think we should contact a lawyer? Jack is a good man, but he's going to protect his own interests first."

"Jack's interests are mine, too. I want him to protect his land. I want him to help me get out of this marriage."

"Do you?"

"Yes. Yes, Dad, I do. It was never my intention to *marry* him."

Her dad cocked an eyebrow. "Just go through a wedding ceremony?"

"I didn't plan to go through with it, Dad. Probably the lawyer will say it's not valid. Which would be a relief since Jack wants Grace."

"And if he didn't?"

Lexi suddenly found the pattern on the old wooden table fascinating. Anything to evade her father's gaze.

"I'm not blind, Alexis. I know you had feelings for Jack before Grace came home. I was mighty proud of how you handled those feelings without making a scene when she went after him, but now you're married to the fella."

"What are you saying?"

"She left the gate open."

Was her father advocating that she go after Jack? Take advantage of the situation? They *were* married, after all. She swallowed the heartbeat that raced into her throat.

It would never work—she wasn't even considering it. The gate might be open, as her dad said, but Lexi could no more try to win Jack's love than she could dance that naked hula for him.

"That's neither here nor there, is it?" She stood, too agitated to sit. "We are where we are, and I have to deal with reality. Jack and I never even flirted with each other. He doesn't like women vets, or maybe it's just me he doesn't like on his ranch, treating his animals. So it isn't as though Grace stole anything. I hope she feels the same about me when she returns."

"If that's the way you want it, that leaves only one question. Where in the blue blazes is your sister?"

Lexi tapped on Jack's bedroom door that evening after Crusty went to his rooms on the first floor, and Anna settled in the kitchen with spelling homework. Entering the large masculine room again raised goosebumps on her skin. The king-size bed with a dark chocolate comforter loomed in the middle of the room, drawing her eyes despite her best intentions. She'd sat on the bed only that morning, with Clint and Jack beside her. Alone now, at night, with the house quiet, and no one likely to interrupt, lent the moment an intimacy she didn't welcome. Her father had encouraged her to win Jack's affections. She could picture him in that huge bed, bare-chested, and grinning with anticipation.

The problem was she pictured herself with him, inspiring that eagerness.

Jack led her to two comfortable wing chairs meant for reading or watching TV.

She perched on the navy seat, leaning toward him. "What did the police say?"

"It was a break-in. Sheriff Matson is a fan of yours, by the way. He thinks you could have taken the door apart with your special abilities."

"My what?"

"Do you carry tools?"

She blinked, nonplussed. "Well, sure. I have some in the truck."

"Maybe that's what the intruder used. Did you get hold of your cousin yet?"

"Not yet. There are several messages on my phone from last night. None from today, when she was driving. Maybe she got home tired and went to bed without checking her messages." Lexi shook her head. "I forgot to ask Dad if Rachel mentioned going by my place to look for me."

"He probably convinced her not to, given that he knew the truth."

"Oh, right. Good point." She sighed. "I just get Grace's voicemail. Maybe Clint found her. Have you heard from him?"

"Just a message saying he got cornered at the gas station. He's sorry about the Vegas story, Lexi and so am I."

She shrugged. "It's a good cover."

"I'm sure he'll check in somewhere once he has good cell reception."

"So the sheriff didn't have any ideas?"

Jack shook his head. "He'll have a patrol car go by on a regular basis since the house is empty."

"But that means I can't go home."

"That wouldn't be safe, Lexi. Not until the police learn who broke into your house."

"Yeah, I guess." She frowned. "What happens if your lawyer says we're not married? I'll have to go home then."

"Not unless it's safe," he repeated.

She tensed, her back stiffening. "What do you mean? Of course I'm going home. It doesn't look like Grace is coming back. I'm sorry. I don't mean to be hurtful, but she would have returned or contacted you by now."

"I never said I'd take her back."

"Of course you would. You were going to marry her."

"She asked me, and I didn't object. It was a sensible solution to Crusty's ultimatum about giving the ranch to my cousins. If she hadn't jumped in and said we were getting married, I would have thought of something else. She took all of us by surprise." He shrugged. "It was easier to agree than call her a liar, and we get along well enough."

Lexi rose and walked several steps away. Did he mean he didn't love Grace? He wasn't devastated? Her heart raced as quickly as the thoughts running through her head.

She'd seen him totally dazzled by Grace. Her sister had a larger-than-life personality that drew in strangers and a magnetic pull that made men flock to her side. Everyone loved Grace. Jack might tell himself otherwise to save face and to avoid admitting his current misery, but Lexi didn't buy it. Couldn't. The temptation was too potent.

After composing herself, she turned and stood before the entertainment cabinet. "We need to figure out our next step. What do we do tomorrow if your lawyer says we're not really married and there's no fraud? And what do we do if he says we are and there is?"

"Maybe we're married and there's no fraud. Or we're not

and there still is."

"Are you trying to be difficult?"

"My point is we can't plan what to do until we know the obstacles. Either way, you can't go back to your house."

"Unless we're not married."

He rose. "Lexi, someone broke in. It's not safe there."

"I'll go to my dad's."

Jack stared at her for a full minute. She hated when she couldn't figure out his thoughts. Jack had always been easy to read. He got annoyed when she came out to the ranch instead of her dad. He hated her truck. He questioned her vet skills. And he loved Grace. But now, she couldn't tell what turmoil brewed behind his calm facade.

"What if this trouble follows you to your dad's?"

"That's ridiculous. Everyone knew the house was empty because of the wedding. Maybe someone didn't get invited and wanted to cause a disturbance. Maybe someone wanted a soon-to-be-famous painting. Whatever the motive, it was a one-time opportunity while the house was empty." Her voice didn't match her conviction. Or perhaps it did, since she didn't feel sure of anything at the moment.

"Yet he didn't take anything. Your jewelry and electronics are still there, as are all of Grace's paintings, according to the inventory list in her room. I checked it over with the sheriff."

"Something scared off the intruder. Or he changed his mind. Got religion. Whatever, he's gone. It was an impulse, taking advantage of an opportunity."

"Taking advantage of your absence but not *taking* anything?"

"I don't think it's personal, if that's what you're getting at. No one dislikes me enough to break into my house just to scare me." Lexi couldn't think of anyone who even disliked her a little. People either accepted her, befriended her, or never noticed her. The anonymous vet, much like the postal carrier, always on the property and taken for granted. Trusted enough to be ignored. At the moment, she found comfort in the thought. "It has to be tied to Grace since this never happened before. Everyone knows I don't have anything worth stealing. I don't think there's any real danger."

"Are you willing to risk it? Are you willing to drag your troubles to your dad's door when you could just as easily stay here? At the Rocking W, there are always people within shouting distance."

She didn't want to admit he had a point. "I want my own life back."

"I know."

He probably did understand. Jack didn't have control of his own life right now either. Her grousing seemed petty in comparison. She sighed. "So what do you propose we do?"

Jack's chuckle sounded hollow. "Finally. A Marshall female who waits for me to propose something."

Her breath caught. They stood in his bedroom, feet from that inviting chocolate dream bed. Would she say yes?

"We'll hold tight until tomorrow," he continued. "I'll go in to Dan's office first thing to get answers. Clint's worried if I state the facts then, as a lawyer, Dan has to turn you in if you're guilty of fraud. But don't worry, Lex. I'll protect you."

"I know you will. Despite our past, I trust you, Jack."

He frowned. "What do you mean, despite our past?"

"Well, you don't want me on your ranch. You don't trust me."

"What makes you say that? Why wouldn't I want you on the ranch?"

"I mean working here. You don't trust me with the animals."

"I never said that. I've never thought that."

She put her hands on her hips. "You frown every time I come. You second-guess every decision I make."

"That's not true."

"Jack, be honest."

She meant it as "you're not fooling me," but he paused as though thinking through the situation. What was there to rethink? It was what it was.

He blew out a breath. "Okay. You want honest?"

Suddenly, she didn't think she did.

"I don't like the thought of you—or any woman, but you're the one I deal with—driving a broken-down, rusted-out, unreliable vehicle alone in the back country. I don't like you going to ranches and dealing with men on your own. I don't like you facing down a bull—and I've seen you do it. I know you can, Lexi. I know you do it all the time. That doesn't mean I like it."

Her heart raced away with her breath, as though she'd run a marathon. She would have sworn Jack had never thought twice about her, let alone worried about her safety. She softened toward him, wanting to hug tight to his tough, angry body and assure him she was always careful. His tension and hard scowl made it obvious he resented admitting this much concern for her. Which only touched her more deeply. This was the sweet man he'd shown her in the past two days, despite the glare he now wore.

"I don't doubt your abilities," he continued. "God knows, you've proved yourself time and again."

She drew back, stiffened a little. He made her "abilities" sound like a character fault.

"I don't distrust women in men's jobs, so don't paint me

with that brush. I just don't think you should be going toe to toe with some of the jerks in this area. You drive alone, and everyone knows it. Someone could follow you, intercept you."

"Jack, no one would do that. Besides, I carry a gun."

The corner of his mouth quirked. "Like you'd ever shoot anyone."

"If I was in danger, you'd better believe I would."

"I'll let you have that one. You're just hot-tempered enough to do it. And then you'd patch him up."

She grunted, knowing the answer would depend on the man and the situation, and therefore she couldn't dispute it.

"It's the driving around alone that's the worst, Lexi. You've heard how my wife died. It's just irresponsible for you to do the same thing."

Actually, Lexi hadn't heard anything that would connect Sarabeth to her. Given the framing of the conversation, she tamped down her resentment at being called irresponsible. "She fell while horseback riding in the hills on the north range. How is that anything like what I do?"

"Sarabeth was alone. As an excellent horsewoman, she rode out alone all the time. Much like what you do." He leaned forward to make his point, four inches from her face. "Until the day she fell off the damned horse. We assume he got startled, but we'll never know."

"I'm sorry." Now she understood. His concern stemmed from grief and guilt over not saving his wife. It was only aimed at Lexi now as the likeliest female to run into a similar situation.

"The thing is," he said, "independence is fine when things are going the way they should. But what happens when your truck breaks down when you're out of cell range or the batteries in your satellite phone are low? When some yahoo backs you into a corner of the barn and no one's around? When some half-addled beeves turn nasty and one gores you wide open?"

Lexi took a minute to gather herself. She felt like an idiot, disappointed his worry didn't stem from some deeper feeling. Now she understood it centered on his wife's accident. What he'd felt—worry, concern, anger—had been about Sarabeth.

It seemed Lexi was always meant to be a substitute for Jack's wife, in one way or another.

CHAPTER EIGHT

Rachel Marshall peered out into the twilight gloom to discover who pounded at her door. She'd only arrived at her home in Longmont, Colorado, a few hours before. She'd had enough to deal with for the day. For two days, to be more exact, if one counted the wedding, non-reception, her missing cousin, and having outstanding sex with Clint Walker.

And Rachel certainly counted the sex. Clint had been amazing, both fun and considerate in bed, seeing to her pleasure and taking his own. She'd felt like the most alluring woman in town.

She shook off the memory with regret, but it came crashing back when his handsome face appeared at the other side of the door's peep-hole. Her heart raced, her breathing accelerated, her thighs tingled.

No, she told her body. Just, *no*. Not going to happen. Not

again. No matter how delicious the night before had been—and it had been—she wasn't making love with Clint Walker. He was supposed to be a vacation fling.

She hadn't foreseen him trailing her home. Had he actually followed her on the highway? How else could he have known her address?

Then she realized: Lexi told him, of course. She wouldn't know not to. Now Rachel had to give him the polite brush-off. Despite being flattered he'd tracked her down, she closed her eyes with sorrow. She didn't want this exchange to overshadow the memory of her time with him. Still, he wasn't likely to just leave and never return, so she braced herself and swung open the door. "Clint, what a surprise."

His grin lit the dim porch. "Rachel."

She shivered at the deep tone, remembering him calling her name as he climaxed. "What brings you here?"

As if she couldn't guess. Hopefully, he'd hear in her voice there wouldn't be a Round Two. She hid a grin of her own. Make that Round Three, as Two had already been celebrated in the wee hours before dawn.

He tipped his hat off. "I came here looking for your cousin."

Disappointment slammed her mouth closed, thankfully. Otherwise she might have cried out, so strong was her surprise. And hurt. She admitted the feeling to herself, just so she could set it aside. "Why would you be looking for her here? Why would you be looking for her at all?"

"Can I come inside?"

Rachel glanced behind her, knowing the house was empty. Nothing seemed out of place. She glanced at the driveway where his rental car sat in plain view. "I suppose you should. We wouldn't want the neighbors to wonder about the man on my porch."

He stepped over the threshold and she instantly regretted his presence. She'd have the memory of him here, in her home. His scent—fresh air and pine mixed with man—filled her foyer. His strong form made the area smaller. Crowded her. Drew her in despite her efforts to resist.

"How are you?" he asked.

"Fine. Would you like a drink? Tea or water is all I have ready." She turned away and mentally slapped her ingrained hospitality. She couldn't have him here, for so many reasons, yet she offered him an excuse to linger over a beverage.

Maybe she should admit she wanted him here. Wanted him, period. Was thrilled to see him for whatever his reason, but wishing he'd come to spend the night with her. She shouldn't let it happen, not in this town where she taught school. Not with her plans for the future set. Plans that didn't include him.

"No drink, thanks. I, uh, wondered if you know where

Grace might be."

She blinked, ready to deny knowledge of anything, including her own name. Then she recalled the whole wedding fiasco and took a calming breath. He flustered her in all sorts of ways. "Didn't she and Jack make it back to the ranch?"

"Not like you'd expect."

"What does that mean?" She placed a hand on her chest, quieting her heartbeats. Deep breath in, *pine*, deep breath out. Deep breath in, *Clint*. Sexy, sensual, arousing. Her breath whooshed out and she gasped in another, placing her hand on the wall for support.

He reached for her, his warm hand closing around her arm. "I'm sorry, Rachel. I should have thought how that sounded. I didn't mean to alarm you. Here." He led her to the couch. "Sit down."

"I'm fine."

"Should I get you some water?"

"No, no. You just took me by surprise."

"I'm sorry. I'm sure Grace is fine. I didn't mean to scare you." He rubbed her arm.

Rachel let him, enjoying the sensation, the care, the memories. She met his gaze, knowing hers revealed too much. Asked for too much. Offered too much.

Clint leaned toward her, green eyes darkening with desire.

His lips brushed her mouth, too light, too quick, too dry. "I didn't come here to sleep with you."

"Then don't." Her voice came out husky with regret and invitation.

"I don't seem to be able to stop myself."

She put her hands against his chest, blocking his approach. "That's not exactly flattering. You're drawn to me against your will?"

"No, not at all. I'm very willing." He winked. "And able."

She didn't want to be charmed by him. "Yet you didn't come for sex. You didn't come to see me at all."

"Rachel." He lifted her hand to his lips and kissed it. "I drove three hundred miles out of my way to come here. I missed sunset in the canyon I had earmarked for the trip home. It would have made a stunning photo and pushed the art world into a bidding war for my work."

She smiled at his exaggeration but paused. She hadn't seen his work. Maybe he had sacrificed a spectacular shot. For her.

"Sex with you," he continued, "would be a bonus, since I only needed to see your face to make the journey worthwhile."

She blinked, speechless. Then gulped as her wits returned. Despite her insides melting, she had to get a grip. And not on him. Could he be that smooth? Was that just a line? A great line, admittedly, but she didn't want to fall for it if he lacked sincerity.

His tongue played with the crevices between her fingers, making her shiver with longing. She wanted him, and the school board could just deal with it. Who would know, after all?

"Do you want something to eat?" She improvised an excuse for a moment alone to make a call. "I just did the same nine hour drive. You must have been right behind me."

His smile screamed sexual innuendo, causing her face to heat as though she'd said something outrageous.

"I ate on the way, thanks." He wisely didn't follow up on her comment, yet the image of him behind her, close and personal, remained. "I carry water at all times. Long habit from on the ranch, so I could use the bathroom."

She pointed the way for him then grabbed her cell phone and headed to the kitchen. Repeated rings met her ears and made her grind her teeth. She waited to be sent to voice mail. Was she being screened? Rachel didn't have time for games.

The timing couldn't be worse as Clint stepped into the doorway and smiled at her just as the recording started.

"Listen," she said into the phone. "It's Rachel. I can't meet you for that movie, after all. You'll have to go without me. I'm going to be busy at home for a few hours. I'll call you later, when I'm free to talk."

They stared at each other as she hit End.

"Am I interrupting something?" he asked.

"Nothing that can't be rearranged."

He stepped into the room. "Let me rephrase. Did you have a date?"

"No. If I were seeing someone, I wouldn't have gone to bed with you last night. And I wouldn't be moments away from taking you to my bed today."

His smile came slow and sexy. "That's a good answer."

"Grace!"

Lexi spun toward Anna's voice. The apple she'd been peeling for a pie dropped to the kitchen counter. Fortunately she held tight to the paring knife rather than cutting her finger off. "What is it? What's wrong?"

The girl swung around the corner, catching her balance on the old kitchen table. She sucked in air as though just crossing the finish line of a half-marathon.

Crossing the room, Lexi assessed the child. Although messy, Anna didn't appear bloody or bruised. A little of the tension eased in Lexi's gut. She couldn't relax until she knew no one else on the ranch was injured. "Is someone hurt?"

The girl's black waves flew around as she shook her head in the negative. "It's... There's..." Anna gulped again. "Molly, the barn cat, had her kittens."

Thank God. Lexi could admit her fear for Jack's safety now that she knew he was unharmed. With that relief, she remembered he'd gone into town to talk to his lawyer and wouldn't be here, in the path of horns or hooves. "That's good. We probably need more mousers out there."

"But, Grace, she had too many babies, and now there's a little black and white one that can't get to Molly to drink. The others are pushing it aside."

"Oh. I see." Lexi started to tuck her hair behind her ear, then noticed the paring knife she still grasped. Setting it down, she rested her still trembling hand on the back of a chair. How to inform a six-year-old on the ways of Nature? She tried to channel her own mother's calm manner when she'd explained things to her and Grace, from the perspective of a vet's wife. "I don't think they're pushing away the runt on purpose. Kittens aren't very aware of their brothers and sisters when they're first born. They're each just trying to get their own teat to drink from."

She hoped her plain-speaking suited Jack's parenting methods. Most of the children she'd come across doing her rounds on ranches grew up hearing straight talk.

"But if Panda can't get any milk, she'll die. Maybe Aunt Lexi could help her."

Oh, boy. While appreciating the girl's faith, Lexi had to divert her. "Aunt Lexi" couldn't attend to the kitten. "Panda?"

The girl dropped her gaze. "I named her that 'cause she's black and white."

"Of course you did." Lexi held in a sigh. Once the kitten received a name, ownership followed as pretty much a done deal. She wiped a smudge of dirt from Anna's cheek. "And you know it's a girl?"

"I didn't handle her. It's a guess because she's so pretty. But I won't really know until she opens her eyes. That's when Dad always knows."

"Does he?"

Anna nodded. "It's because the girls have the pretty eyes."

"You don't think boys ever have pretty eyes?" Lexi waited while the child shook her head. "What about your dad?"

"I guess so. Do you think Dad has pretty eyes?"

Trapped in a net of my own weaving. She'd be humiliated if Anna told Jack. "Yes, I do. Uncle Clint has pretty eyes, too."

"I guess so, but what are we going to do about Panda? Her brothers are blocking her from their mama's milk."

As an animal lover, Lexi wanted to adopt the runt and make sure it thrived. As a vet and pretend-ranch-wife, she had to be practical. "That's sad, but it happens, doesn't it?"

"It does?" Anna barely paused as Lexi nodded. "Why?"

"Moms only have so much milk. The weak ones probably won't live for long."

The girl twisted her fingers, frown intent. When she lifted her gaze, tears pooled in her big blue eyes. "But that's not fair."

The last word emerged on a choked sob. Anna launched herself against Lexi, grasping her waist. The front of Lexi's shirt grew wet before she could ease back and squat to Anna's eye level. She hugged the girl and rocked for a moment, then set her back and wiped her tears with her thumbs.

"This is the way Nature takes care of her creatures. The strong ones grow up to be mommies and daddies. If the weak ones can't watch out for themselves, they wouldn't be good at caring for babies later, would they?"

Anna shrugged, a reluctant concession, but her frown indicated she didn't want to agree. "So if someone is going to be a bad mommy, Nature doesn't let her be one?"

"Something like that. People don't know if they'll be good parents until they have babies."

"So Panda won't be a good mom?"

"Parents have to be strong." Humans as well, she thought. "Good hunters with quick reflexes can keep their babies safe. There needs to be enough milk for the rest."

Anna's eyes went wide. "Wait. We have milk."

"Well, yes, but—"

"We can feed Panda." Her face glowed with excitement. "I'll feed her every day and keep her warm and everything. I promise."

Danger, danger. Lexi could just see herself explaining this to Jack and tried to back-pedal. "Oh, baby, that's sweet of you, but it's not very realistic. We can't save every critter."

"Dad brought a calf in a couple of days ago, just before the wedding. The hands are feeding him in the barn. I'm just trying to save a teeny, tiny, little animal." She tilted her head to the side. "Maybe I should ask Dad about the kitten. He saved the calf. I bet he'd save Panda."

Lexi looked at the child and accepted her fate. Jack wouldn't deny his little girl much of anything, certainly not a cat. Lexi could almost hear him justifying it as teaching Anna about responsibility. She pictured the next few days where she'd play nursemaid to the kitten.

It wasn't as though she had anything else to do. "Grace" couldn't work as a vet. The real Grace would be painting, but Lexi couldn't even stretch a canvas with any credibility. Every time she ventured out to the barn, she felt the men's eyes on her. Doris maintained the house, freeing up Lexi's days. If Dan Higgins didn't set her free today, the inactivity would drive her crazy.

And if she were freed, raising the kitten would be Jack's problem. The idea made her smile. "Okay, we'll ask your dad. Then we'll talk about what you'll need to do."

"Should Grandpa look at Panda?"

Lexi blinked. "Why?"

"My friends take their pets to the vet."

"This will not be a pet, Annabeth. This kitten has to grow up and work in the barn, keeping it clear of mice."

The girl's chin firmed. "I don't think she wants to. I think she wants to be a house pet."

Jack hadn't allowed any animals in the house. She wasn't in a position to change that. Hardening her heart, Lexi locked gazes with her young charge. "Then we should take it to town where people keep pets in their houses."

The two females stared at each other, neither willing to back down. Lexi almost broke first, just because the kid was so darn cute when determined to get her way. Jack better stay alert with this one.

Fortunately, Anna's gaze fell to the floor seconds before Lexi was about to concede. "Well, you could take her brothers to town," the girl said. "You could put up a sign at the feed store, maybe with a picture. If you want, I'll go in to town with you."

Lexi laughed at her manipulations. "They'll all have to stay with their mom for several weeks, so they can grow strong. Let's go see how many we'll have to find other homes for."

"They're super-cute. I bet they'll get adopted real fast."

"Maybe." Lexi covered the apples she'd been slicing for a

pie and put the container in the refrigerator. "When someone shows an interest, though, you have to let the kittens go."

"I know." The girl shrugged and tugged on Lexi's hand to hurry her along. "We never get to keep all of them."

Lexi stopped, pulling Anna to a halt beside her. Had she just been conned? Maybe Jack would have refused to bottle-feed any of them. "What do you mean?"

"Daddy only keeps one or two because he says we have enough cats. He says next time, he's going to fix the one he calls Tom, but I can't see what's wrong with him. He doesn't limp or anything."

Lexi hid her smile. "I'm sure your dad has plans to help him, whatever the problem."

"We should take their pictures now while they're little. Dad keeps the camera on the shelf over his desk."

Lexi hesitated. "We shouldn't go in his office when he's not there."

"I can have Doris get it. She cleans in there all the time. Where is she?"

"Laundry room."

Anna ran off, and Lexi shook her head at herself. She could marry the man, but entering his office made her uncomfortable?

She seriously needed to rearrange her priorities.

Lexi inspected the kittens, handling them as little as possible. Molly had found a quiet, dark corner of the barn to deliver her babies. Their tiny faces gave Lexi a pang, as she too experienced the hankering to adopt all of them. Their closed eyes and stick-like tails made them clumsy and defenseless. She shook off sentiment and finished looking them over. Panda would undoubtedly remain theirs, and he would need nursing, as Anna had pegged his vulnerable runt status correctly.

While Anna coaxed Panda to accept a bottle, Lexi picked up a dark gray furball, keeping an eye on the mother, who, in turn, watched Lexi. Healthy enough, the kitten kneaded Lexi's finger with its tiny paw. "Looking for milk, my pirate beauty?"

"Why's he a pirate?" Anna asked beside her.

"He looks like a cat the Prescott family owned."

"Dread?"

Lexi looked at the girl. "Yes, the Dread Pirate Roberts, in fact. Do you know Genny Prescott?"

"She's in the second grade, but we play jump rope on the playground sometimes. Dread just died. Genny said an owl got him." Anna cocked her head to one side. "Do you think that's true?"

"That's possible." Lexi nodded, glad Anna could relate it matter-of-factly. "Do you think Genny would like a kitten?"

Anna grinned. "She'd like two."

Lexi laughed. "Then let's keep an eye on Pirate in the next few weeks and see which sibling he bonds with. In the meantime, we can run a picture of Pirate over to the Prescotts' house. Invite them out here to see the kittens."

"Miz Walker," a male voice said from right behind Lexi.

She whirled then put a hand to her chest, relieved to identify the ranch hand. How much of their plan to adopt the kitten had he overheard? Would he tell Jack before Anna could butter him up? "Oh, George, you startled me. What is it?"

"Some of the men are heading to town. Do you need anything?"

"No, nothing I can think of, but thank you. You might check with Doris."

"I already done that, miss." With a finger to his hat brim, George ducked back and away.

"Darn it," Lexi said. "If we'd had the pictures taken and printed, I could have asked the men to hang the flyers around town."

"We could hang a flyer at Lee's Freezes." Anna's hopeful expression made Lexi laugh.

"Good idea. But we're just having a cone. Nothing that would spoil dinner."

She set about shooting some pictures, group shots and a few singles. With their eyes still closed, the kittens didn't show much personality, but they did look lovable. That might work for the townsfolk. Narrowing down the best photos involved some debate between her and Anna.

Dirt smudged Anna's face and knees. And hands. And shirt.

"Go run a washcloth over yourself and change your clothes." Lexi felt like a mother as the girl scampered off without protest. A glance at her own attire had her heading to her room. Two of a kind they were, both tomboys at heart.

Less than an hour after taking the photos, she and Anna had hung several flyers in town. Her father hadn't been in his vet office or in the house, which made Anna pout for thirty seconds, until Lexi asked where to best position the flyer.

Lee's Freezes put one in their window, down low enough to catch the notice of children. Lexi and Anna ate their cones and discussed good places to advertise free kittens.

"How about at my school?"

"The kids would see the flyers, but the school wouldn't let us hang them. Anywhere else kids go a lot, other than here?" she added with a wink.

Anna licked vanilla ice cream from the side of her hand, melting in the heat faster than the girl could eat. "I see kids at my doctor's office, but it's a sad place where people get shots. I don't think crying kids would want pets."

They settled on the grocery store, feed store and pharmacy

as their next stops.

They placed the grocery store flyer at a lower spot, hoping to attract children. At the feed store, Lexi looked for the Rocking W truck carrying Jack's men, but without luck. They must have already headed back to the ranch. Fritz Peters, Darryl's father, tore down some old flyers from the window to make room for theirs. As the vet's daughter, she'd always received personal service from the owner, but not until she'd become Mrs. Jack Walker—sort of—had Fritz hurried and kowtowed. *Jack must spend more money in here than I thought.* While her father held prominence in town, he was still a hired professional, not the one with the money.

"You need more tape, Miz Grace," Fritz said. "We wouldn't want this paper tearing every time the door swings open."

Darryl walked up to them. "That's true, Pop. Can't have the Walkers unhappy."

Lexi maneuvered the girl just behind her hip. Darryl's Feed Store T-shirt clung to him. Sweat stains testified to his exertion tossing feed and grain bags around the un-air-conditioned back room.

He glinted a look at Lexi. "How's that wandering sister of yours? Any word on when she'll return?"

Lexi forced a laugh. "I don't expect her to check in with me at her age."

His smirk made her want a bath. "I reckon she's too busy having a fun time in Vegas. I can't wait till she gets back. She's a hot one."

"Darryl," his father scolded. "Don't talk about Miz Lexi like that."

Lexi suppressed a shudder. Being called "a hot one" by the likes of Darryl Peters felt like having naked pictures of herself hung around town.

"Don't mind him, Miz Walker." Fritz rubbed his hands together, brow creased. "He doesn't mean anything by it."

"I'm sure he doesn't." Lexi kept her voice and expression as cool as Grace's. Sometimes portraying her twin had advantages. "Lexi wouldn't think a thing about his comment."

Or about you, her stare said to Darryl. She could tell he got the message when his jaw tightened and face hardened. Good. Maybe he'd back off. She didn't want to be harassed when she "returned" to town. A guy like him took a polite smile as a lusty invitation. Hopefully, he'd understand a pointed set-down from her meant hands-off the family.

She turned her back to Darryl, addressing Fritz. "Do you think Allison would let me hang a flyer in the pharmacy?"

"She'd be happy to."

"Sure, Mom will fall all over herself to make you happy."

"Darryl." This time the reprimand came sharper.

Darryl made a disgusted noise and headed toward the back of the store. Where he belonged. Poor Fritz watched him go, a sag to his shoulders.

"I'll head on over," she told the older man. "Thanks for letting me post this here."

"I hope you get some takers, Miz Walker."

She smiled at him, keeping it in place when she glanced at Anna. She could sure use some fresh air. "Feel like a walk?"

The girl nodded and Lexi hurried them out, not wanting more apologies from Fritz. It must be hell for him to have a son he couldn't be proud of. One day, he'd turn his life's work—a business vital to the area and a family inheritance from Fritz's grandfather—over to Darryl.

Lexi bent and kissed Anna's head.

Smiling up at her, the girl asked, "What's that for?"

"I just love you."

Anna beamed, and Lexi continued on as though nothing had happened to shake her world. She *did* love Anna. The nearest possible relation she'd be to the girl was her aunt. Nevertheless, no matter what happened, Lexi would ease Anna's hurt.

Allison Peters had too much work to spend more than a minute with them, for which Lexi was thankful. The deferential treatment afforded "Mrs. Walker" made her uncomfortable. After hanging the flyer in the spot Allison designated, she waved to the older woman and hurried Anna back to Jack's car. Lexi tucked Anna in to the back and double-checked her buckle.

"I can do it myself, Grace."

"I'm sure you can. But I'm new at this, so bear with me, okay?" Lexi went around front with barely a glance at the non-existent traffic and pulled open the car door.

Brown leather work gloves lay on the driver's seat.

Lexi paused. Had she sat on them as she drove into town? Seemed unlikely. She picked them up, noting the plastic tab securing them together.

Hairs rose on the back of her neck. Glancing around, Lexi didn't see anyone lurking to watch her discover the gift. Maybe the gloves had been there all along, she reassured herself. Maybe she'd just overlooked them on the drive in to town. Maybe they hadn't been placed here just now, in her unlocked car, fresh off a hanger from the feed store.

Darryl? The connection occurred to her as naturally as one plus one equaling two. She turned to gaze in the direction of the store but didn't spot him watching. Why would he put work gloves on her seat? Was it a message saying...? What? He couldn't wait to get his hands on her? But, no. He thought she was Grace. So, maybe it meant he would have to put on gloves to touch her? These weren't the dainty white gloves one associated with afternoon teas. These were thick and brown. Had they appeared in her Christmas stocking, Lexi would have been happy to have them. But Santa gave without wanting anything in return. Without manipulation. Without malice.

Without scaring the bejeebers out of her.

Shaking off her unease, she slid in, threw the gloves on the seat beside her, started the engine, and pulled out smoothly, trying to appear unruffled.

Just in case anyone was watching.

Jack barely had time to clean up and change his shirt before Lexi set dinner on the table. Pot pie. The buttery scent of crust hit him as he entered the house, along with the vegetables and chicken. He'd have preferred a longer shower first after a hot June day. The kink in his neck could have used some easing under the hot spray as well. But the aroma nearly buckled his knees while he stood under the tepid spray, recalling the quick lunch he'd had so long ago. The trip into town to check into his marital status had cut into his day, doubling his work load back on the ranch.

"Where's Doris?" He pulled his chair up to the table.

"Doris done gone on home," Crusty said. "Thought she'd stay, this being your bride's first night and all."

"We'd expect there to be changes." Jack glanced at Lexi. "I'm sure she knew you could serve up a meal."

She shrugged. "I didn't know her usual routine. I asked her to stay and eat with us or take some with her."

"Let me guess, she didn't take any." He smiled as Lexi shook her head. "She knows it's my favorite meal."

"She used to not leave until she served dinner," Crusty said, "at least to the girl and me if Jack was running late. But that was afore we had another woman in the house."

Lexi set down her fork. "I don't mean to disrupt routine. I'll talk to her tomorrow."

As long as the two females settled it and he didn't have to referee, Jack didn't care who cooked or served. He found himself eager for a peaceful dinner with his family. For the past few years, he'd been half-attentive and half-asleep at dinner, as his mind filled with work yet to be done on the land and in the office. He and Crusty usually went over anything of importance after dinner. His body would long for the comfort and solitude of his bedroom, even though his bed had become so lonely.

Now he looked forward to hearing about everyone's day. Record-keeping could wait while he caught up with his family. Even Crusty's expected gruffness held a certain appeal tonight.

And after dinner, he'd have to tell Lexi what he'd learned from Dan Higgins.

Remembering the conversation at hand, Jack said, "Not a big deal. I don't care how you two decide to run the house."

Jack paused mid-scoop. The glint in her eye told him he'd said the wrong thing, but he didn't know what. He thought she'd be glad to have carte blanche. Women. He never would figure them out.

Otherwise, he wouldn't be in his current predicament.

"Anna," she said, "you should tell your dad what you did today."

His daughter darted him a glance then stared at her mashed potatoes.

"You went to school, didn't you, sugar cube?" He frowned for a moment when he realized Lexi never called Annabeth by her proper name. What was going on there? Was she keeping a distance from his child, preparing for the time she'd return to her normal life? Or was she becoming too attached, as the assigning of a nickname suggested? "You have a few weeks left, right?"

Annabeth nodded, her fork making ski trails on the slope of spuds.

"Anything exciting happen?"

A negative head shake.

"Then what did you do?"

"We found Molly with her new kittens." Cornflower eyes met his as he held back a groan. "They're so cute, Daddy. You have to see them."

Lexi didn't meet his gaze. In fact, she appeared a little too innocent.

There went the peaceful part of his dinner. Yet another problem to tackle, despite having travelled this path before with his daughter. His hand found the tight muscle in his neck and rubbed. The conversation alone could give him a headache. "You know we can't keep them."

"I know." She sighed. "Grace explained. We already put up signs in town."

He cocked a brow in Lexi's direction. "Did you, now?"

Annabeth nodded. "Grace took pictures and we said on the flyer to call us, but they gotta wait more weeks to take them away. How many weeks?"

"Six," Lexi answered. "That's when they'll be weaned."

"Did you learn that from your sister?" Jack said, to remind her of her role.

When she shook her head, he froze.

"My dad."

He relaxed but sent her a reproving glance for teasing him. "You got those pictures up fast."

"We're gonna give a couple of kitties to Genny 'cause she don't got Dread no more."

Jack blinked. When had his precious angel started sounding

like a grumpy old codger?

"We're going to *ask* the Prescotts," Lexi corrected, "if they would like a kitten or two because they don't have Dread any longer."

"Why would they have dread?" Jack felt as though he'd missed something. Although he could relate. The idea of more cats on the place filled him with dread.

"Dread's their old tomcat," Crusty said around a forkful. "Any darn fool'd know that."

"They had a charcoal cat, much like one in the barn," Lexi said.

Good Lord a-mighty, the woman hadn't been joking about being a terrible liar. Grace wouldn't know that. If his uncle and daughter were more alert, they'd have exposed Lexi by now. "Another thing you learned from your dad?"

She blinked. "From my, uh, sister. Lexi always laughed at the cat's name, Dread Pirate Roberts."

Jack smiled. "And was he a thief?"

"Dread was known to snatch anything edible left unattended. It didn't do to set down a sandwich or even a slice of apple. According to Lexi."

"Not a good mouser?" Jack guessed.

"Why not?" Annabeth asked.

Gaze on his bride to quell her from answering, he replied,

"If he had to steal food, his stomach wasn't full of mice like it should have been."

"Coulda been a clean barn," Crusty countered.

Three sets of eyes turned Lexi's way.

She shrugged. "I never asked."

Jack narrowed his eyes. Of course she knew. She could have found a way to tell them while maintaining her pretense. Claimed she overheard some boring conversation about the cat between her dad and sister.

He frowned at the severe depiction of Grace. Why did he automatically add "boring" to her supposed opinion of the conversation?

Lexi rose and picked up her plate. "I don't know how it used to be done with Doris, but while I'm here, we all help clean off the table."

Surprised, Jack glanced at his empty plate. Dammit. He'd eaten like a starved animal, barely tasting his favorite meal.

And now he had to talk to Lexi on a full stomach and unsated appetite.

CHAPTER NINE

Lexi's homemade apple pie garnered praise. Jack hadn't minded delaying their talk, especially once the warmed dessert filled his mouth. Apples, sugar and cinnamon comforted him like a crackling fire in winter. The cheese she'd melted over the top had him closing his eyes on a silent moan. Who would have thought she had any domestic skills?

The minute the door snicked shut behind Lexi, Jack realized they should have talked in the office. Not in his bedroom. *Their* bedroom, although she'd yet to sleep there. She'd snuck out to the guest bedroom as soon as she deemed it safe the night before. After their talk about the break-in, he'd disappeared downstairs to the office and the never-ending paperwork. Waited, he'd thought, for her to settle into bed, maybe fall asleep. Tried to be a gentleman, only to find his bride had fled.

An apparent pattern with the Marshall sisters.

Tonight might be different. She probably wouldn't run. After she heard what the lawyer had counseled, she might jump out the window though.

The homey scent followed her into the room. "You still smell like home cooking. You always do."

She blinked and sat in the same wing chair as the night before. "I guess that's the vanilla lotion I use for my hands." She smirked. "And believe me, I don't always smell like this. I'm usually sweaty, dirty and covered with animal hair—or worse."

"I think I'd have noticed that."

"Not when you probably smelled as bad yourself."

Jack chuckled. "Good point."

He sat across from her, easing down as gingerly as he meant to ease into relating the day's news. He stretched out his legs, trying to convince himself he didn't feel worried. The kink in his neck could use stretching as well, but he didn't want to appear weak in front of Lexi. He wanted her to feel she could depend on him.

"Sounds like you and Annabeth had a big day today."

Lexi smiled and leaned back into the cushion. She looked almost delicate in the over-sized navy chair. "We did. After Anna found the kittens, we had to take pictures and go into town. Which meant a stop at Lee's for a cone."

"I should have thought of ice cream when I was in town."
He reached into his pocket and produced two keys. "I did
remember to replace the lock on your back door."

"Oh, thanks. You didn't have to bother. I meant to do it
when I didn't have Anna with me."

"Now you don't have to." It hadn't occurred to him that
Lexi would do it herself, but given the sheriff's praise the day
before, he should have expected it. "I wanted the house secured
as soon as possible. Thanks for taking Annabeth around with the
posters."

She smiled. "Anything for an ice cream. We went by Dad's,
the library, grocery store, feed store, and the pharmacy." Her
brow furrowed as she studied her fingers. She seemed about to
say something, a look of hesitancy on her face. "Places like that.
Everyone let us hang a flyer so we should hear soon."

"So what's wrong?"

"Nothing." But she didn't meet his eyes. "You don't mind
if I go in your office, do you? I had to print out the flyers since I
don't have my printer here."

Was that what had her so uneasy? He almost laughed with
relief. "Lexi, whatever I have is yours. Make yourself at home."

She chuckled. "That's how you get yourself into these
messes, Jack. Inviting women to take advantage of your
kindness."

"Well, as I recall, that's not exactly how I got into this current predicament."

She straightened as though called before a judge, perched on the edge of her seat. Every muscle had tightened. "I'm ready to hear what Dan had to say." When he hesitated, searching for words, she added, "Or maybe I'm not. Am I in big trouble?"

"Don't worry. I won't let anything happen to you."

Her shoulders slumped as she relaxed back again. "Of course you wouldn't. I know that."

Who were her words meant to convince?

"The good news is there's no case against you for signing the marriage license if I don't press charges."

"Press charges?" Her fingers twisted together.

"Which I wouldn't do. It's only a fraud case if I bring it to the attention of the law."

She puzzled it out, her face a study in concentration. "So it really is fraud, but I won't get in trouble because you won't turn me in."

"Something like that."

"I guess that's a relief."

"It should be." Jack wanted to quiet her fingers. Rub them to stillness. Hold on in reassurance. Instead, he pressed against the tight spot in his neck. "It's not as though you can marry anyone under any name, but if I don't contest it in civil court, then it's not a legal matter. You are 'A. Grace Marshall.' There's only trouble if I object."

"Okay. Seems like a law should be upheld no matter who realizes it's been broken, but since I'm benefiting, I guess I shouldn't complain." She took a breath. "And the rest?"

"Unfortunately, Dan's going to have to do some research on the QT. He didn't have a firm idea whether we're legally married or not."

"Oh."

She pretty much summed up their problem with that one hollow syllable.

"He's looking into it further, but until then, if I don't disown you, we're married."

Her brow arched. God, she was cute when she was irritated.

"You'd have to own me before you can disown me, buster."

"Wouldn't even try, honey." Jack smirked as she scowled over the endearment. "Dan's checking into the ramifications either way on the deed being in Grace's married name."

"Wouldn't her not having a married name nullify the deed? Turn it over to you alone?"

He shrugged. "Or turn it back over to Crusty. Or as long as Grace can prove he intended to give it to her, the name might not matter."

"Is that what Dan said?"

"I could use a drink." He stood with that intention then spotted her questioning look. "I need something to do with my hands. You can get away with twisting your fingers, but I'd look idiotic."

Her hands stilled. "I've seen you do stupider things."

He bit back a retort when he saw the slight curving of her lips. He'd never noticed how pink they were. How lush.

"Jack?"

He snapped back to reality, appalled. Had he been thinking about kissing her? Kissing Lexi? He remembered the sweetness of their kiss in the taxi. Now that vulnerability and hesitation made sense. He'd traced the outline of her mouth with his tongue, the indentation of her upper lip, sucked the lower—

"Jack."

"Oh, uh, sorry. I got lost in thought." Hopefully, she wouldn't notice his physical reaction. If he'd still been sitting, he could have put a pillow in his lap. Standing made her effect on him more apparent.

She shifted in the chair, perching once again as though to flee. "So we only have one answer from Dan. I'm guilty but it won't be pursued unless you or someone else turns me in."

"I'm the only one it would affect."

Except Grace.

Neither of them said the words, but the thought floated

between them as their gazes locked.

"She wouldn't," Lexi assured him.

He wished he could agree. It would be a low thing for Grace to do, turning in her sister in order to steal his land. Grace had already done one pretty low act by jilting him. Who could guess what else she'd try?

But the woman he'd meant to build a life with couldn't be that devious. He refused to believe it. No one would treat her own sister that badly.

"So what happens?" Lexi rose and faced him. "Do I stay on until Dan gets back to you? Did he have any idea how long it would take him to find answers?"

"He didn't know. Looks like you're here for a while longer."

"My week isn't up yet anyway." She tried to smile.

"And we don't have any answers from Matson on the burglary."

Her lips firmed. Which was a crying shame, hiding their plump invitation.

"I'm not hanging around out here forever, waiting for your lawyer and the sheriff to get their acts together." She crossed her arms over her chest.

Which was a cr— No. He reined in his thoughts, refusing to even think it. "I'm trying to protect you."

"I don't need protecting."

Her comment pierced his ego. He stepped closer to make his point. She aggravated him that much. "You damn well do. You could go to jail for fraud if I choose *not* to protect you. You could find yourself tangling with a burglar in the middle of the night. Show some sense, woman."

She poked a finger in his chest. "Don't call me *woman*."

"Fine. Use some sense, *honey*."

For a minute, they faced off, inches apart, both breathing hard. Jaws tight, eyes hot. The blue of her gaze burned him. So intense. So deep. So pretty.

His hand raised and cupped her cheek. Her jaw unclenched and her expression softened.

Her hand covered his, not pulling away as her eyes darkened. As her lips parted.

Was his palm too rough against the smooth pink of her cheek? Self-consciously, he stepped back. Rubbed his hand on his hip before sticking it in his back pocket.

"Anyway." Jack cleared his throat. "You should stay here."

She nodded, gaze on the floor.

"Well, I'm going to check Crusty's numbers on some reports." He had no idea what he was talking about, just knew he had to say something to change the mood. To make his feet move toward the door. "The old coot won't check his figures on a calculator or let the computer add for him."

The lifting of her lips in a sham of a smile haunted him as he walked away.

Lexi barely slept that night, which didn't surprise her. Dreaming of Jack during her brief hours asleep didn't surprise her. That she'd almost kissed him did surprise her.

That *he'd* considered kissing her before he came to his senses and hurried from the room shocked the living daylights out of her.

Under the heat of the afternoon sun, she meandered toward the new house on the pretense of gathering wildflowers for the dining table. If she gathered weeds, flowers, or dried grass didn't matter. The walls had closed in, trapping her, and she'd had to get out of the ranch house.

The wraparound porch provided shade and a gorgeous view any time of day. The house stood two stories high with shiny white clapboard siding. Its position into the hillside and whimsical touches of gingerbread trim made it look like a friendly cloud.

Crusty would love living here once Grace returned. Lexi had to keep her sister's imminent arrival in the front of her mind. The dining table at the ranch house which she planned to decorate with a jar of flowers was Grace's table, just as the husband, the child, and the land were. Lexi's role was as a stopgap, and she'd best keep that in mind.

But for one heart-stopping moment the night before, it had seemed all too real.

She closed her eyes and gave herself the luxury of remembering. One more time, then she'd set it aside. She'd never again think of Jack's strong arms encircling her, pressing her body to his. She'd never again recall the intensity of his gaze, the heat, the desire. She'd never again relive the thud of his heart against her, the way he'd swallowed as though his mouth watered for the taste of her lips.

She would forget the tingling of her skin as she'd yearned for his touch, for his taste. She'd deny her heart had pounded, her flesh had heated with desire and ... more.

Because she couldn't feel more. He wasn't hers.

Lexi opened her eyes to the bright hot sunlight and felt almost dizzy. Sun, not lust, she assured herself.

A motor started down near the main house, about a quarter of a mile away, out of her view. Not willing to be interrupted yet, Lexi scooted around the side of Crusty's house toward the hill, hoping to go undetected. She peeked around the corner like a child escaping chores and decided she'd feel silly if she were spotted. With a chuckle, she glanced up the hillside for flowers.

The house extended out from the second level. She stepped

back, shielding her eyes with her hand. Siding circled the first three feet of the level and supported ten foot high glass walls. Sun streamed into the room via skylights. Lexi frowned. A greenhouse? Conservatory? Was Jack experimenting with grasses or oats? Why would he put such a room on the house he'd planned to share with...Grace.

The natural light. The elevated view. The privacy. An art studio.

The buzzing in her head couldn't be attributed to the heat. Lexi put a hand to her temple, overcome with reality. He'd loved Grace so much he'd built her a studio.

She set the empty jar on the porch rail, taking care to balance it before letting go. Letting go. She'd have to practice a lot of that in the coming days.

"So you found it."

Lexi twirled, saw Crusty approaching on a motorized scooter. The buzzing she'd heard earlier had been his motor. Gathering her wits and burying her feelings, she gave him a smile she hoped looked genuine. She felt pale, as though the blood had drained out of her complexion. Clearing her throat, she dug for an answer. "It's a pretty big house. Hard to miss."

"Didn't mean jest the house. What do you think of that?" He pointed to the studio.

"It's quite...a lovely gift."

"Humph." Crusty shook his head. "That all ya got to say?"

She opened her mouth, closed it. Fought for composure. *Act like Grace would.* She gathered herself. "I'll thank Jack when we do a walk-through. He should show me the house himself."

Crusty rose and steadied himself with his cane, both hands resting on the handle as he propped it in front of him. "Hard to believe yore grateful for the studio…Lexi."

She jumped in surprise, her heart racing. "What? What did you call me?" She tried a laugh, stopped when it came out thin. "You've mistaken me for my sister. Happens all the time."

"I doubt that. For all you look alike, you shore don't act alike."

Panicked, she patted his shoulder. "You should sit down. The heat is getting to you. I'm Grace. Jack's wife."

Crusty shook his head.

"Lexi is my sister. She cares for the animals here sometimes."

"Yore Jack's wife, name of Lexi, and you care for the animals. You care for him, too, in yore heart. And the girl."

"Crusty…" She let the denial trail away. Her sigh released all the tension of keeping up the facade.

"'Course I knowed it was you. Minute you stepped into the house. That sister of yores would smile all pretty, but she made a point to never spend much time around me. You stand up for yoreself, even when you pretend to be her. You found ways to make yore point, git yore own way, but without that trickery." He snorted. "People call them 'wiles.' I'm too old to fall for a pretty face. That's why I like you."

Lexi faltered at the half-insult, half-compliment, then bit back a smile. She'd been about to defend Grace, but hearing that this hard-to-please man preferred her set her back on her heels. "We have the same face, Crusty. We're twins."

"She uses hers differently."

Lost for words, Lexi could only goggle at him.

"If'n it had been up to her," he continued, "I'd a been put in an old folks home somewhere. Maybe down in La La Land with Clint so she didn't have to visit or pretend to be concerned or even think about me."

"Grace isn't cold-hearted, Crusty. Artists are a little self-absorbed." Lexi rushed on since her statement didn't sound like an endorsement. "They have to be, to look into themselves and bring it out on canvas. To be able to see the nuances of a scene so that viewers will feel like they were there."

He squinted up at her, one eye nearly closed as he cocked his head in question. "She feed you that line of bull? And you swallowed it?"

Lexi shook her head. "It's not bull, Crusty. You and I will never understand the devotion it takes to produce the masterpieces Grace paints. She sort of *absorbs* a scene, then releases all those emotions to flow through paint onto canvas. Have you seen her works?"

"Naw. I ain't much a one for *gallery showings*." His tone equated it to chaperoning a sleepover of six-year-old girls, hyped up on candy and caffeine.

"I'll take you. Once you see Grace's work, you'll understand her better."

"Don't need to understand her. She ain't coming back, and if'n she did, Jack wouldn't keep her to his wife. Not after what she done."

"You can't know that." She glanced over her shoulder at the studio, a monument to his feelings. "Jack loves her. He'll forgive her."

Crusty snorted. "He don't love her. She tricked him into marriage, even more'n you did. Agreeing to marry him so they could have my land. He wouldn't a proposed himself."

Lexi suppressed a defense of her own actions. "Maybe he would have. They'd been dating—"

"Don't matter. Yore his wife now." Crusty leaned against the scooter's seat.

Lexi relished the freedom of being herself again with someone other than Jack. "It's complicated, Crusty. I can't be his wife, but I can't leave yet, either. Jack will explain the details tonight."

"Jack will do no such a thing."

"The three of us will meet in the library after supper."

"No reason for us all to meet up."

"You don't want me there?" She swallowed. "Well, of course, you wouldn't. I'm not family."

"Not what I meant, girl." Crusty scowled. "It's Jack that won't be there. I'd be more'n willing to hear them details, but from you alone. Jack don't have to know I know."

"I don't understand."

"And here I thought you was the bright one." With both hands, he lifted his left leg over the seat, then settled his right. The cane fit into a built-on slot out of his way, but reachable.

Afraid he meant to start up the scooter and leave her, Lexi grasped the handlebar. "Wait. Crusty. What's going on?"

"I always did aim to leave the land to Jack, which is why I was prodding him about sons. I just didn't plan to do it so soon." The old man looked at his hands. Sighed. "I been to the doctor, Lexi. Hell, I been to a lot of doctors. It don't look good."

Sorrow clutched at her throat, closing off her air. She could barely croak out a response. "What do you mean?"

He scowled at her. "You ain't dim, girl. Jack's gonna need someone to stand by him. Someone who knows about ranching. Someone he can build a family with."

"Crusty, I'm so sorry." She blinked away tears. "What's wrong? Can't they do anything for you?"

"Docs can't do anything, but you can. I'd go a lot more peaceable if I knew you was here taking care of Jack. Of the land. Of that little girl."

"Oh." Lexi put a hand to her chest where her lungs squeezed and her heart beat a hollow rhythm. "That can't be me, Crusty. That's not your decision. It's Jack's."

"You mean to say you'd leave Jack to deal with this now? With the stuff he'll have to go through in these next months, all alone?" Crusty grunted and turned the key. "Then you ain't the girl I thought you was."

She watched him go, a thin dust trail following all the way back to the house.

Crusty dying. She couldn't believe it. Didn't want to hear those words together. He'd been a fixture around Little Tree her entire life.

Poor Jack. Clint and Anna, too, of course, but Jack would be the one dealing with Crusty's declining health, doctor visits, hospital stays. Then funeral arrangements and legal issues, along with managing the land.

He'd handle all that alone. Doris would take care of the house and food, but the rest would be on Jack's shoulders. She could see them bowing with grief, with overwork. How could he comfort Anna, explain things to her, be there when grief hit the girl in the middle of the day? Just be there for her.

Just be there. The words echoed through her cells.

Lexi closed her eyes, shutting out everything around her. Going still, she listened to the quiet, listened for guidance, to find the right path. Instinctively, she wanted to back away before she got hurt. Before she became too enmeshed in their lives.

But it was too late.

Jack passed through the day working the ranch with half his mind on that almost-kiss the night before. He must have been crazy. Must have imagined her reaction. Up until three days ago, Lexi'd barely had two words to say to him that didn't involve animal care. And then those words turned into "I do," and all hell rained down.

She didn't trust him. Barely liked him. Or so he'd believed.

But he was a man, and some things a man just knew. Like when a woman wanted him, especially when he held her in his arms, felt her melt into him, felt her heart race. Some things a man recognized in his blood, down to his deepest core. Lexi had wanted him.

And he'd wanted her. *Her*, not her sister, not an imitation of her sister. He'd wanted Lexi, with all her contrariness, strength, sass, courage, and goodness.

Eyes closed, he rubbed a gloved hand across his forehead. Clint had pegged him correctly, but since his brother's departure, Jack had graduated from "one screwed up cowboy" to just being a damned fool.

He couldn't jump from one woman to another this fast. Lexi would get out her vet bag and inject him with something in his sleep.

He slapped his hat against his leg. Why couldn't he have hankered after someone softer, easier, more pliable?

Like Grace?

Jack scowled at the snide voice in his head, laughing at his folly. Seemed like neither Marshall woman fit the bill.

Yet here he was, coming home early to be with the one who married him. The one he couldn't have. The one he shouldn't want.

The one he yearned to see.

Spotting the jar of wildflowers on the porch rail, he grabbed the makeshift vase and carried it inside. Precarious place to perch a glass. He couldn't imagine Lexi or Doris—the only ones who'd pick flowers without supervision—being so careless. What had distracted the women into leaving it there? Was someone hurt? His heart nearly stopped, then raced like a thoroughbred.

He entered the house, set the flower jar on the kitchen table and searched through the lower level, calming to find the place so orderly. No signs of catastrophe. No Lexi, no Annabeth, or Crusty. Even Doris was gone, although she'd left a note about dinner.

Jack frowned at the silence. Checking his cell phone for messages regarding their whereabouts, he noticed his lawyer had called. What news did Dan have?

He'd call him after he found his family and made sure they were all okay.

The door to the kitchen burst open and in spilled Annabeth, laughing and chattering, Lexi with an armful of groceries, and Crusty, thumping along with his cane and muttering.

"Dad!" was all the warning Jack had before his daughter flung herself into his arms. He laughed, holding her close.

"Where have you been all my life?" He watched Lexi set down the bag, smiling in their direction. Crusty pulled out a chair and fell onto it as though he'd never move again.

Annabeth grinned, giving Jack's cheek a loud kiss before sliding down to touch the floor. "We took the picture of Pirate over to Genny's."

"That was devious of you."

"I went to buy produce from their greenhouse." Lexi indicated the vegetables spilling out of the canvas tote bags on the table. "We just happened to have Pirate's photo with us. And the flyer with all the other kitties."

"Just happened to?"

She sniffed, devilment dancing in her blue eyes.

"Her family wants another cat," Annabeth said.

Lexi nodded at his dubious expression. "Maybe more than one. We'll let them pick—"

Annabeth inhaled.

"Although not Panda." Lexi shook her head. "I'm sure Panda will stay here."

"You'd better not name the others, okay, sugar cube?" Jack tugged on his daughter's black braid.

"Okay. Except for Butterscotch." She stuck her hands in the front pockets of her cut-offs and studied the floor.

He lowered his brows, trying to look stern in case she glanced up. "We don't need any more cats, Annabeth. We're only keeping the one kitten."

"Yes, sir." She turned to leave the room, a huge, heartfelt sigh following behind.

"Well done."

He turned to check if Lexi's expression betrayed sarcasm, although her tone sounded innocent enough. She looked sincere, but he wandered over to make sure.

Oh, who was he kidding? He wanted to be closer to her.

Three days ago, he'd planned to build a future with a

beautiful, sexy painter. Have more children, raise them to love the land, and to one day inherit the Rocking W. Maybe some of them would have an artistic bent like their mother and uncle, which would have suited Jack just fine.

But three nights ago, he'd found himself married to a firecracker who challenged every notion of what he'd thought he wanted.

"I'm going to spend some time at my dad's office." Lexi put two purple eggplants in the fridge, effectively avoiding his gaze. "With my sister gone, the filing and paperwork have become overwhelming. I talked to Dad today and he would appreciate the help. I can work it around Anna's school hours."

Jack adjusted to the idea that she wouldn't be here during the day. Funny how he'd gotten used to thinking of her at the ranch house. But Annabeth was at school for another week, Doris had the house under control, and Crusty usually closed himself in the office with record-keeping or reading. Unable to care for the animals, Lexi didn't have anything to do. "Sounds like a plan."

"It's just for a week, until my sister returns."

He nodded at the reminder. While Crusty might mistake her meaning, Jack understood Lexi wanted to keep up with her regular life, despite this interruption.

Crusty gestured to the table behind Jack. "You got time to

go around picking flowers? You're as moon-eyed as that calf yore feeding in the barn."

Heat rose up Jack's neck. "I didn't pick these. I was busy directing a delivery of grain from the feed store."

Crusty's thick white eyebrows lowered. "The men shoulda been able to handle that without you."

"Shoulda," Jack echoed. "But Darryl Peters was being as useless as usual, and the boy he brought from the store couldn't have two brain cells to rub together. He also had glassy eyes, exaggerated, slow-motion movements, and a distinctive smell of pot on his clothes."

"Pot?" Lexi and Crusty exclaimed, almost in unison.

Jack shook his head. "Never saw the kid before. Once Fritz hears about it, we probably won't see him again. Made me wonder if Darryl had been smoking, but only the kid had the giggles."

Lexi frowned. "I've seen Darryl drunk on weekends pretty regularly but nothing else."

"We all been drunk on a weekend," Crusty said. "At least at some time in our lives."

Jack grinned. "Too true, but from tales around town, I think you had more than your share of weekends, old man."

Crusty cackled with pride. "I been known to raise some hell, back in the day."

"Bet you did." Jack turned to Lexi. "I found the jar on the porch rail. Not a safe place to leave glass, honey."

Lexi gritted her teeth at the nickname, making him hide a smile. "I didn't pick them or leave the jar there. I started out with that in mind today." She glanced at Crusty for some reason. The old man scowled at her, and she turned back to Jack. "But I never found any flowers and forgot about the jar. Guess I left it somewhere."

"Then who picked you flowers?"

"Who's to say they're for me?" Her light scoff made him wish he'd thought to bring her a bouquet.

"So someone just picked flowers and left them on the porch?"

She shrugged.

"Do you have a secret admirer I should know about?" Jack reached out and drew her into his arms, an imperceptible nod at Crusty warning her to play along. "Only married three days and already having to fight off your beaus. What's a husband to think?"

Her mouth tensed in a smile that wouldn't fool anyone, including the old man watching them with interest.

So Jack kissed her.

He meant it to be light, teasing, brief. But the warmth of her skin made him linger. The scent of sunshine in her hair made him draw closer. The taste of her mouth made him tighten his embrace.

The pinch on his ribs made him jump back. He barely restrained the yelp that wanted to escape.

"Don't worry," she said. "Those other men don't mean nearly as much to me as you do."

He had to smile at her cute butt swinging out of the kitchen, sure she was joking about the other men.

Pretty sure, anyway.

During dinner, Lexi found her gaze on the flowers more often than she'd have liked. Who had picked them and left them on the porch? Were they for her? Had someone found the jar at Crusty's new house, filled it, and brought it over? Who?

Was it coincidence Darryl had been on the property this afternoon? He'd been nearby when she'd discovered the gloves in the car. She hadn't asked Jack about them, not wanting to give him reason to worry.

Nothing sinister had happened, after all. A pair of gloves and a jar of flowers didn't equal a death threat.

But the break-in at her house worried her. When added into the equation, the gifts made her skin crawl. If she told Jack, would he try to forbid her from leaving the ranch? She wanted to go in and work at the office, and by God, he wouldn't—

"Whatcha scowling 'bout, Grace?"

Crusty's comment snapped her back to the dinner table. "Oh, sorry. Lost in thought."

"A danged fool could see that much."

"You shouldn't call her a danged fool, Uncle Crusty," Anna said. "It's not polite."

Lexi smiled over at the girl. "You tell him, sugar cube."

Anna blinked. "That's what Dad calls me too."

"Oh. Right. Sorry." Lexi didn't dare look at Jack as she encroached on his parental territory.

"It's okay. I like it. Genny's dad calls her ginger bean." She wrinkled her nose. "We looked it up and there isn't even such a thing."

"Is her proper name Ginger? I didn't know that."

"Nope. That just makes it more silly." Anna smashed peas with the back of her fork. "She's afraid to adopt Pirate in case the owl comes back and gets him."

"I'm pretty sure it wasn't an owl." Jack patted her hand. "Their cat probably ran off to have babies of his own. Maybe he chased a field mouse through their vegetable garden and is still off playing with Flopsy, Mopsy and Cotton-tail."

The girl giggled and her face cleared of worry.

Dinner passed as Anna and Crusty argued the merits of cursive writing, the girl's arguments impassioned, the old man's terse though half-hearted. Jack remained quiet for the most part, although Lexi felt his gaze on her. Since she didn't check, she couldn't be sure he hadn't just been staring into space, thinking of stock projections. After everyone finished, Lexi scraped dishes as the family brought them to her in the kitchen.

She helped Anna with math. The lattice method of addition made her head ache, and she doubted Anna needed her "help." Still, sitting together was pleasant. After they finished and Anna had bathed and dressed in her pajamas, Lexi taught her how to crochet a chain. A spare ball of yarn and an extra hook had the girl enraptured until bedtime as she struggled to make even-sized stitches.

A sweater for her own dad half-completed, Lexi smiled fondly as she watched, remembering her early attempts as her mother taught her to crochet and knit. She'd have to think of something Anna could make for Jack for Christmas. He and Crusty could always use warm scarves, which made an easy first project.

The girl's eyes lit when Lexi suggested it. "Let's see how you like crocheting first."

"I like it lots." Anna held up her chain, displaying large and small stitches. "I'm not very good at it yet, is all."

"That's better than mine looked when I started. But now it's bedtime."

"Can I keep my projects in your bag so Dad and Uncle Crusty won't see them?"

"Sure." Then Lexi wanted to kick herself. She'd have to leave the girl and her yarn behind when she left in a few days. "Or I have an extra tote bag. You can keep the hook, but I'll take you to pick out yarn if you decide you want to continue. It won't hurt my feelings if you don't, sweetie."

"I'll try a couple more days."

"Good idea." That's about all the time they'd have.

Later that night, a scream startled Lexi. She dropped the book she'd been reading and raced into Anna's room, her heart thudding wildly. The girl's eyes were open, but Lexi doubted she was awake. It unnerved her to see the girl staring at nothing while she cried.

"What is it, baby?" Lexi stroked her hair, her arms, her back. Anything to soothe the child. "You're dreaming. It's just a dream."

A shudder shook the girl's small frame and Lexi pulled her into her arms and rocked. Tears wet Lexi's pajama top as Anna snuffled and settled into her. Lexi kissed her head. "I'm here. You're all right."

"The owl. It was flying down...to get at Panda." She sniffed and wiped her face against Lexi.

Stupid owl. "It's okay. Panda's okay. She's in the barn with her mama."

"That's why the owl took me instead." Fresh tears broke through on a wail. "It flew off with me in its claws. 'Cause I don't have a mama."

"No, no, baby. You're okay. I've got you."

Anna clung tighter.

"I'll protect you." Lexi kissed her head and rubbed her back. "I won't let anything bad happen."

It took another ten or so minutes to settle the girl into bed. She hugged Lexi hard until Lexi scrunched down beside her.

A little hand fisted into Lexi's pajama top. "Don't go."

"Just for a minute."

"A big minute." Anna scooted over.

Lexi stretched out gratefully, as her back twinged from balancing half-off the bed. "How long is a big minute?"

"As long as it takes to eat supper?" the girl suggested.

Lexi smiled. "How about a medium minute then?"

Anna had just dropped back into sleep when Lexi heard a sound in the hall. She'd left on her light when she flew to Anna's side and now a shadow passed along the hall.

Jack stuck his head in the door. "Everything all right?"

"Yes," she whispered back. "A nightmare." Her slight shift had the sleeping girl's hand tightening. "The owl came for her."

"Damned owl."

She imagined his scowl just beyond the angel night-light on the bedside table, and smiled.

He came in to stand over them.

"Did you hear her clear down in your office?"

"No. She doesn't have nightmares. It never occurred to me to use a monitor at her age." A hand moved to his neck and rubbed where he sometimes got a frustration knot. "At least I didn't think she had nightmares. Now I wonder if I just didn't hear her."

"Genny Prescott might have embellished the owl story a bit today. That could have set her off." Lexi shrugged then went still as Anna clutched at her. When a moment passed without the girl waking, Lexi relaxed. "The story sounds more menacing now that Anna has the new kittens to protect."

"I know that feeling. Are you okay there? You look like you're barely balanced on the edge."

"It's a good thing she has a full-size bed because I might be staying the night."

"You shouldn't have to do that. I could sit with her."

"You've had a long day. I'll be fine."

Silence stretched between them. The dark room added to the feeling of intimacy.

"Are you done with paperwork already?" she asked.

"I was hoping to be, hoping to spend some time with you,

but I might as well go back down for a while." A short laugh escaped him as he leaned over and kissed Anna's forehead. The girl didn't stir. His lips brushed Lexi's forehead. "Make sure you get some sleep."

"'Night." With the imprint of his kiss searing her, she doubted sleep would come no matter where she lay.

CHAPTER TEN

The next two days passed with little interaction between Jack and Lexi. She didn't consciously avoid him, nor did she seek him out.

She was making herself crazy with indecision. One night he'd seemed ready to kiss her, but then he'd pulled away. The bedtime kiss on the forehead hadn't been at all romantic. Jack didn't feel anything that matched her feelings for him.

Admitting that attraction didn't help. Lexi wanted to flee this place and never look back. Yet part of her wanted to stay forever.

Clint had no news but checked in every day. Back in L.A., he couldn't do much to help after the initial phone calls he'd made hadn't panned out. He reported that Rachel hadn't received a call from Grace. Grace had either hidden from her friends or they were covering for her. She didn't respond to Lexi's messages or return her calls.

Crusty shooed her away each time she'd tried to talk about her identity, or what to do from here forward, or his health. Watching him like a wolf, she'd noticed him rubbing his chest or arm when he thought she wasn't looking. He often seemed to have difficulty catching his breath and sat abruptly when he'd been walking too long.

With no one to talk to, she'd have gone crazy vacillating between options if it hadn't been for the quiet moments at her dad's office, filing, billing, filling out insurance forms, and updating charts. Posing as Grace meant no one expected her to do much of anything else. For the first time, Lexi found a reason to enjoy the charade.

Picking up Anna after school provided Lexi a chance to get to know her as more than a cat-loving tomboy. The girl had a fierce passion for animals and often snuck out to the barn to check on the bottle-fed calf.

"Some of my friends are forming a basketball team," Anna said.

How high was the hoop for that age group? Lexi smiled to herself. "Would you like to play basketball?"

"I won't be able to. I have chores and homework."

"You won't have school after next week."

She could have kicked herself for building up the child's hope. Would Jack have time to drive her into town for practices and games? Could they form a co-op of parents to pick up and supervise, alleviating the burden on the families? Even as Lexi tried to figure a way to transport Anna herself, reality intruded. Soon, she'd either be the girl's aunt or ex-stepmother. In either role, she'd be back at her vet job with little time to spare.

"It's okay, really," Anna said into the silence. "If I have to choose, I'd rather be at the ranch."

"I understand that feeling."

"You do?"

Uncomfortably reminded of her current role, Lexi nodded. "My sister is the same. As a girl, Lexi gave up on a lot of opportunities to work with our dad, but you know, she never 'missed' any of them. Being with Dad made her happy. That's how she knew what she wanted to do."

"How did you know you wanted to paint?"

"Well." Lexi carefully swerved the car to divert Anna, her mind working furiously. "Sorry. Rabbit in the road."

Anna turned to look out the back window. "I didn't see it."

"Fast little guy." She thought back to Grace's early attempts at art. "I saw things differently than the rest of my family, even my sister. Considering we're twins, it didn't make sense to me at the time."

"Because you're an artist and she's not."

She smiled. "She's definitely not. Because I could draw,

Lexi tried to sketch. It was awful." Lexi laughed at herself and with fondness for the memory. The incident marked the first time she and Grace had realized they were different. It had made them stand on their own and also made them cling tighter, as though forces could now separate them. "Dad and Lexi see things more practically. I can't really explain why I see what I see."

A pang in her chest made her realize how much she missed Grace. Despite being angry, Lexi worried about the distress that had driven Grace to abandon the man she "cared about too much to marry." As the days passed, worry over Grace's physical safety grew. Had tears obstructed her vision and caused an accident? Had she run out of gas in the middle of nowhere, which described a lot of Montana and the surrounding states? Had she run into that fictional drifter and met a bad end?

Grateful to arrive home and settle into chores, Lexi parked Jack's car in its usual space. Wishing she had her truck back, she longed to take a drive into the country. Instead, she'd concentrate on making dinner since it was Doris's day off.

Almost immediately when she and Anna stepped in, Crusty took her arm and led her out of the kitchen. Anna skipped alongside them to the office he and Jack shared. An iced tea and an art book sat by the wine-colored leather arm chair.

Crusty had a gleam of wicked humor in his eye as he

indicated the reading material he'd selected. "Thought you could use some time off a yore feet. Since you do so much fer us and yore dad, figured you would 'preciate some time alone with this here book on—" He squinted at the title. "Impressionism for the Modern World."

His cackle made her narrow her eyes. The old coot knew she didn't care two twigs about art, but with Anna as witness, Lexi couldn't rebuke him. A fact he enjoyed at her expense. "I'm not an impressionist painter."

He snorted. "I shorely do know that."

Lexi crossed her arms. "I have to make dinner. Doris isn't here."

Anna fairly hopped with excitement. "We're making dinner."

A glance from Anna's beaming face to Crusty's near-to-busting grin made her clench her teeth. She'd get even with the old man for putting her in this position.

While her great uncle stood red-faced with suppressed laughter, Anna's face clouded. "Don't you like your surprise?"

Lexi dropped her stance and set aside her ire. "I'm not in the mood for reading, but maybe I'll crochet and listen to some music. A brief rest sounds good." She glanced at Crusty. "Then I'll come help with dinner."

"No," Anna cried. "It's a special dinner for you and Dad.

Uncle Crusty is going to show me how to cook."

"Is he?"

"I done my share of cooking, young lady," he said. "I can rustle together some vittles without even thinking hard. Show the girl here how to cook for her family one day."

Lexi curbed her protest. Assuming Anna would cook for a family someday wasn't outrageously chauvinistic, especially coming from Crusty, who had a firm idea regarding gender roles. Everyone needed to learn to cook. Imagining what he'd "rustle together," she wished he'd provided some crackers, cheese and fruit to go with her tea. A snack might be necessary to face the coming meal, especially if he "didn't have to think" about his cooking.

"This is very kind of you," she said to Anna, darting a pointed sidelong look at Crusty to let him know what she thought of his part in it. "I haven't had any alone time for a while."

While the others chattered away, Lexi considered what she'd do with her newfound freedom. Inspiration struck, her knees going weak with longing. "I'm going for a ride."

Closing her eyes, she let the idea wash through her. It would be heaven to be alone, just her and a horse and the hills and valleys. "I should take a couple of apples and a carrot." She'd give the horse the carrot and fortify herself with the apples.

Crusty scratched his beard. "Well, now, I don't know 'bout you riding off like that."

That brought her upright. "Why not?"

He gestured toward Anna with a nod. "Jack don't cotton to anyone riding off alone."

Some of Lexi's joy evaporated. His first wife had died while riding out alone. Every cell inside her protested at being denied this treat. One look at Anna studying the floor curtailed any objections. "Okay. I won't go riding."

"You could go take a bath."

Surprised, Lexi turned toward Crusty. "Are you saying I smell?"

His face turned red, this time with embarrassment. He stuck his hands in his pockets, shifted his feet. "No, no. I wouldn't say such a thing even if'n it were true. And it ain't."

She hid a smile at his consternation. Dipped her head to her shoulder as though to sniff herself. When his shoulders hunched, she congratulated herself on getting back at him. Maybe she couldn't take a ride—and she'd tackle Jack later about that—but she could repay Crusty for putting her in this awkward spot. Free time shouldn't come with strings.

"I jest meant women like soaking in the bath. Bubbles and smelly salts and such."

She relented. The two faces before her appeared so hopeful

and so eager to have her gone. Maybe she'd call Grace's friends. She might have better luck getting answers as the worried sister than Clint had as the jilted groom's brother. "Okay. I'll go busy myself upstairs. You have to promise to call me if you need my help with dinner."

"We won't. Have to call you, I mean." Anna tugged her hand, carting her toward the door.

Lexi laughed. "What about my tea?"

Crusty handed her both the tea and the art book with a solemn expression and a gleam in his eyes.

She leaned close to him. "I'll get even."

He gave a gleeful cackle and waved her toward the stairs.

"I'll wait here," Anna said, "and make sure you go up."

Shaking her head, Lexi finished the climb alone, mind already fixed on who she'd call.

Later, facing the "feast" on the table in front of her, she wished she'd stolen some apples.

Jack had washed up and enthused over getting a treat. His face fell when he spotted the food, although he made a manly effort to regain his smile. "Fish sticks? We haven't had those in a while."

Lexi placed two dry pieces with burnt breading on her plate. She looked for something positive. "I love peas and carrots."

Jack's smile almost slipped. "Carrots are one of my

favorites."

Probably not the shriveled brown variety sitting cheek to jowl with peas, wrinkled and dry, resembling hard green raisins. Lexi scooped a small spoonful onto her plate, hearing the clink as peas hit ceramic.

"We made mac and cheese, too." Anna's grin revealed a dark space.

Lexi thanked the food gods for providing something edible then blinked at her stepdaughter/niece. "Did you lose a tooth? I don't remember one missing when I brought you home from school."

"Aw, it weren't a big deal." Crusty patted Anna's hand on the table. "She took it like a trooper."

Jack's hand stilled from ladling bright orange pasta onto his plate. "She took what like a trooper?"

"The fall. 'Tweren't nothing."

"I slipped off the stool Uncle Crusty pulled up to the counter for me. It tipped. But I'm okay," she rushed to assure them.

Lexi spread the meager servings across her plate so it would appear she'd eaten. Did she have anything in her purse to supplement her meal? An emergency candy bar? A lollipop? A breath mint?

Not surprisingly, the fish stick tasted of burnt breading

around a smidge of fish product. Lexi drank almost half a glass of tea to wash it down.

"How long have these fish sticks been in the freezer?" Jack chewed on the undercooked macaroni, his jaws working as though eating a piece of taffy.

Crusty squinted at the ceiling. "Well, let's see. I bought it when Doris went on vacation, so a while, I guess."

Jack stopped chewing, swallowed with visible effort. "You mean when she went to Disneyland with her grandkids? Crusty, that was last year. No, wait, it was about a year and a half ago."

"Nope. It was when she went to Seattle."

Jack coughed, a napkin quickly covering his mouth, and probably receiving the fish bite he'd just taken. "Three years ago?"

Crusty's nod radiated satisfaction. "That'd be it."

"But..." Jack looked at his plate, then at his uncle. "Why hasn't Doris thrown it away already?"

"Told her not to. Good food shouldn't be wasted."

Silence fell. Lexi could almost hear Jack's unspoken response, defining "good" food.

"Don't you like it, Dad?" Anna's expression teetered between hopeful and heartbroken.

Lexi held her breath.

"Of course, I do, sugar cube." With a smile, he scooped up

some peas and carrots and stuck the spoon in his mouth.

Lexi hid her smile around a mouthful of mac and cheese. Big bites would hurry the meal along.

"What where you doing on the stool?" Jack asked.

"Stirring the cheese stuff into the macaroni." She frowned. "I'm not sure where my tooth went."

Lexi froze. Her throat closed and she tried not to gag.

Jack stilled also. "So your tooth could be in the food?"

Lexi couldn't breathe. Her napkin covered her mouth as she spit out the mac.

Anna looked from Crusty to her dad, to Lexi's wide watering eyes and napkinful of pasta. "I don't think so."

"'Course not. We stirred through the bowl and didn't come across nothing."

"Did you look on the counter and the floor?" Jack asked.

"Shore we did." Crusty scowled. "You think I'm a danged fool? I looked. We didn't find it."

"Well, it must be somewhere."

They all looked at the bowls of food on the table and at their plates. No one spoke. Anna reached out and stirred through the peas and carrots. She glanced at the adults. "Nope."

Lexi stared at the macaroni. Shared glances with the other three. And giggled. The dinner had been such a sweet thought but with bad execution.

Anna burbled, Jack's lips twitched, Crusty's scowl softened, and then the four of them laughed with uncontained humor. They rocked on their chairs and turned red in the face. If one of them calmed, the occasional hiccup of laughter started another of them up again. Crusty slapped his leg, guffawing.

"What's with you, old man?" Jack asked.

Lexi worried so much excitement might be bad for his heart. Or whatever ailed him.

"I'm guessing—" He could barely get the words out. "You won't want the brownies we made for dessert."

An hour after the meal ended, a knock sounded on Lexi's bedroom door.

"Come for a ride with me," Jack whispered.

Her heartbeat quickened with excitement. Being alone with Jack as the sun set conjured all sorts of romantic fantasies. "A ride?"

"Marco needs to stretch his legs now he's a dad."

A *horseback* ride? "Did Crusty put you up to this?"

Jack tipped his head in acknowledgment. "He suggested it."

"Why are we whispering then?"

"I don't want company. Just you and me and this." He brought something from behind his back.

Lexi opened the door farther to see he held a knapsack. Her

eyes widened and her mouth watered. "Food?"

"Shh."

"Real food?" She grinned. "Tooth-free food?"

He stifled a chuckle. "You're going to get us caught."

"Let me grab a few things." She found a faded sheet and pulled on her boots.

They tiptoed down the stairs like teenagers sneaking out to a party. Lexi held back her giggles. She hadn't done anything even slightly mischievous in years. Jack took her hand before running across the yard to the barn. The flash of his grin in her direction made her heart thud. She wouldn't have picked him as her partner-in-crime, but they'd been working well together all week.

"Your dad came out today to see Marco's Miracle."

"Dad was here? He didn't mention he planned to stop by."

"He gave me the evil eye and asked pointed questions about your well-being." Jack chuckled. "I wouldn't want to encounter him in a dark alley if anything happens to you."

"He sees me every day at the office." She should have known her dad would check up on her, despite her assurances to him that everything was going fine. "Sorry."

"I don't fault him for it, Lexi. I'd do the same if it were Annabeth."

Her lips twisted in self-deprecation. "Anna will have the

sense not to get herself in a situation like this."

She checked the cinch then swung into the saddle, found the stirrups already the right length. Jack watched her from atop the bay he'd been riding recently. He secured their picnic in a saddle bag.

"Efficient," she said, indicating the stirrups.

"I can judge how long your legs are." The corner of his mouth lifted, a knowing smile that lit his eyes and had her face heating at the implied intimacy.

He'd probably estimated the length of her legs from how tall she stood against him during their one kiss. One hot kiss that sent goosebumps across her flesh. Warmth spread from her center outward.

Or he knew the length of Grace's legs. The reminder crashed into her gut. She didn't want to think how he'd measured Grace's stirrups and tried to banish the image of them lying together.

They left the buildings behind and moved the horses into an easy trot. Lexi kept her attention on the horse's gait.

"Why don't you call Annabeth by her full name?"

Lexi looked over at Jack, so easy in his seat, a natural horseman. Despite growing up around people who rode, the sight of Jack in the saddle made her breath catch. So masculine. So rugged. So sexy. She wanted to pull him off that horse and down onto the grass, stretching his long body over hers.

"Lexi?"

She cleared her throat. "Well, she doesn't seem like an Annabeth, I guess."

"Because she's a tomboy." His voice held disapproval.

"Because she's strong. She's not interested in tutus and pink frills."

"You never know. She might want to try ballet."

Lexi shook her head. "She doesn't want to take time away from the ranch, but if she did, it would be for basketball."

"No kidding?" Jack thought for a moment then his expression softened. "I can see that."

"Exactly. 'Annabeth' seems like a mouthful for someone so down-to-earth."

They rode in silence for a few minutes while Jack visibly digested that, easier than the fish sticks. Just the thought of food sidetracked her. What had he brought in the knapsack?

They skirted the range where the men kept watch over the cattle, staying south along the property line as they rode. The wind cooled her body as the sun lowered toward the horizon before them. The movement of the horse soothed the restlessness that built in her when she didn't have the chance to ride.

"I bet you played basketball."

"I did. I can also spin *en pointe* so many times and so fast you'd get dizzy watching me."

A click of her tongue moved Marco into a canter. A moment later, Jack rode beside her. Lexi lifted her face into the breeze, trying to regain her enjoyment of the ride.

"I'm sorry," he said. "I didn't mean to hurt your feelings."

She tossed her head, shaking him off. He didn't speak again until he pointed toward a flat area atop one of the many hills. They dismounted, dropping the reins since the Rocking W ground-tied its stock.

"I brought a cover." Jack shook out a red and yellow checked tarp.

Lexi smiled. "I brought a sheet from the back of the closet."

"We work well together."

Settling the sheet over the tarp, Lexi then placed some of Montana's ever-present stones on the corners to anchor it in place. The sweet scent of the grass filled her nose as she sat. Jack opened the knapsack and handed her a water bottle. Her mouth salivated as she wondered what goodies the sack might hold.

"What's in there?" she finally asked, only to see his eyes gleam as he glanced at her. She narrowed her eyes. "It had better be good, Walker."

"The good news, *Walker*," he emphasized the name, causing her to start in surprise, "is that it's not brownies."

Lexi laughed. "We wouldn't want to risk choking out here

so far from help." She picked up a sandwich wrapped in waxed paper. "PBJ?"

He shrugged. "Sorry, it was all I could think of fast. PBJ has been my go-to sandwich since I was twelve. I took the jars and bread to the office so Crusty and Annabeth—Anna wouldn't see me."

"Clever." A bite had her moaning. He'd piled on the peanut butter, making the strawberry jelly a sweet afterthought. Glad he'd brought a drink, she swallowed several times to get the bite down.

He took carrots to the horses before sitting next to her. Stretching out long legs encased in clean denim, he leaned back on an elbow. "This is nice."

A mere six inches separated their bodies. Her skin tingled with longing. Ridiculous longing. As a distraction, she glanced at the setting sun, bright yellow in the sky, lining the clouds with pink, red, and orange. The blue sky deepened on the edges to indigo. Birds made last flights. "Thanks for thinking of this and including me. I miss riding."

"Me, too."

"You're in the saddle all day." She gulped more water to wash down the sandwich. At least, she told herself that was why she need help swallowing. Not his nearness.

"Sure I am, but it's not for enjoyment. I'm watching the

men or cattle, not taking in scenery."

"It's a nice view."

"It definitely is from here."

She turned to find him looking at her. "Are you getting sloppy on me, Walker?"

"I might be."

Her breath caught but his amused smirk made her relax. His eyes twinkled. "Let's be real, Jack. You don't want me, even as a substitute for Grace. And I won't be a stand-in."

He sat up so fast she didn't have time to back up before his hand fisted in the hair at her nape. "I wouldn't use you as a stand-in. That's insulting. To both of us."

Her mouth went dry. She tried to swallow. Wanted to lick her lips to bring moisture. Her heartbeat accelerated. Inches separated them. Then she felt his breath on her. His eyes darkened to emerald. An inch away. She noted his dark lashes, so soft in his masculine face. Her mouth opened of its own accord but she didn't snap it closed. Didn't want to.

"Jack." Unsure whether she meant it as protest or plea, she closed her eyes.

His mouth covered hers. Took hers. She melted, accepted. Put a hand in his hair and brought him closer. The silky strands barely covered her fingers.

He leaned into her, bearing her down on the sheet, levering

over her. His tongue invaded. She welcomed it inside, cozied it with hers. Sucked on it and heard, felt, his sharp inhalation. When he withdrew she almost whimpered at the loss. Tiny kisses landed on her cheek, in her hair, at her ear. He sucked at her jawline and her breasts grew heavy, wanting his touch, as his lips trailed down her throat.

"Jack." This time it was a plea. They both knew it. She found his shirt buttons, opened one, two. Ran her hands inside, against hard muscle, warm skin, silky hairs. Arching into him, she hoped he'd take the hint.

Never slow-witted, he put a hand to her breast, making her shudder with need. Lifting, molding, he nuzzled into the vee, nudging aside her shirt with his chin. His tongue on her breast had her panting. He tugged aside her shirt and air hit her breast just before his mouth covered her, hot, wet, pulling. She tightened, gulped in breaths when he sucked her nipple into his mouth.

She hooked a leg around his, pulling him closer, wanting his weight on her. His erection pressed into her, thrilled her.

He looked into her face, his dark with desire. "Lexi."

Her name confirmed he knew who was in his arms but also asked. Was she sure?

"It's probably a bad idea," she managed, wanting him to disagree. To convince her.

"Probably." But he didn't move off her, nor did he shift his gaze to her exposed nipple, tight with need. He let her decide.

Only two things influenced her decision: she wanted him and she loved him. A step this momentous should take more debate, but it felt like the most natural act in the world. Like breathing. "Are you ready for this?"

Jack rested his forehead against hers and closed his beautiful green eyes. "No. I didn't know we were going riding, let alone…anything else."

He pulled her shirt over her and moved off to the side, stretching out with his arm crooked over his face.

He meant condoms, while she meant emotions. Men.

But his caution gave her a second to think. Was *she* prepared, mentally, to make love to a man she'd have to leave in a few days? They could be married with benefits, she thought with a choked laugh as she buttoned her shirt, and then they'd part without remorse. Two adults with common interests and healthy desires. No entanglements. No messy emotions.

Except hers.

Jack rubbed a hand over his face and sat upright, leaning on his hands behind him. "We should probably think about it first."

"First?"

His grin came lopsided. "I mean, if we do it at all, we should think about it. Not just jump into it because—" He waved a hand at their surroundings. "Of the sunset and the hills on fire and the peace."

Cold water in her face wouldn't have snapped her back to reality any quicker. Outraged followed. "You jumped me because of the sunset?"

He scowled. "That's not what I said. And I didn't jump you."

"You wanted to."

"Yes, I did." He held her gaze. "I do. Anytime, not just sundown. Any place, not just a peaceful hillside."

A shiver coursed over her. Need, longing. She tried humor to diffuse the power arcing between them, drawing them closer. "Married with benefits?"

"Not sure we're married, but making love to you would be a definite benefit of our relationship."

The man had a way with words. "Making love," not having sex. She'd bet her last dime he'd be good at it. She suppressed a sigh for lost chances. "We should get back. Tuck Anna into bed."

His smile made her giddy as she got to her feet.

"I'd like to tuck you into my bed," he said.

She could picture them in his big bed, the chocolate and navy colors warming up his room. Desire warming them.

"Ready?"

She started, looked around to see he'd packed up their trash and the tarp. Only flattened grass gave witness to their interlude. As though nothing had changed.

Jack stared at the computer monitor, not seeing the cattle report displayed. The encounter with Lexi played in his mind. In his body.

Who would have thought Lexi inspired that depth of passion? She'd ignited under his hands, under his mouth. Ignited him in turn, so much that he couldn't concentrate on his work. He stared at his hand, recalled his palm cupping her curves, the feel of her silky skin, her plush warmth. Recalled his mouth on her breasts. The intoxicating taste of her. The laughter deepening her blue eyes when she located Anna's tooth, and the gentle stroke of her hand over Anna's hair as his daughter wrote a note to the Tooth Fairy.

With a growl of impatience, he switched off the computer and rose. Work could wait. He glanced at the ceiling, over-aware of Lexi above him. She often read in his bedroom until Anna fell asleep, then she would hasten to the spare bedroom. Tonight, he'd stop her from leaving. Maybe it was time to pursue that married with benefits idea.

But Lexi wasn't in his bedroom. Or the guest room. Jack peeked in Anna's door and located his wife.

Lexi lay beside his daughter, stroking Anna's hair and murmuring softly. Leaning into the door, he heard the words. "It's okay, baby. I've got you. It was just a bad dream."

Jack frowned. Anna had been having nightmares on and off, but more frequently in the past weeks.

Anna's whimpers tore at his heart. As he stepped closer, Lexi shook her head, stopping him while continuing her cooing. Perhaps his presence would set off his daughter again. He didn't want to undo Lexi's good work.

Jack stepped forward and leaned close. The fresh scent of the wind still lingered in Lexi's hair. "Is she okay?"

"Just a bad dream," she whispered. "The owl and the pussycat again."

"What?" Then he remembered, not the poem but the Prescotts' cat, supposedly snatched by an owl. He eyed her cramped position, propped against the headboard and bent over his daughter. "Are you okay there?"

"Yeah."

Jack tucked a strand of hair behind her ear. Trailed the back of his fingers down her cheek. So soft.

Their eyes held, as he communicated his desire by glow of the angel nightlight. The hitch in Lexi's breath underscored her understanding. She didn't pull away from his caress or break eye contact. His pulse thudded as blood raced through his body.

Pooled in his groin.

She shifted—to rise? To come with him?—and Anna moaned. Her little fingers tightened their hold on Lexi.

Lexi stroked Anna's hair and looked up at him. "Looks like I'm busy."

"Looks like." On impulse, he leaned over and kissed her lips lightly, lingering. At the door, he turned and saw her watching him.

She'd make a good mother to his little girl. No, he corrected himself, she already was a good mother. She took care of Anna, lightened Doris's work load, and even made Crusty a little less sour. Lexi had been a godsend for his family.

As for himself... Well, he'd almost married her twin, so looking at her was no hardship. Lexi had an earthiness Grace didn't. She fit in here at the ranch. If the picnic had proven anything, it showed they would be companionable in bed. Or on a picnic blanket. Or on the hay-strewn floor of the barn.

He cleared his throat. All their lives would benefit with Lexi in them.

Now he only had to convince her to stay.

CHAPTER ELEVEN

For the next two days, Lexi obsessed about the desire in Jack's gaze. He hadn't made a move since. Waiting for him to act made her jittery. Had he changed his mind?

Saturdays in their vet office tended toward small animal check-ups. With few appointments listed, she had time to check in with Grace's voicemail and catch up with her dad while he restocked the medicine shelves. He hemmed and hawed about his dates with Iris, and Lexi caught him up on the doings at the ranch.

After relaying the adventure of the "surprise" dinner—but not the picnic ride afterward—she added, "I don't go out to the barn as often as I'd like. I feel like someone's watching my every move."

Her dad put down his bag and looked at her with patience. "Lexi, you know why you're paranoid. You're waiting to get caught in that lie you're living."

She nodded, rebuked but glad to have a reasonable explanation for the unease she felt on the ranch.

Carrie Moore's call of a mare in distress during delivery came through at eleven, and Lexi itched to go with him. Turning a foal took strength and several helpers, and to be honest, her smaller hands made the mama-to-be more comfortable. But in her pretense, she could only stand on the sidelines.

Carrie was also a good friend. Playing Grace and having to pretend to be "out of town" herself meant Lexi couldn't meet with her friend, have lunch as usual, or seek Carrie's advice.

"Call if you need me." She cornered her dad in his office, gathering medicines from the locked cabinet. "I can be out at the Moores' in twenty minutes.

He slanted her a look. "Carrie or Adam will be there to help out. You need to get back to your family."

Oh, he was so funny this morning. Although glad he'd accepted her role as Jack's pretend wife, she glared at him for finding humor in her situation. "Adam Moore is probably still sleeping off last night's drunk."

"Now, Alexis, you and I can't know what bedevils that young man to drink. Until we can walk in his shoes, it's best to hold back judgment."

His hand on her shoulder burned her with guilt. He was loved as much for his compassion towards humans as his expert care of animals. "I'll try to remember, Dad. It just riles me to see Carrie doing everything on that ranch and having to deal with Adam as well."

"I didn't say it was easy." He kissed the top of her head before turning to finish packing up.

Since the waiting room remained empty until noon, Lexi hung the Closed sign and completed her paperwork for the day. Filing, insurance, reminders for vaccines, inventory and reorders. Necessary minutiae of the vet business that would drive her crazy if she didn't get out to treat an animal soon.

Needing to reclaim a piece of herself, Lexi headed to check on her house. Jack wouldn't like it.

Lexi didn't care.

She was meeting Anna and Jack for a lunch date in town at 1:00. Crusty had insisted "it were too much trouble" to go all that way just to eat, making her wonder if moving around pained him from his old injury or from his undisclosed diagnosis. Lexi wanted time alone before meeting them at Kerr's Grill. Playing Grace for the past week had exhausted her. Watching every word and action. Being unmasked by Crusty. Keeping the secret of Crusty's illness from Jack.

She stopped first at the pharmacy to pick up personal

feminine items she would be mortified to put on a list for Jack or the hands. Doris could have added them to her weekly shopping, but Lexi hated to ask. The woman's chores had been lighter with Lexi helping, but Doris didn't know that was a temporary situation. It felt like trickery, which made Lexi cringe with guilt every time the housekeeper thanked her.

Pulling into her driveway afterward, she took a satisfied breath and relaxed. Home at last.

The new lock on the back door gleamed its reminder of unpleasantness. Stiff with disuse, the key turned with a creak. The sound raked along her nerves and had her looking over her shoulder. Paranoid, she decided. No one watched her, despite the hairs on her neck standing at alert.

Setting the bag on the table, Lexi dug the extra key from the side zippered pocket of her purse. She made sure it worked in the front door then squatted to move the ceramic turtle near the porch. Anyone watching would assume she'd left the spare key there. No one was watching, she reminded herself. Her neighbors to the left had planted a row of hedges, while the ones on the right only visited family in Little Tree at the holidays.

She pulled some weeds from the dying ferns at the side of the porch, sneaking the key into a fake stone under the thick fronds. Grace would know to look there if she returned. When she returned. As Lexi walked back to the house, she sent out a psychic message to her sister, calling her home. She didn't actually believe in that twin mystique, but right now she'd take any help possible.

Her week was up. Tomorrow she would move back home and reclaim her identity.

It would have looked suspicious to buy groceries, but she wished she'd thought to grab a candy bar at the pharmacy. A little chocolate therapy before facing Jack and Anna sounded like heaven. She secured the door behind her, double checking that it locked easily.

"Hey there."

Lexi let out a thin scream. Her heart bucked like a wild bronco. Darryl Peters leaned back against her kitchen counter, arms crossed, amused smirk in place.

Breathing hard, she swallowed. The coppery taste of fear coated her tongue. She braced her feet apart. "How did you get in here?"

"Came by to say hi." He straightened, dropping his arms. "Just being friendly."

She measured the distance between them at eight feet. How long it would it take her to flip the deadbolt and open the front door? Stocking huge bags of grain and feed kept him lean and strong, despite weekend drinking binges. He could catch her. Easily.

She glanced around, searching for a weapon. "We're not friends. My friends knock before entering."

"Aw, now don't be like that." He stepped forward.

She stood her ground, breathing shallow. Knitting needles poked out of the basket on the far end of the sofa. The vase on the shelf would work, but she'd probably cut her hand while smashing it against his head. If she got that close with it. "You've said hello. Now leave."

"That's not very neighborly." He stepped closer.

She stepped back. "We're not neighbors."

"You shop at my dad's store. You were just at my mom's. I'd say you should be nicer to me."

"You followed me from the pharmacy?"

"I saw you from across the street. It's my lunch hour." His leer made her shudder. "You interrupted my meal, but it's worth it just to have you alone."

"Get out." She edged sideways, two steps around the sofa. Would she actually skewer him with the needles?

His face hardened. "Now, why do you want to talk to me like that? I was being nice. Paying you a compliment. Saying I like the way you look."

His gaze traveled down her body, making her feel unclean. She slid toward her knitting basket.

He countered, closing the distance between them. Six feet.

She swallowed, needing to distract him, but how? "Did you leave those gloves in my car?"

His expression didn't change. "You don't like presents?"

"What about the flowers? Was that you?"

"You're not very appreciative, are you? Do you have so many admirers you're not sure who gives you gifts?" His lip curled. "Bitch. Expecting men to drop at your feet just because your daddy is the county vet."

He lunged. She ran around the couch, into the kitchen. He grabbed her. Slammed her face-first against the wall. Pressed his body tight against her back. Breathed hot and hard into her hair. "Not so smart now, are you?"

She shot an elbow backward into his ribs. He released her to clutch at his side.

"You bitch!" His fingers dug into her arms when she made to escape. He swung her around, shoved her back into the wall. Her head thudded and tears sprang to her eyes.

Get free. Run to the door. Three feet—you can make it. Her keys were in the ignition. If she could get away, she'd drive hell for leather out of here. Unless he'd thought to look in the car and taken the keys.

She couldn't think like that. First, get free.

Eyes glittering, he smashed his mouth on hers. Blood pooled as her teeth cut her inner lip. She struggled against him.

The wet slip of his lips against hers made her gag. His tongue shot in, hot, huge, disgusting.

Blind with fear and rage, she raked her nails down his cheek then stomped on his instep.

Darryl leaped back, swearing, a hand to his face.

Lexi raised her knee and caught him between the legs, a little off target, but effective enough. He howled and bent over, cupping his groin. Two quick steps and the door opened under her hand. She raced to Jack's car, almost wept with relief to see the keys dangling from the ignition. Door closed, locks engaged, she started the car just as Darryl raced out of the house. She noted his limp with dark glee.

She reversed as he grabbed at the door handle. She swerved away, and he fell to the side, off-balance, onto her gravel drive.

She didn't look back.

Lexi was halfway to the Rocking W before she remembered her lunch date. She palmed tears from her face, checked the time. Ten till one. She pulled over and parked on the side of the deserted country road, letting the tears come. Reaction could be a bitch. She shook and screeched out her fear and anger into the empty countryside.

After a few good long screams, she rested her head against the seat. Deep breaths and the air conditioning helped calm her. She felt around for her tissue box, remembered she drove Jack's car, and reached for her purse. Which sat on her kitchen counter along with a bag containing tampons and condoms.

A giggle formed, erupted. Another followed. Stress. She wiped her face with her shirt sleeve. Her upper arms sported red marks from his fingers. She shuddered and pulled her sleeve down. No one would notice them if she kept her arms lowered.

What would Jack do if he knew Darryl had attacked her? As much as Darryl deserved a good beat-down, she couldn't let Jack take on more trouble on her account.

But Darryl wouldn't walk away—or limp away—scot free. She would beg off lunch with an upset stomach, which wasn't a lie, and drive straight to the sheriff's office. Since she'd left her phone in her purse at her house, she'd have to make the report in person.

At the sound of tires on pavement, she tensed, hand already on the ignition as she checked the rear view mirror. No car. Glancing ahead of her, she spotted her truck.

Relief and welcome swept through her before panic returned. He couldn't see her like this. Instinct told her Jack would go after Darryl. Jack didn't love her, but he would stand for her.

She fluffed her hair and wiped her cheeks again even as she heard the engine wind down. He stopped next to her and rolled down his window. She turned the car on and did the same.

"Hi, Grace," Anna called.

Lexi raised a hand, tried to smile.

Jack shifted into Park. "Did the car break down?"

"No." She cleared her throat, swallowed. "I forgot about our lunch. I'm not feeling well and thought I'd head home. Then I remembered."

Jack backed to the side of the road and unlatched his seatbelt. "Stay here, Annabeth."

"No, it's fine." Lexi didn't want him any closer. Not only would he see her ravaged face, but she feared she'd break down. She only had a tenuous hold on her emotions. "I was just waiting for you here to head you off."

But he stepped out of the truck and crossed to her. The bones in his face stood out as he took in her appearance. He leaned his elbows on the door frame. "What happened?"

She shook her head, pushed the hair out of her eyes.

He yanked at the door then reached in the lowered window and flipped the lock button to open. "Who did this?"

If he'd roared it, she wouldn't have been more surprised. But the quiet menace in his tone had her recoiling.

"Lexi." With a fingertip as gentle as his tone when he spoke her name, he lifted her shirt sleeve. The muscle in his jaw clenched. "Someone grabbed you."

She nodded, unable to admit it aloud, unwilling to relive

the fear.

"Who?" This time, his tone wasn't gentle. Nor were his eyes. They cut like shards of diamonds.

"Darryl. He...he was in my house. I stopped in after work."

"Just now?" Jack glanced down the road toward town.

"Jack. Don't do anything rash."

His gaze met hers, softened with a visible effort. "Did he hurt you other than this?"

"No." She shook her head to emphasize the point. "I'm okay."

"You don't look okay." He pulled a folded bandanna from his back pocket, reached out to wipe her face.

Lexi pushed it away. "I'm fine now. I was just scared."

His expression blanked. "Can you drive? Otherwise we can leave your car here."

"No, I'm fine. I was shaky, but I'm fine now." She wanted him to head back to the ranch or on to Kerr's with Anna so she could go to the sheriff's.

He straightened. "Take Anna home. Give her lunch."

"No, I'm going to the sheriff's." Lexi scrambled out of the car after him. She grabbed his arm even as he leaned in the truck window.

"Sorry, sugar cube, we can't do lunch. You're going home with...Grace."

"Why?" Anna's gaze stayed glued to her dad's face.

"Jack." Lexi tugged on his arm, his muscles tight under her hand. Clenched fists would do that.

"Grace has an upset tummy," he said. "I'm going in to town to get her something to take care of it."

"Jack."

"Okay," Anna called. "I'm sorry about your tummy, Grace."

"Don't," she said with quiet force, but in a tone that wouldn't reach the girl. "Don't do anything you'll regret."

He eyed Lexi. "I won't. Get back in the car."

The truck door opened, and Jack went around to catch Anna as she jumped to the ground. "Go home, ladies. I'll be a few minutes behind you. I'm just going to lock up the house."

He nudged Anna toward her and climbed into the truck.

"Jack, don't do anything stupid."

The look on his face didn't reassure her.

"Walkers take care of their own."

She watched her truck pull away. *Dammit.* Could she get to the sheriff's and back to her house before Jack found Darryl? Jack had murder in his eye. Old West justice meant he'd handle this himself, regardless of whether they were married. If she went to the sheriff's now, they'd arrest Jack for assault.

She could follow him, possibly stop him. A downward

glance toward the sprite at her side nixed that idea. It wouldn't do for the girl to witness her father in a fistfight.

Resigned, Lexi settled them both in the car and went home to the Rocking W.

An hour later, Jack fumed and drank some more whiskey. He'd been reduced to drinking from the bottle while sitting out in the barn like some schoolboy sneaking his first drink. He couldn't face Lexi. He'd failed her. Husband or not, his job as the man in her life included keeping her safe.

He drank to blur the image of her deep, wounded eyes, haunting him with that expression of shock and pain. Of violation. Peters had broken her confidence, her expectation of safety. He'd bruised her, body and spirit, and for that alone, Jack would see that the son of a bitch paid.

Peters hadn't been at Lexi's house. The man wasn't a fool. He hadn't gone back to the feed store nor had he headed to his parents'. Logically, the next step should have taken Jack to the sheriff's office, but logic had nothing to do with this. He wanted to, *needed to*, bash in Peters' face himself, the law be damned.

A check mark against me. Jack hadn't avenged Lexi. Yet.

The sun had set before he'd given up his search and headed home. Headed to the barn. If he was half the man his father had been, he'd be inside comforting Lexi, checking on her wounds.

Instead, he'd phoned Crusty and had the old coot confirm her condition as stable but jumpy, with Doris attending her. The jumpy part sent Jack looking for a bottle. A fist in Peters' face would have been more satisfying.

It must be the danger of the situation that had him thinking this way. Protective feelings that she'd laugh at. Any man in the county, in the state, in the West, would feel the same. No way would he be stupid enough to fall for another Marshall woman, so this murderous rage must be genetic.

Jack would be damned if he'd let her go back to her house with Peters still in town. She couldn't go to the doc's where she'd be alone whenever her dad went out on calls. Lexi had to stay here on the Rocking W where Jack could watch over her.

It wasn't lust ruling him. He hadn't fallen in love with her in the past week. She'd always gotten under his skin with her independence and reckless ways. Her sassy mouth used to drive him up the wall. Now he wanted to cover that mouth with his, take her breath inside him so she couldn't sass, couldn't think.

He took another swig then set the bottle aside. Walkers protected their own. Lexi fell under his protection through their circumstances.

Simple as that.

Rachel reached for the phone, hesitated when she

recognized the Los Angeles area code on the readout. *Clint.* Her heart raced and she considered letting it go to voice mail. The desire to hear his voice, to have him close in some way won out. She clicked the answer button and put pleasured surprise in her tone.

"I didn't expect to hear from you." Her hands sweat and she alternated holding it to either ear while drying her palms on her shorts. "How's L.A.?"

"Lonely."

She closed her eyes against the longing the single word conveyed. Her knees weak, she sank onto the sofa, also feeling the loneliness and the longing. For him. The house echoed around her as she sought for a reply.

"How's Longmont?" He sounded hopeful. Did he want her to say she missed him?

The hell of it was, she did. But she had other plans for her future and now had saved enough to fund them. She had to let him go. As much as it pained her, she wouldn't tie him to her. It wouldn't be fair.

"Lonely," she heard herself say and couldn't believe the slip. Even as his relieved sigh brushed her ear, she regretted leading him on. That had to stop. "But I'm busy, busy, busy, so I'm sure that'll change. I start next week teaching two summer classes. In one, the students are high achievers and will keep me on my toes. In the other, the students are struggling, so they're a challenge in a different way. One group wants to be there, the other not so much."

She swallowed into the silence.

"Sounds like you have your hands full."

"Yes." Hearing his disappointment made her chest ache.

"I hoped you could come down here for a visit. A long visit. I didn't realize you were working this summer."

Rachel kept the earpiece pressed tight, unwilling to miss a word, not matter how each hurt. She'd love to see him again. "I'm sorry."

"I could come up there for a long weekend over the Fourth of July." Clint cleared his throat. "If I'm invited. Two weeks feels like a long time away, but I can be patient when I want something. And I really want to be with you."

She clutched an arm across her stomach. "Clint." Denial wouldn't come. Neither would she allow herself to cave in and invite him. "I can't."

"Can't?"

"This isn't L.A. People would notice." Angry with herself for sidestepping the issue, Rachel struck her thigh with her fist. "What we had was lovely, Clint. I—"

"Don't talk about it in the past tense."

"It is, though. It has to be. Don't you see, this was just..."

She forced out the hateful word. "A fling."

"No," he said with force, "it wasn't. Not to me."

Remember the plan. "We had a great time together. Can't we just leave it at that? Don't ruin it with an argument, please." She held in a sob.

"It wasn't a fling. It was a beginning. True, we haven't known each other very long, but there's something between us."

She gave a laugh, hoped it sounded convincing. "Yeah, several thousand miles and a couple of mountain ranges."

"Not geography. Romance."

Her breath caught in her throat. *Romance.* How many men used that word, especially so early in a relationship? He would have been great if she'd met him ten years ago. Except he'd have been jailbait then.

The reminder of time passing stiffened her resolve. "Not all romances end happily. Goodbye, Clint."

"Wait."

His plea had her hesitating. "What?"

"Just tell me why you won't give us a chance. Did I do something wrong?"

"No, of course not." She took a breath and forced herself to uncover the courage she would need in the near future. "I made some goals before I met you. I still want to—need to—carry out the steps to achieve those goals. I'm sorry this sounds harsh, but

I met you at a bad time."

"Maybe I could help with your goals, Rachel."

"I wouldn't ask you to. Because—" Saying it out loud would make it real, which made her smile. She yearned for it to be real, but there were a lot of steps before achieving her dream. Step One, she knew, was admitting what she wanted. If she couldn't even say it, she'd never go through with it. So with another deep breath, she told him.

"I'm going to have a baby."

CHAPTER TWELVE

Lexi couldn't hide from the world forever, although she gave a good imitation of it on Sunday by reading in her room. She had an early breakfast and let the family fend for themselves at lunchtime. Only when Anna knocked on her door—a tentative *tap, tap, tap* Lexi could barely hear, to announce they'd made sandwiches for supper—did she stir.

Her gaze met Jack's once during the silent meal. His red-rimmed eyes burned into hers, then slid to her arms, where three-quarter length sleeves covered the bruises. She didn't want to alarm Anna or have to answer questions from Crusty.

Although the hawk-eyed Crusty probably knew, if not the details, then he'd guessed the gist. She'd cowered long enough. She turned to Anna. "Do you want to take a ride after dinner?"

Anna nodded even while Crusty scowled and Jack glared. "Where do you think you're going?"

"Riding." Lexi tossed her hair behind her shoulder,

borrowing Grace's gumption as well as her gesture. "I've never seen Anna on a horse. It's time to fix that."

Jack stared at her, several emotions flitting across his expression in rapid order. "I'm going with you."

It wasn't a request for permission or invitation. The man had made up his mind.

Lexi set her fork to the side of her plate and rose. "I wouldn't have it any other way."

Crusty grumbled them out the door, insisting he could get through kitchen chores on his own. "I wouldn't go with you three even if'n I could. You'll be showing off for each other."

"We didn't ask you to come along, old man." Jack adjusted his hat. "Why don't you whip us up a cake while we're gone?"

"Jack!"

"It don't matter what this one says." Crusty put a hand on her shoulder and pushed her out the door. "You three go do something family-like."

Once outside, she turned on Jack. "Should you talk to Crusty that way?"

Jack jogged down the steps. "If you baby him, he never stops, although he gets more cranky. If you agree with him, he shuts up."

She glanced over her shoulder then realized she was watching for Darryl in the shadows. "That's no reason to be disrespectful. What are you teaching Anna?"

"Survival." Jack cocked a brow. "That poor girl will have to deal with the old man when I'm gone. And he's ornery enough to out-live even her."

Lexi giggled, surprising herself. Some of her tension eased. "You're impossible to argue with."

"You didn't have a problem doing that, way back eight days ago."

"True. I guess you've mellowed since the wedding." She ran ahead to check on Anna, although on the ranch the girl couldn't be safer. She'd be with the kittens. Still, the dark corners of the barn made Lexi nervous.

Jack waved off her offer to help saddle the horses so she inspected the kittens and watched him. He lifted the saddles with ease, demonstrating that rangy strength of the cowboy. His hands on the horse were gentle as he talked to them in a soothing tone. Her gaze stayed fixed on his hands, imagining them— remembering them—on her body. His low murmur became the sweet sound of seduction. Her mouth grew dry while her stomach clenched with desire. Not a good idea at the best of times, and having Anna with them didn't qualify as that.

Saddles cinched and stirrups adjusted, the horses quivered with excitement. Lexi could sympathize.

They rode slow and easy, with nowhere in particular in

mind. Marco accepted Lexi as a trusted friend. Anna's mare, Patches, had probably carried Jack as a child. She had a gentle gait and didn't spook. Lexi frowned at the roan mare Jack rode. "What's your horse's name? I thought I knew all your stock."

He patted the roan's neck. "This is Bathsheba, an appropriate name since she'll jump into any water she sees. Originally, her owner called her that to honor her strong will."

"Really? How'd you get her?"

"She's on loan. The idea is to run her around dry land until she forgets about swimming."

"Can she swim?" Anna asked.

"Like a champ. They should have called her Mermaid."

"Is the dry land approach working?" Lexi asked.

His wicked grin flashed. "Do you want to take them to the creek and find out?"

She laughed. "Let's save that for some other day."

He sobered, staring at her. "I'd like to go swimming with you. Alone."

Lexi pictured them together in the water, clothes plastered against their bodies. Or him without his clothes, since in her fantasy, he'd discarded them on the bank.

She couldn't think of him in that way. He wasn't hers. Lexi reminded herself over and over until she couldn't stand the thoughts in her head.

After another ten minutes, she checked on Anna who rode along with her attention on Patches. Did Jack limit her saddle time because of her mother's accident? Anna showed no fear, but rode stiff and uncertain.

"Let's head back. I've had enough for today." And she thought Anna had as well.

Once the horses were turned over to the stable hand, Lexi propped a boot on the lower rail of the corral fence. She smiled as Anna ran into the house to see about cake. "I'm going back to work in the office tomorrow."

He turned in her direction. "The hell you are."

His low, raw tone didn't carry farther than the two feet between them.

"I can't hide here."

"Why not?"

She blinked, surprised he didn't deny she'd been hiding all day. "I have to face my fears, not give in to them."

"Lexi, just wait. Give it a few days. You're safe here." His hands gripped the top rail. "I can't keep you safe in town."

"Then I'll keep me safe. Don't you understand? I'm on edge, even here."

He studied her, now only a foot away. So close, except for the distance in his eyes. "You know I don't want you to do this. But if you're determined to disregard my concerns, I can't stop you."

"I have pepper spray. I'll put it on my wrist band." She set her hand on top of his. "Darryl can't believe he's won."

"I don't want you to be afraid of anything."

"Pardon me, boss." George Brooks spoke from the barn doorway. "Did you mention Darryl Peters?"

Jack turned. "Yes, what about him?"

"I heard he's in bad shape. Went to the hospital yesterday. Broken ribs, all bruised up on his face." George's gaze shifted to Lexi then back to Jack. "Heard he fell from the loft of the feed store. Lucky to be alive, folks say."

Heart pounding, Lexi watched as George and Jack exchanged information without words. She couldn't see Jack's face and George's was a blank slate. Was that story circulating to cover the truth? If it was known Darryl had been beaten, the sheriff would investigate. As much as Lexi wanted Darryl brought to justice, she couldn't risk Jack being arrested.

Not for one second did she believe Darryl had fallen. She didn't want to picture him bloodied, bruised and broken. Yesterday, still in shock, she might have found peace with the idea. Today she only wanted him to stay far away from her.

The next day at work, Lexi jumped at the slightest sound. Her dad looked at her strangely and asked twice what was the matter with her. Fortunately, none of her bruises showed. She didn't want him involved. He'd insist she move in with him. He might refuse to let her make calls alone. She had to free herself of the internal scars, and the only way to accomplish that was to face Darryl.

"I'm going to the Feed Store while we're quiet. Want some lunch on my way back?"

Her dad shook his head, gaze on the chart in front of him. "Iris packed me a vegetable pita."

"Iris?" Lexi smiled then hid her amusement before he looked up from the desk. "Are we going to talk about this?"

"No."

"Dad, I like her. I think you're cute together."

He sighed. "That's very condescending of you."

"I don't mean to be."

"But you only view me as your father. Dating Iris isn't 'cute.' I'm not a ninety-year-old man trying to rekindle my lost boyhood with a twenty-something girl."

She held up a hand, definitely not wanting to hear about any sparks kindling. "I'm sorry. I didn't mean to belittle what you and she have." She cleared her throat. "Is it serious?"

Her father nodded. "She's important to me. I've had other female friends since your mom died. Iris is more than that."

Lexi nodded. Her father had a life of his own. "I've been

your sidekick for most of my life. If Iris Browning makes you happy, then I'll get used to it seeing you together." She tilted her head, considering. "I never saw you get ready for a date or heard you talk about anyone in particular. You can dance, but I've never noticed you dancing with any one person at Kerr's."

A smile ghosted across his face, lighting his eyes. "I don't go to Kerr's on the nights you do, kid. When you were teenagers, I made myself busy. Dating wasn't important. When you and Grace went to school, I had time alone, time to see that I'd be alone. The first dates I had were awkward."

"Because they weren't Mom."

He nodded. "Because they weren't Mom. I wanted a companion, so I didn't have to go to a movie by myself or have dinner for one. And I had more...intimate relationships."

She nodded, determined to get through this talk, knowing her face gleamed as red as her dad's.

Think of Hawaii. Coastal beaches. Do not picture your father having sex. Coastal beaches, coastal beaches.

"I never looked at Iris romantically until two years ago."

Her father had been dating someone seriously for two years, and she hadn't noticed? Lexi felt like the worst daughter ever born. "I bought my own house about then."

"Convenient timing, huh?" He winked. "I can't imagine sneaking a woman to my bedroom past my little girl."

"Thank the Lord I wasn't here. Talk about awkward."

"But it's more than that between us." He met her gaze with the serious expression he wore to tell someone they needed to put down their favorite horse. "I expect you to be respectful."

Lexi took a breath, decision already made. "I've known her as Little Tree's librarian my whole life, but I'd like you to introduce me to her sometime."

"You'll always be my best girl, Alexis, because you say the exact right thing." He hugged her close, and she breathed him in, hugged him hard. This was the last moment he was truly hers.

Her family was changing. Her dad had fallen in love again, although he hadn't said it in so many words. Grace had disappeared. And Lexi had fallen in love with her sister's groom.

That protective feeling drove her to discover in what condition he'd left Darryl. His parents would know, but his mother might not speak to Lexi. Allison had always been a bit standoffish. His dad might be more open. More anxious about retaining the Rocking W's business, certainly.

Swallowing fear several times on the drive over, Lexi locked the car behind her and stared at the Feed Store. She couldn't stand here all day, despite her legs wobbling like gelatin. *You can do this.*

As soon as she walked in, Fritz appeared at her side as though he'd been watching her on the sidewalk, bolstering her courage. She cringed to think of him seeing her so afraid and straightened her spine. "Fritz, how are you?"

"I'm well, thanks for asking, Miz Walker."

Miz Walker. So he didn't know her identity. Had Darryl not told him or didn't he know either? Did it matter which sister Darryl thought he'd attacked? "I saw Allison briefly the other day." Lexi watched his expression as she mentioned the day his son had come after her. "She's busy. That's good for business."

Fritz nodded, no discernible change crossing his face. "I'm busy here, too. Is there something I can help you locate?"

"No, I'll just wander. Have a good day." She did wander off, feeling his gaze on her like spiders creeping across her back. But that was her imagination surely. Apart from being a little brusque, which could be attributed to the busy store, Fritz hadn't given any impression he knew of her part in his son's injuries. He hadn't mentioned his son's "accident" either. But then, would he have told Grace, especially after their encounter in the store when she hung flyers?

Lexi strolled along the aisles. She recognized most of the people from her ranch calls, but they merely nodded or said a quick hello to the vet's "other" daughter. Grace's friends didn't hang out here.

She browsed through the catalogs on stands. With no one within sight, she slipped through the swinging doors to the warehouse. Sweat coating her chilled skin, she forced herself forward. She had to face Darryl and show him she wasn't afraid.

Prove it to herself.

Fifty pound feed bags piled high to the loft beside a few equally heavy seed bags left over from Spring. The large equipment and parts were shelved in boxes. Dust motes danced in the air.

Not seeing anyone, she realized he might be in too much pain to come in to work. Her gaze drifted to the loft twenty feet above. If Darryl had fallen to the concrete floor from there, he'd likely be dead. The silent cavern gave her the creeps.

With quick steps, she rounded the corner to the office, intending to ask about his condition. To her surprise, Darryl sat behind the high desk on a stool. She'd imagined him as a stock boy, not the back room manager.

His condition made her stomach turn. One puffy purple eye provided a slit for a glare. The other was swollen shut. He wore a sling on his right arm, but no cast. His jaw sported purple and blue shades, along with a severe-looking bandage on the left side of his face. Her nail marks, probably.

"Come to gloat?" He could barely lift his swollen lip to sneer at her.

"I won't lie. You deserved this."

He grabbed his ribs. "I fell off the loft."

"Did you?"

"Broke five ribs, dislocated a shoulder, busted my face some." He leaned back with visible pain and hooked the heel of his boot on the bottom rung of the stool. She noticed then that he wore loose, cut-off sweatpants. "Got some other injuries down here. Did you come to kiss them better?"

She stepped back in revulsion then cursed herself for letting him get to her. She wanted to flee, but they lived in the same town. And by God, she wouldn't be a victim. "Why did you fall? You've worked here since you were a kid. Don't you know where it's safe to step?"

"Don't act all innocent. It's just you and me back here." His gaze darted around the warehouse. "This is as much your fault as his. Did you go back to the ranch all traumatized, just because I kissed you? Is that what set him off?"

Lexi forced herself not to react to his accusation or his remark about his assault being "just a kiss." She'd seen what lurked in his expression when he held her against the wall. He hadn't intended to stop at a kiss, hadn't cared—or worse, *enjoyed*—the fact she didn't want him to touch her. She bolstered her courage. "Don't act innocent, Darryl. You attacked me and would have done worse if I hadn't gotten away."

"If you hadn't kneed me in the balls, I would have gotten away, too." He shook his head. "I should have just left instead of searching your house. You don't keep anything there. No money, no jewelry of any value." He gave his best smirk under the circumstances. "I did enjoy going through your panty drawer. Nice stuff."

She shuddered and determined to give away every item of clothing she owned.

"I took a couple of the more enticing pieces with me, but I must have lost them sometime between getting beaten near to death and the hospital."

She quashed the image of her personal items littering the highway. Better blowing in the breeze than in his possession. "What did you tell them at the hospital?"

The scrape of a shoe on concrete behind her had her turning. A large man stood backlit by the sun streaming in the bay delivery doors. "You okay?"

Lexi let go of the breath trapped in her throat as she recognized the ranch hand. She should have known Jack would keep an eye on her. Sure, he "let" her go to work, but that didn't mean he'd left her unprotected. "I'm fine, George."

He walked over to them. "Boss sent me for some oil for the ATVs." He ran cold eyes over the cowering Darryl. "Nah, that's not true. I volunteered to come. Make sure you didn't have car problems. Or anything."

She recalled he'd been the one to tell them about Darryl's

"accident." Did the entire ranch, maybe the entire town, know what had happened? His presence lent her confidence. "I'm heading back to work in a second."

He snorted, not happy to be dismissed. She raised a Grace-like eyebrow, and he backed away. "I'll wait for you right inside the store here," he said.

Darryl had gone pale under his bruises. He knew George would tell Jack they'd been together. Did he fear retaliation?

"Stay away from me." Darryl tried to glare. "Trouble follows you. Trouble for me, anyway."

She leaned in, inches from his face. "Remember that."

For the next few days, Jack watched Lexi and was satisfied she showed neither fear nor pain. George had told him of the encounter in the feed store, making Jack grateful the man had suggested going in to buy oil. They always needed it, but if either had looked, they'd have found containers in the shed. Jack didn't make a habit of running out of essentials.

He'd struggled with the idea she might be afraid in town, but instead, she'd brazenly gone to challenge the monster of her nightmares. As much as he'd hating hearing of it, her facing down Darryl had chased the fear from her eyes.

When he tapped on her door Thursday night, he felt confident about taking her to town. As confident as a man could be in this situation. Although most men didn't ask their wives out on a first date after the wedding.

"Hey, I was thinking," he said when she cracked open the door. "Other than going in to work, you've mostly been stuck here. I thought you might like to do something different."

She cocked her head in question.

"I wondered if you'd like to have dinner with me at Kerr's tomorrow night."

"Oh."

"Is that a bad idea? I thought we could do some dancing after we eat. You like dancing, right?"

"I do."

Tension slipped away. "Every time you say those words, there's trouble."

A smile lit her eyes. "I'm not sure if that's a slam or just the truth. But I'd love to go dancing. With you."

Instantly nervous, he didn't know what to do with his hands. Not put them on her. Not draw her close. Not mold her body to his. So he rubbed his hands together and felt big, clumsy, awkward. "Good. Uh, pick you up at six?"

She chuckled. "You know where to find me."

He knew all right, he thought as he forced himself to turn away instead of putting his mouth on hers and drawing that laugh into himself. Every night as he walked down the hall to his room, he passed her bedroom door. Crusty couldn't climb stairs easily, but who was to say he wouldn't try? Discovering her set up in a separate bedroom would blow their cover.

The deception bothered him. All day Friday as he worked the fence line with his men, he considered how and when to tell Crusty about Lexi. Whether the old man would approve, Jack didn't know. His uncle had a perverse streak that could sway the matter either way. But Crusty, a Western man to his cells, would agree she needed to stay on at the ranch now. Their arrangement deceived people but it protected Lexi.

Jack wouldn't allow her to return to her house. Not until... Until what? He wiped sweat from his forehead with the back of his arm, feeling new beads of perspiration form under the hot summer sun. If Lexi filed charges against Peters, he'd stand by her while the man was arrested. Peters' family would bail the bastard out, then he might await trial for weeks. No way could Jack stomach the idea of Lexi in town alone. She'd have to stay on the Rocking W. And to save her reputation, she'd have to be his wife, which meant she'd have to continue her charade.

Unless...

No. Crazy. Jack removed the water bottle from his work belt. What if Lexi agreed to stay married to him? They could announce their marriage as a *fait accompli*. Say the switch at the wedding had been on purpose. Lexi had said "I do." They'd signed the marriage certificate. Maybe it was official enough.

He snorted. Official *enough?*

They might have to get married for real this time. Except he might already be married to Grace. Maybe.

He'd asked Dan Higgins to look into whether he and Grace might be married by proxy, but was the lawyer checking whether he and *Lexi* were legally married? Did he want to know the answer? Discovering he and Lexi were married would smooth the path for her to stay on the ranch. Learning they weren't would cause complications.

Anna would have to be the ace up his sleeve. Lexi had a soft spot for her. Was that enough to convince her to stay? To convince her to quit her dangerous job and help him on the ranch instead? Mother his child, and, he swallowed, more kids to come? He could picture her pregnant. She'd be radiant. And getting her pregnant wouldn't be a hardship. He felt himself harden and cleared his thoughts. Would building a family be enough of a draw?

As long as she quit her job, they could make a life together. That was a deal-breaker for him. And very likely, a deal-breaker for her. He could lose her on that point, but he'd be damned if he'd become a widower twice over.

Jack shook off the memory of that dark time, the grief that cut him to his knees. He wouldn't risk heartache that severe again. He'd convince Lexi to agree to stay married or to marry him again. They could do it at the ranch.

He chuckled. And then they'd *do it* at the ranch, just as Clint had suggested in his toast. Just as Jack had been daydreaming about daily for almost two weeks.

Footsteps on the stairs that evening had Jack jumping to his feet. He ran a hand over his shirt, smoothing nerves as much as wrinkles. Why should he be anxious? It was just dinner. Dancing. Holding Lexi in his arms.

He stepped into the foyer as she descended the last three stairs, Anna at her side. His breath caught. She wore cut-off jeans that exposed sexy tanned legs and short boots that made him imagine tugging them off. A yellow buttoned blouse exposed her neck but concealed her breasts. He could fix that.

Jack shook off the crazy thoughts. Tonight was their first date, although hardly traditional. "You look nice tonight."

"Thanks. You, too."

Silence fell, awkward and heavy. Jack couldn't think what to say. How the yellow of the shirt made her hair gleam? How her sky blue eyes sparked a fire in his gut? Seconds ticked by. They continued to look at one another, gazes locked. He stepped forward, thinking to pull her into his arms.

"Can I come?" Anna broke the spell.

"Not this time, sugar cube." Jack ruffled her hair while she scowled. He smiled at his child then his wife. "Tonight is for grown-ups."

Lexi blushed and looked away. The tension that had held him immobile dissipated.

"Let's go, honey." He held out his hand.

Lexi narrowed her eyes but didn't mirror Anna's scowl.

"Git on outta here." Crusty limped in from the dining room. "The girl and me have our own plans for tonight."

"We do?" Anna's eyes were wide. Jack was surprised, too. Crusty had never singled out Anna for special time together.

"Shore." Crusty nudged her shoulder with his elbow. "We're having popcorn and orange soda pop for dinner, then I'll find us a movie and we can have some ice cream. If'n I can hit upon where Doris hid the chocolate bars, we'll have those for a bedtime snack."

Jack opened his mouth to nix that idea when Anna shook her head.

"I don't think we should have popcorn for dinner."

At least someone here had sense. Jack felt safer leaving Crusty in the girl's care than vice versa.

"We should save the popcorn for the movie," Anna said, "and have ice cream for dinner."

Crusty winked at her. "What was I thinking?"

She had a crafty gleam in her eyes. "And I know where Doris hides the candy bars."

The old man laughed. "Kid, I think this is the beginning of a beautiful friendship."

His daughter didn't catch the *Casablanca* movie reference but smiled at the idea. Lexi kissed the top of Anna's head and surprised Crusty with a hug. "We'll see you later."

Jack glared playfully at the old man. "Don't keep her awake all night."

"Back at ya, boy." Crusty waggled his eyebrows.

Jack locked gazes and refused to back down, although he hoped like hell his face didn't broadcast his intentions for the evening.

"Let's go." Lexi touched his forearm and he looked over, breaking eye contact with his uncle. The old coot would consider it a win. With a kiss for Anna, he headed out, a hand to Lexi's waist.

He held the truck door for her then slid in. A sound escaped her before they'd traveled fifty feet. Jack tensed, hoping she wasn't upset at his uncle's teasing. He started to pull over when he recognized laughter. A hand covered her mouth, but her bright eyes shone and her shoulders shook.

"Sorry," she said, trying to control herself with deep breaths. Success eluded her as giggles escaped. "He's just so...Crusty."

Jack's lips twitched. "That he is. I thought you were embarrassed."

"Nope." She wiped tears from her eyes. "He's got it all wrong between us, which only makes it funnier."

Not all *wrong.* "He thinks we're a newly married couple. It's natural to assume we're going to end the evening intimately."

Lexi's mouth opened then closed again. What didn't she say? That they weren't likely to be intimate later? Well, they'd see how the evening went, but he wasn't marking the possibility off his list yet.

They rode in to town in companionable silence. They'd be surrounded by music at Kerr's. Vehicles jammed the parking lot. Without a theater in town, Kerr's was one of the few places to take a date. Maybe some night, they'd play pool at Harry's, a billiard hall run by a friend of Jack's dad. Imagining Lexi stretched over a table, sliding the long cue stick through her fingers, made him smile.

Booths along the walls offered more privacy than the four tops around the edge of the dance floor. Jack guided Lexi toward an empty alcove.

"It's busy tonight." Lexi didn't glance out. "I hope I can pull off the pretense if anyone comes over."

Some of his enjoyment faded. Others would assume he was out with his wife, Grace. Jack hadn't realized the evening might be stressful for Lexi. "I'll keep them away."

As though to prove him wrong, a waitress stepped up to their table. "Hey, Jack. I know who you are, of course, Grace, but I don't think you'd remember me. I'm Rose Schwartz. I used to bring my dog, Smoky, in to your dad."

"Rosemary, of course."

The woman winced. Jack hid a smile. She hated her given name, which Lexi well knew.

"How are your parents?" Lexi asked.

"They're well, thank you. What can I bring you to drink?" Rose smiled. "The first one is on the house in honor of your wedding. Congratulations, by the way."

"Thanks." Jack waved at the owner tending bar. "Thank Hans for me. I'll have a Bud on draft. Do you want your usual white zin?"

Lexi beamed a gorgeous smile. "Maybe I'll go crazy tonight and have a beer, too."

"You don't usually drink beer, honey."

"Then I'm definitely in a rut." She turned to Rose. "A wife can't become too predictable or her husband will stray from sheer boredom. Bring me a Bud draft also."

Rose left the table with a bemused smile. Jack shook his

head. "I'm unlikely to ever be bored with you."

"That's not necessary. No one can hear us now."

"Doesn't make it less true." Lexi fascinated him. Not all tomboy, definitely not a princess. Once, he'd had her neatly pigeon-holed. Now that he'd spent some time with her, he wouldn't know how to describe her. If she'd confine her vet skills to treating puppies in town, they could make a go of the marriage. "Are you stepping out of your rut with dinner, too?"

"Steak, rare, with scalloped potatoes and asparagus."

He groaned. "What's so great about asparagus? They're nasty little green sticks that taste like wood."

"Not the way my mom made them, and not the way Hans does, either." She smiled. "I can assume you won't be snatching them off my plate?"

"Not in this lifetime."

Their beer came and they ordered steaks, baked potato with the works and brussel sprouts for Jack. Lexi made a face. "You won't eat asparagus but you'll eat little balls of slimy greens?"

Rose covered a laugh.

"You haven't had them the way Hans makes them," Jack echoed. "Roasted with some seasonings. If you're good, I'll let you try mine."

She fluttered her lashes. "I'm never good."

"You two are so cute." Rose turned to put in their orders.

Jack leaned over the table to speak quietly. "See? You're doing fine. She'd never know it was you."

"We have lunch together about once a month."

Surprise had him sitting upright. "Seriously? Then you're better at pretending than I thought."

"Thanks?"

He nodded. "I know the Marshall girls love to dance. Want a spin while we're waiting for our food?"

They danced to Florida-Georgia Line then Blake Shelton and Luke Bryan. Jack spun her through Keith Urban's "Kiss a Girl" until they were both breathless. On the closing note, every guy there grabbed his partner for a kiss. Jack reeled her and set his lips to hers. She kissed him back, a hand to his nape. He blinked when she pulled away grinning.

Jack frowned as they returned to their table. He'd kissed more than two women in his life. Why did it bother him that Lexi had done her share of kissing, too?

"This beer isn't bad, even a little warm." Lexi winked at him. "I may have to order it more often."

He shook off his bad humor. "Glad you tried it."

They watched the dancers until their food came. A few people stopped by to congratulate them, mostly known more to Jack than to Grace, so Lexi nodded hellos. When asked about not showing up for the reception, Jack remained non-committal, which only made everyone believe they'd snuck off to consummate their vows. After too many interruptions along those lines, Jack found his steak less tasty.

"Sorry," he muttered. "They should save the ribbing for when you're not around."

She shrugged. "No big deal. It's what I would be thinking if it were another couple."

They ate and danced, sat and drank, danced some more. After dinner, he switched to iced tea and Lexi drank water. Every time he pulled her into his arms, he felt drunk on her.

When they dimmed the lights and played "Making Memories of Us," he became a lifelong fan of Keith Urban. Lexi melted into Jack, pressed against him, seduced by the lyrics, lulled by the tune. He wished he had words, but he wasn't sure where their future led.

She looked up at him. "Want to take me home?"

CHAPTER THIRTEEN

"You're wearing too many damned buttons." Jack fumbled with Lexi's shirt in her dark bedroom.

"Not up to the challenge?"

"Oh, I'm definitely up for something." When she laughed, he narrowed his eyes and grasped either side of her collar. "How fond of this shirt are you?"

"Very." She pushed his hands away and started on the buttons herself. "Save the he-man antics for when I'm wearing rags."

That sounded promising, as though there'd be a next time. "Rags are easy to rip."

"You have that much experience, huh?"

He smiled, feeling cocky as he tugged off her boots. "Yes, ma'am, I do."

"Be careful saying those words. Trouble always follows."

Oh, he meant to cause some upheaval, all right, he thought,

as he rid himself of his own boots. Then she parted her blouse, and all thought fled. The curve of her breasts begged for his mouth. He pulled her up and into his arms, then pushed aside the shirt to reveal a skimpy pink bra, the satin smooth to his fingertips. She shivered as he traced the material to just above her nipples. The lace exposed enough to draw him in and concealed enough to drive him crazy.

"Jack." His name was pure need on her lips. His body tightened in response.

"Lexi." He kissed the side of her neck and she tilted to give him better access. "Lexi." He scraped his teeth down the cord on the side, to her collarbone. Kissed her, sucked. "Lexi."

He'd repeat her name every second of their coupling if she required reassurance. He knew who he held, kissed. Wanted. The woman in his arms had snared him with her tender ways. Ways he hadn't acknowledged before they were married. "You're so beautiful."

Her fingers caressed his skull, causing him to shiver. They twined in his hair, held him close.

Maybe "beautiful" didn't convey his meaning. "I love the way you are with Anna." He stopped to kiss the top of her breasts. "I love the way you put up with Crusty."

She gasped when he sucked. Jack fought the urge to mark her as his, despite knowing no one would see a love bite on her breast. He stroked a finger down the side of her neck again, considering. Just there.

She pulled him close, lips locked on his. Lust washed over him. He walked her backward until her legs met the bed, then he tipped her, coming down swiftly on top. His clumsy fingers fumbled at her belt while he consumed her mouth, drawing in her every breath. He wanted all of her. Working the snap and zipper took concentration he didn't want to spare. Though he regretted having to move, he pushed away to work on her shorts. When they opened, he took care of his jeans, then sent both pairs flying over his shoulder.

Matching pink satin and lace covered her. Barely. Her arms came up to cover herself, and he shook his head. "Let me look at you."

He trailed a finger from just below her breast down over her stomach to her knee. When she shivered, he made a path down the other side. Goosebumps rose and her nipples tightened. Primal satisfaction surged in him. "Let me discover if you taste as good as you look."

He bent his head. There wasn't an inch he didn't kiss, nip, lick. He disposed of scraps covering her along the way. Her hands explored him; their lips met, devoured. She moaned with frustration when he moved on.

"Jack," she urged.

He remembered how she hesitated over words for sex. Maybe next time she'd be confident enough to say she wanted him. In a flash, he covered her, parted her thighs, slipped between. She wrapped her legs around him, making words unnecessary. Desire threaded through her actions.

A storm swept over them like a sudden tornado, but hot enough to scorch. He thrust with his heart as much as with his body, guiding her up, driving himself.

He coaxed her pleasure from her. She gripped him, held on, whimpered his name as she climaxed. Satisfied he'd given his woman all she needed, his release followed.

He nuzzled her neck, sucked the cord there until she giggled and pulled away. "No love bites. Certain people would question how I acquired them."

Her dad. Anna. He rolled to the side and propped his head on his hand. "I'd enjoy hearing your explanation."

"Well, I won't have to explain if you maintain control."

He chuckled. "Babe, being around you blows my control to bits. It's not like that with anyone else." He felt her withdrawal although she didn't move. "No one. You make me crazy."

She slanted him a look. "So it's my fault?"

"Of course." He trailed lazy patterns across her skin, over her breasts, down her stomach, back up to her chest. Gooseflesh followed, puckered her nipples. He vibrated with anticipation.

"Since I can restrain myself with other women, it must be you."

She shivered and captured his hands. "Sorry I'm such a trial for you." Looking into his eyes, she brought his hand to her mouth. Kissed a finger. Scraped her teeth over it. Bit the knuckle.

He grew hard in an instant. No longer a randy youth, he wouldn't have believed it possible.

After another round of loving, he lay back, searching for his sanity. The woman reduced him to a boneless mass. He panted, all pretense of having discipline lost. She wrecked him.

Hopefully, she'd make a habit of it.

He rolled his head sideways to look at the clock on her nightstand. It took all his strength. "Let's go to my room. It's just after midnight. I have a bigger bed for round three."

"Midnight?" She laughed. "Happy two week anniversary."

"It certainly was. Never mind what I said about moving. Just give me a couple of minutes and we'll celebrate again."

"You know where to find me."

Oh, yeah. He knew. And he found her.

Two glorious weeks of passion gave Lexi hope for a future with Jack. She now slept in his bed. Just the night before, when he came in from work, she followed him into his customary shower before dinner. They were late to the table.

Hopefully, he wouldn't be late to the lunch table now. He'd promised to sneak in some time together. To ensure privacy, she'd set up a snack in Crusty's unused house. A note with her location sat on the dining room table at the main house, secure from Crusty's nosy habits in a sealed envelope marked "Darling Jack."

Patience came naturally when she dealt with animals but not so much when she waited for her husband. Or, if not her husband, at least her lover.

Establishing a toehold where her sister should have been was low and dirty. But Grace had willingly given up her place in Jack's life. Lexi would fight her sister for Jack, but she couldn't be sure she'd win. Grace exuded everything feminine, much like Sarabeth. Lexi only reminded Jack of his beloved wife when she did something he considered dangerous.

Jack still hadn't said he loved her. Maybe it was too soon for him. After all, he'd been about to marry another woman only twenty-six days before. In the past two weeks, he didn't mention checking in with the lawyer and she didn't push him about it. Neither wanted to go looking for trouble. If they made it to July first, she'd bake them an anniversary cake. To eat in bed.

She hadn't told him of her feelings, although she suspected her love for him had grown over the past year. No other rancher made her snap, although ornery ranchers littered the county. No other man thrilled her with a smile or made her burn with desire under his steady green gaze. She'd withdrawn from what she'd seen as dislike but had been concern for her safety. Now she understood him better, and while she didn't agree with his stance on her being a country vet, she sympathized with his loss and the resulting apprehension.

A noise on the porch had her tingling with anticipation. Until the knock came before the door opened.

"Miz Walker?"

She stepped into the foyer, and frowned when George closed the door behind him. Had Jack sent him with a message saying he'd been held up?

"Don't want to let out your air conditioning." He wiped his boots on the rug.

"Of course." She kept her disappointment from showing. George didn't look anxious, so she assumed an ordinary ranch emergency had delayed Jack. Afternoon quickies were fun, but the cattle were vital. She'd catch up with Jack later. The thought steadied her. "Would you care for a cold drink?"

"I'd sure appreciate that, ma'am."

Lexi went to the kitchen and returned with a tall glass of iced tea she'd made for lunch.

And almost dropped it when she saw the jar of wildflowers on the table.

George grinned. "You like flowers, right?"

"Yes." Her voice came out reedy. He could have seen them on the porch when Darryl left them there. It was sweet, really. George wouldn't know the sight gave her the heebie jeebies. She forced a smile. "Thank you. They're very pretty."

"The far side of the north hill by the creek is full of them. All kinds and colors, throughout the summer."

"I'll have to remember that."

"You don't have to. I'll bring them to you."

His eagerness should have been endearing. But he was too big and too strong. And they were too isolated. She shouldn't be anxious—it was only George, after all. Knowing it was silly, instinct had her putting up a wall, anyway. "I'm sure Jack will bring me flowers, but thank you."

His expression went flat. "Is that drink for me?"

"Oh, yes, of course." She extended the tea, shuddered when his hand brushed hers. Hard hands. Strong hands.

She shifted, feeling foolish for allowing the memory of Darryl's attack to shade her view of George. He was a big teddy bear. Nerves had her jumpy, that was all. George emptied the glass and set it beside the flowers.

Lexi waited for him to convey Jack's message. Waited while his gaze stayed on her. Waited while his eyes heated.

Her mouth went dry. "Do you have a message from Jack?"

He shook his head.

Sliding back a step, she tried to make it look natural. "How did you know I was here?"

"I always know where you are, Miz Lexi."

Her head jerked in surprise. "What did you call me?"

"Don't worry none. I didn't tell anyone else." His smile suggested the secret bound them together.

"How did you...? I mean, what makes you think I'm Lexi?"

"I didn't, at first. When only one of you showed up for the wedding, I got worried. Went looking for you, but you weren't home."

Ice ran over her skin. "*You* broke into my house?"

"Nah. I was just checking on you. I'll always make sure you're safe, Lexi." He scowled. "Unfortunately, I was too late with Peters."

Heart pounding, she steadied herself with a hand on the back of a dining room chair. "I thought Jack beat up Darryl?"

George's grin had dark corners. "I came into town late that Saturday for lunch, and you'd already left work. When I drove past your house to find you, I saw his truck. Found him going through your things."

Lexi put a hand to her mouth, not sure she wouldn't be sick. At least Jack was in the clear.

"Afterward, I told him to stay clear of you or I'd do worse."

He stepped forward, eyes bleak. "I'm real sorry he touched you. If you were my woman then, I would have protected you."

Afterward? He brushed off nearly beating a man to death with one word. "Did you follow me the day I confronted him at the feed store?"

George nodded. "I'll never let anyone hurt you again."

She glanced out the window, trying to spot movement through the sheer curtains. Nothing. No one coming to her rescue. And no knitting needles here in the new house. "Did you leave the gloves for me in the car?"

He nodded, proud as a schoolboy. "I didn't want the kittens to scratch you. That's when I knew for sure, when you and Anna were in the barn and you talked about the Prescotts' cat. Your sister wouldn't have known about it. She never cared about animals like you do."

His use of the past tense when referring to Grace sent ice through her veins. Mouth dry with fear, she had to form saliva in order to speak. "Do you know where Grace is?"

He shook his head.

"Do you know what happened to her?"

"I don't care about your sister. You're the one I want. That's why I left you flowers."

Oh, crap. She edged sideways until the table stood between them. He eyed her.

"I reckon the boss is keeping you on the Rocking W because Grace jilted him." His face hardened. "But he can't treat you like that, trading in one sister for another. I don't reckon you're even married. Are you?"

What would make him leave? He respected Jack. If she were married, she'd be off limits, right? Would that send George on his way? Or would it enrage him that she'd married another?

"Yes, we're really married."

George's eyebrows drew together in a frown. Confusion puckered his face, as though she spoke a different language. "Did the boss force you into it?"

"No." She shook her head, hoping this was the right way to handle him. "No, I married him on purpose. I wanted to."

"'Cause if he's keeping you against your will," George continued as though she hadn't spoken, "I can take you away. I'll take you anywhere you want to go."

"I don't want to go anywhere else."

"A good hand can always get work, and I'm a good hand."

"I know you are. Jack speaks very highly of you." She hoped mentioning Jack would keep George at a distance. "But I still want to stay here."

A shadow passed outside. Lexi held still, not turning to check if it was a hawk or a person or a cloud drifting in front of the sun. *Please, let it be Jack. I could use some help here.*

"Stay here?" he asked. "You mean in Little Tree? Or here with the boss? As his wife?"

She barely moved her head in a nod. Her heart pounded as she kept her gaze locked on him, ready to counter any shift on his part. "With Jack."

"But you don't have to. We can move in to your house in town." His face cleared. "Is that it? You're afraid to go back home? Because you don't have to be."

He shifted to the right, standing across the table from her and blocking her exit to the door. She'd have to run around the long end of the table and across the living room to the back door. She'd never make it.

"I put the fear of God in Peters. Or the fear of me, anyway." He stated it so matter-of-factly, she thought she misunderstood. His crooked smile made her tremble. He was unhinged. "That lowlife won't come near you again or he'll have to deal with me." He extended his hand. "It time to come along now."

"Where?"

His smile did nothing to reassure her. "To our house in town. So we can be together."

"To my house?"

He nodded. "Ours now."

"Why?" She didn't know which question she needed answered. Why was he doing this? Why did he think it was their house? Why did they have to leave right now?

"Once we're together, the boss won't want you back."

"Together. You mean...have sex? With you?"

"Sure." He reached across the table and stroked her arm. When she pulled back, he grasped her other wrist. "We'll be good together, Lexi. I love you. The boss can't give you that, even if you had been together."

"I was. We do."

His grip on her tightened as he walked around to her side. "Man, I never would have believed the boss would force you."

"He didn't. I wanted to. We're married, Jack and I."

For some reason, George's frown cleared. "Oh, that's okay then. It's like you're a widow or divorced. I can live with that."

"I'm still married." She tried to free her hand to no avail. The pain of trying to wrench free started tears in her eyes. Was he the kind of man to relent when a woman cried? She'd try anything.

George shook his head and dragged her behind him out the door. "You're not really married to him, so you don't have to feel bad about leaving him and being with me. And when you realize you love me back, it'll all be okay."

She looped her free arm around the front porch column as she passed, halting him mid-step. "I'm not going with you."

"Yes, you are, baby. When you're my woman, he won't

want you back."

"George, stop it!"

His eyes narrowed. "Lower your voice or we won't get away without someone noticing."

"That's the idea." She inhaled to scream.

"I'd hate it to be that old man."

Lexi choked back her breath. "Crusty?"

George reached in his pocket, drew out a knife. Flicked it open.

Her heart thudded as she stared at the implement. Cold sweat coated her body. "What's that for?"

"Well, you've made it necessary. I don't know why you're being like this, baby." He closed the distance between them and let go of her wrist. Before she could move, he clutched the bottom of her shirt and hacked at the hem. "I hope that old man doesn't come up here to help you. I wouldn't want anyone else hurt because of you."

"Anyone else? Do you mean Darryl?"

George stopped cutting, for which she was thankful, and glared at her, for which she was not. Lexi didn't want his wrath turned in her direction. How would he react when he realized she wouldn't follow like a calf with its mother? What was his intention with the knife and her clothes?

"Yeah," he replied through tight lips. "That scum. You

should have stayed away from him."

Her mouth dropped open. "He was waiting in my house."

"You should have been with me." George waved the knife near her face as he emphasized the statement. "With me. But now we'll be together, and you'll stay safe."

"I don't want to go with you, George."

"You're confused." He bent his head to her shirt again, sawing with the blade, too close to her stomach for any foolhardy escape attempt.

"What are you doing?"

"Gotta gag you." He grabbed the material in his hands and ripped it across. "I don't want to, baby, but you're making me."

A movement behind him drew her attention. She gasped in mingled relief and fear.

George spun, his knife extended toward Jack. "Back off, boss. She's mine now."

Jack's eyes were flat, his face hard. "I don't think so."

"Back off." George swung the knife in the space between them, creating a boundary.

"That's not going to happen, George."

"I don't want to hurt you."

"That's good to hear."

"You gotta let her go with me."

"She doesn't want that. She wants to stay."

"No, she doesn't!" George lunged.

Lexi muffled a scream as Jack dodged backward.

"Let us go, boss. She ain't happy with you, not like I can make her."

Jack stopped avoiding and stood as casually as though considering the weather. "Where will you go?"

"We're going to live at her house. Our house now. I cleared it of varmints."

"He means Darryl," she said. "He's the one who beat up Darryl."

"Of course he did." Jack shook his head at her and turned his attention back to George, rolling his eyes. "Women. Sometimes it takes them a while to understand what's necessary."

Lexi frowned at him.

"She'll see I'm going to always protect her," George said.

"I understand that you want to." Jack took a few steps to the left, nearer the porch, still using his reasonable tone. "I never thanked you for beating up Peters. And I mean that sincerely."

"My pleasure, boss. And I mean that sincerely."

Jack's gaze darted to her. "What are you doing?"

She didn't know what he meant, as she stood frozen, horrified at the scene unfolding before her. George turned to check on her.

It happened so fast, it took Lexi a moment to realize Jack had grabbed George's hand and pushed it up behind his back, immobilizing the bigger man. The cowboy cried out and his knife fell to the ground.

"Hey," George grunted. "What are you doing?"

He tried to shift, to angle around and free his arm, but Jack shifted with him, countering his moves.

Jack's gaze met hers. "Are you okay?"

She nodded.

George fell back, using his weight and bulk to break free. He twisted and swung at Jack. Off-balance, he missed his mark. Jack landed a punch, then another. George countered.

Lexi watched, heart in her throat. She'd seen the aftermath of George beating a man half to death. Jack couldn't be the next victim. She gasped as a blow rocked Jack back on his heels. He almost fell but righted himself and charged George. Both men went down, but a crack to George's jaw knocked the bigger man unconscious.

Jack swiped blood from his lip. "Call the sheriff."

Lexi retrieved her cell phone and entered the numbers as fast as her trembling fingers allowed. Then she called the ranch house and had Doris send a few men up to help Jack.

Sick to her stomach, she rested her forehead against the wall. She brought Jack nothing but trouble.

*****

Lexi retreated to her room after Sheriff Matson left. The deputies took George away, but the questions continued for almost an hour. Deputies went to question Darryl Peters. Sheriff Matson wanted the case firmly closed.

Her cell phone rang almost as soon as she entered her room. Lexi considered letting it go to voice mail. She had yet to come to grips with the events of the past few hours and felt wrung out. How could she have disregarded her instincts? She'd sensed someone watching her. She'd totally dismissed George as harmless. On the third ring, she glanced at the readout. *Grace.* Heart racing, she answered. "Where are you? Are you okay?"

"I'm fine, don't worry. What's going on there?"

Lexi gave a half-laugh and sank onto her bed, closing her eyes in relief. "Are you really okay?"

"Yes, Lex. Why are you so upset? What's happened?"

Where to start? "A lot, considering it's been less than a month. I want an answer this time, Audrey. Where are you?"

The sigh through the earpiece acknowledged Lexi's reprimand. Grace was only "Audrey" when in TROUBLE. "I had to get away, you know that."

"Old news. Give me the update." Lexi held on to her temper with little patience.

"I don't want to say. You'll just come get me."

Would she? Seeing Grace would alleviate her worry, but Lexi doubted she'd be able to handle any more drama for a while. Trying to be the supportive sister Grace remembered, Lexi said, "Grace, I want whatever's best for you. If that means you need to stay where you are, then you should. Just call Dad again. He's worried sick."

"I will. I wanted to call you first, learn who's angrier at me. So-o-o, how is Jack?"

Lexi had to smile. "Jack's handling things. We might need you to sign some papers. Will you promise to leave your phone on so I can contact you?"

"Only if you promise not to hire someone to trace me through the GPS."

"Deal."

"What papers?"

Lexi didn't know how much to tell her. "Just some things having to do with the marriage."

Silence ticked on the other end, making Lexi nervous. "Grace, are you still there?"

"Yeah. And so are you, right? Still at the ranch, I mean."

"Yeah." Lexi waited.

After a moment, Grace sighed. "I might be able to sign those papers in person. I'm thinking of coming home."

"Coming home?" Lexi gripped the phone. *Not now.* She

and Jack were building a relationship, growing closer, understanding one another. Now Grace wanted to take up with him again? Lexi couldn't fight her sister for him.

Or, God help her, could she? All their lives, Lexi had cleaned up Grace's messes, covered for her mistakes, given in to what Grace wanted. But Grace couldn't have Jack. She'd had her chance, and she'd given him up. Lexi sat upright. "That's not a good idea."

"What?" Her sister's tone held surprise. "Why not?"

"You said you needed space. You should wait until you have your head on straight. Know what you want—what you want to do next, I mean." She thought of the old song about sisters their dad used to sing. Lord help Jack for coming between her and Grace, but, dammit, Lord help Grace if she wanted Lexi's man. She'd put aside her own feelings when Grace returned from Australia and caught Jack's eye. But Lexi wasn't willing to bow out again. "Give Jack some more time, Grace."

"I'm surprised he'd need time. And I thought you'd want me home."

Grace continued speaking, but Lexi spotted Jack in the doorway. How much had he heard? They stared at one another. Lexi lifted her chin and held his gaze. "I'm glad you're safe. Call Dad and tell him that. But don't come back yet."

Lexi hit End, not caring if Grace had more to say. Jack's

eyes burned with emerald fire as he stepped in and closed the door. She stood.

"Your sister is okay?"

She nodded, waiting for the storm.

"Why did you tell her not to come back?" He stepped closer, near enough to speak in a quiet tone. Near enough to draw her into his arms if he wanted to. His expression blank, she could only guess at his thoughts.

"I didn't think you were ready to see her." When he stared, she went on. "Okay, I'm not ready. You haven't said where we stand. What Dan Higgins said. If we're married. What role Grace plays."

"Grace doesn't play any role in my future."

Lexi's heart beat so loudly she thought he might hear it. "What if she owns some of the land?"

"If she won't sign it over, I'll buy it. I'll get the money." His body went tense. "Are you only concerned about the legal matters?"

His accusation made her eyes narrow. "It's a little awkward if you're married to her, Jack, considering we're sleeping together."

"If I believed I was married to her, I wouldn't be sleeping with you."

"Fair enough." She conceded the point. "I don't know if

you're married to me, but I don't think you're married to Grace. I'm with you on that point."

"So if it isn't the legalities, and you're good with us being together, why are you reluctant to have Grace come home?" Jack put his hands on her shoulders. "Do you think I'd take her back? Don't you trust me?"

Lexi's body heated. Her thoughts spun: confusion, hope, fear. Tired of the indecision, she raised her chin, determined for him to make a stand. Pick a bride. "Trust you to do what?"

"I thought we were thinking along the same lines. That we'd stay married."

She appreciated his hands anchoring her shoulders. Hope nearly lifted her off the ground. She felt giddy. *Men!* How could he think she'd known his mind? "You want to marry me?"

His mouth quirked. "I believe I already have."

"Well, the jury's still out on that one."

"Then we'll have another ceremony if necessary."

If necessary? This wasn't the romantic proposal she'd hoped for—or even a proposal, at all. Come to think of it, Jack had a habit of acquiring wives he hadn't proposed to. He wasn't getting away with that a second time. "Why?"

"Why what? Why have a ceremony?"

"No, why do you want to marry me?"

His hands dropped to his sides. "To make it legal, of course.

We're pretty much married already."

And wasn't *that* convenient? "You want to marry me because I'm here?"

"No. I mean, well, yes." He stepped back, probably because he wasn't as witless as he sounded. Or maybe he could feel the tension emanate from her body as her rage built. "We've been getting along well, haven't we?"

Pain sliced her gut as hope dimmed. He felt something for her, she knew. It was in his touch when they made love. In his kisses. In the way his gaze followed her around a room. "Why do you want to stay married to me, Jack?"

He lifted empty hands and let them drop. "You're good with Anna. She needs a mother. I know you love her, and she loves you."

Lexi nodded, cold as granite inside. "You want a mother for your child."

"Yes, and more kids in the future." He tried a smile. "I need a wife for that."

A wife. Not her in particular. She drew a breath just to make sure she could. She felt sliced open. "And?" When he cocked his head in question, she nearly sighed. "Is that it? You want a mother? A breeder?"

His face sharpened at that. "Don't be insulting."

"I'm insulting *you?"*

"Yes."

"Well, too damn bad. I want more than that, Jack. I want a real marriage."

"You mean legal? I said I'd marry you again if I have to."

She raised a brow.

"I didn't mean it that way. Hell, Lexi, you twist me up so the words come out all wrong."

What she needed to hear could be said in three words.

"I'm sorry, Lexi." He glanced around the small room. "Come to my bedroom. It's a little tight in here for me to get down on one knee."

"You don't have to kneel, Jack." *Just say the words.*

"I want to do this right."

Hope fluttered against her ribs, but Lexi remained wary. She nodded for him to continue.

"I'm not one for fancy words, so I'll say it straight out. I need you, and I hope you'll agree to stay as my wife. The sun doesn't shine unless you're in the room. Alexis Grace Marshall Walker, will you marry me?"

Joy burst through her veins. He was her sunlight and warmth as well. What did it matter how he said it? She nodded. "Of course I'll marry you—again."

His kiss expressed all the things he couldn't say. She shouldn't have doubted him after the past two weeks. He'd shown her how he felt every night.

Reluctantly, they parted for air. Jack traced his lips along her jaw.

"I'm better suited to be your wife," she teased. "The vet and the rancher sounds much better together than the painter and the rancher."

He smiled. "The former vet, you mean."

Lexi stilled. "No, I don't mean that."

"You'll have plenty to do around here, Lexi. We have animals to tend."

"I'm not quitting the practice, Jack."

He studied her for a long moment. "But you'll confine your work to the office. Small animals. In town."

She shook her head.

"Lexi." He took a breath. "I don't want you out tending bulls. Driving around in bad weather or in the middle of the night. I don't want you taking risks."

"Jack, I'm a vet."

He squeezed her hands. "And I shouldn't suggest you stop. Just meet me half-way. Work from the practice in town."

"I can't leave the heavy work to my dad. We're partners."

"He would understand."

"Probably. But—" She took a breath. "I don't want to. I've worked hard to be accepted by the ranchers around here."

"Lexi. You don't understand how hard this is for me."

"I do."

A smile ghosted his lips. "There's that phrase again."

She forced a smile in reply, though a cannonball had dropped into her stomach. "Is this a condition of our being married?"

He grimaced. "I wouldn't call it a condition. More like a compromise."

What are you giving up?

She swallowed. "I want to be by myself for a while. I need to call my dad."

To tell him I'm coming home, but she didn't say it. "You should check on Crusty. He hasn't been feeling well, although he's been hiding it from you."

"Okay, I will." His brows lowered. "Are we done talking? Because I'm not sure we settled anything."

"It's settled, Jack. We're done."

CHAPTER FOURTEEN

She'd left him.

Jack stomped through the next day and the next, unable to believe Lexi had gone. Without a word. Without giving him a chance to make it right.

He strove to reassure Anna everything currently in upheaval would settle, just in different pieces. On the third day, he heard the men talking by the barn before they saw him. Lexi Marshall had "come back" to Little Tree and worked with her father again. As the men told it, "Grace" left the ranch, upset over the events leading to George's and Darryl's arrests, and had presumably left town. Jack eased out of sight. The men walked past, speculating why the Marshall sisters couldn't stay in the same place together for two minutes.

Crusty cornered him before he set out after lunch. Jack had been coming home to check on the old coot. The fact that his cell phone received a better signal near the ranch house was coincidence. "Boy," Crusty said, "I could use a hand."

Jack winced. Nothing good ever came of his uncle calling him "boy." The old man rarely asked for help. "What is it?"

"My scooter don't run."

Jack sighed. Without the scooter, Crusty's injury confined him to the house. While Jack wanted to tell Crusty to just stay put, he imagined how crazy *he* would be trapped in the house. "I can take a look, but we're riding fences on the west boundary, so repairs may have to wait. What's wrong with it?"

"I'll show you, if ya let me hold on to yore arm."

Jack hid his surprise. They ambled toward the vehicle shed, which housed the trucks and cars, as well as the tractors and ATVs. Crusty's scooter sat in a wide space, alone. It took Jack a minute to realize Lexi's truck used to sit there. Crusty produced a key from the jingling bits of metal in his pocket.

Jack turned the ignition. No *tick tick tick* to indicate a low battery charge. He popped the engine compartment open. Clean as a whistle, as he'd expect of Crusty's property. Jack pulled over the toolbox and a stool for each of them, then felt for loose parts. If only fixing relations was that simple.

"You been hot-headed the last few days."

Jack didn't look up. "I have not."

"Then you been morose. That's a fine word. Don't know why people don't use it more."

"I'm not morose. My wife left me." Jack swore under his breath. "Which is for the good. That woman could drive me crazier than any person I ever met—including you, which is saying something."

"Jest why do you s'pose she could affect you so much?" Crusty's mild tone showed no interest in the answer, raising Jack's suspicions.

"Doesn't matter why," he countered, wary of a trap. "I don't want to be crazy. Every second with her is a challenge."

"Boy, in my day, we called that a blessing. Don't want no boring woman."

"And when I come home at night, I want peace."

"Pshaw. Real men need a challenge. That's why we struggle with the effects of the weather, with the animals, and with keeping the place afloat."

"I had peace with Sarabeth and never a day of boredom."

Crusty's face softened. "That girl was a blessing in a different way. If she had lived, you two would be living in bliss with a passel of children making noise enough to scare off the coyotes."

"Was that too much to ask?" Jack bent back over the scooter, hiding his expression.

"It ain't," Crusty agreed. "But it also ain't the way life worked out. Sarabeth was the girl of your heart when you was a boy. Yore a man now. You need a different sort of woman, one who can put up with the changes in you since yore dear wife died." He sighed. "You need someone to stand up to yore nonsense. In short, you need Lexi."

"I don't nee—" Jack drew straight with surprise. He hadn't heard her name in so long, unless in reference to *his wife's sister*. "What? I mean, who did you say?"

"You ain't deaf, are you, boy, along with yore other faults?"

Jack narrowed his eyes. "How long have you known?"

"I suspected the morning after the wedding. That gal's too real to pretend to be someone else."

The compliment, intended or not, struck Jack. Real, his uncle called her. Too much her own person for pretense. Honest. Strong in personality—and in opinions. Jack scowled.

"But I knew," Crusty said, "that first night when you two didn't sneak off to bed early. You hadn't touched her all day that I could see, and I was watching. One kiss at the door because tradition called for it, and one in the kitchen because yore brother and I expected it. And she thought to call me Chris." The old man scowled. "I don't like the name no more, but it were a nice gesture."

"Just because I'm not jumping my wife in full view of my family doesn't mean I wasn't passionate about her." He glowered. "If she even was my wife. Damn lawyer."

"You referring to Sam Higgins' middle boy?"

Jack had to smile. Even a sixty-year-old like Dan would be a "boy" to Crusty. "Yeah. Dan has dragged his feet over some matters I asked him to investigate."

Crusty rocked back on his own stool, hands clasped around his good knee. "No, he didn't. That boy is a good lawyer. Got you yore answers straight away."

Jack could only stare. "What are you talking about?"

"He called..." Crusty studied the rafters, eyes squinted in concentration. "Oh, about three days after yore wedding. Tuesday, I suppose it was. I took the message."

"You...?" Words failed him.

"Yep. Took it and kept it." He cackled. "Boy, you shore do make a to-do about everything. If you'd just told me what happened, I'd have signed the land over to you and taken off Grace's name."

Jack's head throbbed. "Then why didn't you? Why not just come and assure me the Rocking W would stay in Walker hands?"

His uncle's eyes gleamed. "What fun would that a been? Watching you rush around, covering up every misstep." He wiped his eyes, tears of mirth gathering in the corners. "Watching you and that gal pussyfoot around each other. It's been a hell of a fun month."

Pain pierced Jack. *Fun for the old man.* But not fun for Jack. Or for Lexi. He turned cold eyes on Crusty. "That wasn't very fair to her. She tried to help me. You could have ended this farce weeks ago."

"But she would have left, and you need her, boy. Anna needs her." He pursed his lips. "Okay, and I need her around here, too. She brightens up this place like yellow paint."

Surprise and amusement dispelled Jack's hurt. "She does. But staying should be her choice. You took that away from her."

"Well, look at what her choice was. She left."

Jack winced. "It's not right to manipulate her, like you tried to manipulate me with threats of turning the land over to my cousins." Something Lexi said about Crusty came to him. He narrowed his eyes. "Did you tell her you were dying in order to keep her here?"

"Well, I am dying. So are you. Every day on this earth is another day closer to being in it. So, no, I didn't lie." He spread his hands in innocence. "I may have suggested the deadline for me is fast approaching, and that I know the end date."

Jack shook his head in disgust. Lexi had been tricked and maneuvered by Crusty and Grace. Even he couldn't claim not to have used her affection for Anna and the old man. He hadn't pushed Dan for an answer, when he knew the man probably jumped right to the problem. Had Jack called back, checked in, or stopped by when he went to town? No, he'd waited for a call and, if he were honest, dreaded receiving it. "We didn't treat her very well."

"I object to that," Crusty said. "*I* was honest with her. Told her right off I knew who she was."

"You let her believe you're on death's doorstep."

"I could be," Crusty muttered.

Jack wouldn't be guilted in to leniency. "No way. I'm not that lucky."

The old man scowled. "You may not be lucky but you shore are a jackass. Rightly named."

Jack narrowed his eyes. "Watch your tongue, old man."

"Ya let her go. She's the best thing ever happened to you, and ya let her walk out the door. Worse still, you didn't chase after her and haul her back."

"Women don't want to be hauled."

Crusty sighed. "Youth is wasted on the young."

"Things have changed since your courting days."

"She's the best thing for this ranch too, not just for you. You go haul her back, boy, or I will."

"Leave her alone, Crusty. I mean it. She has to choose to be with us."

"Look at the choices you made, Jack." For once, his uncle's tone expressed sincerity. "What did you do but try to marry an exact copy of her, but a sleeker model. That says, 'you're close, Lexi, but not exactly smooth enough for me.'"

A punch to his bruised ribs couldn't have hurt worse or surprised him more. "I never said that to her. I never thought it."

"Some things ain't spoken, but they're conveyed plain enough."

Jack shook his head, rejecting the idea. Lexi couldn't believe he found her inferior to Grace. If anything—

He stood stock still, feeling the color drain from his face as his gut turned hollow. Oh, God. He *had* meant to marry a replacement. He'd meant for Grace to stand in for the woman he wanted.

With all her vitality and reckless ways, Lexi scared him spitless. He'd never have married Grace without Crusty's manipulation regarding the land. Still, he'd been coward enough to go through with the wedding for the sake of the ranch, while hiding from his own feelings. Hiding from his love for Lexi.

He ran a hand over his face, vaguely aware of Crusty hitch-stepping across the dirt toward the house. After a few feet, the old man turned. "Here. You might need this."

Jack blinked as Crusty reached into his pocket then flung something into the air. On reflex, Jack caught it as it sailed from sunlight to the shadow of the garage. A new spark plug rested in his palm. Looking to the engine, he wondered when the old man had sabotaged his scooter with an old part.

Crafty old bugger.

A chuckle escaped him, then he laughed until he couldn't stand. Dropping on the stool, Jack set to work. Time to start fixing his problems. The scooter would be the easiest.

Claiming his wife might take a little more planning.

Country music assaulted his ears the moment Jack swung open the door to Kerr's Grill on Friday night. The same local band played as the night he'd brought Lexi here. The first night they'd made love. He should have known how he felt then.

Jack spotted her half-way across the room. Some tall, dark, and soon-to-be-hurting guy twirled her out and back. A dress as blue as her eyes swung with her, her boots quick and light. Her face glowed with enjoyment, and for a moment resentment filled his marrow. His week had been hell, while she danced the night away. Was she on a date?

This had to end now.

He locked his gaze on hers, stalked toward her. She stumbled to a halt, her partner nearly tripping as she missed their next swing.

People stepped aside, showing they could read his mood. He'd come for his woman. Nobody and nothing would stop him.

When he stopped three feet away, she bristled, lifting her

chin. "What do you want?"

"You."

Her jaw set, she shook her head. "I'm not in the mood to talk to you."

People began to murmur. The musicians stopped playing. Being local, they knew the show on the dance floor would steal all attention from their music. They probably wanted to listen.

"Tough. We can do this here or we can go back to the ranch."

Her dance partner stepped closer to her. "Do you want me to take him outside, Lexi?"

Jack cut his eyes to the man, who unwisely didn't step back. If Jack weren't so focused on bringing Lexi home, he might enjoy the other man trying to take him on. At six foot three, Adam Moore matched him for size and strength, if whiskey hadn't destroyed him. "This doesn't concern you."

Adam met his glare without flinching. He didn't seem too deep into his drink yet, but then, it was early.

Had Lexi taken up with Moore? Did she consider the town drunk a safe bet for driving her home? A growl built in Jack's throat, an animal noise he never would have imagined making.

"Lexi?" Moore asked, eyes on Jack.

"It's fine, Adam. He only wants to talk."

Not by a long shot, but Jack let her believe it. For now.

The other man glared at him. He pointed a stiff finger at a table sporting several glasses of beer. And where Lexi's friend, Adam's sister, Carrie, watched with fascination. Maybe Lexi had been out with Carrie, not Adam. Jack let himself believe it.

"I'll be right over there," Adam said. "First sign she's not happy talking to you and you're out of here." Adam moved off, then propped his butt against the table and crossed his arms over his chest. Jack had to admire his guts. Adam would make a hell of a friend if he could stay sober.

"Are you on a date with him?"

"No." She narrowed her eyes at his satisfied smile. "I was having a good time, *with Carrie*, and you're spoiling it. I don't need you here."

"But I need you. Always."

She stumbled back a step.

He moved in, not letting her retreat. "I should have told you that the other night, but I didn't want to admit it. I didn't want to face losing someone I love again, and you don't have the safest job. Nor do you ever back down from a challenge." He gestured between them, indicating their current stand-off. "Case in point."

"You can't smother me in bubble wrap, Jack. I won't live like that."

"I know. That doesn't mean I don't want to. But Crusty, of

all people, helped me see it's your spirit I love. Everything that makes up *you*. I wouldn't change a thing, even if you make me crazy most of the time."

"My job will always have elements of danger, just as yours does."

He nodded a concession. Working with cattle, horses and dogs had its risks. He could—and had—run into snakes, wolves and coyotes as well as ornery cattle and horses. Mentioning his relationship with Grace courted danger, but he had to get it out of the way. "Don't get me wrong, I cared for your sister. She's dazzling."

Lexi shrugged her acceptance, although a little displeasure shadowed her eyes.

"But it's always been you, Lexi." He lowered his voice, gentleman enough to guard a woman's reputation. "Grace was as close to having you as I could get and still protect my heart."

Her hand flew to her chest as though protecting her own. He wanted to tell her he'd take good care of it, if only she'd let him. If only she'd love him.

Color high, she gave a tentative, hopeful smile. "Really?"

"I didn't realize it until you left." Jack lowered his voice again to a near whisper. This part shouldn't be overheard. "I never would have proposed to Grace, not when I was in love with you."

He dropped his gaze from hers, ashamed he'd been so stupid. "I took the easy way when the path opened, when she proposed. Told myself I was content. She's not reckless. I wasn't in any danger of losing her or losing myself with her."

He didn't have the flowery words he needed to convince her, and saying them in front of half the town wouldn't have been his first choice. But she deserved the words, maybe more so because it was hard for him. He met her gaze again and said simply, "All the joy left the ranch with you. I love you."

Tears shone in her eyes, offering him hope he was on the right track. "Rescue me, Lexi. You tried before, at the church. Don't give up on me now."

"How do I know you don't just want a mom for Anna?"

"I don't want just a mom. I want *you* for Anna. I want you as the mother of our future kids, too. But I need you for myself." He might as well go all in. "I have a surprise outside."

She looked toward the door and started as she seemed to become aware of the people circling them. A smile flirted with her lips when she turned back. For the first time, she understood how public his declaration was. "What surprise?"

"I bought you a new Jeep. To make your rounds in."

Her eyes went wide. "What?"

"Your job is a part of you, and I love you exactly the way you are." He shrugged, tension tightening as she continued to stare. He'd offered his heart. "The Jeep is ten times safer than your old truck, but you have to realize I'm never going to breathe easy until you come home at night."

There. He'd said his piece. Their future lay in her hands.

Lexi wrapped her arms around his neck and kissed him. Hoots of encouragement erupted around them as Jack pulled her closer, deepened the kiss. The crowd called out in approval.

Flushed, she pulled back and looked into his eyes. "I'll always come home. To you."

EPILOGUE

Lexi stepped into their bedroom, a sheer lilac dressing gown falling to mid-thigh. "I have something for you."

Her newly-wed-on-purpose husband of three days and two passion-filled nights lay on the king-sized bed, waiting for her. His gaze traveled over her, lingering on her breasts. They'd had time over the past days to confess their love, to discuss when they first knew how they felt. She'd teased him about being in denial for so long. Dan Higgins found a compassionate judge, willing to correct "the mistake" on the marriage license. A quiet ceremony in the judge's chambers had completed their joining. Or renewed their vows. Either way, they were now legally—and knowingly—wed to one another.

Despite the many ways he'd proven his love since leaving Kerr's Grill the week before, Lexi bit her lip with misgivings. This was so far out of her comfort zone. He'd better not laugh.

"All I want is you," he assured her.

She thrilled every time he said it. "You have me. Always. I love you, Jack."

"Then what else could I want?"

She tossed the colorful plastic flower necklace at him. And waited, nervous tingles in her stomach.

He caught it in one hand, his gold wedding band glinting in the light. His gaze swept the cheap lei then his eyes flew wide with understanding before connecting with hers.

Thank God he remembered. Explaining would have been mortifying. She smiled to herself. She didn't have any qualms about what she planned to do to seduce her husband, but she didn't want to *talk* about it.

He grinned and lounged back on the pillows, crossing his arms behind his head. His eyes gleamed with anticipation, just as she'd once imagined. "Bring it on, hula girl."

Want a free short story in the Love in Little Tree world? Visit my website at megankellybooks.com and sign up for my newsletter. *A Risky Proposal* introduces you to Ryan, the hero of book four, *Coming Home*, but you can read it at any time.

Dear Reader,

This book was a labor of love with a long gestation. I conceived the idea at a conference in 2009, and here it is, popping out into the world, in 2015. I'm thrilled to present it for your enjoyment and hope you love my "baby" as much as I loved writing, editing, and publishing it.

If you enjoy my books, I'd appreciate a review posted at the bookseller sites (Amazon, Barnes & Noble, Apple) and reader sites such as GoodReads.

Please visit my website at megankellybooks.com. There are links to my social media pages as well as a sign-up for my Readers' Group. I send out an email only when I have news, to keep my readers up to date.

Thanks so much for buying this book. Grace's story continues in **Runaway Bride**.

Happy reading!

Megan

Love in Little Tree series

Curious what happened to Grace? Read
Book Two in the Love in Little Tree series,
Runaway Bride.

*She ran from her wedding, leaving her twin sister to pick up
the pieces. Now Grace Marshall needs to redeem herself in the
town's eyes, and in the eyes of the man she's come to care for.
Will this* Runaway Bride *find a forever-after of her own?*

Do Rachel and Clint have a future together?
Find out in ***Baby Makes Three***,
Love in Little Tree book 3.

The twins' friend Carrie welcomes her niece
and former brother-in-law back to Little Tree and
hopes they're ***Coming Home*** forever.
Love in Little Tree, Book 4

Ghost of a Chance is a fun ghostly novella,
Book 4.25.

Adam Moore takes ***Twelve Steps to Love*** when
he meets pregnant waitress Brandi. Will he
overcome his drinking or will it sink them
both? Book 5 out now.

Other Books by Megan Kelly

Love in Little Tree series

The Wedding Rescue
Runaway Bride
Baby Makes Three
Coming Home
Ghost of a Chance
Twelve Steps to Love

Christmas in Stilton series

Santa Dear
Holly & Ivey

Returning Home series

The Fixer-Upper

Harlequin American Romances:

Marrying the Boss

Howard MO series:

The Fake Fiancée
The Marriage Solution
Stand-In Mom

Please visit Megan's website:
megankellybooks.com

To keep up to date on releases and news, sign
up for her Readers' Group on the website or Follow
her Author Page on Facebook.

Authors live off reviews and if you liked this book, I'd appreciate your honest opinion. No book report necessary—a few lines or (lots of) stars will do. Just post it to the bookseller of your choice or a book site like GoodReads or Bookbub.   Thank you!

Chapter Two

Over the coms, pleas and panic echoed, but Kat only wanted to see his face. Instead, his body sunk into the floor. A scream ached in her chest. She fell back against her captures, letting them hold her up when her faith would have sent her to her knees. Their four-fingered hands encircled her bicep, and all the synthetics in the world could not guard against that cold. Beneath her helm, tears gathered along her lower lashes. A chill settled in her bones. A world without Jacobi. Impossible. Yet suddenly real.

The lanky aliens dragged her body to the next narrow cell. They threw her inside, leaving her as they chirped and clicked - chatting to each other. Translucent panels formed walls. In full suits, Kat could not identify who surrounded her. On her left, one of the crew of the Intrepid sat against the far wall. They curled their hands around their legs. Drawing their knees to their chests, the unknown member shrunk in on themselves. Closing her eyes, Kat stretched her arms, pressing her hands against the panes.

Creaking, the walls leaked as if crying. Cold spread through her fingertips, and she tore her hands away. Squares of clear crystal encased her gloves. Though protected from the extremes of space, the chemical drew heat away unnaturally fast. Liquid dripped from the walls. It pooled, bubbling up to splash against the ceiling of Kat's cell. Sitting up, she watched it fly. The screams echoed in her ears. Close together, she could hear their pain. Any injuries resulted in death. Unable to bear the quiet, Kat let the screams fill the void where her voice would not sound. Her eyes remained glued to the gravity-defying liquid.

"Helium," a voice crackled through the com above the screams and panicked cries. "The walls appear to divide the ship, exposing pooled tubes to the extreme cooling by the vacuum of space."

"Good to know some lab monkeys survived," another voice joked, more familiar than the first.

Kat leapt to her feet. "Rachel?"

Kat's eyes scanned each cell for anyone calm enough to have spoken. Three cells away, a thin suited human waved. "Came in with Chelsea and Bill."

"Here!" Chelsea called.

Her hand rose from where she lay on the floor as Kat had. Stretching to fill the space with her five foot two frame, Chelsea drummed her fingers along the perimeters but avoided the walls.

One of the three aliens handling them turned. A twirl of clicks twilled through the room. Growling, Kat pressed against the front of her prison. She switched her personal com to project out. Her hands curled around the cold cylinders of metal caging her. Slamming her foot, Kat shrieked. The aliens did not move. As her hand covered in crystals shifted, the metal crushed them into fine particles. It was stupid. Begging for disaster to demand their captors' attention, but Kat leaned forward, clicking her tongue in mimicry. All three of the long-limbed extraterrestrials paused. One, with a blue star on his back, slid a foot back. Without any obvious eyes, she could not tell if the movement was more to redirect visual tissue or audio. Repeating the noise, she pressed her helm against the bars.

Chelsea sat up. The screaming died away as the aliens threw the last crewmember in a separate hold. Blue-Star clicked. Kat replied in kind. From the ceiling, silver orbs descended. They spun, rotating in the hall between the cells. Blue-Star trudged to stand before her. One of the silver orbs followed, bouncing above their heads. The alien clicked twice and chortled. Inhaling slowly, Kat repeated the sounds. The surface of the orb rippled, and Blue-Star gestured with two of his four wriggling digits back at the others. They came closer. All attention rested on Kat.

"Body count!" Rachel exclaimed on closed com.

"Private Brandon Baylor present and accounted!" came the first.

Standing, the human in the cell beside Kat proclaimed, "Dr. Margaret Cho!"

"Science Officer Qamar Karim present."

"Private Chelsea Walker here!"

"Sergeant William Jacobs present," the person on Kat's other side announced.

The number rose to twenty-four all included. Three doctors, two mechanics, and the rest a mix of science officers and military members from the latest academy class called in total. Not a single high ranking officer. Nineteen students trained to be astronauts and anthropologists, not prisoners of war.

Slamming her fist against the side of her cell, Kat spat, "Fuck you!" at Blue-Star before clicking against her incisors then her premolars as if she could translate her hatred into a language she'd only just realized existed.

When she swore, the orbs paused. They hung like ornaments in the air. As she clicked, the ripples repeated, releasing a buzz. Gurgles erupt from their three captures. Rolling its round head, Blue-Star backed away, flicking its fingers at Kat while turning. It left the room, followed by the two. Locked up and without anywhere to direct her rage, Kat muted her com, screaming as she fell to her knees. Nodes and thin lines of illuminants painted the brig in dull green light.

"So…" Chelsea hummed. "Aliens exist."

"Odds were good," Dr. Cho pointed out.

On the far end of the room, Level II Mechanic Cameron McNamara toyed with the liquid helium. "Safety protocol should've automatically sent initial findings to Earth. We didn't get a chance to measure their ship's speed, but it should give them a few hours to prepare."

"Prepare what?" Rachel asked, crouching and fiddling with her cell's bars.

"The military? All the militaries," Cameron retorted.

Releasing harsh laugh, Private Ngawang Pema reclined on the floor. "They tore a hole in our hull in a single shot. Nothing back home could stop them."

"Not necessarily true." Private Amondi Njeri sat on her feet, resting her hands on her thighs.

Ngawang rolled to her side to face her. "Proof?"

"The Russian Academy of Sciences has been working on a nanite shield as a nuclear defense system for the last two decades: Project Svalinn," Amondi replied. "The United Nations will convene. Representative Alexander will reveal we've been aware of the project. Representative Yakovlev will fold. Nanite shield goes up. All a matter of timing."

"Project Svalinn? That's Norse mythology," Private Aisling Thompson pointed out.

"And people never use other people's mythology for code names," Rachel mocked as she sat back.

Kat steadied her breath and unmuted her com. "Whatever happens on Earth, we can't do shit. We need to sort out our priorities."

Dr. Cho nodded. Standing, she leaned against the bars of her cell. "Primary objective: minimize all and any intel provided to the enemy which could endanger humanity's ability to defend itself. Second, acquire all information possible."

"Recon? Yeah, that's a priority when we're locked up and never going home," Science Officer Level I Lupita Henderson snorted. Down on all fours, she traced the edges of her cell. "Priority One: Escape."

A collective groan sounded through the ranks. Kat pressed her back against the bars, sliding down to stare at the wall. Lupita was young. Age seemed so insignificant when she thought about it. Thought

11

about how twenty-two of the twenty-four were between the ages of twenty and twenty-two. At twenty, Lupita was not that much younger than the majority, but she'd been the baby growing up, and when her overly intelligent self arrived at the academy a whole year younger than anybody else, she'd been the baby there too. Kat doubted Lupita realized how young she sounded. Escape made no sense. There was nowhere to go. A ship crawling with enemies surrounded them, and they had no idea where anything was. They needed more information before proceeding, but Lupita was as headstrong as she was smart.

"This tech wasn't made for humans," Cameron offered.

Lupita scoffed. "Doesn't mean we can't outthink them."

"There's probably a failsafe," Dr. Cho pointed out.

Running a finger along a nearly invisible seam, the twenty-year-old did not respond. However, Ngawang did. "If the kid wants to show us all the failsafe, I'm all for it. Somebody always ends up dying revealing the traps. Might as well be little Lupita."

"She's not wrong," Rachel agreed.

A moral label – as if that mattered. Kat shook her head, but her eyes never left Lupita. Though she agreed in discouraging the kid's recklessness and had done so as Lupita's squad leader, a part of Kat wanted her to pull up parts of the hull. Maybe the fail safe would send them all spiraling into space. Cold might linger but not enough to kill. Water systems might even recycle enough to keep them alive for weeks. Everything depended on current dehydration levels. Sleep or suicide would be their primary killer. Most would not sleep while floating through space unless pushed to the breaking. Hallucinations would set in. Falling, floating, flying through the vacuum would break them, but Kat was willing. Let them all freeze. Let them all fall into a black hole's event horizon.

"Private Henderson! You will desist!" Mechanic III Theresa Jane ordered. Her voice vibrated over the lines. A trill of desperation curled around her words.

"Don't care," Lupita grumbled. "I'm getting out."

Theresa sighed, kneeling to press against the same panels. "You're twenty. Here or on Earth, you've got time. If anyone's getting spaced, let it be me. I'm fifty-one. My life's been good."

Dr. Cho rushed to the front of her cell. "Don't you dare, Theresa." She reached out, her forearm stretching between the bars. "Private Henderson! Stand down, damn it!" the doctor commanded, but the science officer struggled on with the edge of the panel.

Lupita struggled with panel, bending it back. Theresa popped out the sheet of metal with an ease born of practice. Though the aliens had taken the humans' weapons, there were subtler tools available embedded in a mechanic's spacesuit. Each one had a basic repair kit. Standing on her toes, Kat balanced to watch as Theresa traced the buzzing gold lines painted on the interior of the metal. Beneath the exterior panel, a line of thin rectangles passed the gold-painted lines from one side of the cell to the other. Withdrawing

13

her circuit tracer, Theresa followed the lines, but her eyes were not on the screen. Instead, she kept track of Lupita's panicked progress.

Tearing off the panel, the twenty-year-old crowed in victory. Her force, however, had bent the edges, curling them upward. If Lupita noticed, she did not adjust her fervor. She tossed it over her shoulder, and the panel bounced over the floor, slamming into a corner. Helium dripped. The liquid ran up the sides. With each minute, it gathered on the ceiling, looming over her head.

"Private Henderson!" Kat spat, and Lupita froze. "Eyes up! That disregard for your environment kept you from achieving a ranking. Move the panel and follow Mechanic Jan's example."

Instinct moved Lupita when reason would not. Grumbling too quietly for her microphone to pick up, she stood, stormed over, and grabbed the panel. Her hands shook as they wrapped around the metal. Falling to her knees, Lupita slammed the panel back in place. Shoulders drooping, she pressed against the misshapen sheet. All the while, Theresa watched and waited. When Lupita fell back against the back of her cell, Theresa released a sigh and slid her own panel back into place. A collective exhale echoed across the com.

Ngawang blew a raspberry. "Now what are we going to do for entertainment."

A portal at the end of the hall opened. Blue-Star and his compatriots sauntered back into the brig. They wasted no time. Two aliens dragged Private Jelle Holt from his cell.

Ngawang sat up. Crossing her legs, she curled her fingers around the bars. Nobody turned away. Everyone kept their eyes on Jelle. As long as they watched, the man being forced to kneel was theirs. When he grunted instead of screamed, their minds became records of his courage. They looked, so he lived even if he died.

Reaching to the wall, Blue-Star clicked and chortled. A quiet moment passed. Blue-Star trudged to stand before Jelle, but everyone waited. Jelle inhaled, swallowed, exhaled, and repeated. Drumming his fingers, Blue-Star rolled his neck. He shook his shoulders, clicking a line. The others gurgled. Kat chewed the inside of her cheek to keep from swearing. Only assholes told jokes to kill time before killing people. Two long minutes passed. Shuffling echoed in the hall; a fourth humanoid alien entered. Entirely black like the two holding Jelle, the fourth had thinner limbs than the rest. Clicking at Blue-Star, Thin-Limb rolled his wrists. He swung his arms back and forth, stretching as if preparing for a workout. Blue-Star clicked in a low tone. More gurgles from Tweedledee and Tweedledum.

And there went Jelle's helmet. Gasping, Kat stepped back. This was not right. Jelle purpled. His eyes bugged out, and he gurgled. Not an alien laugh. A wet, sloshing as his lungs bled inward. Thin-Limb clicked, gesturing at Blue-Star. Blue-Star clicked twice. The air around them shifted. Like a blanket, heaviness fell over them. Above Lupita's head, the helium splashed down. Screaming, Lupita sprang back, bouncing against the walls like a pinball. Nobody paid attention to her. Everyone watched as

Jelle's corpse sunk through the floor, and Blue-Star prowled the corridor.

He took Cameron next. They peeled the spacesuits off him like shelling a lobster. One by one, the men gasped for air where there was none. Each time, Thin-Limb clicked a line, and Blue-Star returned two before the room's atmosphere changed. Cameron lived a few seconds longer. Private James Graves lasted a few minutes. Three dead – not counting Jacobi. Kat had not even gotten to see his face one last time. See the mole on his neck or that scar on his ear where he'd stabbed himself with a needle in ninth grade when Mary Andrews said she liked boys with pierced ears. No, the last human male face she'd ever see alive was William Jacobs. He breathed in an adjusted environment and kept on breathing.

A chortle. A click. Wires descended and no more Private William Jacobs. Thin-Limb shoved a plug between William's two first cervical vertebrae as Tweedledee and Tweedledum held his head down. Two shakes, eyes rolled back. Chortle. Click. Body dropped, and the floor swallowed him whole. Blue-Star tapped two fingers with Tweedledee and Tweedledum. Gurgles all around.

Later, the surviving women of the Intrepid would wonder if the wires just stole basic survival information or something else. Whatever the aliens found, it was enough to feel comfortable dragging the last three men from their cells and shooting them. One by one, the floor swallowed them. Seventeen women remained. Not even a single percent of what had been on the Intrepid. A crew in the thousands dwindled to seventeen.

The number itched. A familiar sort of downsizing. Kat closed her eyes, waiting. This was a cull. Everything on the ship stressed order from the alignment of the cells to the height of the guards versus the height of the room. Whoever ruled would want seventeen to become a clean number. Without knowing their mathematics system, she could not be certain what they'd end on. Seventeen was prime. Maybe that would do. Or maybe they grouped by sevens – cut down three. Grouped by tens, kill seven. Circled three, murder two. No way of knowing yet. The guards clicked, shaking their weapons when a whispered slipped from Kat's lips – projecting when she had not intended. For now, silence and waiting. Reclining on the floor of her cell, Kat stared at the ceiling, counting the twinkling luminescent nodes and praying the goal was not to get down to just one.

Chapter Three

If the adrenaline had not kept Kat awake, the drumming from the upper decks would have. The ceiling vibrated. Each node sparked, flickering like incandescent bulbs on the fritz. Every third glow jumped brighter. All the voices in her head murmured as those over her com jumbled. Prayers and whispers meant for the hallow sanctity of individual helmets echoed. Each - a sign of fear. Maybe this would be the last night. *God help us all. I want to live. Please, God, I want to live.* If they waited long enough, would anybody save them? Rebels? Impossible. Possible. The unknown itched beneath her skin. Not that she could scratch it. Odds were Kat wouldn't touch her own skin before she died.

William had breathed. Taken several gasping breaths after attempting not to, but he had done so and lived. Some of the later men had too. Gunned down or torn apart if they survived the first blow. Though the air pressure had not changed, nobody removed their helmets. Cursory scans showed a mix of nitrogen, oxygen and a scant amount of helium. Breathable air was not safe air. Surrounded by inconceivable technology, none of the seventeen were naïve enough to doubt how dangerous a single breath could be.

Clinging to the edges like caged beasts, they waited. Plans festered. Nothing mattered.

Kat reclined. Her bun pillowed against the back of her helmet, but a single pin poked into her scalp. Every morning, she put them in with ease. Knowing the possibility of sleeping in these suits, she had found a way to organize them to avoid discomfort. But that single pin scraped. She had put it back in too quickly. The last surviving item Thomas had ever touched poked against her scalp. His red hair and sullen eyes invaded her mind. He had roomed with Jacobi first year. They had been fast friends. Jacobi was everyone's fast friend. Sarcastic and blunt – Thomas had been the annoying little brother Kat had never had. Now, he was either a corpse in the wreckage, hurling through space, or dust. If there was any justice in the world, he was dust. She wished she believed that. Believed those were the only options, but the way Blue-Star had gone bit by bit with the air, there was a chance he had been studied.

An autopsy sounded human. Dissection measured the aliens' actions well enough. The sterile, apathetic deconstruction struck her. Thomas – dry-witted, lovable Thomas – naked and cut apart. Would they start with a Y-incision? Kat had seen shows about doctors and police. Blue lights and carefully positioned blankets. Aliens would not do that. Not ones who experimented with air like they did. Kat imagined Thin-Limb. He had been brought in for the helmet removal. Maybe he was their delicate hand. Thomas's pale flesh flashed through her mind. The way the mocha skin peeled and blood spurted wasn't right. Dead men did not bleed. Thomas was not dark-skinned.

Curling up into the fetal position, Kat closed her eyes. They would not spare Jacobi. His body might be sitting on a cold table. An alien, multiple or even the one who shot him, might touch him. Blue-Star would see Jacobi's smooth jaw and slightly crooked nose when Kat could not. She would die having only his panic as a last memory. He had been screaming. Deaf and screaming. The desperation and love in his final words clawed at her from the inside. Sniffling, Kat clenched her hands into fists. Sometimes, some uncertainties had to be believed. Even if Jacobi could not hear her, he knew she said it back. Every time since they had met in elementary school, she had always looked right back at him and said it too. First as a friend then as more. He knew. All the doubt in the world beat like a gorilla against her throat, but he had to have known because the universe could not possibly be any crueler.

"Going to cry yourself to sleep?" Ngawang mocked over an individual com line. Now that they knew names, it was easy enough to hone in on one person.

"Has anyone ever loved you, Ngawang?" Kat asked, but she did not bother waiting for a reply. "Nobody is alive now, so I suppose it doesn't matter. If you want to pretend you're fine, go ahead. But if you continue to attack your own, I certainly won't lose sleep when they kill you."

"Good. Be angry. Be apathetic – just don't be pathetic. There are more idiots here than I can stand.

Stay with me, Parker. We might just survive if we work together," the other woman replied.

Rolling onto her back, Kat stared at the ceiling. Surviving meant living in a world without Jacobi. She could not remember a time before him. They had grown up right next door. Most people knew them with a conjunction: Kat *and* Jacobi; Jacobi *and* Kat. The two tied so tightly together she never imagined a world without him. Now, her naivety would haunt her because deep down inside, she already had decided to live. Tomorrow or the day after, her last day would come, but a little voice screamed from deep inside. Her nerves thrummed. Even with Jacobi six-feet under, Kat wanted to live. Death loomed too close, too big to lie.

"Do you remember Lieutenant Collin's field exercise?" she asked.

Ngawang hummed. The vibrations sparked static over Kat's audio transmitter. "Too much information – cut it down into bites. Pass the plate."

"Conductive paint in the floors," Kat offered. "Numerous lines intersected on Theresa's panels."

"Suggests either the paint is multilayered with some separating element, or…" Laughing, the other woman said, "It's a fucking trap."

Running her hands over the floor, Kat traced the outline of the same panel in her cell. None of the walls had panels. The ceiling transitioned smoothly across the room. Besides the square panels on the floor of each cell, the room offered no obvious ways into the system. Sitting up, she glared across the room. Blue-Star had pressed a hand to the far wall in a gap hall between the cells. Before she could even look, her heart sunk. The cells were split into sections of five. Ten crewmembers imprisoned along one wall. Seven spread along the opposite.

"At least two of us are going to be killed without reason," Kat posited, folding her legs beneath her.

Ngawang rolled onto her stomach, resting her head on her arms. "Probably."

"The panel wall is smooth. No obvious sensors. Bio-scanning electronics? Or their eyes are more finely attuned to tell the differences in the metal surfaces," Kat continued. Though her eyes studied the far wall, her heart raced, and her mind debated why she was certain the aliens wanted a clean number. "Females remain. Males weren't picked randomly, so they had to have some type of scanning system."

"Our suits are difficult to gender identify regardless of familiarity with the human species. They shouldn't be able to smell us. Air-tight and all, so yeah…scanning system. We didn't pass anything overt, so maybe it's an inlaid system. Did you see the spheres? Could be one of them," Ngawang suggested.

Resting her elbows on her knees, Kat balanced her head in her hands. The dark metal beneath her feet stood still. If the ship moved through space, nothing in the room gave it away. A lump gathered in her throat. Any type of self-comfort would either endanger her or give away the fretfulness charging like static around her mind. Like the jolt right before a video paused, the world blurred. The crew of the Intrepid faked sleep, but their minds twittered around her. Scores batted around her head. Some couldn't kill. Other wouldn't. If the battle for survival turned inward, they would be a slow bleed. Not because some, like Ngawang and Lupita, would hesitate to do what they needed to survive. No, any slowness would be the fault of people like Kat, Theresa, and Amondi. Those capable and willing to do what it took to delay the inevitable.

Clearing her throat, Kat told Ngawang, "The orbs reacted to known sounds."

"So they'll learn languages next. Odds are pretty good on them picking a polyglot, and we're all bilingual," the other pointed out. "If their process is the same, giving them English would be easiest."

"Keep other languages to coordinate, sure." Though she agreed, Kat's mind had already moved onto the how. Extracting a lexicon took time and cooperation.

Another voice crackled over the com, disrupting her thoughts. Rachel called, "Are you okay, Kat?"

"Cooperation shouldn't hinder Earth's efforts. We've spent eons fighting people who spoke the same language. Make it easy for us. If it can be easy. Wonder how they'll do it," Ngawang rambled. Her voice thrummed. Each phrase rose to a higher note at the end as if she were asking a question, but it wasn't confusion or anxiety. Kat closed her eyes, sighing. Ngawang was excited.

Switching to address Rachel alone, Kat said, "I'm fine. If you can rest, you should."

"Pot meet kettle," Rachel joked.

When the walls trembled, all seventeen women stilled. Kat stood. Her heart racing as the panels between each cell rattled. Helium leaked. The liquid climbed the walls to drip down from the ceiling. It evaporated before hitting the bottom. In the gap, darkness crept. Shadows of the vacuum whispered through, but something burned them away. The luminescent nodes on the back wall of Kat's cell puttered out. Black metal glimmered; then steam rolled down the edges, fogging up the side panes. Waves of heat rolled over Kat. Backing away, she pressed her back up against the thin metal.

A few cells away, Theresa stretched her hand, pressing it to the hot wall. "An attack?" She wondered over the open com.

The ship shuddered. Above their heads, the quaking traveled. It worked its way across the ceiling, and the heat followed. Crouching low, Kat corrected, "We're boarding."

"Boarding? Who's boarding?" Chelsea asked. "Or are we docking?"

Neither offered much hope, but a planet-docked ship might just be an easier escape than one in space. Perhaps their presence and the thorough securing of them explained why Kat doubted they'd landed. Gravity hadn't shifted, and the smooth flight wouldn't have explained how little pressure changed upon a possible reentry. At the base of the great black metal behemoth of a ship, surely a spark of green would appear in the gap. Flames followed light in a landing. A quick glimpse of the landing platform's color flashed before darkness. There had only been light and heat. Darkness returned too quickly. Though heat remained above and behind, cold crawled back into place.

"Boarded," Dr. Cho informed them when Kat remained silent. "Heat only traveled along one wall."

"Great," Rachel griped. "More faceless assholes."

"I don't think they're faceless," Chelsea murmured.

Sitting cross-legged on the floor, Aisling hummed. "I wonder who it is."

Leaning with her back against the bars of her cell, Lupita scoffed. She fiddled with the distorted edges on her floor panel. "Who cares?" she grumbled. "We aren't gonna meet them."

Kat rolled her eyes. Arguing with Lupita served no point. The younger wanted a reason to pitch a fit, so Kat ignored her. Wondering wouldn't hurt. Speculation offered a release from the pressure of not knowing. With so many unknown variables, a guess had a chance of being right and a certainty of easing tension. Ignoring their situation didn't help anyone. Regardless, the worst case scenario and the best likely overlapped. Blue-Star appeared to be in charge. In charge of the brig, however, didn't mean in charge of the ship. The docking vessel could be a recon or conflict craft. Though the basic warp tech was too large for any American or even any human vessels, the alien ship moved faster than the highest warp drive gear. Compared to the Intrepid, the alien craft had a different form too. While the Intrepid formed a circular, almost doughnut ring, the quick glimpse of the alien vessel appeared triangular with four bended appendages. Intrepid curled space around it like a crochet ring. This ship pierced space like a needle.

25

Worst or best case, the boarding ship had returned from Earth. Best had the ship damaged and the lone survivor. Best case meant Earth remained free. Worst case set a cruiser returning with tales of victory. Stories of how quickly humanity fell. If there even was a fleet. Most books, shows, and movies painted aliens invading. One ship wasn't the end in them. However, they had no way to know if the aliens knew about Earth. Maybe they had destroyed the Intrepid and left well enough alone. Kat hoped they had. Doubting she would live long, she settled her heart on the lives she would never see again.

Her mind filled with unwanted images. Black ships swooped down over Earth. Children scattered in their yards. Screams and blood flooded the black top, leaving charred wood chips and curls of plastic and melted metal. Likely, at least one would survive. Smallest or quickest – someone who'd live a life running, hiding, bleeding beneath the heel of an inhuman hunter. Burning rays set every park to smolders. In a single blast, the ships could start a blaze across the west coast that no one would live to see put out. Curling in the sky, smoke blocked the sun. Darkness descended.

And what of the more familiar scene? Her mother in a straw hat glared up from her garden. Surrounded by green beans and eggplant, she squinted up at the sky before a laser reduced her or the house to ash. If the latter, Kat could hear her mother's cries of panic as her father died in his office. Their dogs would howl, and maybe Blue-Star's species wouldn't care. Maybe they would leave the dogs trapped in the yard. Citizen and Graham towered, behemoth hounds.

They would protect her mother, but from what? Not the alien ships. Maybe alien soldiers.

After they devastated the cities, they would be able to pick off the stragglers at their leisure. Or they might not bother. If they attacked, the aliens would likely have a reason beyond destruction. Resources left Earth a barren rock or, alternatively, a culling of people to make everything green again. Without more information, Kat could only guess.

"Maybe they're one of the fleet sent to Earth," Theresa suggested as if she could read Kat's thoughts.

"Maybe it's someone in charge," Chelsea replied. She sounded almost peppy over the com.

Ngawang snorted. "Cause we're so important."

"We likely are," Dr. Cho retorted, pacing the two steps from one clear panel to the other. "We're the first humans out this far."

"New species – I'd think scientists before leader," Amondi offered, stretching.

A chill ran down Kat's spine. "Dissection?"

"Probing," Chelsea joked, but a dark hush fell over the seventeen.

No one had commented on how they'd killed the men. Though Blue-Star and the Gurgle Twins seemed more like dolls than possibly sexual creatures, none of the Intrepid crew could be certain. Some of the most famous scenes in science fiction involved alien babies bursting through people's abdomens. Rape wasn't an uncommon reality. As a woman in the armed forces, Kat attended at least one lecture every year on sexual assault. A new regret rolled like a stone into her stomach. As she and Jacobi came from conservative families, they had waited. Kat sunk, twisting to sit facing the outer wall. She spent her life driven to be on the Intrepid. Now, the most basic human experience eluded her. She'd never wanted it. Sex never jumped to mind. Jacobi's presence had always settled like sunshine around her, and any consideration for more had been from a desire to have children with him.

"They wouldn't..." Chelsea whispered.

Ngawang huffed, a barking laugh. "They massacred thousands. Hell, they just killed seven men. But, sure, using us as broodmares or just sex slaves is – I mean, seriously, that's just too far."

"That is why I want to escape," Lupita said, peeling up the panel to study the interior compartment once more.

Swallowing, Kat stood. "We need a better plan."

"There's no intel, and we're each in compartments set to be spaced. Even with the suits. That won't go well if we've left in a jarring wake. Maybe if the ship were still..." Theresa trailed off. Shaking her head, she sighed. "But we're not."

"Then what? We just sit here like cattle waiting to get killed?" Lupita demanded, slamming her fist against the bars.

"I have no intention of dying," Science officer Marie Lane stated, folding her arms over her chest.

"None of us want to die," Dr. Cho retorted. Drumming her fingers on her hips, she paused – staring at the solid black wall where the door appeared when the aliens came. "We need to learn the workings of the ship, but not while risking our lives."

"Our lives are already at risk. Odds are we end up dead," Kat informed her.

"Then we do this right." Dr. Cho reached toward Theresa, saying, "Can you use the wiring on the floor panel to access anything outside your cell?"

"I should be able to trace the circuits back if they're connected. At least partially. It depends on their system," Theresa confessed.

Nodding, Dr. Cho shifted to face Rachel. "Then we need -."

The ship rumbled. Flashing blue, the nodes went out. Before the doorway opened, a ripple ran along the black metal. Against Kat's back the bars shook. Each of the seventeen stood at the ready. Kicking the panel back into place, Lupita stood on it, tilting back and forth as she glared at the wall. Any expectations of someone new were soon disappointed. Blue-Star trudged in with three silver orbs. They hung over his head, rolling and shifting along their surfaces as he clicked in low tones as if mumbling under his breath. If he found his work inconvenient or exhausting, he was more than welcome to let them all go as far as Kat was concerned. However, for his low clicking, Blue-Star didn't hesitate.

He walked up to Theresa's cell. Rubbing a hand along his opposite shoulder Blue-Star flicked his fingers at her. She stood frozen, watching him. Reaching above him, he grabbed one of the orbs and offered it to her. A trail of clicks and chortles followed. All eyes honed in on that round metal ball.

"What do I do?" Theresa asked; her voice rose in pitch with each word. Clearing her throat, she pulled it down an octave to add, "Should I take it?"

"No way! It's too dangerous!" Rachel exclaimed.

Ngawang's fingers twitched. "Do it."

"Don't, Theresa," Dr. Cho discouraged.

Blue-Star groaned. A strained hissing emitted from him like a boiling kettle. With a flick of his hand, the bars on Theresa's cage dropped. He held out his hand again. Lifting it up twice, he clicked then tossed the orb to his opposite hand and gestured with it as he chortled and clicked in an alternating pattern. When Blue-Star fell silent, Theresa didn't move.

"Run!" Rachel yelled as Lupita screamed, "Kill him!"

Theresa did neither. Exiting her cell, she circled round. As she moved, she kept her eyes on Blue-Star. The alien did nothing. He simply watched as she moved, stepping back to face her. All the while, Blue-Star held that little silver ball between them. Though free of her cell, Theresa had nowhere to go. Blue-Star stood between her and the door. Behind her, there were only more cells and a tall black wall. Even if a door existed within it, Theresa had no idea how to open it. She ground her teeth. Blue-Star released a nasally whistle. Staring each other down, neither the human nor the alien moved.

"Maybe it's a peace offering," Chelsea suggested. "Maybe he thought the men were a danger to us."

"Bull," Kat retorted.

Amondi hummed in agreement. "This is a trap. Don't touch it."

"I don't think he's gonna give me much choice," Theresa murmured as Blue-Star shoved the orb at her.

She slowly extended her arm, wrapping her fingers around the orb. Kat's heart thundered in her chest. She didn't dare breathe as Blue-Star let go. Seconds ticked by them. Everyone watched, waiting for disaster to strike. After thirty seconds, Blue-Star clicked. The orb rippled.

"Tingles a bit," Theresa said. "It's moving, but just like…vibrating."

"Not really dangerous then," Ngawang huffed, sitting back down in her cell.

Theresa passed the ball between her hands as Blue-Star had. Nothing happened. The metal rolled smoothly from one gloved hand to the other. "It's not moving anymore. Vibrations only lasted as long as the alien kept clicking. Maybe it's a translation device?"

"Probably," Kat agreed.

"So what do I…" Theresa's question never finished as her whole body tensed. Electricity scattered along her suit.

"Theresa!" Dr. Cho slammed against the bars of her cell.

Screams and panicked whispers erupted along the communication line. Kat knelt, bowing her head against the metal. She switched her com to a private line. "Ngawang?"

"Yeah, this was always gonna go wrong," the other woman replied.

Frowning, Kat shook her head. "Theresa's first language is Spanish. She spoke it at home growing up."

Ngawang sighed. "So much for straight forward. But hey, it might not be anything like that. Seriously, she's being electrocuted. Not much language formation there. The orbs are probably just torture devices," Ngawang told her.

Pressing a hand against her helmet, Kat asked, "How many words do our suits know?"

"The tech's a modified artificial intelligence. They know as many as…oh," Ngawang growled. "God damn it."

Switching over to the general frequency, Kat commanded, "Separate Theresa from your communication system!"

"What?" Chelsea gasped, but the rest reached up, removing Theresa from their general grouping in a single, unified movement.

The action didn't go unnoticed. Blue-Star turned as if to check when those within his sight lifted their hands to their temples. He clicked several times, tapping his foot and rubbing his shoulder. Grabbing the sphere from Theresa, he stepped over her as she fell to the ground. When the alien pressed his hand to the same spot on the wall, he clicked those same tones he'd done the first time Thin-Limb showed up. Bile rose in Kat's throat. Chewing on her cheek, she clenched her hands in fists. Recalling his 'joke,' Kat put her com to project and released the same line of clicks which Blue-Star had said to Tweedledee and Tweedledum. The two orbs over Blue-Star rippled. Rolling his shoulder, the alien stepped back. His neck twisted toward Kat. Though she couldn't be sure he had eyes, she recognized the weight of a glare.

"Back off, Parker," Dr. Cho commanded, and Kat stepped away.

Blue-Star clicked. But the portal opened, and Thin-Limb entered. While his appendages had been long before, his arms hung like elephant trunks at his side. They swung back and forth as he moved. At seeing the other, Blue-Star threw up his hands. Thin-Limb gurgled, but he yelped like a wounded dog when Blue-Star grabbed his arms. Running his fingers up the side of Thin-Limb's arms, Blue-Star clicked as the black arm lit up orange. A whirling sound echoed, and Thin-Limb's arms shortened. Clicking rapidly, he pulled his arms back. He rubbed his hands up and down them, grumbling like a whistling kettle.

Lying on the floor, Theresa twitched. Blue-Star waved an arm her way, and Thin-Limb slid his foot across the floor. Metal looped around Theresa's arms and legs. A table rose from the floor, twisting the woman until she faced downwards. Kat's pulse raced. Chelsea whimpered, and Rachel turned away, crouching down and pressing her hands near her ears as if she could drown out what was happening. Wires descended from the ceiling. Thin-Limb reached up, grabbing a wire in each hand. He tapped them together. Sparks jumped, and the bastard gurgled.

With a swing of his hands, he tore her suit apart. The material fell in tatters beneath the table and drained into the floor. Theresa's dark brown eyes darted back and forth. Without her suit, the block on the com did nothing to silence her panicked cries. Black curls fell from her bun. With one hand, Thin-

Limb guided a piece of metal over the back of her neck, shaving her hair. Running two fingers down the back of her neck, Thin-Limb clicked the same sing-song line of five clicks on repeat. Then he shoved a wire into her spine. Her screams ripped through the ship.

On a closed line, Ngawang huffed. "That could work."

"If shoving wires like a horror movie villain into a neck steals language, I'm shocked we haven't done it," Kat drawled.

Despite her shield of sarcasm, fear filled her. Thin-Limb moved with an ease which came from practice. He tilted the wires, clicking his little song. As the wires stretched, Theresa's hands flexed and twitched. The orbs orbited around Theresa. Images projected around her face, and when Theresa tried to close her eyes, a shock tore through her. Spiking mountains and valleys along their surface the orbs drew closer. A spot of red bubbled up from the wires. Spinal fluid and blood mixed around the metal wires. Her brows furrowed. Bearing her teeth, she cried out. Eyes rolling back, Theresa fell limp against her restraints.

"We're all going to die," Lupita lamented, pressing herself toward the back of her cell. "We should've fucking escaped before. This is insane."

Sitting down, Ngawang started doing crunches and turned off her communication device. Amondi crossed her arms, leaning her face into her hands against the bars. They and the majority of the seventeen looked away. Only Kat and Dr. Cho kept their eyes on Theresa. Blood leaked from her nose.

34

Twitches passed along Theresa's face, but she didn't regain consciousness. Kneeling, Kat pressed her helmet against the bars. The five-note song stopped. Thin-Limb tore the wires from her neck. The table and Theresa sunk down through the floor. Blood and spinal fluid smeared across the floor. As Dr. Cho shrieked and wept, Kat swallowed back an unexpected surge of relief. Jacobi's quick death had been a gift in a way. A painful, nearly unbearably cruel gift.

"*¿Do you want to talk now, monster?*" a deep voice asked in Spanish.

For a moment, the words flowed over Kat. Her eyes lifted to meet the featureless mask of Blue-Star. Beside him, one of the silver orbs rippled. Standing, she repeated the line of clicks of his joke. As she spoke, the orb moved, and words came back: "*I guess we shouldn't be surprised that a gaseous lifeform is as slow as a fart.*"

"That was his joke?" Aisling sneered.

Stepping up beside Blue-Star, Thin-Limb scoffed. "*Frankly, I doubt an insect would ever have the opportunity to measure the speed of a fart - let alone release one.*"

Rachel groaned. Sitting down on the floor, she called, "A translation, please? For the rest of us?"

Clucking her tongue, Aisling replied, "Kat repeated the wider one's joke. Apparently, the thin one is some type of gaseous lifeform. The first said, 'I suppose we shouldn't be surprised that a gaseous life form is as slow as a fart.' When the thin one heard Kat's repetition, he said something about the other one being an insectoid and measuring the speed of a fart"

"I can't believe these are the first words shared between our species," Amondi lamented.

"And the first words among three species at that, apparently," Chelsea added, stretching her arms over her head.

Aisling switched her com to project. *"Excuse me, but we come in peace. ¿Why did you attack us?"*

"For the glory of Mah-Wærm. God of the Empty Sea," Thin-Limb informed them.

Lupita translated this time. Standing, the young science officer set her hands on her hips. "Do they mean space?"

"Great, a bunch of fanatical cultists," Rachel grumbled. "Just our luck."

Thin-Limb shifted between Kat and Aisling as they spoke, but Blue-Star kept facing Kat. His fingers drummed along his thighs, mirroring her every move. Stepping up to the bars, Kat held her breath as Blue-Star drew closer. Though the orb translated Thin-Limb's claim of Blue-Star being an insect, his body didn't match. Perhaps the words didn't translate correctly. Maybe his suit hid another set of appendages. Her gaze dropped to his side. Maybe he could pull in his arms.

"The majority of us don't speak this language," Kat informed them.

Dr. Cho growled, "Don't tell them that! They'll take someone else if they realize we don't all speak Spanish." Ngawang hummed in approval on their private line.

36

"Well, they were going to find out eventually," Chelsea offered in placation.

Blue-Star hissed like a cockroach. The kettle sound fell into place, and the picture of their captors became a bit clearer. Though the helmet seemed mostly in proportion to the body for Blue-Star to have a human shape, Kat imagined a small head with a set of mandibles. Antennae crushed to his skull or small enough to easily be covered. Besides his four-fingered hands, nothing marked him as separate from the average human. However, they hadn't sent a human this far. If they couldn't speak human languages, odds were they hadn't come across any humans to torture before. The contrast irritated her. Humanoid appearances without humans. Someone had enforced the look, but beyond the individual being an incredibly prejudice humanoid, she couldn't imagine why. A unified appearance for unity perhaps. If Thin-Limb was a gas life form, they could've given him a fifth finger, so whatever appearance they wanted aimed for just four. Her eyes scanned the thinner alien. Frowning, she crossed her arms; when Blue-Star did the same, she glanced back at him.

"*We will harvest your main language. We are not deterred,*" he assured her.

Sighing, Kat reached through the bars. "*Of course. Then use me. I'm up for a good time one-on-one.*"

Blue-Star gurgled, and the orb projected a deep, monotone chuckle. He leaned forward, pressing his helmet beside hers. The black of his mask shifted. As the opacity lessened, Blue-Star's face came into view. Shadowed, his gold skin shined with a waxy sheen. Two human-sized compound eyes stared back at Kat. He had no hair. No eyelashes or eyebrows, but the shape of his face followed familiar, human lines. Where she imagined mandibles, he had thin lips. Blue-Star smirked. Opening his mouth, he revealed his lack of mandibles was only external. Two twittering black appendages vibrated; snapping them together, he laughed again.

"How lucky you are to be so minimally malformed," he whispered, and the orb came close to keep the information from being overheard. *"But don't worry. We'll fix you. Mah-Wœrm will reconfigure you in his image."*

"Shit," Kat muttered. "We're on the island of Dr. Moreau."

Blue-Star sneered, and Kat's eyes widened. She hadn't intended to project that part. Her ears echoed with the rush of her own blood. Dr. Cho reached out, wrapping her arms around the clear panels toward Kat's cell. Snatching her wrist, Blue-Star stepped back. The moment he stepped away, his helmet became opaque once more.

Keeping his gaze on Kat, Blue-Star proclaimed, *"This one - we'll use her."*

"Fine, fine," Thin-Limb grumbled. *"It isn't like I have a laboratory to run or anything."*

Blue-Star snorted. *"Your asteroid bacteria can wait."*

As her bars fell, Dr. Cho tensed. The fingers of her free hand twitched. Tugging her forward, Blue-Star didn't bother looking at the petite woman. Perhaps he thought Dr. Cho was too small to be dangerous. He was sorely mistaken. In a shift, Dr.

Cho twirled, and Blue-Star flew over her shoulder to land on his back. Thin-Limb retreated to the wall. His hand slammed against the panel, but nothing happened. Twisting his wrist, she flexed it backward, frowning when Blue-Star simply laughed. He stood, letting his arm fall off. Dr. Cho held the prosthetic as the alien stretched. Where an arm had seemed to be, there was only a scarred shoulder. In the dim luminescent green of the nodes, his waxy skin glimmered.

"Explains why he was so light," Dr. Cho grumbled.

"*We all have flaws, but Mah-Wærm is fixing mine*," Blue-Star said; his scars wriggled.

Lupita scoffed. "Apparently, this freak show Mah-Wærm fixes people."

"Now I'm getting the Moreau reference," Rachel commented.

Thin-Limb released a long trill and then wheezed. The orbs spun, shifting. Two more descended. Near Blue-Star, the translators clicked and chortled, but those around the humans kept to Spanish.

"*I'm the one constantly having to fix your insect ass*," Thin-Limb complained. "*Mah-Wærm might have designed the modifications, but I'm doing the work*"

Kat smirked. Any dissent provided an opportunity to sow chaos, and chaos opened doors that conformity kept closed. Though immediate action would raise suspicions, Thin-Limb's discontent soothed her. His simmering grudge humanized him. If a gaseous, Mengelian alien could be a spiteful shit, he could be manipulated. Thin-Limb remained by the panel as Blue-Star faced Dr. Cho. His severed arm stretched, wrapping around her like a boa constrictor.

"We will finish this," he murmured.

The metal prosthetic arm and Dr. Cho as a result flew back to Blue-Star. He rotated, slamming her into the table where Theresa had been. His arm reattached. As the table grabbed hold of her, his arm unwound. A bright curl shimmered around the rim of his shoulder. Rolling his shoulder, he sighed. Blue-Star crouched down, whispering in Dr. Cho's ear. The more he spoke, the more violently she struggled. Step by step, Thin-Limb pulled away from the wall. When he reached the table, Blue-Star stood and waved the other back.

"Cut me off," Dr. Cho whispered; her voice wet and thick.

Hands rose, and one by one, the remaining fifteen cut Dr. Margaret Cho from their communication line. Swallowing, Kat closed her eyes. "I'm so sorry."

"Don't be," Margaret replied. "I'm getting out of here."

Blue-Star raised his hands. His fingers shifted. The rounded edges sharpened. With a wave of his hand, the insect-alien tore her suit apart. When Thin-Limb had removed Theresa's suit, she's been entirely uninjured. Each peeling piece of her suit had fallen without blood or skin. Her hair only received cutting attention afterward. Unlike Thin-Limb, Blue-Star gave Margaret no mercy. Synthetics dropped to the floor in tatters. Blood and flesh joined them. Tears flowed, dropping to the ground. Clenching her jaw tightly shut, Margaret glared down at the floor.

"*You believe you are so smart,*" Blue-Star clicked.

Kat gritted her teeth as she translated, "You believe you're smart."

Grabbing the wires from the ceiling, Thin-Limb buried them into Margaret's neck. Blood bumbled over her lips, but she didn't scream. Blue-Star knelt beside her. He drummed his fingers on the floor. The orbs buzzed, and rippled as the insect-alien clicked.

With each new translation, Kat spoke the alien's words in English: "You think you're safe. You live and die by the will of a God many of you will never meet."

Thin-Limb shifted the wires, making Margaret fall limp. Her short bob of black hair cascaded over her high cheekbones. Red colored her body. A pool of blood collected beneath her. Margaret seemed so small. In life, she'd been an unreachable giant. Everyone on the Intrepid struggled through her physiology coursework, but the doctor's skin peeled away. Any titles she had earned vanished. Everything she made disappeared. Like a ruined statue in a desert, the intimidating accomplishments her resume left only a hard reality: they would all die here. When Margaret's jaw released, chunks of flesh splashed down in the blood below.

Thin-Limb nodded, removing the wires. Twisting around, the black metal spun the corpse of Dr. Margaret Cho, burying her beneath the floor with the rest. Whether fire or a metallic tomb awaited her,

Kat didn't know. Blue-Star stepped into her blood. The liquid drained around his feet. His helmet shifted, folding back in upon itself in waves to reveal his bald, gold head. Smirking, he rolled his shoulders. Crossing the room, Blue-Star stood in front of Kat. As he moved, his compound eyes bore into hers. She didn't dare look away; however, her periphery caught Thin-Limb retreating. Running his hands along his arms, he unwound them, letting the length return to what it had been when he entered the room.

Lips spreading to let his mandibles show, Blue-Star wrapped his metal fingers around one of the bars. "One by one, you all will fall."

"Then knock me down," she challenged.

From the crown of his head, thin coils lifted. The translucent antennae shimmered as he moved them. Folding around his face like a diadem, they entwined above his hairless brow. Thin stands poured over his face. A curtain formed, brushing the tip of his nose before inching to align. As the nodes lit, the strands shifted. Blue-Star's face vanished behind a projected screen, and Kat blanched as Jacobi stared back at her. The contours of his face rippled, but his warm brown eyes blinked at her from the string antennae. Biting her lip, Kat kept her eyes level. Tears lined her bottom lids. They rolled down her face. Trails of salt staining her cheeks.

Blue-Star gurgled. The orbs spiked with his laughter. All the while, Jacobi's face remained. Kat trembled. Fury and grief warred as she stared into the alien's death mask. With two fingers, Blue-Star gestured at five more cells. Thin-Limb pressed his hand to the wall, and each of the cells that Blue-Star had gestured to shook. The bars grew, melding together to form a solid wall. Shifting, the metal back wall and floor retreated into the ceiling. Each of the five women was left floating in space. In their suits, they were alive. One, Sergeant Lena Vilanova, stretched and grabbed the ceiling. Her fingers slipped against smooth metal, but she clawed until she found a hold.

"Pull to the outside!" Lupita yelled.

Slamming her hands against the panels beside Lena, Rachel demanded, "Try to get through the bars! Use the boosters on your boots!"

Blue-Star's lips slid together into a smirk. His helmet rose and encased his head as a web of lasers shot through the cell, tearing the five women apart. Their limp, torn bodies floated in the space where their cells had been. Curling his metal hand around one of the bars to Kat's cage, he leaned in close.

"Knock, knock."

Chapter Four

Left to stare at the floating, tattered corpses of their comrades, the surviving ten remained silent long after Thin-Limb and Blue-Star left. Kat collapsed. Sliding down against the bars, she muted her microphone. She clenched her jaw, struggling to swallow the sobs crawling up her throat. Her tears continued. Through the blur, her eyes alighted on the floor panel. Life or death seemed no different. When Blue-Star came for the Intrepid's crew – her crew, she only agitated. Dr. Cho had died because of her. A talent for mimicry and a good memory served no purpose here. The latter tormented her. The former seemed useful only to draw negative attention. Crawling forward, Kat reached out when a voice peaked through the coms.

"Lupita! Stop!" Rachel commanded.

Swiveling, Kat gasped as Lupita lifted the plate of metal over her head. Lupita slammed it down on the thin panels within the floor box.

"Please!" Chelsea begged. "Don't make us watch you die too!"

Ngawang curled onto her side. "Let her die already."

"Shut up! Shut up! Shut up!" Lupita bellowed.

Kicking the wall, she redirected the leaking liquid helium onto the circuits. The liquid dripped down onto the conductive paint, but nothing happened. Whether the paint's other components insulated the current sufficiently to prevent a reaction or the helium simply wasn't conductive enough to cause the circuits to cross, none of the remaining crew could know for certain. Except, perhaps Lupita herself. When Lupita swung the plate into the bars, the plate shattered.

"What the hell! Who makes spaceships with temperature sensitive metal without a polymer coating?" Marie cried as Lupita sifted through the pieces of metal. "Wait…" The youngest of them picked up a piece. Holding it up to the luminescent nodes, she shifted the light along the sharp edge. "Lupita – don't!"

"For the love of science, Marie. Shut the fuck up," Lupita muttered and brought the sharp edge of the metal down between the conductive panels, scraping the paint off of the plates.

Sparks jumped up with each hit. Though electricity traveled along the edges of her suit, the insulation protected her. Surrounded by the dead, nothing would stop her this time. The floor may have swallowed some, but a mass grave grew around the remaining ten, and as horrifying as another death would be, Kat stood back. Her heart ached.

Down came the shard. Up went the sparks. Helium leaked. Running up the ceiling, it dripped and leveled out, evaporating as the atmosphere heated it to a gas. Some of the liquid collected in the circuit box. A pink glow passed along the floor.

"The bars!" Aisling cried. "Lupita! You have to stop!"

The thin bars had grown, melding together inch by inch. As they sealed her cell off from the rest of the block, the pink illumination spread between the panels. Electricity crackled across the clouds.

Slamming against her bars, Amondi screamed, "Please, Lupita! Your suit won't be able to handle that much electricity!"

"Just let her die," Ngawang said with a sigh.

Turning her eyes upward, Kat exhaled slowly. She pressed her right hand to the side of her helmet. As she removed Lupita from her communication line, Marie, Ngawang and Rachel followed suit. Qamar hesitated before following. The bars on the youngest woman's cage sealed. From the center of the metal, a clear panel grew, revealing the growing pink hue as the helium transformed into highly conductive plasma. In the midst of a storm of electricity, Lupita knelt. Her hands rose over her head, but with each downward slam, her reaction slowed, and the pink light flashed brighter like a blinding pulse.

"We'll figure something else out," Chelsea pleaded. "You don't have to kill yourself. You took every piece of tech apart on our dorm block and put it back together in the same night! You can do this. Please, Lupe, just try!"

Over her head, Lupita's arms stilled. Her shoulders shook, and she dropped the shard. The bit of metal clattered to the ground. Reaching into the panel box, she removed each board, disconnecting layer after layer of circuitry. All along her walls, the nodes dimmed. Hissing resounded. The pink light grew brighter until it enveloped everything within Lupita's cage, including her. Amondi and Aisling pressed against their coms, quickly removing Lupita, but Chelsea reared back, falling across the floor as her com recoiled against the explosion. Tearing through her suit and body, the bright storm of electricity ripped Lupita apart. With a click, the walls retreated. The light and anything that remained of Private Lupita Henderson drifted off into space.

"What is wrong with all of you?" a voice came from the far corner of the block.

Between the different course groups, Kat had known most but not all of the Intrepid's crew. This voice wasn't familiar. Light and with a curl to the vowels not native to any part of the United States, the tone offered numerous clues; however, all the names and biographies provided to the crew didn't include any non-Americans. Regardless, the cell opposite of where Lupita had been, the speaker sat, leaning against the back wall.

"Oh damn, I had money on the Chinese getting on board," Ngawang joked.

Aisling snorted. "Who had money on the United Kingdom?"

"Not me. I bet on Israel," Rachel replied.

"How inhuman can you be? One of your crew committed suicide, and you're joking," the woman spat.

"Log says: Private Emma Sugg," Kat read off her suit's internal computer. "Definitely didn't share any classes with you."

"She wasn't in the biological sciences coursework either," Marie added.

Tapping her foot, Aisling noted, "Emma Sugg wasn't listed in linguistics."

"Not in politics with me," Rachel muttered.

"How the hell did you get on the ship?" Kat asked.

Emma snorted, standing to glare at the rest of the crew. "Hundreds are dead, and your big concern is a Brit made it to the final nine. Typical."

"Get off your high horse, princess. You're the one who drew national lines. If you were border-blind, you wouldn't have started with separating yourself from 'all of' us," Kat retorted. "And frankly – you aren't a big anything. Do we want to know how and why you boarded the Intrepid? Sure. But I think we all know who'd be the quickest to pull a gun on the other if it meant surviving."

"Spies – the two-faced shits of the military," Ngawang drawled.

"Nobody likes a liar," Rachel agreed.

Leaning against the bars of her cage, Emma tapped the side of her helmet. "And nobody asked the good old U.S. of A to send a ship the size of London beyond our solar system. In fact, I specifically remember several United Nations' representatives speaking against the entire project – Academy and all."

"Hey now, how are we ever going to be *Star Trek* with that attitude?" Marie scolded.

"Joke all you want. Forget Earth's quite likely a pile of smoldering ash. Forget we're the only survivors of the Intrepid – the bloody Titanic of space. When those aliens return, die – one by one – or speed up their timeline. Taunt them," Emma seethed. "Mock them in their language or another. We still have no bloody idea what they want, and if that bastard is to be believed, they're well on their way to getting it."

Before any of the American crew could respond, the black metal of the entry wall rippled. Blue-Star entered followed by Tweedledee, Tweedledum, and almost two dozen of their cousins. A pair of Tweedles stood outside each of the ten survivors' cells. Their slick black suits shifted. Spots of darker and lighter blacks pooled along their spines like monsters waiting beneath the surface, straining to break free. Standing in the center of their cells, the women shifted from bickering humans to caged animals. Shivering, Kat forced her eyes down and bit her tongue. Reaching Lupita's cell, Blue-Star chuckled. The deep voice of the orbs vibrated across Kat's skin.

"And now there are nine." He turned to face Emma. "True. We're well on our way to what we want, and it's time you know what you've been brought here for – for the glory of Mah-Wærm."

"Whores?" Ngawang posited along the closed com.

The orbs spun, clicking onto the signal and translating. A snicker slipped from Blue-Star's mouth. "No. You have no reproductive value to us. Your genetics do offer some interesting new elements to our breeding programs, but we don't need you alive for that. Plus, with all of your dead comrades, you're really not necessary."

"But we're the ones that survived. Survivors are winners. Winners…" Ngawang trailed off, letting the points connect themselves.

Blue-Star rolled one shoulder, rubbing his metal hand over his shoulder. "Survivors are winners...such an optimist. No, we don't want nine of you."

"You just want one," Chelsea guessed.

"Yes," the insect alien confirmed. "You've been selected as Species Four."

"An honor, truly," Kat grumbled.

Shifting to face her, Blue-Star swaggered over to her cage. "Species One through Three already have their offering in the Riders, but now, the empire will have a full set."

"Four Riders?" Kat murmured, and her lips twisted into a smirk. "Like horsemen? Let me guess, the four will be called: Conquest, War, Famine, and Death."

"Yes," he confirmed.

A gasp rolled through the communication line, but Kat couldn't place who'd slipped until Marie asked, "So one of us is Death?"

"Don't be ridiculous." Blue-Star clapped his fingers against his palm. "First in, last out. Last in, first out. One of you will have the honor of being Conquest." Stepping back, the insectoid pressed a hand to the wall. As the bars clinked together and slid into the ceiling, the Tweedle guards shifted to face each other outside each cell. "Your genetic code and language are now synced to the mainframe, so let's get you all into some better housing." Glancing between the two outside her cell, Kat waited. None of the crew moved. With a wheezing sigh, Blue-Star crossed his arms behind his back. "Must we?"

50

Running her tongue along her teeth, Kat stepped outside between her cell's two Tweedles. "I'm half convinced your entire existence is some strange karmic justice for my habit of feeding bugs to my dog."

"Cute," Blue-Star clicked.

"Would I be able to kill you if I were Conquest?" Ngawang asked, stepping outside her cell. "Like – without consequences? Because if that's the case…" Her lips curled into a smirk. "I accept that title right now."

"You creatures are so…chatty." Blue-Star clapped the fingers on his right hand against his palm. "Grab and go."

The Tweedles grabbed Kat by her upper arms, dragging her through the entryway. Allowing them to lead her down the black halls of the ship, she glanced over her shoulder. Ngawang was behind her. Over each trio, a silver orb hung. Blue-Star walked along behind the other woman. His mask swirled, and he gestured at his eyes then pointed forward. Turning back around, Kat studied the long corridor. Seamless sheets of black metal spanned the length. Webs of glowing white nodes wove across the ceiling, lighting their way, but the nerve-cell like illuminants randomly painted the metal without any clear pattern. Like Bowie's Labyrinth, any other doors and rooms were hidden.

The Tweedles made a sharp right, walking straight at a wall, but they never hit it. Crossing through, they shifted direction, so Kat faced Ngawang. Between Kat and Ngawang, a semi-translucent wall lowered. When the floor shifted, Kat stumbled, but the Tweedles kept her in place.

"So…I'm calling you Tweedledee and Tweedledum," Kat admitted. No response. "Do you have names?" Still silence. "Okay…well, you are Tweedledee, and you," she said, looking at the man on the right, "are Tweedledum."

Neither masked extraterrestrial spoke. After a few seconds, Kat sighed. Tweedledee shifted. His fingers tightened, and the elevator jolted. The panels on Tweedledee's side cleared, revealing a star system never charted by humankind. She desperately tried to place the bright clusters of white dwarf stars. A lifetime love of astronomy meant she'd studied any image available of space, but the red giant which loomed closest matched nothing she could recall. As the ship glided through a system, a trio of planets caught her gaze. Artificial satellites orbited two of the three. However, the ships which passed between the two had Kat's jaw dropping.

"We're not in Kansas anymore, Tweedledee," she whispered.

The door to the elevator opened. As the Tweedles walked her down a new corridor, she struggled to slow their progress. Rooms lined the hall with large arched doorways. White stone rippled in gold. A large fountain sent crystal blue water up into the air. Stretching across one side of the hall was a pool the size of a lake. Plants in a thousand shades filled floating vases, and they were all empty. Footsteps echoed behind them. When Kat shifted to glance behind in hopes of seeing Ngawang, Tweedledum jerked her back around. Rising before them, pillars outlined a staircase into the most self-congratulating throne. Gold flared like an exploding star. Wires curled with colored glass, encasing a humanoid form. Dressed in a deep crimson robe, the alien wore the same opaque black helmet as the rest.

"I've never seen a motorcyclist in a toga. I can now die happy," Kat drawled, watching the orb above her head spike as she spoke.

Tweedledee and Tweedledum grabbed her shoulders, shoving her down. Her knees cracked as they slammed against the marble. The Tweedles released her arm. Though they stepped back and folded their hands behind their backs, tension tightened the muscles in her shoulders. If they had pressed a gun to her head, she wasn't certain she'd be any more stressed. On his throne, the alien didn't move. However, from behind, Ngawang and her Tweedles joined them. One by one, the remaining nine women were lined up on their knees before the marble throne. Blue-Star came up to stand between them and the throne.

"Glory to Mah-Wærm!" Blue-Star proclaimed, slamming his fist against his chest.

In unison, the Tweedles slammed their right fists to their chests: "Glory to Mah-Wærm!"

On his throne, the creature sighed. The echo sounded far more human than any noise Blue-Star, Thin-Limb, or the Tweedles ever had made. He lifted a single hand, pointing two fingers at each of the women as if counting. A second sigh followed.

"There's only nine," the alien said. "Where's the tenth?"

Blue-Star bowed his head. "The tenth activated the plasma failsafe."

Tossing his head back, the toga-wearing alien groaned. "Fucking bitch."

"You would've done the same," Rachel accused.

"Actually, I didn't," the alien informed the group. "I watched my comrades die, and I grew stronger. I learned what it is to be powerful. Last time the Riders gathered, I knelt before Famine. My brother begged for his life beside me, and when Gamalt slit his throat at Famine behest, I saw the weakness bleed from my species." Slouching, the new alien rested the side of his head against his fist. "Strip them."

The Tweedles turned and in a unified fluid motion, they tore apart each space suit, leaving the women naked before the marble throne. Ngawang puffed up her chest, glaring stalwartly ahead. Chelsea crossed her arms to cover her breasts, and Emma collapsed around her knees. Exposed to the alien's gaze, Kat gritted her teeth. While Blue-Star and the Tweedles had no interest in their nakedness, the seated alien leered. Marie arched her back. Though Ngawang and she struck the same pose, Marie's flirtatious smirk held the alien's gaze longer than Ngawang's fierce glare.

"You," the man pointed at Marie, "Stand."

Marie clucked her tongue, rolling her eyes, but she stood. Of all nine, she was the only one with curves that rivaled Marilyn Monroe's. Her brown curls bounced over her shoulders, and she slid one foot to a point to stand like Botticelli's Venus. Rising from his seat, the alien tossed his toga aside to reveal a swirling red and black suit as he approached her.

"You're the first guy to see this much without giving me a name first," Marie told him, and the alien chuckled.

"I am War," he proclaimed.

He spoke each word as if they made him a giant. Perhaps to those in this alien empire, it did. All Kat could see was the way his red melded into the black like blood absorbing through the floor. Then he slid his hands up to his neck. Cracking open along the midline like a zipper, the helmet detached from the suit. The sides folded backward, falling about his shoulders like a hood. Any metallic sheen faded, but the glinting swirls remained across his chest and limbs.

"I am War," he repeated.

Though heavily accented with a lingering hiss, he spoke the words. Hearing English from her enemy sent Kat's heart racing. Having translation tech know English had been bad enough. To hear it spoken raised bile in the back of her throat.

Marie's eyes widened. Pressing a hand against her left collar bone, she tilted her head, watching his face emerge. Tan skin appeared. Crimson red hair fell about his well-defined jaw. High cheekbones cut across his face. They looked more like prosthetics than bone. A line of black scales covered the left side of his neck. Those scales closest to his tan skin curled with graying edges like peeling calluses. Amber eyes blazed, absorbing the mixed reactions of the women before him.

Ngawang frowned. Her nose wrinkled while Emma and Rachel glowered down at the floor. Amondi, Aisling, and Chelsea watched him, but Marie remained the only one to respond with a smirk. Her eyes bounced between War's crotch and face. Qamar's brows furrowed.

War chuckled. His lips curled into a smirk. "I've been around lesser species for so long," he lamented. The words tumbled over each other as if the space between confused him. "How do I look?" he peeled off his suit, letting it fall about his waist.

From his pectorals to his abdomen, every muscle rippled as he put himself on display. With a spin, he flexed. Scales lingered on his right side beneath a scar running along the underside of his eighth rib. Every bit of hair fell perfectly into place. His eyebrows arched like a painting. Along his jaw line, there was the shadow of stubble.

"Not bad," Marie admitted.

Gasping in horror, Rachel glared at Marie, but the long-haired brunette ignored her. Shifting her arms to further cover herself, Rachel glared at War. Her eyes narrowed as Marie cocked one eyebrow. Marie's eyes sparkled as the bio-science officer tossed her hair over her shoulder. While the move seemed flirtatious, Kat watched her friend's focus. Blue eyes jumped from War's pupils to his neck's left side to his crotch. Kat followed. Dilated pupils – dark and consuming the yellow hue – a sign of attraction. He swallowed, and there was some definite downstairs movement. Kat frowned. Not that it guaranteed anything remotely penile. For all Kat knew, a third hand or second face could hide in his pants. Unlikely but possible. Still, based on Marie's smirk, she'd gotten what she'd been after.

"They're not contagious," War informed her, running a hand along his scales. "Curing yourself takes time."

Stepping closer to him, Marie stopped a few inches away. "May I?" she asked.

He tilted his head back and forth, but when she didn't move, he whispered, "Yes."

Her fingers ran down his side. They slid across the scales on his ribcage. "Does it hurt?"

"They itch," War stated, and their eyes met. Running a blue tongue across his bottom lip, he continued, "Before my selection, my nerve-endings were…different. Cold sent me to sleep. Now, I just shiver."

Marie slipped closer. "Shivering can be fun," she whispered.

As War moved to wrap an arm around her waist, the air beside him shimmered. A wraithlike being in a black suit appeared. It towered over War by a foot, and grabbing War's arm, it wrenched the red-haired alien back. As this new creature shifted, its spine bent like a question-mark. With a low sigh which resonated like a hollow tree, it stretched back into a humanoid spinal curvature. War's jaw dropped. The cocky alien babbled wordlessly as the black-suited one dragged him back, placing War on his throne. His fingers clenched around the arms of the golden wires. Sealing the red-head's helmet, the other alien stepped back.

"Thank you," War murmured, bowing his head.

The black-suited alien shrugged. A ripple passed along the long lines of its body. "You are young," the creature intoned. "Your body ready. Mind...not so much."

Marie slid back into place, but her eyes never left War's, and though his helmet hid the amber of his gaze, Kat would've bet anything he held Marie's too. Whatever plan rattled around Marie's head, Kat prayed it wouldn't be turned back on her. Lust motivated, but there was no endurance to it. If drawn out too long, it sputtered or burned everything down.

Beside the throne, another section of air shimmered. Waves rose and fell like heat off pavement. A white-suited alien arrived in its place. "This is why I didn't trust you to greet the new tributes," the white-suited man informed War.

"He is young," the black-suited alien repeated.

Crossing his arms, the white-suited alien sighed. "You don't have to defend him."

A rippling shrug passed through the tallest of the three. "He is my younger."

Kat glanced up at Tweedledum. "You've got a gun you can shoot me with?"

"He does; he won't," War called.

Rolling her eyes to look back at the throne, Kat shook her head. "Then get on with it."

"I do not like that one," the black-suited alien murmured.

Ngawang snickered, and Blue-Star growled, "Quiet!"

"Oh, Bel'von, let the poor things speak," War commanded with a wave of his hand.

58

The white-suited one tilted its head. "I doubt any of them have anything worthwhile to say."

"Let me go, and I'll kill every single one of these idiotic peons with my bare hands," Emma offered. She sneered, and all three tilted their heads. "Hell, I'll do it with my teeth."

"Famine?" The white-suited one glanced up at the black-suited.

"I do not like that one either," the black-suited alien stated.

"Well, by all means," Kat drawled. "Pick your favorite naked woman. I'm sure however we're acting now is exactly how we'll be in any circumstance."

"Pale horse?" Rachel asked, pointing at the white-suited alien. "Let me guess…you're Death."

"Old, white, condescending – it's like we never left Earth," Ngawang snarked as she leaned forward to look at Amondi.

Famine's shoulders drooped. The angle between them and his neck went obtuse, closer to one hundred and eighty degrees than they should have been. Even faced with at least three species of human-shaped extraterrestrials, Kat could not wrap her mind around how inhuman these humanoids were. They stumbled along an uncanny valley. As her mind adjusted, she sought humanity where there had no reason to be. Cracking her neck, she rolled her shoulders. Life or death – the decision was no longer hers. Kat stretched. Tension tightened the muscles in her spine. Beside War's throne, Famine mirrored her.

"There isn't much point in this," Bel'von muttered. "They're mentally unstable, emotionally feeble – a species evolved in looks alone."

Death shimmered, disappearing to reappear in front of the insectoid. Bel'von flinched; his whole body curled, recoiling, but Death grabbed his neck. His white suit flared, stretching to fan around Bel'von's neck. Nodes flashed a pale green along Death's arm. They slipped over to the black of Bel'von's suit, traveling down his chest and pressing against the blue star on his back.

"Do you question the wisdom of the Mah-Wærm? The emperor of a thousand galaxies? The God of the Empty Sea?" Death growled. The edges of his body vibrated. He shifted from opaque to translucent as if he were a ghost.

"No!" Bel'von clicked. Though his hands twitched, he kept them at his side. "Never."

"Then you believe War incapable of training them? Sorting them? Curing them?" the white-suited alien demanded.

"I do," Famine volunteered, raising its hand. Qamar smiled, lifting her hand as well. Famine pointed at her; its shoulders jumped back to a ninety degree angle. "That one, I like."

Throwing Bel'von back, Death transported to Famine's side. He slammed the taller alien's arm down. "Don't get attached," he warned.

"Yes, Jimmy," Kat mimicked, dropping her voice to a lower octave. "We can't keep them."

"Name: James – diminutive," Famine said. He tilted his head. "I don't understand."

War harrumphed. "She's mocking you."

Shoulders dropping, Famine bowed its chin to its chest. "I very much do not like that one."

"You need the practice. Your language acquisition speed isn't fast enough," Death commented.

Massaging the forehead of his suit, Death sighed. The gold wire swirled behind him. It formed a mobile around the three. Slipping between the marble stairs, the wire revealed the immateriality of the tier. War hadn't stepped far, but the wire passed through the marble with each pendulum swing. Famine lurked like a specter behind War. In all black, he stood in sharp contrast to this level of the ship, but a light sparked behind his mask. With each pass of the wire, two glowing spots flashed where his eyes might've been.

"As splendid as your forms may be, they are weak, quick aging, and feeble in mind. We will cure you," War proclaimed. His fingers wrapped tightly around the arms of his throne, but his left foot tapped.

Eyes dropping to his hands, Kat counted his finger and drummed her own against her thighs. Five stood out, a thumb and four more. Nothing external varied too greatly. His scales peeled, remains of whatever he had been. Biting her lip, she studied Death. Five-fingers and familiar proportions stared back. He moved like an athlete – a human one save for how he shimmered. Though he stood by War's side, the edges of his suit wavered, becoming translucent. A fog rose from his feet as if he stood in liquid nitrogen. Slouching back in his throne, the red-haired alien stared at the remaining nine. A decision lurked in his sudden silence, but Kat couldn't read any of the three well enough to guess.

Her eyes drifted over to Bel'von. His hands twitched, but he kept them down at his sides. Even a few feet away, she could see the crack. Long dull lines ran from his neck down his shoulders and across his upper back. Death had left marks. They ran around his neck. At their ends, there were thin, blue lines. Around his neck, white dents pressed scattered across his suit. Curving over the insect's shoulders, the longest trailed down the surface to pierce the star on his back. However, the ends of the lines sealed back together, inching their way back to completion. Not enough to vanish as she watched, but with time, they undoubtedly would. His fingers sharpened. Four knives brushed against his upper thigh. Shimmering in the deck's bright light, they didn't speak of malfunction or rebellion. Someone had to die. They were all waiting for War to say which.

"Kill me," Kat offered.

Death's face snapped around to look down at her. "What?"

"Kill me. If someone has to die right here, kill me." Inhaling, she held her breath, but none of the trio spoke. Clenching her jaw, she counted the seconds. Her teeth scratched against each other, grinding. "You're gonna kill one of us. I've got nothing left. I won't kill any of the women next to me. Given the chance, I'll let them kill me even if I have to make them do it, so if you need to assert your stupid control over us, kill me."

Death tilted his head. The mist shimmered around him, stretching as if to frame his shifting movements. As War sat forward, Famine fell back. The black-suited alien dropped down to sit on the arm

62

of the throne. Pressing a hand to its chest, Famine's shoulders drooped and stayed low even when War tapped the other on the side. Helmet bowed, Famine shimmered as if transporting away and back again in a loop. Death shook his head. The face of his white suit glimmered a pale green.

"No!" Aisling cried. "Kill me!"

"Don't you dare! If anyone's dying here, it's me," Rachel spat.

"Please, kill me instead," Amondi begged, reaching her hand around Ngawang toward Kat.

Ngawang's lip curled into a sneer. She shoved Amondi's hand back before any of the Tweedles could move. "She's not fucking Spartacus. If she wants to die, kill her. Some of us want to live."

"And some of us understand the desire to die," Amondi retorted.

"Ridiculous," Emma grumbled. "You are all the most dramatic women I've ever had the displeasure of working with." As she spoke, Ngawang whipped around, glaring at the Brit. Ngawang launched forward, but the Tweedles closest pulled her back.

"You fucking spineless bitch. Sold us out and now complaining about us. You aren't one of us," Ngawang accused.

Climbing to her feet, Kat yelled, "Enough!" Ngawang and Emma fell silent. A smirk twitched into place on Ngawang's face, but her eyes narrowed into daggers. Facing the throne of War, Kat held open her arms. "If you want someone who'll have a chance of standing beside you, kill me. If you want someone emotionally compromised and guaranteed to kill at least one of you." She pointed to Bel'von. "Definitely him." Waving her arms at the Tweedles, she added, "A good number of them probably. Then yeah, let me live. Waste your time and mine."

"Why?" War asked, watching her intently.

Crossing her arms over her chest, Kat explained, "One of them killed Jacobi. " Her eyes shifted to Famine. "It's a name. A male's name – a good name." Glancing back at War, she bared her teeth. "I can't stop you from attacking Earth. My guess is you've already got a crew sent that way. My parents and friends...I can't save them, but I saved Jacobi. I got us to the escape pod, but you took him from me. You stole him. One of these things," she tilted her head at Tweedledum, "shot him. And he wore Jacobi's face," Kat gestured at Bel'von. "Jacobi was mine, and I was his. We're a matched set. I won't live in a world without him, but as long as I'm here, I'll destroy anyone and anything that took him from me. You can stick me with wires, set me against them, I don't care. I love him, and you took us from each other. I won't be kept here, not without destroying myself and everything that's not human on this ship. I won't be your weapon."

Death hummed. In a flash, he stood before her, but any hope she had for relief vanished. At the far end of the line, Emma doubled over. Blood poured from a hole through her neck.

"You'll learn," Death told her. "We always learn."

Chapter Five

Though no face haunted her, the wraithlike helm of Death remained even after the remaining eight crew members of the Intrepid had been left alone. Like an archaic sanitarium, padded walls and floors formed their new prison. Eight black suites hung on the far wall. While the smooth, soft texture reminded Kat of cotton, the interior bore black metallic lines like the floor panel. She pulled one on, and it conformed to fit the athletic, straight lines of her body, but when Kat lifted her eyes, the suits melded to the varying sizes and curves of the women around her.

"Hey," Marie grinned. "It's our traveling pants."

"Shut up, Marie," Rachel grumbled, crossing her arms over her chest.

Ngawang snorted. Bumping hips with the biologist, she smirked at Rachel. "Shut up yourself."

"I still feel naked," Chelsea grumbled. Her hands traced down her sides against the deceptively thick material. "No helmets though."

"Course not. When they have us kill each other, they want us to know we did it willingly – knowingly," Amondi stated.

Flexing her arms, Kat watched the exterior material shift. Armor plating rose across her body. A metallic sheen flashed. Contained beneath synthetics once more, Kat breathed a sigh of relief. She stretched her arms and fell back against the padded floor. Everything around them reflected light. White floors, ceilings, and walls without a door in sight. They had come through the wall like Bel'von down in the brig, but Kat didn't want to try to open anything just yet. A door without boundary offered numerous dangers. Now wasn't the time for risks. Unable to sleep since the fall of the Intrepid, she stared up at the ceiling before closing her eyes. The floor bounced when people fell on either side of her.

"Sleep sounds good," Marie murmured from Kat's right.

Ngawang familiar scoff sounded from her left. A finger flicked against Kat's ear. "Don't be stupid again."

Opening her eyes, Kat whispered, "Jacobi's dead." Every time she said the words aloud, Kat's heart ached.

"Yeah. He's dead. You aren't, so you're going to pull yourself back together, and we're going to get this done," Ngawang informed her, flicking her ear again. "I plan on surviving, but I'd prefer not to do it alone."

"Then you weren't paying attention," Rachel scolded.

"Yeah, yeah - all but one of us is going to die. I heard the shtick. Doesn't mean everyone has to jump on that grenade early," Ngawang retorted.

"Someone's going to be stuck being brainwashed and experimented on for who knows how long. Least the rest of us can do is last as long as possible," Marie agreed.

Sitting beside Marie, Rachel pulled her knees to her chest. She wrapped her thin arms around them and rested the sharp point of her chin on her arm. Her brown eyes fell to the white floor, staring blankly at the padding spread beneath them. Qamar shifted from one foot to the other until Marie held open her arms. Curling against her friend, Qamar released a dry sob then buried her face in Marie's shoulder. Sitting down between Kat and Marie, Amondi tugged the two closer, so the group of four huddled together. With a huff, Ngawang shifted closer as Aisling wrapped her pale arms around the other's waist. The red-headed woman pressed her cheek into Ngawang's back.

"Come on down, Chelsea," Aisling called, and the blonde scuttled down beside her friend.

In a pile, the last eight survivors clung to each other. Human and vulnerable, they silently mourned what they had lost and what was to come. Their voices faded into the walls. Every bit of padding took away the echo. The soundlessness left them floating as if they sat on a cloud. Kat frowned up at the ceiling. They would never survive the fall. Exhaustion weighed down on her. With each blink, she kept her eyes closed a bit longer. Danger remained, but surrounded by the warmth of her comrades and the coldness sitting inside her heart, Kat did not care if she woke.

Between one blink and the next, she slept. The explosion replayed in her mind. A sudden form appeared on the radar. Screams echoed. Fire erupted through their level, but she had urged Jacobi onward. He would have tried to save everyone given the chance. There was the difference between them. Though Jacobi had followed her to space, he had been the idealist of the two. Kat wanted adventure. She wanted to get away from the uncertainties of Earth, but Jacobi was a good person - empathetic, heroic.

Somewhere in the mix, War invaded. His amber eyes lurked like double suns, watching everything inside her head from afar. As her dream world shifted from the Intrepid to Tatooine, Kat screamed. Red light shot through space, swallowing the planet.

Sitting up straight, Kat gasped for breath. Her pulse raced, spiking further when she realized the black spot before her was War. He crouched over her. The blood red splash across his chest swirled.

"Do the humans have that weapon? The...Death Star?" he asked.

With a sigh, she glanced around at her crewmates. They were all still soundly sleeping. Biting her tongue, she studied War with a frown.

"Sound military logic tells me to say no," Kat informed him.

His helmet slid down around his shoulders to reveal his grinning face. Bright white sparkled, but his large canines drew her attention. While the rest of his teeth appeared capped, the fangs were a slightly different shade of white than the rest. Running a hand through his hair, he slipped back to kneel in the gap between Kat's hip and where Marie had sprawled across Amondi's stomach. His hand fell from his hair, sliding beside the arm Marie had thrown over her head.

"Mah-Wærm doesn't have a centralized planetary system. Well," War hummed, tilting his chin up. "He has a single planet in close orbit to a white dwarf, but he's only there when curing us."

"What if we don't want to be cured," Kat asked.

"You won't survive like you are. He has plans for you…one of you. They understand it takes time. You need to become used to the idea, but one of you will get there. Then, you'll take the role on willingly. It's always a choice in the end," the red-haired alien explained.

When his eyes slid to Marie again, Kat looked away. If Marie wanted to use her beauty and intelligence to manipulate War that was up to her, but there was a childlike wonder in his eyes when he looked at Marie. She was a strange and wondrous star. War could not resist falling into her orbit. Jacobi had looked at Kat like that long before she recognized what that look meant. Every little piece of the familiar and the foreign reminded her of him; the ache burrowed deeper with each recall. Sliding out of the group pile, she stumbled. Her hair and body pulled upward as if gravity failed to hold her down.

"Wires," she whispered. "You've got us plugged in. This room…?"

"Famine designed it. Mah-Wærm wished him to understand emotions and their uses. He created this to learn. My cohort was the first in this room. Yours will be the last," War told her. His eyes never left Marie.

Kat frowned, furrowing her brows. "This is a dream."

"Yes."

Her fingers curled into fists by her side. "Good."

When she threw the first punch, he flew back. His eyes widened. They closed only once he slammed into the padded wall behind him. War's brows furrowed. Pushing away from the wall, his eyes widened as his hands sunk into the padding. The harder he pulled, the harder it held him. As if in a microwave, the white marshmallow substance grew. It flowed over War's shoulders, collapsing back and dragging him into the wall.

"What is this?" his eyes narrowed.

"Humans can become lucid dreamers." Kat's lips curled into a smile, but the expression failed to reach her eyes. "Jacobi and his brother got into the idea when we were young, so I did too. Never thought it would be useful. I didn't have the nightmares Thaddeus did."

"The younger brother," War posited. With a curt nod, he tugged against the fluff. "This is unusual."

The world shifted, and the two returned to Tatooine without the other seven women. War knelt. Dark chains curled about his wrists. Stalking toward him, Kat lifted the familiar weight of her Academy-issued pistol. War clawed at the chain around his throat. Towers of black metal erupted through the desert sand. One of the two suns swirls, churning as if being pulled into a black hole. Though the second star remained, the yellow light shined red as it expanded.

Red fiery flares pressed closer. They burned across the atmosphere, threatening to consume the planet below. War's eyes widened, but the tension ended in his forehead. He bore his teeth without any real anxiety. Either he had more control than he revealed, or his invasion wasn't dangerous. If death within the dream wouldn't kill him, there was no satisfaction in pulling the trigger. Lowering the pistol, she ran a hand through her long dark hair.

"You're in theirs too. How much of this will you even remember?" she asked.

War's lips slipped over his teeth and contorted into a frown. "Everything."

Staring into the rage of the growing red giant, Kat closed her eyes. "Good."

Her dream shifted from science fiction and fantasy to memories. A green field stretched for acres. Bright bunches of flowers popped up. None of their colors mattered. Two children raced. A boy and a girl ran, laughing as they pushed each other. Their hands met. Fingers brushed only to slip apart.

Jacobi's smile when they were eight years old had been her favorite sight then. In his batting helmet, he held a slingshot in one hand and a tennis ball in the other. She'd worn his baseball glove on the wrong hand, swinging a tennis racket over her head. With paint on her overalls and her father's beekeeping hood over her face, eight-year-old Kat laughed. Imaginary dragons flew overhead. A pair of knights fought against the impossible.

Watching her memories play, Kat walked over to War. She dug her fingers into his red hair. Her nails scratched over his scalp. "Pay close attention," she commanded.

Years together and apart in classrooms just seconds away played around them. Long summer days spent carrying Jacobi's younger brother, Thaddeus, to the town pool and back again. Kids in charge of a toddler. In her backyard, surrounded by her dogs and a stray chicken, they had built a rocket ship instead of a tree house. Her father walked them through every step. Sitting hip to hip on the porch swing, she sketched the design while he told stories of what they would do. When she had cut her hair in a fit of frustration before high school, he'd shaved his even though Jacobi hated his ears. No matter who tried to come between them, they stayed side by side. He was hers; she was his. Dating didn't matter. She'd never understood the point of it anyway.

Snow gathered on the ground, and Christmas Eve formed. Sitting at the kitchen table, she glared at her hot cocoa. Fifteen and certain she knew everything, the Kat from that time complained, "They keep pushing back the opening date for the National Aeronautics and Exploration Academy. What if it isn't open in time? We're graduating in two years!"

"Then you transfer in," Jacobi suggested, counting his mini-marshmallows.

"It's going to be part of the Air Force. They won't let people just 'transfer in,'" Kat retorted.

War rolled his eyes. "What's the point of this?"

"I spent my life desperate to get out. Not of the town or the house, the entire planet. There was never another option in my mind," Kat stared at the teenager she had been.

Six years separated them, but she drifted worlds away. She was light years away. A whole star system separated her from this girl. Thaddeus entered, just having turned five. He grabbed the bag of marshmallows and set about building a tower, but Jacobi's younger brother ate more than he put into the structure's walls. Fifteen-year-old Kat reached across the table to stop him.

"Hey!" Thaddeus cried. "They're mine!"

"We share," Jacobi said without looking up.

"You can't eat the whole bag. You'll get sick," Kat scolded, but Thaddeus simply puffed his cheeks.

Jacobi sighed. "Now he's going to hold his breath."

"Yeah, well, then keep holding it 'cause I'm stuck pausing my life for the next two years. What am I even supposed to do? They've moved it back to 2131. I mean, seriously, it's ridiculous," Kat grumbled, flopping back in her chair.

Setting his mug back on the table, Jacobi shifted to face her and said, "…"

Frowning, Kat waited. The memory blurred, and she rounded on War in a rage. "What did you do?"

War shimmered then appeared in front of her. "You don't teach me. I teach you."

"And what are we learning in a dream? That I can't escape you. Already learned. That you don't give a damn about invading my privacy? Again, you taught us all that in front of that stupid marble throne of yours," Kat exclaimed. Fire rained down around them. "If you've got a lesson to teach, get it over with. Actually…" She held up her hand. The pistol had returned. "Screw this."

And she shot herself in the head.

***

"I bet you Marie stays asleep the longest," Ngawang said as Kat woke.

"Nobody's taking that bet," Rachel replied.

Opening her eyes, Kat groaned as the bright white of the room blinded her. As she sat up, she glanced around, counting those awake and those asleep. The only ones still under were Marie and Chelsea. Both sprawled comatose on the ground. Everyone else milled around the room as if afraid to fall asleep again. Pressing the heel of her palms against her eyes, Kat groaned.

"Morning, Sunshine," Ngawang grinned down at her.

Sitting up, Kat sighed. "How long was I out?"

"No idea. Not much longer than Amondi," Rachel told her. "Why'd you wait so long to kill him? I thought you'd be pretty quick about it."

Kat's whole body tensed. Her muscles tightened as her mind raced. Raising her left hand, she pressed her fingers against the left side of her head. When the bullet had ripped through her skull, a bang had echoed in her ear. Even awake, a metallic taste coated her tongue. Reaching back, she pulled Thomas's pin out of her hair.

"Kat?" Rachel pressed.

Dropping her hand, Kat hummed. "He wasn't my top priority."

"Nightmares?" Aisling asked, sitting beside her. "A bunch of pink elephants showed up in mine. Then this gigantic coconut crab came after me. War popped up. Killing him was only an accident; I missed the crab."

Running her hands over the pin, Kat shrugged. "Apparently, shooting yourself also works."

Aisling gasped as Ngawang rolled her eyes and walked away. Crouching down, Rachel bit her lip. The brunette's brows furrowed. They wasted their time. No one was coming. Nobody could come. Only one of them would live, and the more they invested in others, the less likely that one was to be them. Guilt settled in her stomach like a stone. Pulling her knees to her chest, Kat pressed her left hand against her head. Her body ached from the inside.

"Did he not show up?" Rachel asked.

When she didn't answer, Aisling ventured, "Jacobi showed up, didn't he?"

One by one, Kat pulled the pins from her bun. "It'll be fine."

Rachel frowned; her lips pressed into a thin line. "That's not what either of us asked."

Kat hooked the pins together. "I know."

"You lucid dream," Ngawang accused, storming back over to them. "How could you kill yourself in a lucid dream? You keep wallowing! It's ridiculous!"

Kat's hair fell over her shoulder. Running her hands through it, she glanced up at Ngawang. "Don't suppose anyone's found anything sharp." As she spoke the gloves on her suit shifted, the fingers sharpened into knives. "Never mind."

When she slices through the first handful, Ngawang huffed and walked away. Hair grew. Kat never found it valuable, and she had worn hers in whatever fashion provided her the easiest mornings for years. Cutting her hair wouldn't bring Jacobi back. No matter how much DNA she left behind, he wouldn't spontaneously leap up from the floor - healthy and whole. That reality haunted her. Every moment filled with a desperate desire to find him. To look over her shoulder and see him standing there. With Jacobi, she could have withstood anything, and that reliance would get her killed. Kat couldn't reach beneath her skin and cut Jacobi out. Whether she liked it or not, he was there. A piece of her. Her hair, however, she could remove it all.

Chunks dropped around her in a dark, misshapen circle. With each strand, Kat imagined a memory of Jacobi drifting away. Every school lunch spent together. Each summer they had been inseparable. Bits and pieces of her fell to the floor. They took pieces of him away, leaving her less herself. Like a metamorphosis, Kat reduced back to the basics. Melting underneath the pressure and the heartache. When she solidified, maybe that person could deal with Jacobi's death. Her crew needed her. The women around her were the last remnants of Earth, and she couldn't protect them if she remained as she was. Grief dragged her down, but cutting the anchor sent her scattered to the sea. Pulling herself back together would take time. Time, they didn't have.

"Here," Rachel stood, bringing her own sharpened fingers close beside Kat's. "Let me help you."

"Shave it down," Kat whispered. "Please."

A small voice in her called out. With those claws, Rachel could end all her pain in one swift move. Kat bit her tongue. Asking that wasn't fair. The universe mocked them all cruelly. In the belly of an enemy ship, they waited for torture. Nothing in this world or the next was fair. Still, she kept her mouth shut. Aisling ran a hand through her red hair. The copper strands pooled, running through her fingers. Her bright blue eyes jumped to Kat's head.

Shifting to kneel before Kat, she asked, "Do me."

Metal hands slipped through red hair, forming a new semi-circle between Kat's knees and Aisling's back. Rachel silently continued her task. Sharp hands slid over the brunette's scalp. Across the newly exposed skin, a chill settled. Amondi watched them from the corner. Her dark kinky curls had been shaved before she had ever stepped on the Intrepid. Ngawang kept a tight bob. Her hair barely reached the bottom of her ears. Sitting down facing Aisling, Rachel sighed. Her fingertips brushed the edges of her brown, shoulder-length hair.

"What about you, Qamar?" She called instead.

Qamar shrugged. Her curls tightly braided and wound into a bun on her head. Though she did not complain, her hands drifted upward about her face as if to adjust the hijab that wasn't there. Against the wall opposite of Amondi, she sat, staring at the white wall.

"Shaved or short?" Kat asked Aisling.

Fingers clenched on her thighs, Aisling replied, "Short as you can without cutting me."

As Kat slid her fingers a few centimeters above the crown of Aisling's head, a laugh rang from the floor where Chelsea and Marie still laid.

"You will be assimilated," Marie proclaimed, doing the robot as she sat up. She chuckled when her eyes caught Kat's. "Man, where'd we get the knife? And why aren't we cutting through this pillow shit?"

A smile curled at the ends of Ngawang's lips. "Hell yeah."

"Wait!" Aisling exclaimed; her hands shot up into the air. "Chelsea's going to wake up last! I win the bet!"

"We didn't bet," Rachel retorted.

Aisling scoffed as Kat finished her hair. Turning, the linguist crawled over to Marie. "Rachel and Ngawang thought you'd be last."

"Well...I don't dream biologically unrealistic dreams." Marie smirked, her eyes narrowing. Jumping to her feet, she threw her arms to her side. "Unless I'm flying! Bam! Plane!"

Watching the brunette run around in circles making motor noises, Ngawang sighed. "I'm going to miss you when you die."

"You know it, bitch," Marie cheered.

Stepping around Rachel, Kat slid up beside Chelsea. The blonde's eyes moved rapidly beneath her eyelids, flickering back and forth. Kat pressed two fingers to Chelsea's neck underneath her jaw. Though her eyes moved fast, her pulsed lagged. Even without a watch to time, the long gaps between beats dropped a solid weight in Kat's stomach. She adjusted the other woman's arm, rolling Chelsea onto her side as if she were drunk rather than in a strange technologically induced coma. Worst case scenario, Chelsea died. As the blond was a self-proclaimed pacifist, dying in her sleep might be the most merciful act.

"You realize we could just kill all but one of us with these," Ngawang commented, wiggling her fingers in front of her face. They shifted back and forth between knives and gloves.

"Sure, let's beat them to it!" Rachel exclaimed, exaggerating her cheer sardonically. "Anyone besides Kat going to volunteer to die? Huh, weird. Nobody's jumping on that great idea."

"Oh, screw you," Ngawang grumbled.

Slicing her hands down the wall, she peeled back the fabric. Tightly packed foam remained beneath. Ngawang growled and pulled out the foam. Somehow, it seemed whiter than the fabric. Everything in the room made Kat want to claw her eyes out. It was like staring into a nuclear reaction. Bright and all consuming, the room set her nerves on edge. Kat sighed. When Ngawang had her arm up to the elbow into the wall, she turned her attention to the floor. The foam melted in its piles like snow. Draining towards the edges of each pillowed cushion, the foamy liquid sunk into the fabric. As Ngawang dug her way through the floor, Qamar leaned against the wall.

"I don't understand. He had access to our heads. Was he digging through our memories? Testing our capacity to kill? Seeking information about Earth's defenses? All of it? Or did the violation just happen because he could?" Qamar asked. Covering her eyes, she groaned. "What sort of world is this? We're stuck here, knowing only one of us will live. We're stuck. Pretending we're alive. Decaying here. In this room."

"Great. First, Kat. Now, you," Ngawang complained, glaring at the wall as it stitched itself back together. "I can't be the only not depressed one."

"Two of eight does not make a majority," Amondi retorted.

Slicing a square of the fabric from the wall, Ngawang bent it. "Whatever. I bet we could embed Chelsea in the floor."

A laugh bubbled up, escaping from Kat despite herself. "We're not entombing her."

Ngawang held the fabric, closing one eye to study the fabric. "She'll die soon, and the floor will eat her anyways."

"Emma didn't get go through the floor," Aisling pointed out.

"Maybe it's the level. Dungeons have self-cleaning torture floors. This is sanitarium chic," Marie suggested, falling to lie beside Chelsea. She reached over. Using a finger to move the unconscious woman's lips, she sang in a higher pitch voice, "Someday my prince will come! Someday..."

"Marie, I'm going to bite those fingers if you keep sticking them in my face," Chelsea grumbled. Blinking, she shoved the other woman back.

"And she's up!" Marie cheered.

When the cool wave of relief failed to arrive, Kat stood. Metal pressed against her skin, and as the suit hummed against her skin, she pushed her concerns to the back of her mind. Modesty hadn't inspired her rush to dress. The suit contained material and technology which she had never seen before. Black knives stretched then receded into her fingers. Clawing at the floor, Ngawang dug onward. Fluff melted into fluid behind her, but even as it poured back into place, she just kept digging. Her brown eyes narrowed, and her brow furrowed.

"How did they even get into our heads?" Chelsea asked, her voice interrupting Kat's thoughts.

Marie shrugged. "The suits definitely. The room might also help."

"There's no tech here," Ngawang announced. "Unless everything is in the ceiling, the signal has to be going to our suits."

"Then fine," Chelsea pulled at her collar, but the suit didn't move. Eyes widening, she clawed at her body. "It won't come off!"

"Who's surprised?" Rachel drawled, and when Aisling rolled her eyes, the brunette clucked her tongue at Chelsea. "Huh, just you."

Their voices rose. A buzzing white noise of sarcasm and distress. Anxiety clashed with defense mechanisms. No happiness would result. Closing her eyes, Kat named and narrow the sensations, running along her body. Every inch of her flooded with a coolness just warm enough to be vaguely comfortable. Her fingers tingled. The bones in them creaked as she flexed and extended them. Pain spread from her lower abdomen. Heat followed, spreading up her spine. No urge to eat. No urge to defecate or urinate. Even the saliva in her mouth balanced level. Running her tongue along her teeth, Kat stretched her neck to one side then the other. She blinked. The noise threatened to drown her thoughts.

"They've already started the transformation," she murmured, but nobody listened.

Qamar remained near catatonia. Unresponsive as she stared blankly ahead. Covering her ears, Amondi whispered to herself. Kat hadn't ever mastered lip reading, but as the phrase repeated, she had some idea of what the other said.

Over and over again, Amondi pleaded, "I don't want to die. I don't want to die."

Rachel's cheeks flushed. Arms crossed over her chest, she spat, "How did an idiot like you survive but Dr. Cho's dead?"

"I'm not an idiot," Chelsea retorted. "And it's not my fault she died."

"The surviving ten were all between twenty and twenty-five," Aisling pointed out as Ngawang hacked through the floor.

"Stop that, Ngawang!" Rachel commanded, tugging at her dark brown hair.

Dark eyes rising from her task, Ngawang glared. Her arms continued to slash into the floor, digging through the fabric and the insulation without a solid exterior in sight. At the tips of Kat's fingers, claws extended. Eight women scattered around the room, but all she could see were spots of black in a white expanse. With a sigh, she trudged to the far wall where Bel'von had opened a doorway. The white wall seemed no different from the rest. They all stood in large expanses up to the white ceiling. Smooth fabric spread in diamond pillows over every inch. Retracting the sharp edges of her fingers, Kat pressed. Through the gaps in her fingers, the slight rises of the white fabric protruded like the ridges of a skeleton's spine.

Lips pressed into a thin line, Kat pressed her palm against the wall. She recalled the large archway in her mind, but while she had transformed her hands in a similar way, the wall stood unchanged. Any change in the suit remained in the suit. War and the others had given the human survivors tools to kill each other but no escape. Standing her fingers on end, Kat pushed. Her pointer finger sharpened. The claw burrowed into the fabric. With it, so too did Kat's perception. Like a piece of her body, she could feel the spiraling black metal pierce inch by inch. A chill ran down her spine. On the back of her neck, the small hairs stood on end.

When the wall shook, Kat sensed the trembling through the claw before it trembled up her arm and sent her stumbling backward. Her fingers returned to normal size. As the doorway reopened, Rachel and the rest fell silent. All eyes turned to the door. Dread crawled like corrosive foam up Kat's throat. Tension tugged at her muscles. Every inch of her body screamed to run, but there was nowhere to go. Catching her footing, Kat bent her knees, sliding into a boxing stance. Her fingers flexed. Knives expanded from their edges. From her spine, long twisted tubes of black stretched. They dove into the floor and walls, blocking the rest of the women from view.

"If you're that eager, by all means – you can go first," Bel'von taunted.

Free of his helmet, his golden skin and compound eyes shimmered in the bright room. His mandibles receded. Lips closing, they contorted. The ends twitched up and down as if connected to a string. Rising from the crown of his head, his antennae cast the stringy curtain in front of his face. Kat steeled herself, certain he would show her Jacobi's death mask; instead, a different face arose. Blue eyes looked out at her. Thick, ash brown hair gathered around high cheek bones. When thin pink lips spread and exaggerated laughter lines, Kat swallowed and blinked, hoping to spread the tears gathering in her eyes rather than shedding them. Before she died, this would be the last time Kat saw her mother's face. Every freckle wormed into her soul. Though she wanted to look away, she couldn't bear to move her eyes. Warm hands belonged to those blue eyes. Loud laughter and soft advice came from those lips.

"I'd say you know better, but a doubt little larva you even knew your mother," Kat said. All her spite fell flat.

Bel'von's gurgling laughter broke through the veil. "I know my God's face. Can you say half as much?"

Raising her left arm, she wrapped her right hand around her elbow. The black suit shifted. Dark metal spread, covering her fingers. Coils wrapped around and formed the barrel of a gun. Warm curled around Kat's back. As Bel'von's antennae recoiled into his golden skin, she laughed. Bouncing off the walls, her laughter thundered through the room. Clarity flooded her. Within her bones and blood, certainty curled inside her flesh. Everything was absurd. Every single creature in the universe had been born to die. Nothing she did could matter. Like Jacobi, she would die. Anyone who loved her would too. An abyss swallowed every accomplishment of men and women far greater than her. Meaning came from one place. Plasma crackled in the metal tube.

"God is dead, and we have killed him," she said and discharged her gun.

Bel'von's eyes widened. One of the Tweedles jumped in the way, but as the blast surged into the nameless alien, the Tweedle slammed backwards, colliding with Bel'von and throwing them both backwards. Tweedles bled red. Thicker than human blood, the Tweedle's corpse splattered across Bel'von's body. Pus-colored globs gathered around his joints. It oozed alongside the tomato-paste blood. Heat poured off the metal spikes connecting her to the walls. Hitting the metal frame of the room, the spikes spread along the walls toward the doorway.

"Ridiculous," Bel'von growled, tossing the dead Tweedle off of him. Blood and pus slid down his suit. "Do you really think we'd just give you our suits unchecked?"

Kat sent another plasma bolt at the insectoid. The blue star on his back migrated to his arm. Black metal spread, forming a shield with the blue marking at the center. He ducked, slamming into the blast with his shield. Electricity dispersed along the edges. Snapping and crackling against the edges of metal, a large portion slid off to hit the Tweedles behind him. Another fell. Tacky blood and pus gushed from a small hole in his side. Red spurted as the Tweedle clicked, begging to be saved. Stepping over their injured comrade, the rest of the Tweedles formed a shield wall. Their armor expanded to blockade the door.

"Hell, yeah, Parker! This is what I'm talking about!" Ngawang cheered.

Her fingers sharpened as she raced forward. Sliding beneath one of the spikes, Ngawang threw herself into the fray. She swiped her hand across a Tweedle's chest. Slamming her fist into the creature's throat, Ngawang roared victorious as the alien fell to the ground.

From her wall, Qamar screamed. Her suit swirled. Black crawled up her neck like living liquid. Crossing over the top of her head, the suit formed a hijab as Qamar raced across the room with Marie at her side. Above their heads, the silver orbs shifted, jumping about the room as if seeking unsure of what to do with themselves.

Kneeing a Tweedle in the groan, Marie smashed his face into the ground, shattering the black helm. Green and gold skin covered a narrow face. While lips covered Bel'von's mandibles, the Tweedle's displayed without any skin folds and his compound eyes took up the majority of his face. Whatever transformation Mah-Wærm gave to Bel'von had clearly not been passed along to the rest.

Detaching from the wall, Kat slammed against Bel'von's shield. He pressed her backwards even as the long tendrils rounded him. When the first one pierced his back, Kat's mind blanked. His blood was thinner. It poured across the white floor, smearing red in their wake.

"You think you're the first primitive I've dealt with?" Bel'von growled, snapping the metal tendril in two. He shoved her back. His hand slammed against her jaw and threw her against the floor.

Pain radiated along Kat's back. Spots danced across her vision as her head back hit the metal floor. "Primitive? I've seen your Riders; I'm your evolutionary wet dream."

"An emotionally weak creature incapable of placing progress before its own petty vendetta?" Bel'von gurgled, laughing in her face as he pinned her to the ground with his shield. "I could kill you. Slam a spike right through your head, and none of them would complain. You're only alive as long as I let you live."

"Then do it," Kat growled.

Bel'von's eyes crinkled as his mandibles contorted his smile. "You'd like that, wouldn't you? I know you're kind. Think death will fix it all. No...I'm going to make sure you live a long time."

"Bug thinks he can elect me Conquest. Wonder what Death would think," she retorted.

The Tweedles contained the other seven women. Blood dripped from Ngawang's nose, and a bruise purpled around Marie's eye, but she grinned at the ground even as a Tweedle shoved her to her knees. From face to face, Kat's eyes shifted, and each one glowed with pride. A cruel trick of fate clawed through. Though there was a chance they would fight beside each other again, a greater likelihood remained their next battle would be pulled punches. Their next enemy – each other.

Lifting Kat to her feet, Bel'von wrenched her arms on top of one another. Like magnets, they slammed together. Blue spread out, binding her arms to each other and to her abdomen right below her breasts. Defenseless, she ground her teeth. The Tweedles escorted the other seven out, and as the insectoids dragged them from the room, Bel'von lagged behind the rest. His shield retracted. Shifting back onto his back, the blue star shimmered.

"I'm going to kill one of them," he whispered to her. "And you won't be able to prove a thing."

"You just admitted it, so…" Kat tried to shrug, but he shoved her into the wall.

Leaning in close, Bel'von clicked. The silver orb flew in close to translate. "I don't think you understand the situation. I'm the next phase. You think that dream invasion was just for fun? War's found your weaknesses. He knows what you fear, and now I get to push you until you break, and I get to decide when it's over. Be a pity if one of you pathetic ape's died."

"Not much of a threat. Eight of us are going to die anyways," she reminded him.

"But which whose death is going to set off the worst chain?" Bel'von asked. "Kill Ngawang. Things calm down. Kill Marie, and the tension increases."

"Pretty sure War's not going to be happy if you kill Marie."

The insectoid laughed. "You stupid woman. You really think one lustful overture would be enough to emotionally manipulate War?"

"I think he has a strong mating instinct," Kat drawled. "And females of the ideal species are finally around."

Before he spoke, Bel'von's lips curled into a smirk. He held her neck in his metal hand. "You don't

88

believe that." His eyes shifted. The glimmering planes lifted just enough for her to guess where his gaze fell before his hand slid from her neck to her shaved head. "Deep down, you know that whichever one I kill, I picked because of you. Nobody else thought about it. Just you."

"And you don't believe that."

Pulling back, he dragged her down the hall. His lips pressed into a thin line. The long bright halls and overflowing decadence fail to take her eyes off the orb shimmering over her head. If it translates, it hears, and if it hears, there was a chance the thing recorded. Spies in the air. Kat would be lying if she said she had never imagined ruling the world. Every child played pretend after all. She had never thought of such a simple way to control the world. Let them rely on robots to translate everything. Every linguistic group in every species would grow lazy, and their secrets spilled down the line. Her lips curled at the corners. A strange kinship warmed the abyss Jacobi left within her. As cocky as Bel'von's proclamation was, any chance of the orbs being a recording device added a new layer. Either his arrogance stemmed from an erroneous belief that he could control what had been heard or ignorance that such a device could be used against him.

They reached a short dark corridor with four chairs on either side. Tweedles stood in between them. Pulling her arms in front of her, Bel'von ran his hand along her forearms where they were bound. His eyes met hers. Though his lips curled into a smirk, the muscles about his eyes remained motionless. He tossed her at a Tweedle, who shoved her into the last empty chair. Bel'von marched down the hall.

With a hum, he grabbed Marie by her long brown hair. "Lucky girl. You're first."

Chapter Six

Seconds passed into minutes. Silence reigned, and all eyes flicked to the door at the slightest noise, but it remained closed. With their hands in fists at their sides, the Tweedles remained. Marie's life hung in a constant state of unknown. Like Schrodinger's cat, she was both dead and alive as long as she stayed with Bel'von beyond the other women's sights. Leaning back against the wall, Kat forced her eyes to the ceiling. In the otherwise bright level, this corridor stood as a stark and misplaced black rectangle. Light flooded in the end from whence they came. Darkness swallowed the opposite. Shifting her shoulders, Kat held back a groan. The angle of her bindings left an ache in her upper back. Without dislocating at least one elbow, she couldn't shift her shoulders enough to ease the pressure.

When the door finally opened, Bel'von walked out. Marie lay unconscious on the floor. Blood caked her neck. It trickled from her lips and dripped onto the floor. Bel'von's eyes met each woman's. His smirk grew as he dragged Marie by her wrist. Her chest rose and fell. Kat bit her lip, swallowing a sigh of relief. Bruised and bloody but still alive. As horrible as the pain would get, it was the last part which mattered most.

"Get her out of here," Bel'von commanded.

Two Tweedles stepped forward. They took her under each arm and carried her away. No one moved to protest. Each woman watched without a word. Fear might have kept some silent, but guilt held Kat's tongue. When Bel'von grabbed Qamar, panic sent Kat's heart racing. Qamar set her eyes forward, but she jogged to keep from being dragged. When the door swirled shut behind her, a breath Kat hadn't realized she held slipped out.

"Well, this sucks," Rachel grumbled.

None of the Tweedles moved.

Raising a brow, Aisling frowned. "They weren't going to space her, right?"

"Hey!" Ngawang kicked the Tweedle to her left. "Where did they take her?"

The Tweedle didn't move even as Ngawang kept kicking him. Aisling shifted in her chair to look at the Tweedle to her right. Grabbing her shoulder, the other Tweedle turned her to face forward.

"She gets to kick one of you guys," the red-head complained.

"How are you guys?" Chelsea asked. Before any of the women could answer, she looked between the Tweedles beside her. "I know my friends killed some of you. I'm sorry if they were anyone important to you."

"Seriously, Chelsea?" Ngawang snorted.

Chelsea shrugged. "They're people too."

"Probably had their vocal cords or whatever removed," Amondi suggested.

Aisling shook her head. "They made noise earlier."

"We know they can laugh," Kat stated then mimicked Bel'von's joke, but the Tweedles remained silent.

Their discipline reminded Kat of the guards before the Tomb of the Unknown Soldier or the King's Guard outside of Buckingham Palace. Blank faces and stiff muscles always made Kat's own limbs itch. Shifting in her seat, she gritted her teeth. Stillness frustrated her. Each shifting moment strained her joints, but that had likely been Bel'von's intent. As time drained on, waiting for a second time pressed on her patience. Roiling the acidic guilt building in her gut, her anxiety shifted into rage. Nobody would save them. Kat couldn't save anyone, and the more the world pushed into that thought, the less she cared.

Tilting her head, Kat studied the Tweedle to her left. She named him Tweedledum, giving Tweedledee to the one on her right. From the sole of her foot, blackness spread. Against the already dark metal of the hall, the aqueous metal traveled, weaving across the ground. Tweedledum remained still. If he realized what was happening, there was no outward sign to tell. By the time it reached his thigh, his notice didn't matter. Needles dug down, and Tweedledum twitched. A shiver ran down the other's body, but he corrected himself, freezing back into place. When the black metal of her suit pierced his flesh, white and red bled into her mind. He experienced no pain. The sensation reminded her of sitting behind a small fan. Air moved. A slight wisp crossed unfeeling skin.

Words slipped through the metal. Vibrations from a mind unlike her own burned, and it scratched against her ears. Dreams of golden earth and violet skies stole her sight. On this world, there were neither stars nor night. The sky dimmed for mere minutes to a dark purple before growing light once more. In the background, buzzing droned. Clicks and gurgles sounded without silver orbs. Peace towered with a silver beauty. Iridescent wings – limbs promised and lost. An unspeakable want lurked beneath the surface, and in this creature's mind – Hez'i-bibs – the name passed between them.

"Hez'i-bibs," the word slipped out, and Tweedledee tensed at his companion's name.

Hez'i-bibs bowed his head. Through the black helm, his compound eyes studied her face. They watched her. The possibility of death stretched like a long sleep. Coldness followed by nothingness. A place without pain – without grief. There was nothing resembling sympathy. Hez'i-bibs reflected no understanding that his torture and hers matched. As he dreamed of sunlight and flowers large enough to sink into like a pool, she longed for golden fields and dusty roads.

"What'd you say?" Rachel called.

Kat pressed further. "His name is Hez'i-bibs."

"Who's?" Aisling asked.

A face shimmered. A light descended from the firmament. All at once, nations fell. Children cried in the streets, but orbs flew down. Promises of peace came false. A pale face surrounded by dark hair appeared. Thin lips sulked beneath a straight nose, and no pity could be found for anyone who looked like him – like Mah-Wærm. Gray eyes stared her down through Hez'i-bibs's memory.

"Can you see it?" Kat whispered.

Red flooded her mind. Fire consumed those who fought back. Anger burned then simmered into helplessness. Worlds fell. Galaxies swallowed whole without a single voice left to cry into the night. Silver collapsed into anguish, leaving the destiny of their species to a mad man. Bel'von wasn't supposed to be gold. Cut off the arms. Cut off the wings. Though the world shattered, the instinct remained the same. Paralyzed into silence, they buried themselves.

Darkness slinked into Kat's mind. "They want to die. He wants to die."

A blast blew across the corridor, sending Hez'i-bibs backward. He collapsed downward. Slumped against the wall, he twitched, and as her mind wrenched away from his, her last sensation was a wash of cold. Nothingness promised. The hole in his chest bled pus and thick, red paste. Falling back against her chair, Kat blinked. Spots danced in her vision. Through them, she saw Bel'von. The cylinders of dark metal retreated into his arm, but smoke rose from his fingertips. Qamar limped beside him. Two Tweedles held her up.

"There now," the blue-starred insectoid proclaimed. "He's got his wish. Anybody else want to slink back into their hiber-hole?"

None of the Tweedles moved. Kat's mind reeled as she struggled to refocus. Somebody was screaming. The noise echoed through the dark hall. Every inch vibrated, but none of the other women moved. The Tweedles carried Qamar away, taking her wherever they had brought Marie, and when Bel'von grabbed the next one, his metal hand wrapped around Aisling's bound arms.

"You won't win," the red-haired human warned him.

Bel'von scoffed, dragging her with him toward the room. "Mah-Wærm always wins. If you had learned that, you might have survived."

"What?" Rachel whispered. Standing, she threw herself forward only to have the Tweedles at her side slam her back into the chair. "You can't! Stop!"

"Don't take her!" Kat pleaded.

Tears poured down Chelsea's face, and Amondi's dark eyes widened. Her chin quivered. Kat's eyes flicked to Ngawang, but the dark haired woman glared down at her feet, refusing to watch as the insectoid walked away. Rachel screamed. Black needles flew from her suit, piercing the Tweedle across from her and slicing across Ngawang's shoulder. For a second, her skin showed through, and a trail of blood trickled down, but the metal grew back, sealing the gap. Bel'von threw Aisling inside, turning to face the hall.

"One of you was already chosen," Bel'von informed them. "The second your insignificant parasitic selves entered the Mah-Wærm's territory, he sensed Conquest aboard your ship. If he hadn't, you'd all have been able to explore – measure out how much of the galaxy bowed to him before he slowly, painstakingly conquered your hearts and stole your people's loyalty, but any planet with one of his Riders has to face desolation. A Rider is a survivor – the last of their kind – like our great leader himself."

"War seemed to think he had a choice," Rachel growled.

Lips curling into a smirk, Bel'von laughed – his mandibles breaking the illusion of normalcy. "I've lived through two Riders. Only Death existed when Mah-Wærm brought my people into the fold." He reached up, holding the top of the door with one hand. Leaning forward, he studied the faces of the women before him. "In the end, the one Mah-Wærm sensed always makes the final choice."

"Then why bother with this charade?" Amondi asked.

"Some bones must break before they can be mended," Bel'von proclaimed, and stepping back, he let the doorway close.

"He won't kill her," Rachel said.

If her words assured anybody, it was only herself. Whether time passed quicker or he kept her for a shorter time, Kat couldn't tell. The door opened. Bel'von left the room. Blood painted his suit red. Helmet down, his golden face showed; crimson painted that too. He nodded back at the room, adjusting his arms as he hummed. A droning buzz translated to a tune by the silver orbs. Each note drilled into Kat's memory.

"Clean it," Bel'von commanded.

The closest two Tweedles vanished into the room. One emerged seconds later with Aisling's dead body over his shoulder. Her skin paled to blue. All color vanished from her lips. None of her limbs came out attached to her. Tweedle Two carried them like logs. They dripped blood like her torso, and the floor didn't swallow the trail of red. Tears streamed down

Rachel's face. Chelsea sobbed, folding in half to bury her face against her knees. Collapsing back against her chair, Amondi moved her lips, but no sound came out. Ngawang remained silent. Her eyes lifted, avoiding the floor where blood remained.

An arm wrapped around Kat's shoulder. Her eyes jumped up, and Bel'von smirked down. Without a word, he forced her to stand. His hand slid to the back of her neck, and he shoved her forward through Aisling's blood and into the darkness ahead. None of her crewmates watched. Holding her head high, Kat kept her chin parallel to the ground. Tears blurred her vision, but breathing slowly, she held them at bay until the metal wall behind her sealed. Darkness crowded around her. Like thunder, lights blinked on above her head. Blood covered the floor. Bits of flesh and black scraps of fabric sprinkled over the huge empty room.

"Let's begin," Bel'von's voice carried, echoing through the large empty room.

Circling to face him, Kat asked, "Begin what?"

"I really shouldn't tell you," the insectoid taunted. "It might skew the results."

He smirked. His hands slid across his body through the dripping vestiges of Aisling. Heaviness overtook Kat's limbs. Stepping further into the room, she held up her arms. Spikes of black metal flew, slamming into the walls. The lights swung overhead. Electricity shot down. Particles spread throughout the air ignited. Nanites, too small to see clearly, shifted. Golden fields took over the darkness, and in the distance, her childhood home stood. The vegetable garden was the same as the day she left for the Academy though winter's first frost would've already hit. Bodies littered the field. Fires consumed the house. Red blazed against the storm. Gray clouds lumbered over the hills, drowning all light below.

"This isn't real." Kat sighed.

Her hand brushed against the wheat surrounding her. The rough stalks brushed against her, but even the solid weight of the rain-filled air couldn't convince her otherwise. From the house, her mother's voice rose. Screams filled the emptiness between them, and howls pitched, but her dogs were not there. Her family remained beyond her reach.

"Heartless," Bel'von proclaimed. His gurgling chuckle plucked at her nerves.

"I'm emotional, Bel'von. Not an idiot. If you want to test my mind, try something a bit more realistic," Kat retorted.

The world around her collapsed, leaving the large metal room. Though the blood shimmered in the illusion, Aisling's recorded screams were achingly real. Each gasp for breath between them pierced Kat like a bullet. No doubt lingered in her mind as Kat watched the video play out. Aisling died terrified, screaming and in pain. Cowering, the red-haired woman tried to shield herself, but something shattered the shield her metal suit formed. Her left forearm fell first. Whatever attacked her sent it flying against the wall. Jaw dropping, Aisling fell back, staring at her arm in disbelief.

"Get up!" Kat yelled despite herself. "You have to get up!"

Blood gushed from Aisling's severed arm. Rolling as if to dodge, something pinned her in place. The next blow came down separating her right arm at the shoulder and gliding down through her collar bone. Blue eyes rolled back in her head. Red flooded the floor, and invisible claws raked down her torso, tearing apart the synthetic metal of her suit. When they reached her legs, the joints stretched, skin tearing like a rag doll along its seams. Kat wrapped her arms around her waist. Her eyes watched as Bel'von drummed his fingers against his thigh. A silver orb lurked just above his head.

"Phase Three - complete," the insectoid stated.

If the orb had translated his tone accurately, Bel'von sounded as pissed as Kat felt. Her fists clenched and unclenched. Tension traveled the length of her body, without any clear way to leave. Across her body, the suit rippled as if waiting. Lights flickered; they sounded like thunder as the nanites discharged, letting the illusion fall. The blood lessened, but still, dark red stains dried against the metal sheen of the floor. Aisling had died here. Scared and alone knowing her friends would stand here too. Nothing had attacked her, but her body ripped apart just the same. Kat's fingers slid against her black suit. Though the strange fabric fit like a second skin, it proved to have more potential as a weapon than first suspected. Each blow landed against suit-covered flesh. Whatever Aisling had seen, her suit likely cut her down.

"Do I get to see Qamar's go next?" Kat asked. Her voice reverberated across the room, growing larger than she had intended. "Or Marie's?"

Footsteps clanged against the metal floor. Standing beside her, Bel'von sighed. He raised the skin above one eye where an eyebrow might have been and shrugged. None of his expressions matched Hez'i-bibs memory of their species. Every aspect of him from Bel'von's humanoid silhouette to his lips contrasted with the more familiar insect-like appearance Hez'i-bibs recalled. Trauma blacked out a portion of the Tweedles mind, but if they'd all been surgically modified, Bel'von appeared to have most passionately embraced his transformation.

"How do the orbs translate names?" Kat asked, narrowing her eyes.

"Familiar labels. They have a catalog of names on both sides to pick from. They select ones which are unused if no direct translation can be found. Everything has meaning - even the most basic naming conventions muck about in history," Bel'von explained. "My species don't call me by my true name. Even if I said the word for it, you'd never hear anything different than what Death spoke."

"Because you were meant to be a Queen Bee but your dear god turned you into a drone?" she offered.

He made a clicking noise, and the orb remained silent. A smile tilted up the corners of his lips. "It means your prior words contained grievous errors that suggest you aren't of sound mind. Like a scoff or a tapping of the tongue muscle." Shaking his head, the insectoid sighed. A vibrating sound like someone bouncing sand on a speaker. "I can't wait to have a tongue."

"He's still modifying you?"

"Of course. He modifies any who wish it." Turning toward the door, Bel'von laughed. "And many who don't."

Following him at a distance, Kat frowned when the portal open. Waving his arm toward himself, Bel'von stood in the doorway as the remaining Tweedles brought in the last of the Intrepid's crew. Ngawang stood. Her arms clapped together beneath her chest. If her muscles ached, nothing in her posture gave the pain away. Rachel and Chelsea both shifted their weight as if trying to ease their backs like Kat had done earlier. Eyes closed, Amondi barely breathed. Only Ngawang kept her eyes trained on Kat. When she blinked, she did so deliberately and paused before repeating the pattern.

"As I said, the great Mah-Wærm felt Conquest's presence on board your ship. He's known it was you from the beginning. We simply had to determine how to awaken the Rider in you," Bel'von informed her. "You were easier than War. His bloodlust was obvious, but his heart hadn't traveled with him. He fell in line of his own choice when his mate and brats were dead."

"Whatever you think you're doing," Kat said. "Stop lying to me."

"I haven't lied to you once, Katelyn Parker. I have no intention of lying to you though you can understand my temerity to believe you worthy of what you will become," Bel'von replied.

Leaving the women standing, the Tweedles left the room. Metal rose up to encase the other four women's legs. The liquid flowed up to their knees, trapping them in place. Still, Ngawang blinked her code over and over, but Kat already knew what it said. Illusions didn't often give themselves away so willingly, yet the letters spelled only one thing over and over again: N-O-T R-E-A-L. If everything happened outside of her head, it made no sense for the nanites to project Ngawang passing code to her. It was possible, in the vaguest sense, that – like Spanish and English – this was just another language stolen from one of her dead crewmates. Dr. Margaret Cho hadn't known Morse Code, but Theresa had.

"Kill them," Bel'von commanded.

Kat frowned. "No."

"Kill them," he repeated. "Or I will."

"If you wanted somebody willing to kill their comrades, you should have picked Ngawang then," Kat told him. Crossing her arms, she hummed, repeating the noise he'd performed earlier.

"True."

The word hung in the air for mere seconds before their suits turned on the four women. Chelsea fell to the ground, screaming. Her arms still bound to each other and to her chest as she wrenched away from an attacker she couldn't perceive. When Rachel tried to run, she fell over; her feet stuck to the ground, but the sickening crack of bones echoed. Blood spurted, and a cream-colored shaft stuck out of her shin. Twisting from side to side, the brunette exacerbated her injuries. While panic unfolded further misery for those two, Amondi stood still as deep gashes tore through her suit and flesh. Ngawang growled with each blow. Her message remained the same: N-O-T R-E-A-L. Their pain bled into every fiber of Kat's being. Her mind swam in their screams as blood painted her vision, clouding sense even as she read the words flashing with Ngawang's every blink.

"Kill them," Bel'von pushed. "Or I will."

"By inaction or action, the choice is mine," Kat murmured.

Rounding on Bel'von, she bent her knees and lunged, but her feet stuck to the ground just the same. She threw her hand up, sending spines of dark metal at Bel'von, but the floor shifted, sending a shield up to block every single one. Clasping her hands together, Kat formed a spear, but when she launched it at the alien, he whacked it aside. The dark metal melted, slithering across the ground back to Kat's suit.

"Did you really think we would give away a weapon we couldn't defend against? Any nation which launches a weapon it is incapable of defending its people from does not deserve to be a nation. Such arrogance - to think anyone can hoard knowledge after the sight of its results," Bel'von clicked. Mocking her in his untranslatable gesture. Even as his mandibles retracted, his lips curled into a condescending smirk that wrinkled his nose and furrowed the space above his eyes. When she braced her arm, he gurgled. His laughter rolled low and deep. A twitter crossed his inhuman mouth. The plasma sent charge after charge at him, but each one dissipated against his shield.

All the while, the four women screamed. Their suits inflicted shallow wounds, prolonging their torture as Kat struggled to land any sort of attack on Bel'von. With each failed attempt, her pulse raged. She struggled to lift her feet. Metal crumbled and reformed around her legs.

Each rise saw the metal go higher. Every crash nearly sent Kat to the ground, but nonetheless, she persisted. All the while a voice too similar to Jacobi's to ignore questioned if Ngawang's message was real or not real. If her eyes deceived her, Kat subjected the four to torture without reason. Faced with this circumstance and knowing the women were real, she doubted she would have hesitated to put them out of their misery. It would have been merciful.

"Are you so heartless that you'd let them suffer? Every horror they imagined, I could make real in this room. You can't stop me, but you could save them. I'd let you stop their pain," Bel'von offered. His words circled around her head like poison.

"Liar," she spat.

"Please!" Chelsea begged. "Make it stop!"

"We're going to die anyways. Suck it up and take the shot," Ngawang bellowed, but her eyes kept blinking the same message.

"This isn't real!" Kat screamed. "None of you are real. This is just another illusion. Shut up!"

Metal dripped down from the ceiling. Splattering over shoulders and down cheeks, it slid against the four women's skin to seal their lips shut. Like iron angels, they stood frozen as the metal spread. Rachel's back arched. Her eyes watered as the metal gag sealed her screams inside her. Shoulders sagging,

Amondi bowed her head. Tears streamed down her cheeks. Ngawang just kept blinking.

"But what if it isn't?" Bel'von asked.

Kat ignored him, clawing at her legs in an attempt to get free. Her fingers sharpened, and she paused. Not real. Standing up, she surveyed the room. Blood and liquid metal bubbled over everything. Not real. Her legs were bound, melded to the ship. Not real. Bel'von drummed his fingers against his thigh. A nervous tick - a cadence clicking through the air. Over his head, a single silver orb rotated. Not. Real. Real or not real. Nothing in this room mattered. If anything existed, she did. Chills ran up her legs, but as she lifted and drummed her toes, they moved unrestricted. Bracing her left arm, she took aim. Metal rings rose and slid down her hand, forming the body of the plasma cannon.

As plasma built, a warm heat crossed along her back. Kat pulled her right hand back, and aimed it parallel to the first. Black metal expanded, sliding down her forearm to envelop her hand. Between the two, the plasma jumped. Metal shifted into spiraling coils, and as snaps of energy leapt back and forth, a song rose between the two. The drumming of her heart kept the beat. Bolts fired down, hitting walls and smashing into the ceiling. Thunder rumbled overhead. One of the gigantic lights swung into view. On the ground below, blood vanished and reappeared from the floor. A flood of nannies scattered, forming back together when the light flickered back off and back on against.

"You, me, them…any of us at any time," Kat yelled over the crackling music of her self-made

Tesla Coils. "You, me, them…I don't give a damn who lives and dies, who's real or not real."

"Good," Bel'von's mandibles seemed like the huge fangs of a spider in the flashing bursts of light. "Kill us all."

"This isn't a game of chicken," Kat warned.

A bolt slammed into Chelsea's chest. She writhed for an instant, but when she stilled, steam rose off her charred chest. She flickered like a bad connection. Then the nanites which formed her collapsed. They rained down onto the floor, clinking like raindrops. Amondi fell next. Her body arched backward like a dancer before she erupted into tiny robots. Tears ran down her face as Rachel dislocated her shoulder struggling to escape. Bolts slammed into Rachel's legs, snapping them in two as the nanites dissolved. Ngawang blinked through the O and exploded. As small as ash, the nanites littered the floor, melting into the deck below them.

"Open the door," Kat whispered. "I'm done."

"Airlock?" Bel'von offered.

"Don't care. Airlock. The same door I came in from. Frankly, I don't care," Kat replied, breaking through the metal holding her legs.

She crossed the room toward the wall where they'd enter. Beyond her exhaustion, her lack of injuries lurked in the back of her mind. Marie didn't walk out of that room. Though Qamar stood on her feet, she hadn't been moving entirely under her own power. Blood dripped from both. Bruises bloomed.

Bel'von sighed, pressing a hand against the wall; however, the door remained closed. The lights overhead shut off. Nodes illuminated the room a dull.

107

Thrumming low enough to echo in Kat's bones, the red pulsating light synchronized with her heart. As her pulse slowed, the room fell into darkness for longer lengths of time. She inhaled. Letting the metal around her hands slid back into place, she slammed her palms against the wall where the door had been. Electricity traveled across her back. Bolts of static climbed the walls like a spider's web, leaving disrupted illuminates in her wake.

"I never understand why you each try to run," Bel'von commented as he removed his hand from the wall. The nodes matched Kat's heart regardless.

Gritting her teeth, she sharpened her fingers, but the knives slipped down the wall leaving nothing but a screeching in their wake. When he leaned against the wall beside her, a spike wove round her shoulder to attack him. The alien flicked the metal spear away with a twitch of his wrist like one might shoo a fly. All around their heads, the silver orbs levitated. Swirling and spinning back and forth. Kat roared, baring her teeth at the metal. On her hands, small hair-like extensions grew. Arachnid legs sprouted from her back, ramming into the wall. Their tips crashed against the metal, but while they held fast, they barely made it an inch into the wall.

"I'm going out on a limb for you," the insectoid proclaimed. "War doesn't want you to know. It is tradition, but you all run into the same blockades, and I'm the one who has to fix you."

The double tones of his clicking and the translations pressed against her nerves. Everything he said, everything he did was a lie. She wasn't Conquest. Human, empathetic, sane - none of those things matched with the other three Riders. If anyone fit, Ngawang belonged among them. Beyond the Riders, the only image of Conquest in Kat's mind came from lack more than anything else. Pratchett and Gaiman replaced the title with Pollution, and Famine had, at times, been switched for Pestilence. No name would've fit. Bel'von lied. She wasn't Conquest. If they tortured her for the next hundred years, she wouldn't be Conquest. Mercy killings meant nothing. They signified her exhaustion and frustration. Those were a symbol of her humanity. A shallow term with less and less non-species-specific meaning the more aliens came into the picture. Climbing up the wall, she measured the distance with the metal legs until she reclined at the height of the hall's ceiling.

"Action is a choice," Bel'von paraphrased Kat's earlier words. "What sort of choice would killing off the rest of your competition be?"

"You took Qamar and Marie elsewhere. I'd just be ensuring whoever succeeded wasn't who you wanted," Kat replied.

She pressed her palms against the door, relying on the spider-like legs of metal to keep her in place. Black rings expanded, descending over her hands once more. Warmth spread across her back. Across the floor, the nanites' dead shells rattled. The air shifted, flowing toward Kat to crash across her back as she charged the blast. The metal rose from the floor. A cyclone of robotic corpses flared to life from the far wall to the center of Kat's back. Like bullets, they slammed into her, melding with the synthetics of her suit.

Bel'von sighed, rolling his silver compound eyes. "You all fight as if you actually think you have a chance. Why would we give you what you need to escape?"

Heat swelled around her hands. Lights lit along her suit, and along each arachnid extension, electricity sparked. A circle wider than the doorway had been buzzed with the charge. Thunder swelled in her ears. Releasing the trigger, Kat flew back with the recoil. Bolts jumped across her arms. A tingle traveled up her spine. When it reached her neck, black spots swarmed her vision as buzzing filled her ears. Over her head, thunder sounded, and the lights turned off.

Metal footsteps clanked against the cold floor. The blur of Bel'von's face danced in and out of focus as he knelt beside her. He made the sound again. An untranslatable click condemned her stupidity.

"As if you could ever be Conquest," Bel'von said, making the noise again. Then black consumed her, and unconsciousness pulled her down.

Chapter Seven

Sound came first. Not buzzing or thundering but humming. The noise droned on then passed only to begin again. Opening her eyes, Kat blinked as the world came back into view. They had placed her in bed. A gossamer curtain floated around the bed's dark wooden canopy. Familiarity rung in her head. She had been here before. Sifting through her memories, she chased the déjà vu. Nothing came to mind. With a sigh, she rolled over only to tense. Beside her, Death reclined in a metal chair. His face fully exposed. White stretched on either side of him. Metal walls reflected light. Against their backdrop, his suit blended, but the paleness of his features hovered in a sallow hue.

Black curls coiled around his head. Gray wires curled in his eyes, and the coldness of steel stared back at her. His tongue darted out, running across his top lip. Shifting, he leaned forward. Yellow sat about his eyes in stark lines. They shifted to purple behind his ears.

Blinking, she sat up on her elbows, but Death pressed her back into the mattress. In the movement, white blankets shifted, catching her version. Standing over her, he sighed and sat down. His weight shifted the mattress. Again, his eyes shifted to the far corner of the room, casting his face into profile. High cheekbones and a flat nose weren't what she had envisioned.

"You sustained minor injuries before you decided to electrocute yourself," Death said, not even bothering to look at her.

"Wasn't intentional," she retorted.

He clucked his tongue. Glancing down at her, his silver eyes flicked back and forth over her face like she was a book. "Don't bother lying to me. I'll hear it."

"No, you won't."

Death's eyes narrowed. "Lie."

When she tossed her head to look the other way, only more white walls greeted her. "So, what? We're all separated now."

"Something like that," he admitted.

"Why?"

Death shifted, lying down beside her. There were certainly enough pillows or pillow really. Just one stretched the bed's length. Death raised his head and hit it against the pillow, rolling back and forth. Wiggling, he settled. His fingers drummed against his chest. Whether his actions were avoidance or comfort, she had no way of knowing. Inhaling, Death let out a deep sigh.

"Separation causes anxiety, but it also forces the participants to show their capacity for self-reliance and their adaptability," Death explained, tapping his wrists below the thumb. His gloves retracted, showing hands a slightly paler shade than his face. "You were the fourth; therefore, you are aware that at least one of your number has died."

"Was murdered," Kat corrected.

Death sighed. His fingers entwined over his chest more like a dead man in a coffin than a comfortable position to rest. Purple tinted the edges of his fingernails, but he breathed steadily without any sign of a chill or oxygen deprivation. Perhaps the ideal had naturally violet nails. Pressing her lips together, Kat glanced at the far side of the room. As the taut white fabric stretched, Death's gaze followed the rippling movements.

"There were four others who might also be dead. Two more returned from the room injured, so we might have killed them." His right leg crossed over his left, jostling the mattress. "We'll visit the survivors one at a time."

"All seven of us," Kat replied.

With a shrug, Death grabbed the edge of the blankets on his side and threw them over himself. "It's an utter waste of my time."

"None of you like this process. Why bother? If Mah-Wærm knew who he wanted, just kill the rest of us. It's like he's a fucking cat playing with a mouse before eating it. Just get it over with," she complained, frowning when she raised her arm and found it bare.

Her hands fell to her chest. Soft cloth replaced the black suit. When she tugged at the blankets to lift them, Death sighed, shifting to give her more leeway. Without sleeves, the fabric fell around her waist in a shapeless, mid-thigh length dress. Scratching at her recently shaved head, Kat glared at the alien beside her.

"I didn't change you," he preempted.

Scoffing, she furrowed her brow. "What was the point of those suits if we weren't stuck in them?"

"Base biometrics, locator maintenance, quick disposal," Death listed, tilting his head to one side. His eyebrows raised as his lips pursed. Rolling his head to look at her, Death frowned. "Conquest will receive a final suit of armor. Once you're in, you never get out," he said. His hands drummed against the metal covering his chest.

"Figuratively or literally?"

Adjusting his head to stare resolutely at the canopy, Death sighed. "A prison of the mind works better than any bars."

Kat rolled her eyes. Bel'von flared with drama, but at least, he managed to be informative. Side by side with Death, a chill raked over her skin. A shiver traveled down her spine, buzzing like pins and needles in her fingers and toes. Without the suit, her only weapon was her mind, and given enough time, the wood she could break from the bed's frame; however, until Death left, she kept her eyes from staring at the material too long. Curling onto her side to face him, Kat studied the alien's profile. Her eyes trailed over his features. Minor discrepancies between him and a regular human clawed at her mind. He had no earwax or nasal hair. The skin about his ears matched his hands but not his face.

"War is reptilian. Bel'von's an insect. You were some lineage without external ears," Kat whispered, knowing he could hear her. "What were you before?"

Closing his eyes, Death inhaled. As the air filled his lungs and expanded his chest, the edges around him blurred. The steel gray eye she could see shifted to look at her as he said, "Afraid."

"Gaseous life form?" she posited.

"Fear must be overcome," Death replied. He turned his head. The edges of his hair floated like a mane fanning about his high cheekbones. "When a creature wants to die, they don't stop fearing the end – but you...you feared life, feared loneliness. Feared being Conquest."

"Yet Bel'von says I've always been Conquest." Kat frowned. "Then said it was a lie."

He scoffed. "Bel'von has a habit of exaggerating."

"The Tweedles aren't male, are they?" Kat asked, and when Death's edges solidified, she continued despite his furrowed brow. "Bel'von's species. The guards look male, but they aren't."

Death's eyes widened. "Oh. Tweedles? I thought you'd jumbled your languages. Tweedles...I'll have to consult the memory banks on that one. Regardless, Bel'von's species doesn't exist anymore. Name's been stricken."

"Because they fought back," Kat stated, remembering the horror ingrained in Hez'i-bibs as their armies fell from the sky. "They're a hive. All of them asexual females." The word perturbed her. "Asexual? Infertile?" Death gave her no answer. "Mah-Wærm killed the drones and current reproducing queen to destroy the species after they fought against him."

"It was early. He was young," Death dismissed, lifting his hand off his chest in a shallow, dismissive wave.

"I'm sure he's better at conquering now," Kat drawled.

Lips curling, the male chuckled. "Something like that."

"Bel'von was supposed to be a reproducing queen, wasn't he? Hez'i-bibs thought of him as silver, and only the queen in his mind had been silver. Does Bel'von know? Should I be calling him her?" Kat wondered aloud.

Death scoffed. "Bel'von is him. He knows what he was supposed to become and is pleased not to have been activated."

"Activated? Wouldn't he have been born as the queen fell or something? I thought dying insect queen's laid queen eggs only when weak," Kat said. Shaking her head, she pulled the covers tighter around herself. "Marie would probably know."

"Death of the queen, who they call the Mother, triggers a series of hormonal releases in the heir – or the dwarf mother. As you said, they are a hive. Dwarf mothers connect mentally to the reigning Mother. When the reigning Mother fell, Bel'von should've been activated, but knowing what might come if the dwarf mothers ahead of him died, he made a deal with Mah-Wærm to save himself and a section of his species. No queen, no continued species, so you salt and burn a planet, but surviving workers become guards who follow a non-activated dwarf mother." Death stretched his legs then rolled off the bed to stand beside it. "You've wasted your time with me asking about your warden rather than your trials."

"Maybe I'm just not that invested," Kat retorted.

Death's lips twisted downward. His pupils narrowed to pinpoints, and with their whirling movement, the shifting robotics beneath clicked into place more like a cameras lens than a human eye. White liquid spread up his neck from the collar of his suit, expanding to wrap his face in a mask like a motorcycle helmet. The edges sealed together, but they remained as shifting and ephemeral as mist.

"Then you're even less intelligent than I thought," Death said; his voice crackled beneath his helm, popping and clicking like gears grinding stones into words.

As he walked away, Kat sat up, studying the empty square of a room. Smooth white walls formed a fifteen by fifteen foot box with a ceiling at least eight feet in height. Bolted to the floor, Death's chair faced the bed. A clear shifting swirling marked the doorway which opened like a camera's shutters. In the hall beyond, a bland white hall stretched. Everything on the ship seemed pulled to the two extremes. Gold and white or black painted this world as if color was a rarity instead of the norm. A blue star marked Bel'von's rank. Red swirled across War. Only the flowers seemed needlessly colored, but perhaps meaning lurked there as well.

Sliding her legs over the side of the bed, she pressed her bare feet against the cold metal floor. No one came. Her heart beat echoed in the absence. Without stimulation, she'd be hallucinating in three days, so Kat turned on the bed and tore it apart. The gossamer fabric separated from the rungs along the canopy, tearing into long strips she cast aside. Tossing the pillow on top, she tugged at the mattress, dragging it from its frame. When only wood and metal remained, a sigh escaped her lips. They'd bolted the bed to the floor too. Sitting on the edge, she slammed her feet down against the boards running between the two sides. Deconstructing it took time. Hours passed as she slammed against the edges, piling the wood against the far side of the room. Hunger brought food, and thirst found water. When her body needed relief, a hole opened in the far side of the floor. She couldn't be certain they intended it for waste, but she had no intention of using it for anything else.

Quiet carried on. Bruises colored her heels and shoulders when she brought the canopy down. If red smeared against the white floor, she didn't mind it. Tearing the fabric into strips, Kat wrapped them around her wounded feet. Resting a hand against the wall, she steadied herself, peeling the hand away to wipe streets of red down the sides of her dress from her hips to the hem. A glance up finds her face to face with a single, clean print of her hand on the wall. The corners of her lips curved upward. Color bred in her veins.

Pulling up a piece of wood, she slid a hand down the edges. Treated or not, fire might not be available. The metal chair works well enough to split the wood. It's all about the angles. Whatever metal made the nails sparked when hammered against the chair. One blow. Two blows. Then she made light. Warm radiated where only cold reached her before. Carefully, she ran the burning scrap of wood against the metal. Smoke left gray behind, but the scent of chemicals dug into her senses. Without vents in sight, oxygen would run out. Eaten by fire. Not the way she intended to go, but suffocation couldn't be as bad as electrocution or mutilation. Gray consumed wherever

118

fire touched, wrecking the white between the metal and her skin.

   In a world of blood and fire, Kat fell into the apocalypse. The world beyond the door ceased to exist. Though no vents were visible, the air cycled up through the ceiling, leaving not even a single breath of smoke to gather there. Six women were closer to her than Earth, but a dimension away. Stuck in a metal cage, she bent to the time of fire. Measuring her hours by the life of stained wood and fabric. A chill ran down her spine whenever the fire slipped, but even as she kept it tended, her feet drew her in circles, touching each corner of the room to ensure they didn't change her environment without her noticing.

   Sleep offered no escape. Even in her dreams, white enfolded her. Standing in the center of an empty room, she shifted her environment back to her memories, but something immediately reverted even her dreamland back to a square void. War or Famine played in her mind, for she didn't think Death cared enough to block such an escape, but she could not tell whether it was the machine's creator or War who recalled her lucid dreaming. Cast back to her blood covered dress, each waking brought her back to exhaustion and despair.

   Calisthenics helped. Pressing her hands against the floor, she threw her feet into the air and held them there. Her abs tensed as she bent her arms to brush her head against the floor. Up again and her toes drummed as if they might walk on the ceiling. In rare moments, she wished she'd left up the canopy. There was more she could do with a bar, and as if the room heard her thoughts - which seemed well within

119

reason - a bar traveled from one side to the other of her room after her third sleep. Curling her fingers around the bar, she lifted herself, turning her grip as she rose over the bar beyond her waist to stretch out her arms to straight down. Hours in gymnastics when her friends were chasing balls for touchdowns returned to her. As she spun around the bar, her feet missed the ceiling by inches. A thrill burned through her skin. Familiarity swelled like warmth where cold made its bed.

When she exhausted and returned to the dead fire, she stretched beside the torn pile. Sweat dripped from her forehead and abdomen down onto the cold metal beneath her. Even as her lids fell, the lights remained on. The room remained white. In her fourth sleep, she found herself not in a white emptiness but back in the old barn where her mother set up a makeshift beam and where her father cleaned and formed old metal piping into uneven bars. In sleep and wakefulness, she trained. For what, she didn't know.

Once - six sleeps in - Kat imagined she heard Chelsea singing, but having spent so long in solitude, she dismissed it as an auditory hallucination. When Marie's lewd poetry stumbled into her dreams, she woke with a start only to find the crackling of a dying fire to be the only sound. Burrowed in the blanket, Kat closed her eyes, thinking of Aisling, Emma, and Lupita. Lupita died to prove escape impossible. When loyalty came into question, Death slaughtered Emma. Aisling fell to show that no amount of strength was enough. Each death formed a lesson. With every one, the survivors moved closer to being Conquest, but as she curled beneath the torn sheets, Kat couldn't fathom what lesson would come from this.

"They're breaking us down," she whispered to herself in a dream. Standing barefoot in the barn, she took a deep breath and screamed, "This isn't a room! It's a fucking cocoon!"

While her body hardened with constant work, her mind melted down like a caterpillar to be reformed however they wanted. Given enough time, they would succeed. Awake or dreaming, everything melded into each other. She woke, and the wood pile had grown. With little change otherwise to the room; she recognized the different shape of the scraps of wood. Kat sighed. They enabled her fire. Either they thought she wouldn't notice and would become confused about her rough timeline, or her captors didn't care. Calculations of time hadn't even crossed her mind before. Even if the wood was one she recognized, there was no way she could be sure the exact time each piece took to burn.

"This is ridiculous," she growled, glaring at the smoke.

Grabbing a piece, she threw it onto the fire. Green smoke flared. Piece after piece, Kat cast each scrap of wood until a blazing bonfire roared. Blaring green swirled to life. Waves of toxic black smoke rose faster than the vents could clear. Dark clouds gathered along the ceiling. A thin layer of soot stained the walls, building until large slits opened. Running across the whole ceiling, they sucked up the smoke, rumbling and echoing through the small room. Kat clasped her hands over her ears. Her eardrums throbbed, pounding until a resounding pop took away any sound at all. Dropping her hands in defeat, Kat glared up into the darkness above. A shimmer glimmered in the dark. Down through the enlarged vent, spindled tendrils curved around the wood and torn bedding. As they retreated into the grated vents, Kat grabbed hold of one of the sheets.

The grates slammed closed, trapping the sheets. Kat growled. White sheets curved down, cradling her like a hammock. Falling backward, she sighed. She swung back and forth, staring at the bound folds against the ceiling. No smoke, no fire, just soot and ash remained. Boredom itched at the back of her mind. Kept alive by two feet. Reaching out of the sheets, she grabbed a chunk of loose material and curled further into the fabric.

Thousands of years had brought humanity to space. All for nothing. Humanity had won in the end. Mammals outlasted dinosaurs. Sapiens bedded or shredded Neanderthals, and every alien movie pondered if they could do it again. Like the town hero and reigning champion, humanity stepped up to the new contender. Nobody wanted to beat down a hometown hero, so fiction made them strong until winners were losers. Then they made them smart. Eventually, history drew them as both. Nobody questioned why. Maybe writers were too subtle. Neither strength nor intelligence alone permitted their survival. Diversity gave *Homo sapiens* the power to endure. Humans thrived because they were malleable in their behavior.

Yet in a panic, everyone sought comfort in conformity. A homogenous group seemed safe like a school of small fish pretending to be one bigger fish.

Quotes about standing together rose up. Earth had likely adopted some pro-majority slogan against the alien invaders. Us versus them. Kat scoffed. Blood red and gray painted her walls. The true colors of humanity, but all anybody wanted to see – just like the ship's designer – was the extremes. Humanity obsessed with the stark contrast of black and white. Conforming transformed humans into bricks. Lined up, cut to size, stacked, and made into a shield. Nothing more than dominos. Any idiot kid could flick them down. But humans endured in horror. Bled, bred, and wed in cruelty and torment. Some would endure as long as Earth lived.

Again the Death Star crept into her mind. With neuro-responsive suits, what prevented Mah-Wærm from having a fucking laser the size of a moon? Nothing. Absolutely nothing stopped that. Rocking back and forth, Kat glared up at the grim on the ceiling. She stretched her arm, brushing the tip of her finger through the soot. Today, tomorrow, the next day could come and go, but Kat wouldn't know if humankind lived or died. Grinding her teeth, she pushed down the thumping lump of envy rising that Leia at least knew. Hope wasn't hope when Earth took on the role of Schrodinger's cat.

"You could've asked for us to turn up the heat," War joked. Peering over the edge of the hammock, Kat glared at him. He stepped into the room, ducking beneath her hammock to reach the chair. "Love what you've done with the place."

All air rushed from Kat's lungs. Her eyes caught on a single incongruous speck of red, and nothing else mattered. Information poured for a new fount. Equations jumped to the forefront of her mind. Impossible – perfect, brilliant Marie. As complex as she could have gone, Marie had outwitted an empire with a smile and flash of color. Even better, she was alive. A weight lifted from Kat's shoulders. She huffed. A short rough breath.

With War staring at her in confusion, she found her mouth moving faster than her brain when she told him, "Women pirates pled the belly."

His brows furrowed. "What?"

"You came from Marie. She asked. For red lipstick. Did ask. It's on your suit. Marie's alive," Kat laughed, falling back into the curve of sheets. Tears streamed down her face as she swung.

"What?" he spat. "I – she…"

Pulling herself back out, Kat leaned over the edge, smiling at the red-haired. "A master's degree in biology, second best shot in our class, and she got you with lipstick!"

War spun, reaching his hands against the metal back of his suit, but Marie had kissed him where he could not reach. Right in the center of his back, a perfect kiss impressed against the metal. As he struggled, more red lips came into view. One on the back of his left knee – smudged but there. Another plastered on his thigh just below the curve of his ass. None of them places War would easily notice on his own. Kat's heart leapt for joy. Earth was a cat, but Marie was alive.

Chapter Eight

Sitting in the metal chair, War flushed almost as red as his hair. He cradled his head in his hands. "I'm an idiot."

"No. Marie's an intelligent, resourceful woman. What you did was kind," Kat corrected. "Honestly, this was the first decent act anyone on this ship has done for one of us. You brought her lipstick." Kat's lips curled into a smile. "Thank you."

Letting his hands drop, War leaned back. "You are welcome."

As the sheets beneath her swayed, Kat waited for him to speak, but War remained silent. His golden eyes stared unblinkingly at her. Though he moved his limbs like a human man, the longer Kat looked the more alien he seemed. Scars hid beneath the sharp edge of his cheekbones. Fine lines outlined his mouth. Nothing from smiling or laughing, lines where his skin – if it even was his – had been stitched back together. When War crossed his arms over his chest, a flash of red in his armpit caught her eyes. A weight pressed down on her.

"Lipstick on your ass makes you less threatening, but if you're looking to screw up my psyche, you'll have to talk," Kat informed him.

War shook his head. "I'm not here to speak, and the lipstick wasn't a special favor. You each are permitted to request one item. An offer of goodwill from the Riders to the Potentials."

As Kat's lips twisted into a frown, War ran a hand through his red hair. Nothing about the gesture suggested goodwill. This was another test. Any requested item created a more complete understanding of the person requesting. If Marie asked for lipstick, she reasoned against knowledge. Marie loved collecting random facts. Lipstick over books or access to historical information meant none of that was to be trusted. A reasonable assumption as all information would be heavily biased and clear propaganda. Even parted from the rest, a basic understanding of each woman might permit a collection of various useful items. Lipstick sent a message. Meaning Marie had helped.

The rest were a bit more complicated. Chelsea would ask for comfort. Either a different outfit or some piece of furniture to make the room less sterile would be her go-to requests. If able, Ngawang would go for a knife. Betting on War refusing to provide a weapon, she would have wanted a mirror. Wood, rope from the blankets, and shards of glass from the mirror gave her enough to set a number of traps for whoever entered next. In all likelihood, Rachel asked for books. Unlike Marie, she would trust herself to filter through the propaganda to the esoteric truth beneath. Amondi would ask for meat. Not because she wanted to eat it, but out of a possibly futile hope they might provide a knife alongside it. A requested scarf for a wearable impromptu strangulation method would be Qamar's. None of that helped Kat.

She didn't want to know more about Mah-Wærm or his empire. Even lies made them too human. Comfort might be good. Having destroyed the room, a new bed offered a number of new options. Unlike Amondi, Kat wasn't willing to gamble. She couldn't fake an ideological reason to ask for a scarf. Without the wood, Kat risked cutting herself if she requested anything to break down. No chance she'd pick lipstick. Maybe Chelsea had the right idea.

"A clock," Kat decided.

Brows furrowing, War clucked his tongue. "Time? You want time?"

"A way to tell time. I think it's reasonable," Kat said.

"It is," War conceded. He watched her as if waiting for her to explain. When she remained silent, he rolled his eyes. "Out of the survivors, your room is…"

"The most destroyed?"

He nodded, running his palms over his thighs. "Most went after the chair, not the bed."

"Why?" Kat asked. She gestured, reaching over the edge of the sheet. "It's bolted down."

"'Dogs don't shit where they sleep,'" War quoted.

His lips curled upward at one end into a smirk. Kat hid her smile in the folds of the sheet. If the idiot wanted to think he sounded clever, he could keep quoting Ngawang. Joy loosened her lips with the red lipstick, but this time, she held her tongue. Whether intentional or accidental, he revealed two of her comrades lived long enough to meet with him. A chance remained of him admitting to a third, so Kat wouldn't risk ruining it.

"Don't care. I want a clock. Not in the wall clock or some high-tech digital clock tied into the ship's mainframe. I want a self-contained clock." She held her hands over the edge of the sheet. "This big," Kat told him, holding her hands about six inches apart in a box. "And I want it to be an Earth clock."

"Do you really think our chronometers will be so different from what you know?" he asked and then frowned.

"I said 'clock.' You said 'chronometer.'" Kat pointed out. "Not a translator in the room to blame."

He shuffled his feet. Frowning, he inhaled and exhaled slowly. Jacobi used to do the same when Thaddeus tested his nerves. Movement held meaning, and perhaps his twitching meant the same as Jacobi's – a half-hearted attempt to hide frustration. It all seemed ridiculous. He had no reason to hide anything. Affection curbed Jacobi's anger with Thaddeus. She and War had nothing of the sort between them.

"I don't understand you," War lamented, shaking his head. When he blinked, the skin around his eyes grew red, outlining the gold of his eyes.

Kat smiled. Curling one leg over the side of her make-shift hammock, she spun and landed before him. His eyes widened, flicking from the blood on her dress to her bandaged feet. Swallowing, he lifted his gaze to her face, but just as quickly, War looked away. Beneath his red locks, a brighter red flashed into view. Her hand moved without a thought. She grabbed his head and pressed her thumb against the lipstick behind his ear. Marie had touched him there. Pushing against the proof of her friend's survival, Kat stared down at the bright-eyed creature. He seemed so small, yet her life depended on his mercy. The words buzzed across her mind. Tart in their uncertainty, they left nothing positive in their wake. Shoving him back, she let her hand fall to her side. Red transferred a streak against the congealed blood already staining her.

"You don't have to," she told him. "I'm a person, not a puzzle."

"How do you live without hope?" War asked.

His voice came softer than before. The curl of his words dragged down with each vowel. Every enunciation revealed the lack of pink within his mouth. Too dark for pink to stain. One day, perhaps the black would be bleached blue and dyed purple. Scalpels brushed against corpses in her mind. If Mah-Wærm wanted, his men could be harvesting flesh from any number of dead.

"Clearly, you don't know anything about living."

War's brows furrowed. Red bled around his eyes, darkening to near brown. "I have lived long."

"Were your people pacifists?" Kat asked.

War's hand rose, reaching to brush his fingertips against the edge of her skirt. Her lips pressed into a thin line. When he glanced up, she glared, and his hand fell away.

"No."

Kat shrugged, pacing the length of the room. Though she passed out of his view, she kept her eyes on War. He didn't do the same. Running his fingers over the kiss behind his knee, he studied the red which transferred and smudged on his gloves. His eyes remained there even as she moved back and forth within his sight.

"What did you hope for when Famine kept you here?" she asked.

He sighed, rubbing his thumb through the lipstick on his fingers. "Escape."

"Outnumbered in a hostile environment. You have superior weapons, and the ship seems to run on a type of communication system which we don't have. Even with the suits, we weren't able to locate the doors. Now I'm separated from my team. I have a piece of cloth instead of armor. Put that aside, I have to consider that the air available to me outside that door might be toxic. It took a number of deaths for Bel'von and his group to fine tune the brig," Kat explained.

Rocking his head from side to side, War hummed low in the back of his throat. His eyes focused on a speck of ash as it fell from the ceiling, drifting down to settle amongst the remaining wreckage on the ground. Tattered strands of fabric curled through dust and splintered remainders of wood. Broadening her shoulders, Kat grinned. Sterile white might be someone's dystopia, but blood, ash, and wood wreckage suited her far better. A blazing hell consumed her effort.

"Rescue?" War pressed.

Laughter bubbled out of her. "Who's going to rescue us? SpaceX?"

War clenched his jaw, pressing his lips together. "I don't understand that reference."

"Do you know what a warp engine is?" she asked, and when he twitched his head slightly to the left, she took it for a no and continued, "The fastest type of engine on Earth warps time-space around the ship in order to increase its speed. The Intrepid, the ship your people destroyed, was the first manned craft with a warp drive. It managed to go nine billion miles in four months."

"Miles?" His eyes narrowed and shifted up and down as if reading a text. "Ah, approximately one hundred astronomical units - the distance between your planet and its central star - the Sun." War laughed. "Your ships are slow."

"Light speed is the goal."

War lifted and dropped the corners of his lips in opposite directions. "Our ships are substantially faster. Mah-Wærm's war ships ride at upward of ten light years before we even consider our jump gates which permit passage between planets using contained wormholes."

Of course, they had star gates. If he told her his personal ship was a T.A.R.D.I.S., she wouldn't have been shocked. Every piece of science fiction she had ever devoured as a child came back to haunt her. Dreams of uploaded brains and psychic connections to the transmogrification of animals burned like insults when they had once been dreams. Nightmares were cruel like that. Twisting everything she loved into monsters, they stole her breath away, leaving her a hollow shell of the woman she'd been before. With a sigh, she stared down at War.

"Regardless, nobody's coming," she told him.

His eyes fell. Gold glittered as they contracted to gaze upon the red which marred his gloves. "If it matters, they haven't fallen."

"It doesn't. They will."

Ships at light speed with weapons to terrorize ships could rain hell down on Earth. One way or another, they could and would burn and salt every last bit of green. If they wanted to leave Conquest without a home, she had no doubt they would succeed. Mah-Wærm won against numerous species. If War had believed in escape or rescue, his kind had been capable of more than humanity could do for the surviving women of the Intrepid. Kat reached up, grabbing the ends of the discolored sheets. Lifting herself back into the warm confines of the makeshift hammock, she fixed her eyes to the ceiling. Hope killed. Curiosity and hope drew humanity to the stars. Feats of intellect rusted into a snare. Earth would fall. Rachel could argue that Russia and America would join forces until she was blue in the face. Even if the nanite defense system activated, they wouldn't be able to save the whole planet in time. Privilege set lines, and nanites would erect the walls, but this time, any available space would be a vulnerability.

"How long does it take for one of his war ships to destroy a planet," she asked even as her heart ached.

"He's not sending war ships."

Kat sat up, pulling herself to look down upon him. "What?"

"Your planet is too primitive. Even more than we expected if their ships are so inefficient. He sent a number of chimera crafts. A competition to see what the youths on our newer acquisitions could do with soon to be trashed parts," War explained, scratching at the scales on his neck. One flecked off and fell to the floor. "For all your interstellar lag, your terrestrial weaponry is…formidable."

"We're good at explosives," Kat agreed.

Outmatched, humanity had one last grasp even before the nanites came into consideration. Nuclear winter won every time against planetary annihilation. Fallouts would span the circumference of the globe. A temporary reprieve from the heating environment, but cancer rates would soar. In her mind's eye, Kat envisioned the horror across thousands of faces. Stampedes crushed children beneath their feet as they tried to outrun an unbeatable force. Screams echoed around the Earth, and as their cry of pain and fear rang into the dark of the universe, only their enemy would hear them. This war would not paint the streets with blood. No, the surface of the Earth would gain new sediment born of ash and bone.

Falling back into the soft embrace of the sheets, Kat closed her eyes. Images flared as the scent of burning flesh crept up like acid in her throat. War wanted hope. If any light existed in the universe, one by one this empire would snuff them out. Hollow and empty, cold crept in where love had been. Hope died. Buried in a shallow grave, Kat let it rest in peace. Silence lurked on the edges. One day, she'd be silence too. No one needed hope here. Nobody wanted hope here. Like files on a computer, Kat sorted the memories in her mind. She held tight to each face. Dreamed of holding them to her, but one by one, she let them follow hope. They belonged to a better world. A world Kat couldn't bear to remember anymore.

"We will outlast them," War warned. "All they've gained is time."

"If you believe in hope, all they need is time," Kat retorted even as she set aside the last of her loved ones.

A soft scoff escaped him. "Time means very little against an immortal."

"Man is immortal to the fly," Kat offered.

War's brows furrowed. "That makes no sense."

Kat shifted, pressing her heels against the sheet to lift herself enough to stare down at him. Rolling his shoulders back, he winced as his joints cracked before giving way to the movement. Time ticked onward in her mind, but her scale glared back at her with each passing second. Years, months, days, and hours never seemed superficial. Each passing year grew on her and each hour had its changes, but all this stemmed from rotations and orbits of a planet Kat would never see again. If all of time built from her life on Earth, a life without Earth weighed on her like the moment she first realized death was permanent.

"Probably because insectoids live longer than Earth flies. Does time translate?" When War didn't reply, she sighed. "A human lives one hundred years on average. There are three hundred and sixty-five days in the year. Flies live maybe twenty-eight."

"I understood the concept, but immortality is immortality. Your metaphor was incongruous. Time remains constant to the universe, and none but the universe remains constant to Mah-Wærm," War corrected.

Rolling her eyes, Kat slid down. "I'm not disoriented enough for this conversation."

"Fine," War said, rising from his chair.

Through the white fabric, she watched him head to the door. His footsteps echoed. The doorway spiraled open. Bright light filtered from the hall as War's boots kicked up debris. Glimmers sparked as light hit dust. At the door, he paused. Pulling her knees to her chest, Kat slid her hands over her ears. If he intended to say anything, he was kind enough to think better of it. With a thud, the door closed, and Kat was alone once more. Though the last several sleeps left her in light, the brightness in the room faded within moments after War left. Darkness enveloped her, and sleep overtook her.

"You are to wake." Kat wrinkled her nose. No light in the room, just a dream. Again, the soft voice curled in the room. "Excuse me?" A hand pressed against the hammock, shoving her aside and sending her flipping onto the ground below. Crouched low, she sought for a source in the darkness. Green light pulsed along the walls. Long-limbed Famine curved his spine. He tilted nearly parallel to the floor. "You are awake." He tilted, curving to the side until his head was below his waist. "Hello."

Kat's shoulders sagged. "What is wrong with you?"

"Many aspects," Famine admitted. "I had no spine; my current one is too flexible. My limbs are disproportionate." He waved his hands awkwardly at his side. "My new nose whistles when I breathe without my mask as I did not care for it properly post-surgery. Death taught me a number of bad habits to deal with anxiety, but my nails had not grown yet when he started, so they grew in wrong because I chewed them." With a long inhale, Famine tilted his mask to the opposite side and stood up straight.

"Okay!" Kat held up a hand. "You can be done now."

"Oh…" His shoulders drooped too low, but he quickly corrected them. Pressing his palms together, he murmured, "I still dislocate my new glenohumeral joints."

"How are you so okay with being sliced and diced like some Frankenstein's monster?" Kat shook her head, sitting back on the floor. "Are you really happy being cut up like that? Mentally molded like Harley Quinn? You're really okay with that?"

"I do not understand. What is a Harley Quinn?"

She sighed, rolling her eyes. "Shut up."

Famine twitched and flexed his wrists, but he remained dutifully silent. Kat rose, staring up at his blank, black mask. His long fingers wriggled then straightened before Famine released a wordless exclamation and tilted his head. Each movement jerked. Ease combated grace, giving a strange fluidity between movements between harsh conscious corrections. When Kat crossed her arms over her chest, the black-suited alien did the same. Nothing screamed near-human.

"What were you?" she grumbled.

His arms fell back to his sides. "Adaptable."

"Now you're just being purposefully obtuse."

The alien folded in on himself, collapsing backward into the chair. His legs remained straight as he flopped forward. "You ask imprecise questions."

"What species were you? Some kind of insectoid like Bel'von? Reptilian like War? Gaseous like Long-Limb?" Kat rambled. As she gestured with each question, Famine groaned into his knees. "Seriously! What are you?"

"I am Famine."

Placing one hand on her hip, Kat rubbed the bridge of her nose. "What were you before you were Famine?"

He sat up straight, resting his palms on his thighs. "Not Famine."

"Was that your name? Or are you being obtuse again?"

"I was Porfavornomepreguntaseso."

Scoffing, Kat growled, "I speak Spanish! Your name was not 'Please don't ask me that!'"

"Anything else I say will automatically call the orbs. Death told me no orbs with the potentials. We are to converse closely. In your language. I spent seven cycles to perfect my speech pattern," he complained, raising his hands to his throat. "It is so difficult to make these noises. Mah-Wærm promised it would stretch them out, but the vibrations feel funny."

They confined her in a room and rambled at her like some psychopath's therapist. Pressing the heels of her palms into her eyes, Kat groaned. She turned her back to him. Any conversation they had would humanize him. Nothing she said would change his mind. Those who died were tools, and the one who lived wouldn't be much better. Reaching up, she pulled herself back into the hammock. Curling into the fabric, Kat tethered herself within while Famine watched. When she stilled, he stood.

"You are to wake," he repeated.

Kat snorted, tearing and tying the area above her together. "If you don't have my clock, fuck off."

"I do not desire sexual congress," Famine informed her.

"Then you have the clock?" she asked.

He collapsed upon himself, sagging so low to the ground that he seemed to melt. His awkward form fumbled toward the door. Lifting herself to peer over the sheet, Kat watched as the door opened, and Famine left. The green nodes dimmed. Darkness consumed the room, but this time, Kat flipped down to the ground. Her bare feet gathered ash. Dust rose around her legs in clouds. Pressing her hand against the door, she leaned her forehead against the cool metal.

Beneath her touch, the metal receded. Though she regained her balance almost instantaneously, the bright glare of the hall's light blinded her. Kat backed away, raising her hands before her face. Famine's lanky silhouette loomed in the open door. He held out his arms, and when she did not move to take the item from him, he placed it down on the floor and left. As the doorway closed, leaving her in near darkness as the nodes shimmered dimly to life; her eyes fell on the strange new intrusion.

A black box sat on her floor. On its top, a circular gear with sixty teeth clicked away. When sixty clicks passed, the first of six gears on the side ticked forward. Each of the six had ten teeth, and they were separated by a thin band of white. The box formed a perfect six-inch cube, and there was a single gear with twenty-four teeth on the opposite side. Nothing sat on its bottom or back, but there was a clear panel on the front under which the nerve-like nodes glowed: 00:00:02:03. Clicks traced the seconds, and when the next minute came around, the two turned into a three.

When she lifted the clock, her hands slipped over the smooth surfaces where the gears appeared to be. Counting the seconds down, she measured the next sixty carefully. Each tooth lasted the same duration. Frowning, Kat set the box upside down on the seconds gear. The clear surface between the gear and the outside kept the seconds from stalling. Every edge smoothly transitioned into the next surface. Only the transition between the sides and its face could be noted by touch alone. Kat stood. She carried the box to the chair, and lifting it over her head, slamming it down against the metal. Nothing nearly so satisfying as sparks flew. Clanging metal filled the room.

The two remained solid, giving Kat nothing more than a headache. If she couldn't open the damn thing, the clock had no point. Gears and wires, they could be useful. No matter what lay inside, if Kat couldn't open it, the clock would only be a reminder of how long she'd been stuck. Her worries would mount. Lives hung in the balance. An animalistic growl of rage vibrated low in her chest. Squeezing the box, she took a deep breath. Her right hand slid an inch across the back. A click echoed in the room.

Kat dropped into a crouch. "Come on; be open," she whispered, pushing the panel back to reveal the internal wiring.

Connected to the inside with only a thin metallic line, the gear system moved separately from the mess of wires and box of boards. Gold lines intersected with bronze and silver. A single metallic red line crossed, connecting all of the rest. Tapping a finger against the lines, Kat pulled the clock's innards out when nothing shocked her. No tools meant keeping it slow, and without a clear idea of the power source, she couldn't move forward to create an explosive. Escape would take time. Trapped alone, she had nothing but for the foreseeable future.

Chapter Nine

By the third day, Kat took apart the clock entirely. Wires, boards, and gears sprawled the length of the room. Fourteen sleeps beyond that, she'd put it back together correctly twice and counted two days each time before taking it apart once more. No battery could be found. Instead, she found a small barrel of wires which enabled the device to collect free energy from the room. Interrupting the flow to create a buildup of charge wouldn't be too difficult. Timing the explosion offered a number of challenges. If she built up the energy for an explosion, but no one else was around, she couldn't be sure the clock had enough power to slam through the metal. Sliding the panel back into place, Kat frowned.

"Nobody likes to get blown up."

Jumping to her feet with the box in hand, Kat glared at Death. He shimmered. The edges of his suit wisped like mist, spreading from his feet to gather along the floor. A single dark brow rose. Looking straight into his eyes, she swallowed. Empty white orbs stared back. With a single blink, color flooded his irises.

"Is the color for me?" Kat asked. "Or were you supposed to keep it there?"

Death snorted. "Don't ask stupid questions."

"You've covered this. You know how horrible this is. By destroying Earth, you're committing planet-wide extinction." When he sighed and rolled his eyes, Kat frowned. "Bel'von drunk the Kool-Aid, and War's fresh off the mind fuck train, but you've been around. Three times."

"Famine came alone. The richer nations on his planet sent individuals off-world as punishment. We found him in his hundredth or so planetary orbit as punishment for emoting too loudly," he informed her. He brushed his fingers over the wall, sneering down at the dust which came away. "Mah-Wærm gave him a place beside me at my behest. We annihilated the planet and its surrounding infected satellites out of mercy for the rest of the universe. If you wish to speak ill of this process, blame me. I presented the idea of the Riders to Mah-Wærm."

"Why? Why would you do that?"

Pressing his lips together, Death sighed. "Why bother asking? You wouldn't accept any reason I give you."

"True," Kat agreed. "But I'd like to hear you try."

He sighed. "I'm not sure you're capable of understanding."

"Humans have committed genocide over a number of things. Fear's the most common reason. But...you...I'm betting you thought you were doing a service to the universe. Dusting off those who don't match your expectations," Kat offered, placing the clock up into the hammock. "Perfecting the universe in a massive ethnic cleansing."

142

"Is that really so horrible to you? Doing away with murderers? We've breached your informational systems. I've read several texts about human rights. It seems we're in agreement. The difference is that Mah-Wærm follows through. Cultural variance for its own sake has no point. Let them maintain what is right or what does no harm. Traditions of suppression and oppression have no purpose. They inhibit progress," Death explained. His tone exhausted as if this were his hundredth time informing her rather than the first. "Your texts speak of a longing for a world without injustice, yet every time you approach a solution, it is rife with the same sins."

"A bit hypocritical on your part," Kat drawled.

Death flicked his eyes to the floor, and shuffling his feet, he slammed his hand into the wall. Vibrations started in the floor. Panels flipped and shifted beneath their feet, cleaning the debris. Racing to the sheet hanging from the ceiling, Kat grabbed hold of the edge. She spun herself up into its hold as the ceiling opened. Tendrils fell, running across the floor. The sheets moved, drawing upward into the ceiling. Leaping out the opposite side with the clock in hand, Kat landed on the chair as the last of the cloth vanished into the ceiling. Walls descended and blocked out an area of the room where the bed once had been. As the rest of the panels closed, leaving clean white walls in their wake, the walls rose, revealing an identical bed left in its wake.

With a small smile, Death brushed his hands against one another. "Better."

"Yay! More kindling," she cheered sardonically.

When Death shook his arms, his suit retracted and left his chest bare. The mist surrounding him condensed back into the rest of his body. Two elongated triangular patches of ink-black skin ran vertically down his shoulder blades. Otherwise, he had no scars or blemishes. With a skip, he jumped face-first onto the bed. Death sighed, rolling over onto his back.

"I'm stuck speaking with an idealist for the next eighth of a cycle. Forgive me if I want somewhere comfortable to make up for your unpleasantness." He jiggled his legs, and the metallic material around his feet peeled back.

Calluses lined the heels and balls of his feet. Purple colored his toe nails, but they matched his fingernails. His suit loosened, falling around his ankles like sweatpants. He grabbed the long pillow and hugged it to his chest. As the alien's breathing slowed, Kat stood and crossed the room. Death's eyes were closed. One arm pillowed his head while the other held the actual pillow diagonally across his body like a plush shield. If he wanted to try desensitizing her to his presence like a cat, he only wasted his own time. Humanity in the inhuman interested her. She joined the Academy due to a love for science fiction, yet the fanaticism and ideological absolutism drained her.

Retreating back to the chair, Kat pressed against the panel, opening the clock. She tinkered with the system, altering the intact to increase while creating a hold where the charge would build rather than moving cleanly through the system. Destroying the door jumped straight to mind. While killing Death presented a number of exciting prospects – mainly just killing him, the bio-sensitivity of the suits prevented his death from profiting her long term. In a society of body modification, clones weren't off the table.

"Clones offer quick slave labor but for long-term species vitality, variance is more desirable," Death informed her.

Kat sighed. "Get out of my head."

"Not in your head. You think too loudly," Death complained.

"Yet I'm still being allowed to tinker with a possible explosive."

Propping himself up on his elbows, Death hummed. "Famine gave it to you."

"Are we getting paired off then? You and Famine – War and Marie?" Kat wondered aloud.

Death snorted, pursing his lips as he fell back down onto the bed. Pushing the pillow into the air, he batted it back down at the top of the bed. "This isn't about loneliness. Or love. Or friendship. This isn't about your morality. You are here – one of seven in the universe chosen to be tested – because you have potential. You came here of your own volition. Despite several opportunities, you decided to live."

"Cake or death?"

"What?" Death frowned, sitting up to brush his feet against the floor. His lips twitched downward into a frown as his brows furrowed. "What the hell does that mean?"

"Which do you pick? Cake or death?" Kat repeated.

"That's a non sequitur," Death scolded. "If you wish to change the topic, explain your colloquialisms."

"It isn't a colloquialism or a non sequitur. My decision to not view death as an option is ingrained in my society. Dying for a cause, I understand that. I knew the risks coming here. My decision to live isn't approval of your actions," she explained, sealing the box once more. "I can't kill you if I'm dead."

Tilting his head, Death said, "You won't kill me."

"Not today."

Kat trudged over to the door. Placing the box beside the wall, she knocked lightly on the metal three times. Each knock vibrated across the length of the wall. All the while, Death's gaze weighed on her. She chewed on her tongue. Anything she thought could be used against her. Crossing her arms, she turned around with a frown. Decay filled her mind. From the smell of rotted flesh to the slaughter house from the movie that had given her nightmares at nine years old. Adam Scott's tibia breaking, sending bone through skin. Blood oozed and scream roared as she collected her worst memories and threw them at Death like a flash bomb.

He yawned, showing off the crowns of his mandibular teeth. In the back of his throat, there were no tonsils; instead, his mouth connected back into the smooth tube of his throat. Death blinked and smirked. An onslaught of images flooded back. The expanding heat of a rising red giant swallowed her whole.

Screaming wraiths echoed in the dark, swimming like sirens around a black hole. A single ship blazed like a neutron star in the dark. Her bones ached with loneliness even as her fingers curled into fists with rage. Stumbling backward, Kat pressed her hands against her head. The door slid open behind her, and Death's suit slammed back into place, covering his face as War stormed inside.

"Where is she?" he roared.

Death stood. The blank white of his mask reflected War's own black and red. Mist curled around him, blurring the edges of his body once more. "Get out," Death hissed. His words churned as if ground down by gears.

War's trembled. His fists shook. "I decide who lives and dies!"

"Marie's dead?" Kat whispered.

"Where is she?" War bellowed, but when Death remained silent, he turned to Kat. "She's gone. Someone took her. I left her for…" Throwing out a hand, a plasma beam slammed into the bed, setting it on fire.

Knocking War's hand down, Death spat, "She's alive, you idiot. We moved her to a different cell."

"You had no right!"

"Follow the correct visitation pattern, and I won't have to interfere again," Death retorted as he activated the walls to fix the bed a second time.

While the two concentrated on one another, Kat backed away. The door to the hall stood open. Picking up the clock, she glanced back at the two who had reverted into another language. From the ceiling, one of the silver orbs spun. Before it could dislodge from the ceiling, Kat ran. Only the temperature changed between the room and the white hall. As she raced down the corridor, her breath fogged. Nothing marked the doors. In her hands, the clock shook. Static jumped along the gears. Behind her, War ran. His footsteps thundered against the metal floor, but vibrations traveled through the air, preempting Death's transportation before he appeared in front of her. As his form solidified, she twisted and slammed the clock into the side of his helmet. Death's head snapped to the side. Stumbling, he moved just enough for her to drop the box and continue running past him.

An orb glided up beside her, keeping pace as the air vibrated a second time. Kat squinted. Overhead, the lights flickered. Then the bomb went off, sending her flying forward. Electricity traveled along the walls. The bright lights drained, and metal clanked as holes opened along either side of the hallway. With a groan, Kat pushed against the floor, crawling onward as spots danced in her vision. All along the floor, blue nodes lit. They outlined her body, spreading up the walls as metal echoed ahead. A dark form stood over her, and when her eyes focused, Famine stood above her. He tilted his head.

"You are not where I left you," he informed her. Right before a large chunk of wood slammed against his head. Straightening up, Famine glanced over his shoulder. "Desist please."

"Desist this!" Rachel spat.

She smacked him with a beam in the face as Amondi slammed another against the side of the alien's knees. Stepping to the side, Famine tilted his

148

head, but before he could speak, Ngawang jumped over Kat's prone form. With a makeshift knife in hand, the dark-haired woman stabbed into the side of his armor. A hiss of steam rose around the scrap of metal as Ngawang pulled back to stab back into the space spot. Marie and Qamar each grabbed one of Kat's arms, lifting her to her feet. Half-dragging, half-leading her down the corridor, they raced for a tall door leading to a darker side hall.

"He's down!" Qamar roared over her shoulder. "Leave him!"

Ngawang spat on Famine's fallen form, but she ran alongside Amondi as Rachel came slow behind. "Fucking, bastard!"

"Chelsea's not in any of these," Rachel yelled.

Ngawang sneered, sliding around Qamar to take the lead. "Maybe we got lucky, and she's dead."

"Lucky? She's our friend!" Rachel reminded the other woman.

Amondi coughed. "She's friends with whoever is convenient."

"So am I," Marie admitted. Her bright red lips parted to reveal her sharp white teeth. "We've all got our survival techniques."

"Lipstick on his butt," Kat gasped the winced as her ribs ached.

Marie chuckled. "Hoped at least one of you enjoyed that."

"You what?" Rachel gasped.

Ngawang rolled her eyes, but a smirk played about her lips. "Marie kissed War's ass because the idiot's too enamored to question why seduction might be a misstep between an executioner and the head on the block."

"I know. I'm brilliant, right?" Marie cackled.

Kat smiled. Each time she lifted one foot, the other slid in a delay. Heat radiated off her spine. "Big boom, shit, feet," she murmured.

They turned down a dark corridor. The ceilings lowered to hang well within reach, and the only light around them came from the glowing nerve-like luminescent nodes.

"Wait!" Amondi called.

She pointed down a small hall. At the very end, a door stood. Frame to hinges, a common doorway stood before them. Metal covered the rest of the hall, but wood formed the door and its frame. Heading down the hall, Amondi slipped around the three. Qamar positioned herself furthest out. Marie leaned Kat against the wall as Rachel and Ngawang held up their makeshift weapons. Amondi's hand wrapped around the knob, and it turned with a soft click.

"You've got to be kidding me," grumbled Ngawang.

Shoving the doorway open, Amondi cursed. Rachel gaped. The room looked nothing like Kat's had. A deep blue rug covered the whole floor. Rather than a canopy bed, there was a huge low mattress taking over the far side of the room. From the desk in the far corner and the viewing panel above to the lounge set up on the opposite side, nothing in the room suggested Chelsea resided in a prison cell. Chelsea glanced up from the tablet in her hand with a smile.

"You're wearing fluffy boot slippers," Marie said, pointing at Chelsea's feet.

Glancing down, Chelsea tossed her blond hair over her shoulder. "They matched the sweater dress."

"Did they give you a manual for the ship?" Ngawang demanded.

Chelsea frowned. "What?"

"What did you ask for that you got all this?" Amondi asked before Ngawang could comment again.

"I didn't ask for anything," Chelsea frowned. Pouting, she sighed. "Well, maybe for a vegan diet because who knows what that meat was, and they left me with only two different outfits, and both were white, so I asked for a few more - like this one!"

Bel'von lied. Faced with the wealth of luxury surrounding Chelsea, no one else could've been chosen as Conquest. From her perfectly coiffed blonde hair to the shoes, Chelsea stood apart. She had no reason to be so. Rachel took the same classes. The rest went through the same basic training, but for all the sense it didn't make, Chelsea was Conquest, and there was no way Kat had been the only one to realize this. Though Ngawang smiled, the narrowing of her eyes better matched a grimace. Marie set her lips into a straight line and pulled Kat closer.

"Come on," Marie murmured to Qamar.

Qamar ducked back into place without a word. Her tan face drawn and tired in a way she hadn't been before they found Chelsea. Storming into the room, Ngawang upended the desk. In a few kicks, she separated its legs and tossed two each to Amondi and Rachel.

"You shouldn't do that!" Chelsea exclaimed.

151

With a laugh, Ngawang turned her back on the blond and ransacked the wardrobe. Clothing flew, and Chelsea raced to stop her. While the others clashed, Qamar glanced around the corridor. They couldn't escape, but the more they learned, the further they went, the better prepared they would be for whatever was to come. Darkness stretched onward, and as the lights overhead buzzed with static, they did nothing to assuage the dark. Black metal lined them on all sides. Footsteps thundered from the bright white hall.

Shadows cascaded across the far wall, and spheres descended from the ceiling as War marched. Red swallowed the black in his suit. Around a long staff, his fingers curled, flexing and twitching as he stormed down the hall. Electricity jumped across the surface of his body. Static popped, gathering and shooting forward. Death appeared, shimmered, disappeared, and reappeared in different positions; however, the forward motion of his usual transportation gave way to random movements. Steam rose from his metal armor, weaving between his limbs to the ceiling. Like a shadow, Famine lurked behind him.

"You shouldn't have done that," War growled.

He spun the staff, crashing the end into Rachel's stomach. Kicking Amondi back into the side hall, the alien grabbed Ngawang's face and threw her into the corner where the two halls connected. One by one, they fell before War's rage, tumbling down like playing cards. Tweedles paired off - two to each woman. Metal hands tightened around Rachel's upper arms. They dragged her away. Her screams echoed, and when two more stood forward, Amondi ran. A rod of metal extended from one of the Tweedle's arms. Like a whip, she cracked it back and forth, sending a tendril forth. Wrapping around her ankles, the serpentine weapon slammed her to the ground.

"Chelsea!" Amondi called. "Help us!"

"Eyes forward, Parker," Marie ordered, picking up the pace.

"We can't outrun them," Qamar whispered.

Turning down a side hall, Marie glared at the metal walls. "Not running. Hiding."

"With doors we can't open?" Qamar frowned. "Even if we get in, there isn't any way to be sure we could get out."

"Surges seem to work," Kat said.

"Don't think you'll be allowed to touch wires for a while," Marie retorted.

Catching her feet beneath her, Kat pulled back, pushing the other two women forward as she collapsed against the nearest wall. "Go! I'm just slowing you down."

"Kat?" Qamar hesitated, but Marie nodded, grabbing Qamar's arm and tugging the other forward.

"Make them pay," Kat whispered as the two fled.

Kat closed her eyes, pressing the palms of her hands against the metal wall. If she wasn't next on the kill list before, the explosion shot her to the top. Death wouldn't be so bad. Jacobi was there. Wherever there was. Spaced or dissected, neither would bother her after her neurons stopped firing. Shifting, she glared back down the hall. Unarmed and dressed only in the blood-stained white dress, Kat pushed herself to stand unsupported as War stormed around the corner.

"Where did the other two go?" he growled.

Kat sighed. "Chelsea gets a five-star room, yet Marie's your favorite? I'm not buying that."

Splitting his staff in half, War slammed one half through the wall to his left. "Where is she?"

"Why do you care? You assholes took better care of Chelsea. Go make kissy-faces with her," Kat retorted, pressing a hand against her right leg to stop it from shaking.

Rounding the corner, Bel'von led half a dozen Tweedles two-by-two. Mist curled up from the floor, and his electricity jumped between the vapors, and Death appeared. War trudged toward her. Red swirled in different hues along the outside of his suit, and when he towered over her, she smirked. Death wouldn't be so bad. Chelsea was Conquest. The rest of them would just be fodder. One day was just as good a day to die as the next.

"You stupid creature. Step aside." War raised his arm and brought the halved staff down on her shoulder.

As she collapsed, Kat grabbed hold of the same staff. Her body moved automatically. Long hours of combat training taking hold when her body wished to crumble. One leg crossed over as she jumped, wrapping the other leg up from beneath his opposite arm. She hooked her ankles and snapped his head back with her thighs while her hands twisted his, but War wasn't human. Though he fell backward at the sudden change in weight, the red-suited alien easily tore away his hand from her grip. When they slammed into the ground, Kat winced. Gritting her teeth, she slammed her elbow down on his side.

"I'd like to remind you that this isn't a fair fight," Kat informed the alien.

War growled, grabbing her leg. Before he could break it, she twisted, smashing his shoulder with her knee. Tweedles marched past. Their minds screamed out, but they filtered on the edge of her thoughts. Curling to wrap an arm around her throat, War pressed her back against the floor. Bel'von stepped up. His shimmering compact eyes had no pupils to track his gaze, but the weight landed squarely on Kat. Her stomach churned. Empty and sloshing between explosions as Tweedles begged her to stop. If War raged, there would be hell to pay. Death would ravage the halls. Blood red claimed his eyes until it claimed the floor, and only when his feet shuffled through the liquid and pus would anyone calm the berserker within him. Their reasoning fell on ears deafened by her own pulse, but a single word caught her mind: "Please." It knocked the breath from her lungs.

Going limp, Kat closed her eyes. When War's hold loosened, she glanced up at him. Red swirled across his masked face. "Do it," she gasped around his grip. "Kill me."

Death glided across the hall. A phantom menace focused on two figures already out of sight. With the Tweedles, he continued even when Bel'von's eyes flickered back. Kat frowned, and War shoved her back as he stood. Kicking his foot against the wall beside her head, he bellowed wordless syllables. The spheres hung beside his head, and though they spun, no translations came. War punched the wall over her head. When he reconnected the ends of the staff, spikes erupted down one half with a single long scythe blade curling in red at one end. A dagger's point formed at the opposite. Bellowing in one long cry, the red-suited alien whipped the weapon around. Every swing passed the blade close to Kat. However, each one left a long cut in the wall without touching her. Rearing back, War lifted the scythe over his head and brought it down into the wall over Kat's head. When he shifted to draw it back once more, the blade stayed locked in place.

"Damn it!" War screamed.

Frozen in place, Kat glanced up the hall. Death and the rest had disappeared. War paced. With each step, he railed in random syllables. Spinning overhead the orbs rippled every few syllables with a word, but nothing made sense.

"Oil…plumage…undoubtedly...hydrocephalic …magnetic monkey volcano," the sphere translated.

Kat shifted to the left. War kept ranting, and with each violent gesture, the red receded from his suit. It swirled along in ribbons as the black grew. Leaning against the wall, Kat struggled to stay standing. Her legs shook. Pain laced its way up her back. As predictable and startling as the first burst of flame after striking a match, War lunged at her, grabbing her arm and slamming her back against the wall. His helm clicked. The material retracted into his collar, leaving his shimmering gold eyes bare. With furrowed brows, he flashed his teeth and made a low sound in the back of his throat.

"Never met a growling reptile before," Kat commented.

His lips closed over his teeth as the inner edge of his brow trembled. "She's going to die, and there's nothing I can do."

"Six of us will die," she reminded him, and he slammed his fist against the metal beside her head.

"Shut up!"

"Why? So you can pretend Marie's the only one in danger?" Kat huffed. Pushing back against the wall, she ignored the twitching anger in his brows. "She's just as aware as I am. We're fucked. Worst we can do is inconvenience you."

"You have no idea, do you?" War murmured. His eyes blazed as his fists clenched and unclenched. "They said your kind would be smarter. That humans were the second closest species to Mah-Wærm, but all you do is whine."

"We're natural complainers," Kat agreed.

Inhaling as if each milliliter of air caused him excruciating pain, War pressed a gloved hand to his forehead. "I am the last of my kind. There are no others like me anywhere in the universe. When I die, everything about my species will die with me. So I have endured, because my species - my people deserve to endure. I have watched my brothers die. Seen my wife and child burned alive. You have no idea how lucky you are to have found the edge of an empire."

Narrowing her eyes, she stretched to stand as tall as she could. "I watched my partner die. One of Bel'von's kind shot him straight through. His last words reaffirmed his love for me, and you think I'm lucky? Mah-Wærm didn't have to go and drag him here; my love came here with me, so don't tell me I'm lucky. Everything you endured, I'm there now. My people might be far away, but they're still dying."

She made her words weapons and aimed them at his heart. Though the enemy shared a familiar face and spoke a familiar language, they weren't human. More important than that, they weren't family. They hadn't grown with her, suffered with, celebrated with, mourned with her. Death, Famine, and War loomed over her life; living shadows made flesh. Any show of pain didn't make them anything more. Pain made them vulnerable. Vulnerable creatures could be killed. Today, tomorrow, fifty or a hundred or a thousand years from that moment, Katelyn Parker would kill them all. One way or another, and if ghosts existed, not even death would stop her.

War pursed his lips. Stepping back, he gestured back the way they had come. "Go."

"Why?"

Grabbing her arm, he dragged her down the corridor. "I've been soft on you all. Let you rest between the slaughter. My mistake. I'll learn."

"Will you?" Kat grumbled, struggling to keep up without losing her footing. Her back and sides ached.

"Yes, but you might not be alive by then."

War brought her around the corner, storming down the hall like a force of nature. Chelsea's door threw open of its own accord. Back on her plush sofa, Chelsea glanced up. Rachel, Ngawang, and Amondi gathered in the corner. Dragging one of the nails from Chelsea's desk over a pillow, Ngawang glowered up

158

at War. Clothe and feathers pooled around her bloody viscera. Actual blood absorbed into makeshift white bandages around Rachel's forehead and left elbow. Amondi reached out. Her hand held Ngawang back when Chelsea threw aside her book to rush toward War.

"What's happening?" she asked.

War pressed down on Kat's shoulder. Her knees buckled, and when he continued to push, they collapsed beneath her. Falling to the crowd, Kat winced as a resounding crack sounded throughout the room. When Rachel shifted to her knees, War's forefinger lengthened into a blade. He ran it alongside Kat's face. The sharp metal slid beside her ear.

"You think you're ready. You think you're Conquest." War pressed the blade closer to Kat's neck. "Kill her."

Chelsea's jaw dropped. "What?"

"No!" Amondi cried as Rachel blanched.

War pointed his bladed finger at Amondi. "You don't get a say in this!"

"I won't!" Chelsea cried, backing away from War. "I can't. I'm not...no."

Ngawang scoffed. "Not keeping the nice room long if you don't pay for it in blood."

Cold metal slid over Kat's skull. The blunt fingers of his opposite hand clenched around the back of her head. Tugging her head back, he forced her to extend her neck and expose her throat. He brought the blade to slide across her neck. As he moved, his hand dipped in and out of her sight. A chill ran down her spine. Each breath – no matter how shallow – set her further on edge. Her chest rose, and the brush of the blade pressed closer.

Pressing her hands to her ears, Chelsea closed her eyes. She sat on her feet and turned her back to Kat, to War, to the whole mess. Kat's lips stretched. A thin smile painted on her face. She glared up at the alien who held her steadfast in place. His gold eyes darted from Chelsea's trembling form to the three women sitting on the floor. Stepping back, he held Kat toward them.

"You said you wanted to live," War growled, and Ngawang clenched her jaw. "Kill her."

"I'd rather kill you," the black-haired woman informed him.

Amondi's eyes dropped to the floor. Her shoulders tensed. "No one here will kill Kat."

"Why are you called that?" War growled. His gold eyes shifted, the pupils elongated before tightening back to pinpoints of black.

"When you steal language from a head, don't you get the spelling?" Rachel spat. "Kat - Katelyn. It's a term of affection."

"Names have purpose! Shortening them does nothing but diminish the individual," War roared.

"Can you just kill me already?" Kat asked.

Reaching up to hold the hand gripping her skull, she wrapped her opposite hand around his bladed fingers. Though she tugged on the blades, he fought, keeping his blade back from her throat. Rachel yelped. Biting her lip, she looked away, but her exclamation drew War's attention regardless. His fingers tightened around Kat's head. With a growl, he tossed her aside.

160

"You're all useless. Emotional! Weak! He'll destroy you when he comes. Get inside your heads and tear you apart. If you can't even consider killing each other now, how will it be when you aren't in your own heads - when you aren't in the body you know?" War paced the length of the entrance. His eyes darkened. "He'll destroy her. Kills everything good and right in the world."

"Then kill her first," Ngawang suggested.

Amondi cursed, "Don't say that."

"She's right," Kat said. "We're all going to die. Be merciful. Kill us first."

"Before we become monsters like you," Rachel joined in the urging.

War's brows furrowed. "You're tricking me."

"To kill us?" Kat pursed her lips. "Hardly a trick when you need to kill us off anyways."

"If you get to decide who Conquest is, pick Marie," Rachel suggested.

Though she spoke in line with Kat and Ngawang, Rachel's fingers curled into the rug beneath her. Tears lined her lower lashes. Ngawang leaned forward. The muscles in her neck and arms stretched taut. At any moment, she would race forward. If they could unbalance War, they could kill him. With his helmet down, he was vulnerable. Fingers curled around the nails she used on the pillows, Ngawang rose onto her toes as Kat laughed. Jumping at the sound, War glared at her.

"You integrated with the Hive. Extinction is one thing; they underwent obliteration - their species and planet names are taboo. Only Bel'von has a name of his own. The rest are mindless soldiers." War shivered, shaking his head.

Kat quieted with an exhausted smile. "They aren't mindless. They're screaming. Lonely and furious. It's why we'll kill Bel'von the moment we can."

"We will," Rachel agreed. "He's the only thing holding them back."

"I saw their last stand. They hate Mah-Wærm. They hate all of you, and if they could betray Bel'von, they'd do it a million times and a million times again. He's an abomination. A prospective queen that refused to transform. He put his self-image before his people." Kat shrugged. "Can't say I blame him. I would tear out my reproductive system before becoming anyone's broodmare. Last surviving woman or not."

"I did it before we left," Amondi confessed.

All eyes jumped to her. Rachel's brows furrowed. "You…what? What are you saying?"

"I had a hysterectomy before we left. They offered a list of optional surgeries before flight, and I just…I understand why most people just wrote it off, but here we are. Captured. No idea what they want from us, and it's strange, but I take solace in knowing my organs won't be used against me in that way. They can put in an artificial womb or take DNA for a genetically engineered child, but in the end - that wouldn't make me think twice about killing whatever thing they made from me. If it were my baby…I realized I couldn't, so I took the chance away. Had my eggs frozen for future surrogacy, but I doubt anyone's hunting those down just to torment me,"

Amondi explained. Her dark skin shimmered under the bright lights. "If that's what Bel'von did, if that cost his people whatever it cost them...I can understand that intimately."

War tilted his head. His golden eyes shifted, moving from Amondi's face to her abdomen as if he could see through her skin to the scars beneath. The grip on Kat's head slipped away as War's hand fell to his side. Blunt fingers replace the sharp blades of his opposite hand, and with a sharp yank, he pulled fully away from Kat. He blinked. Tucking his chin toward his chest, War backed away, turning and ducking out of the room. The wooden door slammed behind him.

Forcing a smile, Amondi shifted to cross her legs. "Now that was just overreacting."

"Pretty depressing confession," Chelsea retorted, letting her hands fall from her ears.

"Now the princess speaks," Ngawang grumbled.

Chelsea ground her teeth. "I didn't ask to be treated better than anyone else."

Swinging her fist, Ngawang slammed a nail into Chelsea's couch and stood. The dark-haired woman glared. Her eyes narrowed to dark points as she stared the blonde down. Like a predator, Ngawang prowled. Chelsea pressed her hands against the cushions beside her, pushing herself further into the couch, but Ngawang's head lowered; her shoulders tensed, and with a scoff, the black-haired woman leapt forward. Screaming, Chelsea raised her arms and ducked, but Ngawang never reached her. A beam of pale red light surrounded her like a highlighter's outline.

War stepped further into the room. One of his hands extended outward toward Ngawang, connecting them with a thin beam of light. In his opposite hand, he held his spiked scythe.

Chelsea jumped over the back of the couch. Cowering behind the furniture, she peaked over the edge at War. His nostrils flared with each inhale. All around his golden irises, the white showed. He ground his teeth. With a flick of wrist, the alien cast Ngawang aside. Kat flinched as her friend's body slammed against the far wall. She fell limp on the floor like a rag doll.

"Just stop! Stop it!" Rachel cried.

Amondi leapt to her feet, but the red light surrounded her. "Nobody moves," War growled.

Swallowing, Kat pushed to her feet. "Kill us, or get out of our way."

"As you wish," War murmured.

He dropped his hand, and rearing back, he brought it down across Kat. Pain like a fire blazed from Kat's left eye to her right hip. More a rag doll than Ngawang, she split at her invisible seams. Her knees snapped against the floor. Blood poured down her, and only a hand against her stomach kept her organs inside. Red covered her vision. Falling backward, she held tight, pressing down though blood gushed from her.

"Kat!" Rachel shrieked.

The pitch of her voice jumped. A cry almost animalistic in its unrelenting grief broke through her call, but Kat couldn't pinpoint its origin. Cold took hold at the tips of her fingers. Bleeding up her arms, it crept into every crevice of her as black stole her sight away. As her fingers slipped, a hand pressed down in their place. Warmth spread from them.

"I will not let you die," a deep voice told her. It seemed to bounce off the walls, coming from every direction.

Vague lights pierced the darkness. A long shadow loomed over her while another blurred form leant over her from the opposite side. When the longer one tilted, his name leapt to her mind. Famine had arrived. War's raging rang in her ears, but the words which overpowered the echo were Marie's.

"Put that down!" Marie commanded. "Do it! Put that thing down now!"

Metal clattered to the floor as War roared, "She dies! They all die!"

"We will," Marie informed him.

A sob burst forth. "I can't lose…not again. I'm not strong enough. I love to my bones."

"If I say you are strong enough, you are," the voice proclaimed. "Keep the potentials away from this area. I have no need for your assistance in this matter, Famine, step back."

"She is leaking. Should she still be leaking?" Famine asked.

"Bleeding," the voice corrected gently.

"Bleeding," Famine repeated. He hummed. "Stop bleeding human. You will die."

A low chuckle rumbled, and the heat grew. "I'm sure she is aware of that, Famine."

Famine straightened. His shadow became a pillar against the bright light of Chelsea's room. Color leaked back though it made little difference. Everything remained monotones. Grays and creams

165

came as if they could warm the coldness of black and white Heat razed along the wound. Every muscle in Kat's body tensed. Fire lit along her nerves, and as she reared up, Famine ducked, pressing her back down. Tracing from her hip upward, pressure and heat spread. When they reached her neck, two points of quicksilver followed. Orange blurred her vision.

"Should we burn the other side?" Famine inquired. "She is no longer symmetrical."

Heat cleared, leaving only two quicksilver eyes behind. Purples, blues, and opalescent shimmered. A pale face stared down at her. From his slicked back black hair to the brilliant white of his teeth, he matched the room. Even his knitted sweater was a light shade of gray. Kat frowned. The left side of her mouth twitched. Her muscles ached unevenly, but the taunt pull of a scar or stitched wound didn't match. Where taunt cauterized fresh ought to have been, just the familiar numbness after a particularly frustrating dental visit.

"The muscles will tighten back up, and the paleness of the new skin will be matched soon enough," the silver-eyed man reassured the black-suited alien. "Just consider this her first modification."

"You should have let her die!" Chelsea cried.

Amondi lunged forward, slamming her first into Chelsea's nose. The blonde tumbled to the ground. Standing over her, Amondi inhaled. Out of the corner of her eye, Kat watched her pant. A pleased little smirk twisted on Amondi's lips as if she had wanted to punch Chelsea for a long time, but Famine popped up with a high-pitched shriek.

"Back down, Famine," the strange alien man called. "A broken nose can be easily mended, but I rather think she deserved that."

Famine crouched down, pressing down on Kat's shoulders. In a soft voice, he confessed, "I listed her symmetrical features as her one positive."

"Then let us hope you were too severe. I have no intention of fixing her nose. Miss Parker has all my attention today." A smile twisted his lips, but no minute speck of kindness or joy reached his eyes.

Like a phantom, mist moved out of the corner of Kat's eyes. Death materialized. He frowned. Deep lines creased his forehead and around his mouth. Spikes of white jumped from his suit. With a glance at Amondi, he disappeared and reappeared beside War and Marie. The black-haired man sat back, watching as Death peeled War from Marie's embrace. Footsteps shuffled along the rug. Qamar crouched down by Famine's side.

"Kat?" she whispered. "We've got you, Kat."

When she reached around Famine, the black-haired man slapped her hand. "Get back over with the rest."

"Please, she needs someone to stay with her," Qamar pleaded.

Death scoffed as he shoved War toward the door. "What do you want me to do with this idiot?"

Quicksilver eyes stared back into Kat's hazel as he said, "Nothing." Pale lips curled into a small smile. "War?"

"Yes, sir?" the golden-eyed alien stepped forward, pulling away from Death.

"You made a mistake. How will you fix it?" the man asked.

War's eyes dulled. His shoulders drooped, and the tension in his jaw drained. "I will be reeducated."

"Good. Hop to it now," the man commanded.

Bowing his head, War whispered, "Yes, Mah-Wærm," and fled the room.

The master of their fate leaned over Kat. Any trace of a smile faded. White light painted a halo over his head, but his horns appeared as real in her mind as the heat of his hand against the strange numbness spreading down from her face to her hip. Infinity delved into his gaze. Cold like the universe hadn't yet known loomed in him; a heat death no ship could outrun. She had seen such a thirst before, and no one could quench the yawning hole in that sort of soul. They crawled from their mother's womb with an inhumanity branded in their bones. For all he surrounded himself in his likeness, Mah-Wærm's narcissistic ego belied a far more monstrous depravity. His eyes crinkled at the edges. His hand descended upon her face, and with a tap of his middle finger between her eyebrows, darkness consumed her.

Chapter Ten

Propped up on pillows, Kat awoke. Dull pain radiated through her from her bones outward. As her eyes focused, white surrounded her with a single dot of blue. Slowly, her eyes focused, and a blanket folded across the foot of the bed came into view. Variegated blue strands of what looked to be wool wrapped and twined around one another as if to paint the infiniteness of the universe – spotted with whites and golden stars. The urge to touch left her hands itching. When she shifted her foot, pain rippled up her body. A speck of color just beyond her reach – an insult if she ever saw one. It was made all the worse at the slight huff from the man sitting beside her. Mah-Wærm lounged, pulling light from the air. Small orbs of wispy light danced about his fingers as the nodes along the walls shifted.

"I believe the appropriate greeting is 'good morning,'" the dictator said. His quicksilver eyes drifted to her. "But that depends on which side of the planet you lived on."

"I doubt it's a good morning for anyone," Kat retorted.

Mah-Wærm smiled, and the chair drew closer to the bed. "No. I suppose it likely isn't. If it's any comfort, it won't be their last. Not yet."

Frowning, Kat leaned back against the pillows. "Mercy or delayed gratification?"

"Neither," the man admitted. "Your people are rather clever."

Her brow furrowed. Clever meant difficult. She could see it in the way his eyes narrowed when he landed upon the word. The nanites had gone up. There was nothing else capable of having a chance against the fleet of ships under his command, but a hole lurked in the bottom of her stomach. Though Earth had found a defense, the best they could do was erect a golden cage. Mah-Wærm stood immortal. If Bel'von and the rest of the aliens on this ship told the truth, no one could outlast him, and all the advanced technology under his domain would concentrate on destroying the nanites if he wished to do so.

"Where are the others?" Kat asked, shifting their conversation.

Tilting his head, Mah-Wærm frowned. "Together. It seemed pointless to separate you after the mess War made."

"Why separate us in the first place?"

"Humans reshape quite easily. It's your minds which offer the greatest challenge. I need to break down your psyches and reintroduce a new moral code. White rooms with no interaction and minimal stimuli for an extended duration should have warped your perception of time. Providing uncertainty about your teammates' survival and pushing personal time with my Riders would introduce a new dependency which would upset the hierarchy within your command structure." His tone rolled, rising and lowering with each sentence. Like a hypnotist's easy droll, every

170

word threatened to lull her into a false sense of safety.

"Then why reunite us now?" she asked.

Tilting his head, he sighed. "You reunited you."

"But you could separate us again. You could have let me die," Kat pointed out.

Her eyes narrowed when his lips shifted into a small smile. The dark lashes of his eyes brushed against his high cheekbones as he reached for her hand. She quickly pulled it away, and his smile grew as quicksilver stared her down. Any joy on his lips didn't reach his eyes. They were as cold as the translucent walls of the brig. Shivering, Kat tugged on the edges of her blankets. Grabbing the blue blanket, Mah-Wærm spread it over her, running his hands over it as if to smooth out wrinkles which weren't there. Standing to sit beside her on the bed, the pale man stared into her eyes. Her heart raced, and every muscle in her body tensed.

"War is young. He's learning, but Famine placed far too much trust in him. As he made a mistake, he'll be reeducated. Death will fix him," Mah-Wærm assured her, and he leaned across her to press a hand against her hip.

Kat flinched. The edges of the new skin tugged. "Then what?"

"Not then," he corrected. "While."

"Fine, and while that happens, what?"

His lips peeled back to flash his white teeth. "You'll cull your own from here on out. Between each round, I'll introduce the potentials to different aspects of my empire. We're on our way to one of my favorite little planets."

"Who against whom?"

Pale lips pressed together in a straight line. The edges twitched down, jumping right back as if incapable of staying in a full frown. "It would have been you versus Rachel, but I believe Ngawang will take your place."

"No, I can do it," Kat insisted, shifting despite the pain which flared throughout her core as she tried to swing her legs over the opposite side of the bed, but his hand held her in place. "You want a fight to the death. Let me up."

"You are problematic."

Glaring, Kat pushed against his wrist, but he would not be moved. "I'm human. Get over it."

"Marie is problematic as well. Qamar too though they haven't realized such," he admitted.

"Marie knows," Kat corrected.

Mah-Wærm smiled. "You don't know, do you?"

Frowns stayed well enough on Kat's face. Brows furrowed, she pulled her hand back, but he released her hip and grabbed her hand instead. A rough thumb brushed over her skin. His calloused palm pressed against the back of her fingers, and though she resisted, he lifted her palm to face him. Kissing the center, he kept his eyes locked on hers.

"Kill me," she demanded.

Blinking slowly, he chuckled. "Not yet."

"Then tell me what I don't know."

His quicksilver eyes flicked to her hand then back to her frustrated glower. "That would be Qamar's secret, not mine."

"So – Qamar's gender fluid," Kat shrugged. "Not much of a secret."

"Agendered – in my own language and most others, there is a more polite pronoun, but 'it' just doesn't fit. Suggests something rather rude, doesn't it?" he murmured, keeping his lips close to her skin. Each puff of warm breath sent her adrenaline soaring, and if she could have leapt from the bed, she would have been as far from him as the ship would've allowed. "Among you, Qamar is unique."

"Which is problematic?" Kat posited.

A single dip and raise of his chin provided the only acknowledgement of her correct supposition. "You are erratic. One moment, you would die to keep others alive. The next, you tear the world around you down."

Jacobi's warm brown eyes haunted her mind's eye whenever she blinked. Swallowing back the tears, she asked, "Have you ever loved?"

"There's nothing on your planet with a lifespan so comparably short that I might even begin to frame the absurdity of your question," Mah-Wærm retorted. Tilting his head, he smiled. The same cold emptiness filled his eyes. "However, I suspect you wouldn't be able to contextualize my response without further information. You see, I am the last of my species."

"So are all your Riders. War still loves," Kat replied. If he wanted to paint himself a tragedy, she wouldn't give him the ease of playing lead.

"Yes. It's rather new to him though. He hasn't lived long enough to realize how long his life will be. Death knows. Famine…" As if playing demure, he dropped his gaze to the blue woven blanket. Releasing her hand, Mah-Wærm drifted his fingers over the twined coils. "Well, his modifications haven't gone as expected, so there's some freshness to those wounds. Scholars often take the longest to fathom the pointlessness of existence. A desire to accumulate all knowledge –regardless of its utility – clouds any grander idea of how futile the endeavor might be."

His eyes flicked up to meet her own. They sparkled, and his lips quirked up at one corner as if asking whether she understood the joke. She stared back. Refusing to blink, she raised a single brow. He had a plan. She could see it in the way he stared back. The way he touched her suggested things which his expressions failed to delivery, and the more he toyed with her, the greater her desire to attack him grew. It might have been futile, but everything she did was at this point. As if he could read her thoughts, Mah-Wærm rolled his eyes.

With a sigh, he ran a hand through his dark hair. "Contrary to plan, you will be my focus for the next few cycles. Death will assist you, but I'll be keeping a close eye on you."

"I'd prefer you didn't," Kat told him.

His quicksilver eyes narrowed. "Would you? I can focus on Qamar if you'd prefer."

"If there is pain involved, I'd prefer you focus on me. If you think there won't be pain, but you've never bothered to ask, focus on me. If you would prefer some sort of procedure to modify Qamar, focus on me." Kat paused. Her hands knotted into the woven blanket. "If your focus means socializing, go with them."

Mah-Wærm hummed; a light buzzing grated against her nerves. Slipping off of the bed, he brushed his hands down his clothes as if there were some speck of dirt on his black pants or light gray shirt. Nothing clanked when he stood. As the man headed toward the door, his feet came into view. For all the softness of his clothing, she had imagined boots. Instead, the ruler of a horrific empire wore knitted socks. His feet padded against the floor, and when he turned, his legs slid rather than stepped.

"My attention isn't negative or positive. Though you imagine yourself capable of separating the two between yourself and the others, that won't be the case," Mah-Wærm told her.

Cold pinpricks danced underneath her eyes, and until tears poured over her lashes, Kat hadn't realized she was crying. His pale lips curved into an empty smile. Blue tinged the inner edge. Biting her tongue, she glared when he nodded and swiveled to go. The wall closed behind him, swallowing the hall and isolating her once again. Burrowing her fingers in the loops and curled knots of the colored blanket, Kat stretched her spine, screaming as her skin resisted the movement. Her left eye blurred further.

With a cry of savage rage, she threw the blanket to the ground at the bed's side, only catching a knot on its edge before the woven length went to the floor. Kat settled against the pillows. Her eyes slid closed, but her fingers worried the final knot. Fiber by fiber, she unraveled one string from the next. Stars split into dashes upon gradients of blue. They coiled and wound about her legs. A mess of blue over the smooth white of the sheets.

Mist spread across the floor. At her side, the air vibrated before Death appeared. Fanning out on either side of his head, the helm receded to reveal his pale face. Though their colorings were similar, Death better matched among Ngawang's family while Mah-Wærm might've been one of Kat's cousins on her mother's side. When he ran a hand through his hair, however, the gesture united the two - mad scientist and patient - leaving Kat queasy.

"Hanging isn't a pleasant way to go," he said, sitting in the chair Mah-Wærm left behind.

Kat sighed. "I don't plan on dying today."

"How do you decide each second? You don't have a coin or anything? Is it some random generator in your head?" Death asked, and while the questions could've been mocking, his tone was sincere.

Burying her fingers in the coiling strands, Kat bit her lip. "You've got to stop him."

"I have to do nothing."

"Ngawang can't go first! She'll kill Rachel," Kat whispered.

Death didn't have to speak. His answer stood clear as anything else. No one cared about them dying. Though each of them had at least one person they would hesitate to kill, Ngawang's person wasn't Rachel. Philosophical ideas of ethics would restrain the latter. If the two women faced off, Rachel still would be extolling the belief that the remaining crew of the Intrepid would never turn on each other when the knife dug into her back. Chelsea hadn't killed Kat when given the chance. While she hadn't saved her, inaction meant something to Rachel.

Kat's chin quivered. Tears blurred her vision, and pain blinded her further. Even as her body rebelled and screamed at her to be still, Kat curled onto her side, bringing her knees to her chest. White covered her again. Pants, socks, and a long-sleeved shirt kept warmth against her skin, but the heat offered no comfort. A chill remained from which no amount of clothing could ward her.

When a hand pressed into her back, Kat tensed. White spots flashed in her vision. The bed dipped as Death sat down behind her, running his hand down her back three more times before he shoved her over. Tugging the blankets out on one side, he burrowed beneath the covers beside her. His suit pressed against her back, and his armored calf pushed against the socked soles of her feet. Death hummed. His voice echoed across the emptiness, but he fell silent as he shifted, rocking the mattress back and forth. Nothing mattered to him. All he and the rest cared about were themselves, and Kat couldn't fault them for that. If the Rider faced the same horrors, it was no wonder they were numb to the pain of others. Everything always got worse.

"They have a purpose," Death informed her, slipping out of the bed.

He clanked and clattered, and when looking over her shoulder proved too painful, she rolled onto her opposite side to see what he was doing. He'd tossed his suit onto the ground and stood naked beside the bed. Knocking on the wall beside her bed, he opened a panel and tugged on a pair of pajamas similar to her own. As he moved, thin shiny lines shimmered over the surface of his skin. The remains of wounds long healed. Facing her once more, he waved his hands. She raised an eyebrow.

"Move over," he commanded, but she stayed where she was. Throwing up his hands, he climbed in beside her. "You should be grateful. I sent War to be tortured for you."

"No. You sent him because your master told you to," Kat replied. "Nothing you do is for me."

Death rolled his eyes. "Most of what I do isn't for you. I didn't move Marie for you. I didn't insure I was visiting you when War discovered what I had done for you. Every step leading to your escape and the reunion of your crew wasn't done to help you."

Pressing her lips into a thin line, Kat furrowed her brows. "Why then?"

"I need someone I can rely on. Famine was a fluke. Couldn't fight his selection. War…is problematic." The adjective startled her. Its repetition further tethered Death to his maker. If the spike in her adrenaline showed, the pale alien didn't care to comment. "He gets infatuated easily. Once Marie dies, he'll recover quickly enough, but it'll happen again and again until there's just him throwing himself at the next and the next and the next…" Rolling his wrist of his head and wiggling his head back and forth, Death sighed. "Endless cycle."

"And me not fighting helps how?"

Death rolled to face her. Curled in upon each other, they were like children whispering secrets though the room was anything but dark when Death told her, "I want you to be Conquest."

Kat's jaw dropped. Shutting it with a click of teeth against teeth, she inhaled and held the breath. Half-exhale, half-question, she asked, "Why?"

"Not for any positive trait of yours, I assure you. You are the least of the offered evils. Marie lives, and she forms a blockade with War. Ngawang lives, and I have to watch my back. Rachel or Amondi live, they'll go out with a bang halfway into their first round of modifications. Qamar would ruin everything I've done to make Famine bearable." He sighed, glancing at the door. "Chelsea lives – and everyone's out of a job in however long it takes to gestate whatever Mah-Wærm is. And – personally – I'd really like to not see another one of him – especially a child – in the universe."

"But you serve him."

Death snorted. His lips curved up at one side into a smirk. "I've been going through your history, so let's see if I can put this in terms you understand. I don't want Yoko breaking up the band."

"Thought you'd go with Hitler," Kat muttered, curling her fingers into the pillow beneath her head.

Shrugging, the alien scratched at his neck. "I agree with his aims, but I also recognize his weakness. If he has a family, he will forget his original intentions."

"Because if he can reproduce, he'll be a horrible ruler. The universe falls into chaos?" Kat laughed, but Death wasn't laughing. All the blood drained from her face. "You actually think he's a good ruler?"

"Mah-Wærm ensures the peaceful progress of every planet and species he rules. All the horrors you've ever known cease to exist once his rule is in place. No one comments on what brought that peace once it's there. Safety – like they've never known. Opportunity – like their worlds could never have given them," Death explained.

As he spoke, he stared straight into her eyes without blinking. The certainty in his tone dragged her deeper beneath the water. Despite everything she'd experienced, his nonchalant assertion crushed her spirit more profoundly than anything Bel'von had ever proclaimed. Blind fanaticism seemed less daunting than quiet conviction. With a sigh, Death rolled over onto his back. A swipe of his hand sent the tattered remains of the blanket to the ground beside them.

"Turn onto your back," he commanded. "The new skin needs to heal evenly."

Chapter Eleven

Once again without a clock, time dragged on immeasurable with only Death's rare visits to break up the monotony. Death shimmered by her bedside. The vapors around his legs coalesced as soon as the door opened to reveal his leader. Each time, he forced her to stand. They walked the length of the room, and in the gaps when he wasn't, she stretched, gritting through the painful stretching of her new skin and reconnected muscle.

Sitting with her feet over the edge of the bed, Kat glared at Death. "Is Rachel still alive?"

Death didn't answer, but his master did. "For now," the dictator informed her, standing at the door. Stepping into the room, he asked, "Can you move to the chair?"

Though his quicksilver eyes concentrated on her with a forced patience, his fingers drummed against the back of the chair. Kat slid off the bed. Her sock feet pressed against the cold metal, sending a chill up her spine. Walking hadn't proved any more difficult than before. After the first few hours, the pain faded. All that remained of her near-death experience was tautness in her abdomen and face. While there were no mirrors in the room, the tug every time she moved her lips told her that her expressions were lopsided. Death never approached the subject. A weapon didn't need expressions after all. Sitting in the chair, she glared up at Mah-Wærm - taking advantage of the oddity in her facial muscles to smirk.

"I can also kick people in the shins. Want to see?" The smirk fell into a frown when Death grabbed her shoulder and pulled her further back in the seat. "Lobotomy time?"

"No. Your mind will do fine for now," Man-Wærm assured her.

With a twirl, he walked away, and the floor sprung to life, rolling beneath her like a conveyor belt. Death remained behind her. His hand rested heavily on her shoulder, holding her in place as they left the room. Outside the door, two Tweedles stood guard. Neither seemed particularly pleased to be there, and when Mah-Wærm headed off to the right, they ducked away to the left. Their fear and frustration left a metallic bitterness in Kat's mouth.

Furrowing her brows, she ran her tongue along her bottom teeth. The taste waned the further they moved, but a different sensation trembled in her bones - Mah-Wærm's impatience and Death's resignation.

"Where are we going?" Kat asked, forcing the question even when Death's grip tightened.

"The fighting ring," Mah-Wærm replied. "Should be over quickly. Not nearly as exciting as I'd hoped."

"Sorry your soldier mauled me," Kat drawled.

With a cluck of his tongue, he curtly informed her, "Apology not accepted."

"Why not set Rachel against Chelsea instead?" Kat suggested.

Neither would want to harm one another, so their combat would be mainly avoiding each other. Eventually, however, Rachel would attack Chelsea. Not because of a desire to kill her, but a number of grudges brewed between the two, and while neither enjoyed aggressive conflict, they'd had their share of passive aggressive stand-offs during the Academy.

"I could make this more interesting. It would be more entertaining to line up everyone else behind a curtain and have one of you shoot until somebody had died," the dictator mused. "But this isn't about entertainment."

"No," Kat agreed. "It's about completing your collection. A perfect set of matching bobbles for the mantelpiece."

The wall to their left opened. Mah-Wærm swaggered into the room, opening his arms outward at the transparent wall before them. An arena stood on the other side. Black matting covered the floor, and weapons line the walls. Ten feet up from the ground, the room stared down like a private box at a football game. Along the right-hand wall of the arena, the six human women waited. With their arms clasped behind their backs, they huddled together. All six wore the same black suits from before, but a swirl of ice blue marked their backs. Tweedles lined the right wall behind them, and on the left-hand side, Bel'von spoke with War and Famine. Silvers orbs floated around their heads, spiking and dipping between them in pairs. As the conveyor stopped, Kat jumped to her feet. Her nose scrunched; her eyes squinted, but she grimaced through the spike of agony across her front.

"Let me fight," she pleaded. "Rachel's not going to be interesting. You said that, so why not let me and Ngawang go at it."

Mah-Wærm shoved a finger right beneath her sternum where the scar crossed her midline. All of her muscles tensed, and she stumbled, falling back into the chair. Pressing a hand over the area, she ground her teeth together.

"When you die, you'll die having had a fighting chance," Mah-Wærm said.

He clasped his hands behind his back, watching as Bel'von marched across the room. They released Rachel first. Rubbing at her wrists, she moved to get back into line, but the insectoid held a black disk. Electricity jumped around the edge, and an inner wheeled spun as a whirling, churning sound echoed about the arena. Ngawang didn't wait for Bel'von to finish releasing her. With one arm freed, she slammed her knee into his chest. Rachel leapt at him from behind, and the two brought the warden to the ground. None of the Tweedles moved.

"Didn't see that coming..." Mah-Wærm murmured, moving to press a hand against the wall.

Death's jaw tensed. "They had too much time to organize."

Both glared down at Kat. Cocking a brow, she scoffed, "You got your one sarcastic apology out of me for today."

Mah-Wærm harrumphed. "At least Bel'von had his helmet on."

"I informed him you were willing to perform the optic surgery today. I don't think he wants to risk it," Death commented as Kat shifted around in her seat.

Curling her fingers around the back, she ran one foot down the other, removing the sock and repeating the motion until her feet were bare. Her toes curled. A chill crawled up her legs from the metal floor. Death's gaze remained focused on the arena. Raising the disk over his head, Bel'von subdued Ngawang and held Rachel at bay with his hand around her neck. Their suits turned to prisons. Like a remote-controlled soldier, Ngawang marched to the opposite side of the arena. From the wall beneath the viewing room, the weapons unrolled and cut the room in half.

"Pick one! Pick any number," Bel'von commanded, throwing Rachel forward. "Whoever kills the other first, lives."

Rachel sputtered, rubbing her hand along her throat. "We're not -," a cough interrupted her. "We're not going to do that."

Mah-Wærm focused on Ngawang, and all the women still cuffed did the same. Marie stepped forward, but the moment her vocal cords vibrated, her suit expanded to cover her mouth. Gags rose on all four of the other women as well. With a frown on her lip, Rachel furrowed her brow. Kat tore her eyes away, refusing to watch the predictable unfold. Instead, her eyes trained on Mah-Wærm. As Ngawang hurdled the barrier with a long shaft of metal in her hand, Rachel turned to face her, and Kat tackled Mah-Wærm to the ground.

Taut skin pulled at her body, but Rachel's scream of betrayal and terror tore her soul apart. Tears poured down Kat's cheeks as she slammed her fists into the man's pale face. His quicksilver widened, but even as his hands moved into motion, she shifted and pinned them down with her knees. Death leapt into action. His hands grabbed fistfuls of her shirt, and threw her off Mah-Wærm, but rage made her feral. Blood deafened her ears. Down in the arena, Rachel bled out. Metal slammed through her chest, and red soaked into the black. Feet covered in blood, Ngawang stood at her side. Her dark eyes glinted like shards of obsidian. Any humanity in her drained. Desperation to survive took its place.

Death dragged Kat off, but she could see it in the dictator's face. He hadn't seen this coming either. She laughed even as blood trickled hot and sticky down her face. All the Tweedles bowed their heads. They hadn't expected her to win, yet the joy of seeing the murderer of their species bloodied and beaten had been so sudden, the Tweedles had no idea how to return to their forced apathy. Their grief echoed into Kat's mind.

"Obviously, you don't understand mercy," Death growled into her ear.

"You don't get to take credit for Ngawang's actions." Kat licked the blood off of her lips, and for the first time since War nearly killed her, she smiled evenly. "If there's mercy, it sure as hell isn't yours."

Folding his hands together on his abs, Mah-Wærm chuckled. His head rested back on the floor. "You stupid girl."

"What? I'm up for scars," she told him.

Bringing his legs to his chest, Mah-Wærm jumped to his feet. Light gathered around his hands, and above their heads, electricity flickered. Death held her in place as Mah-Wærm pressed his glowing fingers against the reopened areas of her wound. Heat surged through her. Though Death prevented her escape, she grabbed what she could reach. Her fingers hooked in the soft fabric of the dictator's sweater. Stretching his well-fitted clothing matched her petty delight in the red and purple brewing around his eyes and left cheek.

"Every time I heal someone. More of myself is left behind. I generally avoid modifying by hand. This is the second time you've forced me," he lectured. As if he predicted her argument, he pressed harder and dropped his hands to work against the blood along her hip and stomach. "We'll be siblings if you keep this up."

Over his shoulder, Kat kept her eyes on her friends. Grief poured off of them with all the intensity of a tsunami. Even Ngawang's eyes glinted with unshed tears. Turning her back on Ngawang, Chelsea sobbed, but she wasn't who Ngawang looked to for comfort. Marie and Ngawang stared at each other. Tears ran down Marie's face and over the metal that swallowed the lower half of her face to keep her mute. Biting her lip, Ngawang broke their gaze, glaring up the ceiling as she sniffed, swallowing down the tears which threatened to overflow. For all her talk, she hadn't wanted this. When Ngawang's eyes dropped to the ground, Marie rushed forward.

Death gasped, "What the hell?"

Drawing his hands away, Mah-Wærm glanced over his shoulder. "What did I miss?"

Marie raced Ngawang, and though she couldn't embrace her friend, Ngawang wrapped her arms around the shorter woman. Steel glared at the rest of the world, and when War stepped toward them, Ngawang growled, baring her teeth at him like a wolf.

"It'll all be over soon," Ngawang whispered. Her voice carried through the spheres which hovered around their heads. "I promise."

If her rage gave War pause, her words set him flying. "Get away from her!" he roared.

Though Ngawang glared, she opened her arms and stepped back with a slight bow of her head. Rachel died to keep Ngawang alive after all, and the latter wasn't about to press her luck against the Rider. Wrapping an arm around Marie's shoulders, War guided her back in line with the rest. Mah-Wærm stood, and as his eyes focused on War, Kat's smile grew. Backing away with her arms still outstretched, Ngawang straddled Rachel's corpse. Her hands wrapped around the spear, and dragging it from the dead, she threw the shaft.

Time slowed. The spear flew through the air. Set on a collision course with Bel'von, the metal soared. A Tweedle leapt into action, leaping straight into the weapon's path. White pus oozed alongside red liquid when the alien slammed against the floor with a crunch. Down the line, the others of the Hive flinched. Glancing down at the body, Bel'von sighed and waved one arm at Ngawang.

"Well?" he demanded. "Restrain her!"

His voice snapped the rest of the Tweedles back into focus. Surrounding Ngawang, they subdued her. Despite all her rage, she couldn't fight them all. Dark hair clung to her forehead as she roared. Blood seeped along the ground, and with each sweep of her foot, Ngawang sent the splatter upward against the Tweedles' armor. War pushed Marie behind him, but if he expected her to be afraid, he'd be disappointed. If fear existed in the arena, it existed for Ngawang rather than of her.

Mah-Wærm sighed. "Unnecessary."

"The emotion? Or the death?" Kat inquired, leaning back against the metal of the chair. Death's hands remained on her shoulders, but any force behind the gesture faded.

"I hadn't thought humans would be so dependent. You're a troublingly social species, aren't you?" Mah-Wærm complained as he stepped back from the window.

Though he phrased the question as rhetorical, Kat informed him, "Misanthropists don't get into the Academy."

"What does that even mean?" the dictator demanded.

"What? Misanthropist? I thought you sucked the brains out of enough humans to have the whole English vocabulary down? Thought we'd be speaking slang just to scuttle some ideas around you," Kat joked, ignoring the increasing pressure Death placed upon her shoulders.

"The Academy." Mah-Wærm sucked on his teeth as if tasting his words. "We found the location easily enough on your planet. A large metal and glass building with a number of plastic components, yet any memories we were able to synthesize into something nearing coherency, there's a web of nostalgia."

"What else did you find? There are these great stone triangles in the desert. A lot of people like them," she drawled, curling her fingers in the fabric of her pants.

Rolling his eyes, Mah-Wærm waved his hand and focused on the arena. Beneath the chair's legs, the floor spun on a disk. Death remained behind her; his hands tightened when she stretched to see the Tweedles lead her living comrades away. Marie would offer comfort once in private, but watching Ngawang kill Rachel would sow distrust between the former and the others. Most had likely believed Ngawang's willingness to kill to survive was some sort of morbid bravado. None of them would make the same mistake as Rachel.

"When am I back in gen-pop?" Kat asked, looking up at Death as his helmet rose back into place. With a sigh, she corrected, "Gen-pop means general population. Prison terms."

"I understand the significance. I don't understand why you'd want to go back. The sooner you do, the sooner you either die or kill one of your companions," Death retorted.

Each bland white metal wall blended into the next. Holes opened and closed creating doors where none remained once they passed. Smoothed over and painted until nothing remained but conformity - uniformity in all things, yet when they returned to the medical room, she was oddly positioned on the far wall in the second bed in from the right. None of the

190

other beds had chairs. Then again, many items didn't appear to exist until there was need of them.

"We're in a Borg cube, aren't we?" Kat spoke, filling the silence which drained her more than the walls. "Everything just continues on forever. Do you even get to personalize your room? Do you even have a room? Or just some sort of tube to charge?" Death stepped to the side, swinging one arm toward the bed. Kat crossed her arms. "Humans are social creatures. Indulge me."

His arm fell back to his side. Retreating from around his face, his helm revealed his dour scowl. A light purple cradled his eyes. With a sigh, he squatted and scooped her up with one arm beneath her knees and the other under her arms. Tossing her onto the bed, he twisted a piece of suit around his wrist, causing it to expand into a one inch thick ring. Death slid the ring from his wrist and held it to her.

Taking the ring, she passed it back and forth between her hands. "Does this mean we're going steady?"

"Target practice."

"And here I thought you were getting bored with me," she drawled, sliding the bangle over her right wrist. As much as he seemed to be honest, she'd rather not lose her dominant hand. "Dance, monkey, dance."

"Bel'von's giving the potentials lessons, but he wasn't willing to teach you one-on-one." Death paused. Pressing his lips into a thin line, he sighed. "Brat wants you dead."

"Oh, Bel'von, he does listen!" Kat feigned a swoon.

"You've been inside one of their heads. I think he's more so concerned you'll work to undermine his control of his minions," Death replied, pressing a hand against the wall. On the opposite, different sized and colored dots appeared. "Shoot those."

"How?" she asked.

Lifting his arm, he clenched his fingers into a fist. The metal unfolded the same way she'd created the plasma cannon. Three tubes formed on the end. A laser beam shot out the top, and the end rotated, sending beam after beam into the center of one of the smallest blue circles. Small burnt circles like cigarette burns remained for ten seconds before the colored coating spread back down covering the metal and matching the rest of the circle.

When she lifted her arm, the bangle remained just a ring of metal and circuits. She cocked a brow at Death. Frowning, he wrapped her wrist with one hand and the circle with the other. As his hand pressed on the bangle, the metal shrunk until it fit her arm. Death waved at the wall. Raising her hand, she sighed. The white metal expanded, covering her arm from the middle of her forearm past her fingers. Three cylinders forced a triangle on the end toward the upper middle of the space available to them. Shaking his hand, Death placed his fist in front and squeezed his fingers together. The first shot hit slightly off-center of a large red circle straight across from her. Tightening her fist a second time, Kat watched the laser slam against the edge of the blue circle Death had hit as an example.

"The gun you can't put down," Kat grumbled. "How many of these do you technically carry in a suit?"

"Several."

Though she'd expected a vague answer, hearing the general count rather than the actual irked her. Pointing her lasers at Death, she squeezed her fist. Nothing happened. Death scoffed and shoved her arm to face forward once more.

"I'm not an idiot. That gun won't hurt me," he informed her.

Humming, she studied the edge of the gun, keeping it carefully pointed to the side rather than toward herself. "What about someone else?"

"You won't have it when someone else is in the room that I care to keep alive," Death said with a shrug.

"Cocky bastard."

Not that he had a long list. Famine might not even be on it, and War probably would be the first he'd kill if given a chance to ensure the reign of his deranged leader. Bracing her gun arm with her left hand, she focused the beam on the bed nearest to her behind Death. A red laser slammed into the metal, sending the mattress and bed tumbling. Tendrils rose from the floor like Eldritch monsters. Though they were able to put everything back into place, the blast mark remained. Melted metal curled in a spiral outward. Sharp spikes fanned out in spirals.

"How does this ship even work? Is it a biosynthetic metal?" Kat asked, shooting down at the floor a few inches from Death's feet. The white-suited alien didn't even have the decency to flinch. "Bang."

"The Architect designed a way to incorporate genetic material into the external coating. It's allochroous," Death explained. His lips curved downward into a frown as his brows furrowed. "Mainly thermochromic - with free-flowing liquid metal components behind the primary panels. The exterior fungi layer and interior electric paint keep the primary panels in place, but our suits interact with the electric paint causing a break in their circuits."

Clenching her fist, Kat kept it tightly pressed, watching the laser. As she moved her arm, crisp gray lines remained, tracing cursive into the wall. Sliding down she held her fist as she allowed her arm to drop along the edge of the bed. The laser continued, carving a line into the floor which gently skipped around Death. He didn't even pretend to be nervous. Crossing his arms, Death tapped his foot. Each pass and lift shifted the beam, and none of them got even close to hitting him or his pristine white armor.

"So, this ship is just a bunch of squares that you phase through," Kat summed.

"Cubes," Death corrected. "But generally correct."

"Bang, bang," she muttered.

"Lasers don't make that sound."

Each shot sent the beam scattering around his feet. Releasing her fist, she scratched the short rough hair at the crown of her head. Meals included water, but any desire to bath often involved more sterilizing than bathing. After each physical therapy session with Death, he shoved her into a small rectangular like closet which glowed violet and vibrated the air around her. Her skin hadn't broken out, and any grease disappeared in the process, so she hadn't pushed the matter. For all the alternative hygiene methods in space travel, she longed the warm pelting of water against her skin. However, if it meant asking, she'd never feel it again. Of everything she'd lost, submerging herself in water hadn't been one she'd expected.

"Yay," she muttered, keeping her voice monotone, and her eyes glazed with boredom as she spoke. "I have a gun. I shoot the gun but can't shoot what I want to shoot...now what?"

Sitting down in the chair, Death crossed his arms. "We could discuss your ally's death."

"Friend. And no."

"I like to imagine people don't outlive their friends," Death informed her. Tapping a finger against his neck, he activated his helmet. White rose around his head, blocking his gray eyes from sight. "Enjoy the gun."

Kat snorted. "Alone with a gun. Whatever shall I do?"

White and colored spots pulled apart, spiraling into an opening. Glancing over his shoulder, Death informed her, "It won't shoot you either."

Kat smiled, pointed the cylinder at her head, and squeezed the trigger. The gun clicked. A shiver traveled up her arm. She pulled it again, again, and again. With each click, her smile fell. While Ngawang would've thought suicide the easy way out, Kat disagreed. Faced with an unknown length of time in this black and white prison, death was just another escape. Blinking, she laid back. Tension drained from

her shoulders, and the gun retracted into a ring.
Without another word, Death left her behind.

Chapter Twelve

When the wall steamed from the number of scorch marks covering its surface, War came. Kat lifted her arm, pulling the trigger. An annoying click resounded. Shaking her arm, she transformed the gun back into a ring. Though his red and black helm remained in place, he communicated his disapproval in the droop of his shoulders, a scoff, and shuffle of his one foot over the floor.

"Hey, scar for a scar," Kat argued, pointing at the white line down her face and neck.

War shrugged. "It'll all be that pale soon."

"So what you're saying is that I need to go tanning when you finally let us go planet-side," she retorted. With a sigh, she leaned back against the pillows. "If I'm not getting an apology, why are you here?"

"Time to go back into gen pop." War raised his arm, revealing a black suit.

She tossed the blanket aside and slipped her feet off the side of the bed. Standing, she crossed the room to stand before War. A weapon stood in front of her, and while she'd hated the feel of the material against her skin before, being with her surviving crewmates pushed any discomfort to the bottom of a growing list of complaints.

"I'm guessing I can't invade people's minds with this one," Kat asked as she took the suit from War.

He snorted. "You can't shoot yourself. Mah-Wærm thought any other modifications would prevent you from learning to properly guard your thoughts."

Sliding the ring from her arm, she set it on the bed and took the suit from him. Shucking the socks off her feet, she tossed them over her shoulder onto the bed. Pants followed as she pulled the suit on. When she tossed the shirt to fall beside the rest, black covered her from her toes to neck. Armor expanded across her body. A spot of blue like a star exploded across her chest. Warmth radiated inward. Every ache which stretched from the new skin and muscle tissue stopped. Only the scar on her face called for her attention.

"It's like coming home," War told her.

When she faced him, his helm became translucent enough for her to see his golden eyes. Her stomach rolled, and the taste of metal whispered across her tongue. She inhaled slowly. Pressing her lips together, she studied her hands. Shiny, black metal glimmered back at her. Kat bit her cheek. Frustration gathered as water in her eyes, but she blinked them back. Earth was home. Jacobi had been home. A list of loved ones circled round her mind. Walking forward alone would be difficult, and whoever found themselves under Mah-Wærm's thumb as Conquest, life would be an impossibility rather than an inevitability.

"Home is people," she told him.

War snorted. "People die. Conquest won't."

Plush pillows and a wardrobe to suit a princess more than a prison stole her fear away. Lips curling into a smile, Kat shrugged. "I'm not Conquest."

"I hope you never are."

He stepped closer, reaching around her to pick up Death's ring. "You'll need this," he said, offering the white metal ring to her.

When Kat shifted her arm, the black metal of her suit slid down to cover her hand. Plasma danced around three prongs. "Pretty sure I'm good."

"You will need this," War repeated.

Gritting her teeth, Kat grabbed the ring. "Why?"

"Death gave it to you. Keep it."

With a sigh, she tugged on the ring. White metal expanded, and Kat slid it up her arm, tightening it around the middle of her right forearm. Opening her arms, Kat lifted her brows. Death had marked her. Though she could only guess at the significance, there had to be some. Regardless, any differences in her would be noted. Everyone would stare at the paler, new skin stretched across her face. Differences became signs of betrayal behind enemy lines. Add in the ring, and nobody would trust her. Perhaps for the best. Strange emotions filtered across her skin. They passed through her like sensations, leaving whispers behind.

War nodded when white melded with the black to lie smooth. Behind him, the wall opened. White painted the halls. Just like before, she couldn't tell one length from the next. Counting steps didn't help. Storming down the corridors, War raced from one doorway after another, leading her on a different route. Any time she lingered too far behind, the floor shifted and threw her forward.

"How can you even know where you're going?" Kat asked.

Without pausing, War replied, "We do not move. The ship moves."

"That's stupid."

Beneath her feet, the floor lifted, shifting to toss her onto another moving section and then another. Above the level ground, Kat struggled to maintain her balance while War glided as if dancing. The ceiling opened, and sections of the floor lifted. Black halls loomed, but another turn through a ceiling brought them to white once more; however, the luminescent nodes swam across the surfaces of the ship. Spinning around them, the ship mocked Kat, and when they landed in another bland white hall, chills ran up her spine and across her new skin. Her lips twitched into a grimace.

War faced her. Red blurred, growing like a fungus to cover the whole of his chest. "Do not mock the Architect."

"Are we going to meet this biotech genius?" Kat asked, crossing her arms over her chest.

"No." War looked away. "Conquest will. Eventually."

"So he's not a part of the selection process. Good to know."

"The Architect wakes and sleeps in turns. Riders join the pattern several times in the beginning. A few thousand of your planet's years," War explained.

Eons flouted as if they were a pittance. Immortality haunted her. Eternity without Jacobi, without any other humans, could be ignored. Those who endured torture did so with the hope one day it would end. Swallowing, Kat forced her arms down to her sides. Her fists sat heavy there like pendulums waiting to be set to swing. War watched her. Though his eyes remained hidden behind his mask, the weight of his gaze settled on her for a moment longer before his arm reached out, and the hall shifted.

The white wall opened to reveal a square room with six beds. Each one had a side table and shallow open-faced closet with a pair of the soft pajamas, a white dress, and a black scarf. One of the closets didn't have a scarf. Qamar, instead, wore it around her head, tucked into the collar of her suit. A soft gray rug covered the floor, and each bed had a knitted blanket with the same space pattern.

Kat waved. "Hi."

"Be prepared for your next test," War commanded the women, but his eyes remained on Marie. His left hand jerked, but he halted whatever moved him and turned, leaving the room.

The door closed behind War. All eyes focused on Kat. None of them approached her, and Kat held herself back from approaching them. With a scar transecting her face and the extra bangle on her arm courtesy of Death, she didn't look like herself. For all they knew, Katelyn Parker died on that floor. Whatever remained might not be the same. Those same questions lurked in the back of her mind when she'd seen Chelsea's room. Nothing else suggested the blonde faced any sort of other treatment or made any conversions to the enemy's side, but those thoughts lingered.

Stepping forward, Ngawang separated herself from the other woman. Her dark eyes slid down and up before sliding down the scar on Kat's face. Around her arm over which the white band ran, a chill surged.

"You still human?" Ngawang asked.

"I don't think so," Kat admitted.

Bowing her head, she focused on the floor. Her skin stretched. The muscles ached beneath on the curve of her jaw. In the map of her mind, humanity lurked light years away on a blue sphere she would never see again. If the flesh on her body left her disoriented, something had changed. A fundamental piece of her washed away. Scratching at the rough stubble growing across her scalp, she sighed. Nothing gold could stay. Every piece of who she was would be chipped away, and if Mah-Wærm had his say, human would be the marble which birthed Conquest and nothing more.

"Human or not, can we trust you?" Amondi pressed when Kat fell into silent contemplation.

Kat frowned; her brows furrowed. "Probably not. You should kill me the first chance you get."

"Can't use the suits against one another," Ngawang informed her. "Otherwise, Blondie would be a kebab."

"I didn't ask to be given a plush cell. None of this is my fault!" Chelsea waved her arms, but Ngawang just rolled her eyes.

"You have hands," Kat said. "Punch me in the throat until I stop having a pulse."

Marie sighed. "Morbid and blunt. Well, Kat's back."

"Tells us to kill her, and no one's going to beat her up. Why does Kat get acceptance? Sure, she almost died, but how's that an excuse? We all almost died!" Chelsea argued, crossing her arms over her chest. "Besides, Marie slept with one of them. When do we get to talk about that?"

"She did, didn't she…" Qamar hummed, sitting up to stare at Marie.

Marie raised a single brow. "What now?"

"You comforted him," Ngawang accused, clenching her hands into fists. "Right after he'd sliced Kat in half. You hugged him."

Marie shrugged as her lips curled into a red smile. "And then he comforted me."

"So, you're training him?" Amondi questioned, but Marie shook her head.

"Lima Syndrome - I want him to develop positive feelings for me. It'll make it harder to kill me or do something that would upset me," she explained. Her voice dropped low as she spoke until they could barely hear her even in the close circle. "Which could now be ruined if there are mics in these suits."

"There aren't…or they're really good at hiding how much I've insulted them in private. Then again, I'm pretty sure they can read our minds, so War probably already knows," Kat commented as she stretched her arms over her head.

The pale skin of her face pulled, and both Amondi and Marie winced, watching her body shift. Their pity chaffed. Letting her arms fall, Kat pressed her lips into a line and glared at walls. Time would see things mend. It always did, but their clocks weren't the ones that mattered. A quick reunion wouldn't work. Inhaling, she bit her lip. Marie opened her arms. Her bright blue eyes shimmered as her brows peaked in question and concern. Red painted her lips still. Closing her eyes, Kat bowed her head against the hollowness within her bones.

"We're going to get through this," Marie promised, and when Kat couldn't move her legs, the brunette stepped forward and wrapped her arms around her. "You'll survive this."

When Kat had pulled on the black suit, the strange chill which enveloped her since being healed quieted, but with Marie's arms around her, the ache returned. Her eyes watered. Tears lined the edges of her lower lashes. With a sob, they spilled over. Marie's hold tightened, and Kat burrowed her face in her friend's shoulder, stifling the agony bubbling up from within her. Eyes watched from the walls to the five other women in the room. They'd been a crew of thousands; now, only six remained. Human blood spilled across the system, but every moment, the Tweedles' memories and Death's words reminded her so many more had bled for Mah-Wærm's conquest. Extinctions clawed at her. Nanite shield up or not, Earth's day would come, and the best she could hope for was to not be there to see humanity fight its final battle.

They would burn in their ships. Scream would echo across the face of the sun. Fire and darkness would consume in turns until not even a planet remained. Shattered trails of rock like broken gravestones would orbit the sun, and only one of the six women around her would remain. Time was running out. An unknown number of eyes watched them. Soon, another of them would fall. Like a card house, they'd crumble down.

Shaking, Kat bit her lip to stifle another sob. Skin broke and bled. "We're not going to survive this, Marie."

"We will," Marie assured her.

"Know something you're not telling us?" Ngawang asked.

Though she crossed her arms, her eyes shined with emotion. Not hope. Something smaller and altogether less positive – doubt. Not in Marie or in anyone or thing particular. Doubt in existence itself. A cold, rock welling up in every joint, doubt stole bits away. From the shimmer in her eyes to the resigned set of her jaw, Ngawang stood like a mirror. A reflection of everything Kat wanted to deny. Her heart hardened against her crewmates – against her only living allies. One day, and Kat prayed it wouldn't be soon, she'd stab one of the others in the back. Some died without betraying their people. Those few, like Rachel, couldn't fathom such cruel nihilism, but that wasn't Kat.

"Earth's alive. Nanites and all, Earth's alive. As long as humankind goes on, what does it matter what happens here? We'll survive this. One way or the other, and the same can be said of Bel'von and Mah-Wærm and War, Famine, and even Death," Marie proclaimed, rocking back and forth as she turned, so Kat's eyes stared at the far wall while Marie confronted Ngawang. "We might not live, but we'll still be here. Still be human in the end, and that's a win. They don't want us to be human. They don't want us to feel sympathy for one another. That's why Rachel died."

"Oh? Really? Not the spear I put through her chest?" Ngawang sneered.

"You didn't have a choice," Marie replied.

Ngawang laughed. Each exclamation of sound slammed into Kat like a punch. "Rachel didn't try to kill me. None of you have tried to kill each other, but me? I killed her the first chance I got."

Kat pulled away from Marie. Squeezing the brunette's hand, she faced Ngawang. "Everyone knew what was coming. Even Rachel. Nobody doubted what you'd do to survive. Don't torment yourself into thinking she was really surprised."

"And that makes it better?" Ngawang demanded.

Chelsea frowned. Sitting back on her bed, she pulled her legs up. "No. It makes you human."

"And accepting comfort is human!" Marie pointed out, waving a hand at Chelsea. "Offering it," she said, pressing her hand against her chest. "That's human."

Wrinkling her nose, Ngawang tapped her foot. "So…what? War's 'human' now?"

"I'm not pretending I know what he is. Or the rest of them frankly. All I know is that I want to live – just like you do. I want to go home. I want to swim in the ocean when it's near freezing. Drink a cup of crappy instant coffee with my sisters and talk about which movie star is the hunkiest. I want to feel autumn again. The almost chill with the crunchy leaves and everything," Marie confessed. Pressing her fingers to her lips, she hiccupped as she cried too. "I thought it'd be okay, you know? Getting on that stupid ship. I thought not seeing my family for a decade would be fine. Better than the first settlers on Mars. They were told they probably wouldn't see Earth ever again. Ten years wouldn't have been so bad, but here we are, and I don't even know what day it is. Is it winter back home? Is there snow? I don't know. I just don't know." She sniffed, forcing a smile even as more tears fell. "All I know is I'm here, and right now, my best friend is hurting, and I can't make it okay, and I know it's not my fault, but she's pretending not to be my friend anymore, and that's not okay. You're all I've got. You don't get to take yourself away."

Ngawang's features smoothed. Her eyes widened as her brows curved up at the closer they came to the center of her face. Blinking rapidly, she opened her mouth, but nothing came out. Her chin trembled, and she forced herself to look away.

"Only one of us survives," Ngawang whispered; her voice cracked as she spoke.

Marie nodded. "I know that, but I'm not losing you – any of you until I have to."

"Oh, how touching."

All six women turned at once to the door. Mah-Wærm stood by the door. Famine and Death flanked him. Both wore their helms, creating faceless phantoms like an angel and a demon on the dictator's shoulders. However, the man before them needed no warriors at his side. Gone were the soft clothes. Silver armor covered him from his feet to neck. Specks of light sparkled across his joints like stars. Unlike the rest, his collar sat smoothly against his skin. No edge existed for a helm to reside. Strands of silver wove up his neck, seeming to curl not just on but into his pale skin.

"Now that you've been reunited, I think it's time for a trip," Mah-Wærm informed them.

"A trip where?" Amondi asked. Her dark eyes narrowed.

"What was it you called it, Katelyn? Planetside?" When he smiled, the blinding white of his teeth offset the silver on the inside of his lips. "One of my favorite little worlds. A planet called Sin."

Spheres dropped from the ceiling at the planet's name. They danced around, whispering, "Earth."

Pushing Kat behind her, Marie frowned. "Earth?"

"Home?" Chelsea whispered.

Shaking his head, the dictator gestured up to the spheres. "Translating planet names is difficult. The majority of species name their planets after the world for ground. A speck of ground; all the ground. Earth, earth."

"What makes Sin so important?" Ngawang asked, glaring at Mah-Wærm with all the rage she'd turned in upon herself.

"They have a festival every year at this time in my honor. I try to attend at least once every generation. Today...I will attend for this generation. That they may know I am alive." As Mah-Wærm spoke, silver crawled up to wrap around the lower half of his face. It curled over the bridge of his nose and under his eyes. Against the white and quicksilver coloring him, his black hair seemed a wreath of shadows. "I'd suggest you keep together. As potentials, you will be respected, but there are those who will test you. It is expected that you endure without striking them back."

"And if we kill them?" Kat asked.

Mah-Wærm hummed and turned away without answer. He left his Riders behind. Famine stepped forward. His long limbs kept tightly under control. As he approached, the women stepped back as a group. Only Qamar hesitated. She remained where she'd been; her eyes focused on his mask as if she could see the face beneath the metal. Brows furrowing, Qamar tugged at the edges of her suits color.

"Is it moving?" she asked. Her eyes widened as she gasped and grabbed against the black, but the metal spread regardless.

One by one, the metal of each of their colors ran up their necks, coating their lower faces, so from their noses around their eyes and down their cheeks around their head beneath their ears could be seen. Tears welled in Chelsea's eyes. Grabbing at her face, she pulled at the metal to no avail. Her screams rang. Falling to the ground, the blonde clawed her own skin to pull the metal back. Amondi grabbed Chelsea's hands, forcing them down by her side.

"Stay calm," Amondi commanded as Chelsea's eyes watered.

Famine tilted his head. "You will not converse or attack any of the citizens of Sin."

The spheres shuttered, whispering, "Earth."

Gliding across the room, Death came to Kat's side. "You'll be split in groups of three. Famine will take Qamar, Amondi, and Chelsea. Marie, Ngawang, and Kat are with me."

"Parker," Kat corrected. "Only my friends call me Kat."

"Don't be petty, Parker. None of us are friends here," Ngawang spat though the mask stole some of her vehemence, replacing it with a brittle resonation.

Marie sighed, her shoulders sagging. "Where's War?"

"He has not been approved for this mission. His reeducation is still in process," Famine explained as Amondi and Qamar helped Chelsea to her feet.

Each of the former held one of the latter's hands, keeping the blonde from worsening the red scratches down her face. The black-suited alien set his hands on his hips. He tilted his head one way and then the other before shrugging and waving for the three to follow him out the door and out of sight. Death remained unmoved. Ngawang crossed her arms, tapping her foot. Marie folded her arms behind her back, similar to how they had first been held.

"If any of you kill anyone on this planet, you will be immediately put to death in their customary manner," Death said. He paused, shifting his focus among the three. "Hanging. Not pleasant, I assure you."

"Good to know," Ngawang drawled. "Kat, that's how you can attempt suicide today."

"Thanks for the blessing, but I think I'll pass on the lynch mob," Kat retorted.

Death sighed, rubbing the back of his neck. Shaking out his limbs, the white-suited alien about faced and walked away. All three women followed. Ngawang and Kat bumped shoulders gently. Raising one brow, Ngawang glanced Kat's arm and Death's. All the women wore the same suits, so the white ring on Kat's stood out especially as there was an indented ring rounding the alien's arm. Meeting Ngawang's dark eyes, Kat gave a single quick nod. When the wall sealed behind them, the floor spun and dropped.

As her feet left the ground, Kat grabbed Ngawang's wrist and Marie's shoulder. They each reached out in return. Holding tightly to one another, the three women fell, and the hole above them dimmed as black swallowed them. No lights remained. There were no nodes on the walls of the shaft.

"Your first time to the hanger," Death commented. "You'll get used to it. Lucky for you, we actually put oxygen in the atmosphere for you. We don't generally make the air breathable for our pilots."

Slamming back to the metal floor, the three tumbled to their left as the disk moved to the right. Marie grabbed Death's arm. "What's with the masks then?"

"Consider it a precaution," the white-suited alien retorted. His lowered tone shut down any reasonable possibility of further conversation on the matter.

However, Marie rarely listened to tones. She settled on her feet and prepared to argue. Kat squeezed her shoulder as Ngawang tightened her grip on her arm. A wrinkle formed between her brows, but

Marie kept silent. When the plate stopped moving, they stood in a hanger which seemed to go on for miles. Thousands of ships lined up in battalions of a hundred. Each shimmered like a black bullet. White glimmered around gills along their sides. Death led them to two which hovered, glimmering like small white stars. As they marched across the black floor of the hangar, a planet floated below them. If Earth spun as a blue ball, this planet circled as a dusty-beige marble.

Tweedles lined the two ships, forming a path through which Death led them. Famine and the other three women stood beneath one ship. A plate circle lowered, and the black-suited alien led his trio on board. Stepping onto her group's plate, Kat scanned the hangar. Mah-Wærm was nowhere in sight. His lips curved into a frown, but the ground beneath her jerked, and they rose into the dark interior of Death's ship. Seats lined the deck with crossing straps loosened for them. Toward the front of the ship, a circular pedestal sat with another seat.

"Buckle up," Death commanded.

He reclined in the pedestal seat, and rings curled about his arms. Larger rings spun around his body, lifting him up into a higher level of the ship outside of the humans' sight. Sharing a glance with Marie, Kat strapped in. All around them, the metal ship rumbled. When all three settled, the ship dropped out of the sky. Black turned translucent. Sin grew closer; brown consumed the dark, and fire blazed around them as Death guided the ship into the atmosphere. Beneath sparse white clouds, cities loomed. Deserts with golden dunes sprawled below them. Death headed up the globe northward, and a blue river snaked through the desert. Lush green spread from its shores, pushing against the desert. A wall of stones lined the edges where brown turned full and flush with vegetation. Tall trees like soldiers stood in perfect alignment north of the wall for ten miles. Circular, spiraling farmlands carved into the rolling hills.

Toward the northern polar circle, an ocean loomed with a city on its edge. White cliffs lined against the blue and foaming waves, which crashed against the rubble over which the city towered. Glistening skyscrapers broke the horizon. Every hue imaginable painted their sides. Spheres buzzed around the city like bugs. On the top of one of the buildings, Famine's ship landed. Crowds rushed the ship, but a line of black-armored people kept them at bay.

Death flew further into the city. They landed in a large gray area toward the cliff's edges. As the ship ceased vibrating, Death's chair descended from the cockpit. "We've got four hours here. Enjoy the fresh air. Enjoy the culture. If you get hit, ignore it. If you get yelled at, ignore it. To these creatures, you are all gods-in-training. Let them test you. They can't do much harm."

Kat unbuckled. Her eyes scanned the crowds lining up outside the ship. Tall, lithe bodies held round head aloft like cattails. Painted faces stared back at them. Every hue she had ever seen covered the creature's skin, but the more her eyes searched the crowd, the more numerous the different species became. Shorter aliens pushed toward the front. Tubes carried water passed gills on their necks for some.

Others fanned themselves with their elephant-like ears. Silver orbs flew over their heads.

"We stick together," Marie whispered. "We stay alive."

"No killing – no attacking," Kat agreed, but Ngawang merely rolled her eyes.

Smacking her friend's arm, Marie hissed, "No attacking. We're outnumbered. Play along, even if it's just for today."

Ngawang held up her hands, facing Kat and Marie. "Not doing a thing. Scout's honor."

"Come along, Potentials," Death called.

With one last glare, Marie followed the white-suited alien off the ship.

Smaller, multicolored ships hovered over their heads. No lights, strings, or exhaust surrounded them. Higher above, pathways glimmered, connecting the buildings. All along them, people stared down at them. Spirals of spun glass rose like thorns from the concrete ground. Stairs rose around them. While Famine landed high, Death had landed low.

"Death!" the spheres chanted, echoing the call of the people.

Throwing up his hands, Death bowed his head, facing the different angles of the crowd. "Thank you for greeting us. Today, I present three potentials. One may rise to join the ranks of the Riders – our glorious leader's right hand!"

The spheres translated, and the people cheered. A strange hunger flashed in their eyes. An entire species marked for eradication, but the aliens reached with a longing as if touching the humans might transfer some of the damnation for which they

214

yearned. Though the black-suited guards matched the Tweedles, their three fingers and long limbs matched the painted faces. One alien slipped between the guards. A sphere bounced beside her. Painted a metallic green, the alien wore a fedora-like hat with an expanded floppy brim around her face. Her eyes were crystal blue and comically large. Ngawang shifted into a defensive stance at Kat's side, and though Kat's shifted one foot back, she kept her hands at her side. Marie's eyes crinkled, smiling even with her lips hidden.

"Lord Death!" the alien greeted. Her thin lips moved to reveal comb-like teeth. Her language matched though the pitch was far higher than any whale calls Kat had ever heard. "We are pleased to have been selected as the city to host you and Lord Famine." When she bowed, her knees bent, and her body wobbled back and forth, causing her hat to jump. "We've prepared the library as requested."

"Well done, Nel'ul. Lead the way," Death gestured over the crowd to a glass building covered by a golden web-like dome. It looked like someone had tipped a basket over a Rubik's cube.

As they headed from their landing area, the crowd parted, but hands grabbed, running across any piece they could touch. With a quick glance at Marie, Kat shifted to the outside. They flanked Ngawang. The fewer aliens near her, the better. Children rushed around, dashing close enough to touch before racing back out. Holding their hands in awe, the alien children squealed in delight. Nobody blocked Death's way, and any who lingered matched his pace for the duration of their contact. A small gilled child scuttled between Death and Nel'ul before skittering back to walk backward. His large gold eyes stared up at Kat. Every few steps, his gills flared, and bubbles filtered along the tube.

"Hello," Kat whispered. The orbs around their heads spiked.

Skipping, the boy nearly fell, but he quickly caught his footing when Kat offered a hand to help him only to have Ngawang strike her hand back. "No touching," Ngawang warned even as the boy reached out, brushing Kat's thigh as he returned into the wall of people on either side of them.

As the golden dome tossed shadows around them, Nel'ul reached forward, pressing a hand against the glass which slid apart into a more familiar doorway. Her gold nails sparkled against the glass. Leading them into the building, she smiled, and though the intention seemed authentic from the crinkle around her large blue eyes, the way her muscles moved screamed unnatural. Without a clear brow ridge or even a defined nose, the alien moved like an octopus. Each step made with a graceful, albeit dragging, precision. For all that octopi could do, Kat had never heard of one smiling.

Nel'ul's blue eyes glanced back at the three women. "My ancestor built this library," she told them. "Well, he designed it."

Stairs formed geometric shapes which vanished and appeared between rooms. Clear floors melded into gold. The whole building seemed more like an optical illusion than a physical place, but Kat kept silent. As they climb the shifting stairs, Nel'ul recounted her planet's history. Names and rulers meant nothing to the women. Histories painted as running red with blood – especially if that blood was in fact blue - couldn't win them over. None of the doors formed the same shape or stood the same size. Ducking up and down, Nel'ul's fedora flopped around her head.

Children raced around their heels, but the rest of the crowd remained behind them. Painted faces pressed up against the glass. Some more adventurous youngsters, or at least smaller creatures, climbed the golden webbed dome. Their eyes tracked Death and the three with the obsession of a paparazzo's camera. Within minutes, Kat was lost. On a strange planet of empire loyalists, escape made little sense. Regardless, the layout solidified the impossibility. Entering a long corridor, Nel'ul stopped, turning to face the three.

"Though your planet will not be joining our illustrious empire, you still wish to know about our great and glorious leader, don't you?" That strange, twisted smile tugged at her green skin. "Before, we were a primitive species. My people are the planet's natives, you see. Then Mah-Wærm came. A great and powerful being that we could only call a god. Our people bowed to his will, and beneath his rule, our culture flourished. Once, we starved. Over ninety percent of our land once was desert. Within the years of his reign, we have reclaimed thirty percent!"

"As what? Usable farmland? Rivers? Tundra?" Ngawang asked, folding her arms over her chest.

"Tundra? Oh! Ice deserts, no. Farm lands and forests. We're transforming the planet piece by piece. Just over thirteen generations, and we've made extraordinary strides!" Nel'ul exclaimed. Clapping her hands together, she wiggled her head back and forth as if she could not contain her joy. "We've learned to control the drying summers and stop our oceans from boiling. Our population has stabilized. It's incredible. If it weren't for Mah-Wærm, only bearing S'ne'rulic could receive education. Now, fertilizing and ovulating may as well!"

"Do you have a nose?" Kat asked, causing Death to snicker.

Nel'ul wiggled her fingers. "This paint actually maintains moisture for our skin which takes in oxygen naturally. Our respiratory systems and digestive systems aren't connected. We're a sight heavy people. We see vast ranges though…our ears are also rather underdeveloped." She pointed to flaps of skin beneath her flopping hat. Even when they stretched, fanning out to the sides, they were no larger than a quarter. "When my 'mouth' moves, I'm actually releasing vapor particulates which shimmering in a particular way to speak. Our hearing is very limited. Thank goodness for the spheres!" Pointing up at the silver orbs, she clasped her hands together. "They can give us a taste of what music feels like through variances in higher and lower hue projection. I suppose, if you haven't noted such already, they are outside your ocular range."

"A later modification reserved for Conquest," Death assured her.

Giving him another knee-bending bow, Nel'ul pressed her hand against another panel, leading them into a large auditorium. Light dappled across a collection of lower consoles, painting the fogged glass and metal with flecks of color. Following the lines, Kat frowned up at eight panes of stained glass stretching across the wall before them.

The first window was of a desert world with spikes of red and caramel tones. A blinding light leaked from the uncolored panels that depicted the sky. In the second, a creature appeared with blue skin in white robes that was crouched low. Wisps of gray rose from the alien, and blood red blocks traced the outline of its hands. In the third, Mah-Wærm stood with his arms stretched wide like Jesus at Da Vinci's *Last Supper*. Panic fluttered in Kat's heart. These people had accepted the idea of a god made flesh in a heartless conqueror.

The fourth showed Mah-Wærm lifting the alien from the second. In the fifth, the alien was painted a sparkling bronzed hue, and the blood and wisps were gone. The figure of the alien smiled in the fifth holdings its arms in a joyous upwards expression where it had clung desperately to the other in the fourth. Mah-Wærm was integrated into the culture so endlessly he was the core of their very self-perception. Kat's eyes turned to the sixth. A city grew in spiraling towers with blue glass for the sky, and a serene Mah-Wærm sat in the upper right corner watching the city grow. The seventh showed multitudes bowing before the seated Mah-Wærm. In the final panel, Mah-Wærm showed his face without the lower face covering. His skin blazed tanner than he'd seemed in the ship, but whoever created the piece perfectly matched the quicksilver shade of his eyes. Dark black curls framed his curved ears.

"When were those windows made?" Kat asked. "If your ancestor built this…does that mean grandfather? Further back? Was this two generations ago?"

"Ancestor signifies anyone five or more generations apart from me in the past; however, my ancestor came after the alignment. The artist created these within the first generation of Mah-Wærm's influence. Perhaps seven thousand years ago…oh, I'm not sure what that would be in your years." Nel'ul pressed a finger against her mouth.

Death shrugged. "Around two-thirds that."

"He hasn't changed much," Marie muttered, voicing Kat's thoughts.

Nel'ul glowed. Flecks of violet light shimmered where the green paint wore thin. "Unsurprising, truly. Immortals rarely do. Lord Death stood at his side when he first came to us."

"How can you be certain this Death is the same?" Kat asked. "You can't even see his face."

"His magnetic field is the same." Three sets of lids blinked at once.

Kat crossed her arms. "But you weren't there."

"I did not need to be. We've recorded the signatures of all the immortals who've cross our path. Our glorious leader, Mah-Wærm, Lord Death, Lord Famine…we will record your signatures as well as we once did Lord War. When we see him again, we will know which potential rose to the rank of immortality. Just as one day, we will greet Lord Conquest and know who he was before," Nel'ul explained.

Kat glanced at Death. He stood as a statue of white metal in the light of the planet's sun. Shattered beams of multicolored light fell across him. With his hands in fists at his side, he arched his back, and though she could not see his eyes, she traveled the level of his gaze to the eighth panel. Eons spent with Mah-Wærm, yet Death saw no monster in his creator. They were a strange pair. Frankenstein and his monster born of a keen desperation to defeat the very reality after which the beast had been named.

Footsteps whispered across the floor below. A small group of half a dozen gathered within the lower chamber. Their eyes turned up to the windows which silhouetted those on the stairs. Like moths, the aliens gathered, shifting and weaving their ways toward the stained glass, Death, and those who stood alongside him. When the first stone flew, Kat spun in confusion after it hit her back. Standing on one of the consoles, a pair of small children giggled, clutching the fabric of their dresses to carry piles of stones.

Ngawang's fingers flexed before clenching into fists at her side. Marie slipped between her and the people. They watched. Their saucer-sized eyes blinked, but their focus remained. Spheres hovered over the small ones' heads. Giggling, the two tossed two more stones, and while one hit Marie, Kat caught the other. Both pairs of eyes honed in on the throwers, and Kat couldn't be certain which startled the two enough to cause them to stumble back off the consoles. Stones scattered across metal. Crushing the sandy sediment into dust, Kat glanced back at Death. His eyes remained covered. A faceless specter better suited to his name than he had been on the ship.

"If you keep catching the stones, you'll be rather colorful by your return," Nel'ul warned, gesturing down at Kat's hand.

Gold covered her hand. With a smirk, she rubbed her two hands together, spreading the mix before she smacked both Marie and Ngawang on the back. Though Marie rolled her eyes, Ngawang's gaze narrowed devilishly. Whatever competitive nature lurked within Ngawang and Kat had to be held at bay. Neither wished to kill the other, but Kat didn't doubt the frustrated energy coursing in her veins swarmed in a higher fold within Ngawang.

"Do the orbs translate writing?" Ngawang asked. Another colored chunk bounced off Marie. Ngawang knelt to pick it up even as the other woman brushed off the dust from her shoulder.

Nel'ul's face squeezed together. Lines partitioned her head like the innards of an orange. With a hum, Death shifted his feet to be shoulder length apart and clasped his hands behind his back.

"Nothing perverse, ladies," he commanded.

Of all the things he could say, that likely was the worst. Immediately, Ngawang rubbed her fingers in the brown pigment, writing "fuckers" on the floor before she wrote the same up Kat's calf. Even if Death punished them, Marie's giggle made any future pain worth it. Tossing her long locks over her shoulder, Marie offered her own calf for whatever explicative Ngawang opted to place there. She received a crude drawing instead.

Death sighed, causing Nel'ul to tense. Her hands fluttered. Kat smiled as she watched the metallic green painted alien.

"He's just disappointed that he got stuck with the rebels. Famine has the more submissive potentials," Kat explained. "Perhaps you could divert your citizens toward us? We're far more entertaining."

"That's just inviting problems," Marie whispered, but the orbs carried everything.

In a flutter, all three of Nel'ul's lids blinked like dominos. "We do not guide anyone in their welcoming of potentials."

Scratching at the stubble on her head, Kat hummed. "I see. I see. So...what are we supposed to be guided to do?"

Even as she spoke, Kat leapt off the stairs, landing beside the console where the children dropped the rest of the condensed pigment. Riffling through them, she sorted them by color as Nel'ul gasped and looked to Death for instruction. Ngawang smirked, shrugged, and jumped. Slapping one hand against her face, Marie grumbled beneath her breath, and while she was too far for Kat to hear her, the orbs carried the words down.

"Impulsive masochist," Marie's words buzzed from the orbs.

Juggling three different blue stones, Kat rotated to face Marie. "We aren't allowed to hurt the citizens. Never said I couldn't be an impulsive anything."

"Not putting your best foot forward here, Parker," Marie warned.

Death crossed his arms over his chest. "She rarely does."

"Yet, I'm your favorite," Kat reminded him, pointing to the white ring around her forearm. She managed to keep two of the three clods in the air, but one fell, painting her foot blue. "Mistakes were made."

Nel'ul rushed down the stairs. Descending at a slower pace, Death and Marie followed. With them out of the way, the stained panes stood clear. The first blue pigment stone splattered upon impact with the blank face of Mah-Wærm in the eighth panel. If she hadn't known what sort of monster hid beneath his mask, that window would've struck the hardest blow. Biting her tongue even though no one can see her feigned concentration, Kat tossed the second at the cheering crowd of glass aliens. First, the monster. Second, the fools.

"Desist!" Nel'ul shrieked.

Kat's brow furrowed. "Why?"

Gasping like a popped balloon, the alien smacked Ngawang's hand to send the colored chalk she held tumbling. "You dishonor our glorious leader."

"He won't care. Believe me, I've actually met the guy," Kat assured her. Static traveled up her arm and down her spine. Eyes widening, a smile hidden from view peeled back her lips. "A shock collar. You gave me a gun with a built in shock collar."

"That was your only warning, Potential," Death informed her.

Marie grabbed Ngawang's hand. "Stand down."

Crossing to Kat, Death cleared his visor. They were close enough together that no one else would see, but his gray eyes burned into hers. "This is not a game. Respect the Emperor." Kat's eyes narrowed; she remained silent. Appeased, Death darkened his mask once more and turned to face the rest. "Shall we continue?"

Nel'ul's hands fluttered. "Yes, Lord Death."

Her first few steps stuttered, but the alien quickly regained her footing, leading the group further down the hall. Echoing across the room, the spheres cast her words into English. The next group to accost them was a dozen around the same height as Nel'ul. Like a rainbow made flesh, they twittered about, pointing with their eyes before touching and tossing pigments at the trio as they pass. They didn't reach toward Death. One, a vibrant pink painted face, watched him, but their hands stayed firmly at their sides. Kat and Marie flanked Ngawang, but a blue-painted hand grabbed at the ends of her black, straight bobbed hair. Rather than stop or jerk back, Ngawang pressed her head forward, leaving the alien with torn strands.

"Just squeeze my hand," Marie urged.

Kat frowned, watching the blue one croon and show off his prize to the rest. However much the aliens revered Death, they disregarded the potentials twice over. Their selection offered no protection. If anything, their torment opened them to further violations. Her stomach rolled. Acid burned at the edges of his throat, but she bit back the putrescence working its way through her veins. Until they drew blood, indifference served as her quickest weapon.

Nel'ul led them out a side door into a large greenhouse. Stained glass colored the bright sunshine.

Beating down against the green within, the rays drew sweat across Kat's brow. Salty liquid rolled across her forehead and down near the crease at the outer corner of her eyes. Already pale, a hand lifted to brush against her scalp. With the glove, she could not feel any burn even if one brewed. The scar of new flesh across her face stung.

Like a cat waiting to pounce on its prey, Marie went from calm movement to insane action in less than a breath. The lone orb fell. Pressing it into the moist, hot earth, she watched Death and Nel'ul continue before gazing over her shoulder at Kat and Ngawang.

"Fucking hot," Marie complained.

Crossing her arms, Ngawang kept her eyes on Death and the orb above his head. "They're getting cocky. We're mounting toward an attack. They're all edging to see who can be bigger – more daring…"

"Slaves until sacrosanct," Kat muttered.

Death's pace faltered, and Marie released the sphere. Before the white-suited alien flicked his eyes back at them, they had returned to their pace as if nothing had ever passed. Green plants twitched together. Thin needles covered their edges. Their sides curved inward, minimizing space for evaporation. Curling hair-like moss weaved across the ground beneath some. Every plant stood in near isolation if the moss did not connect its ground to another's. Bright red flowers sagged against a wave of small, pale green leaves on a bush barely five inches high. Each bit of green ached. So many memories of Earth blurred to green and blue. Even amongst the multicolored lights and dry beige earth, green carved pieces out of Kat's heart.

"We hope these species will take hold," Nel'ul explained when they came to a stop in front of a contained glass area within the greenhouse. Vapor gathered. The panes fogged, and condensation slid down the glass. "They require a higher water saturation level than the majority of this planet can sustain, but we plan to section off areas beneath a containment field."

"Won't isolating the remaining water result in extreme temperatures and inhospitable regions outside the fields?" Marie questioned as the trio joined Death and Nel'ul.

"Better sections than the whole planet," Nel'ul replied, pressing her hands together.

Ngawang cocked a single brow. Her eyes slid from Marie to the green metallic painted alien. "And you'll shelter all living creatures on your planet?"

"All species which are of use." Nel'ul's face squeezed together like a skinless orange.

Kat shrugged, rolling her head from side to side. When the bones in her neck creak and crack, the alien flinched. Invasive species welcomed, sprawling in vibrant shades across the ground. Back home, fliers and banners cursed the same even if they only crossed state lines. Another blatant display of eugenics – that was all that the plants inside that hot house were. Tearing her eyes off the sight, Kat glares up at the stained glass. Quicksilver stared right back. Everything ended with Mah-Wærm. Her blood boiled in her veins, and the earth trembled beneath her feet.

"What's happening?" Nel'ul cried, throwing herself against Death who pushed her back onto the ground.

"Sounds like the bowl is full. Sigyn must be draining the poison, and while she does…" Kat's eyes narrowed, sliding to pierce Nel'ul. "Loki writhes."

Marie grabbed Kat's shoulder. "Stop. We said we were going to grit and bear this."

Death scoffed. "It's an earthquake; she's not doing anything. Seriously? You really think I'd give any of you the power to move the tectonic plates on an already volatile planet?"

Though no one could see her smile, Kat found herself beaming. Her skin pinched against the mask as the shift of muscles pressed it further into her cheeks. White crawled down her arm. Tendrils spread like whispers in the dark, but Death stormed forward, grabbing Kat's arm. The spheres did not follow. They shimmered in the distance, spinning but silent.

"No one would offer you sanctuary here," he murmured.

Kat shifted, rocking alongside the earth as it quaked a second time. "All your mighty tech, and nobody realized an earthquake was coming?"

Nel'ul trembled. Her eyes lifted to watch the glass though it moved well enough with the shaking. A stampede raced toward them; a group of children with their hands over their heads ran beneath the stained glass. Weaving along the path of planets, the children froze. Their large eyes took in the trio, and holding open their empty hands, they murmured to each other before Nel'ul threw herself forward.

"Back to your houses! Now!" she commanded, and the children continued. Swiveling like a top, the painted alien reached toward Death. "Have we displeased you, Lord Death" Beneath her paint, a glow grew. "Have we displeased him?"

Releasing Kat's arm, he turned to the alien woman. "Rebirth takes time. This planet will be saved if Mah-Wærm deems to save it. I – as you well know – should not need to remind you what occurs when you question the will of Mah-Wærm."

Ngawang's eyebrows rose. Though Death's words sounded like a threat, Nel'ul sagged in relief. Even when another aftershock came, she chirped away. Each historical fact exhausted Kat as much as the last. When they exited the greenhouse, the bright sun burned down on Kat's scalp. Without a thought, the suit expands, covering her all but the eyes. Black metal shimmered across her body. Trembles shook up the towers, releasing a high pitch whine like china dancing in a cabinet. As they walked through the streets, the people darted between buildings. Clouds gathered overhead, and for the few aliens who braved standing still, their eyes focus on the skies. Long fingers pointed to the sky. Gray loomed.

"The winding structures and shifting foundations allow the buildings to move without breaking," Nel'ul explained. Her face remained tight; however, the spheres did nothing to mimic the strain.

Exhaustion and fear permeated the echo before the sphere's translations. Rising pitches and gasped breathes would've told Kat enough, but Nel'ul's fear came in shifting fingers and a light glow beneath the paint as if the moisturizing decorative paste hid another method of communication. If bioluminescence lurked beneath the colors, a whole new collection of questions awoke within Kat's mind. Her hazel eyes drifted across the crowds. Children sparkled the most. A glow beamed from scratches on their knees and hands where their play wore down the layers of paint, but some of the paler painted aliens glimmered just the same. Across them all, the hue remained the same. Orange light threatened like a dart frog. It screamed of poison. An attempt to warn and protect, the light failed to act as a warning when everyone knew what to fear, but the sight stained Kat's memory.

"I was told there would be a public execution," Death stated. His eyes traced the orange glow. "Why don't we cut the tour and go there?" Though he phrased it as a question, there was nothing optional about his tone.

Bowing her head, Nel'ul waved them off to a side street. "We had been informed to keep your path and Lord Famine's from the sight by our great and glorious leader."

Death held a hand up. "As wise as Mah-Wærm is, extenuating circumstances dictate I bring the potentials to the greatest collection of citizens."

"True. The podium is the most stable ground in the city," Nel'ul conceded.

Cross her arms, Ngawang glanced back to Marie. "At least we'll find out what'll happen if we fuck up here."

"You fuck up; you die. Rather straightforward," Death retorted.

230

Without waiting for Nel'ul, Death changed directions, storming down the wide street. Trembling, the green alien followed. Orange brightened beneath her paint. Marie and Kat met each other's gazes. Like each time before, someone would die on this planet. Otherwise, the test seemed pointless to their captors. As patient and peaceful as Famine's trio was, the pendulum swung between Kat and Ngawang. Kat's hand jumped to the white ring around her arm. Fused with the armor, it couldn't be removed. Marie shook her head. Whether to stop Kat from fighting for Ngawang's life or to keep her in line, Death had removed Kat from the equation. Clenching her fists at her side, Ngawang glared at the aliens who covered and raced between the buildings. Beneath their feet, the ground remained still.

A crowd filled a large square plaza. Tall buildings covered in stained glass cast blood-red light down onto the streets. Before all, a platform of black podium rose. Silver spheres flew in circles above the plaza. They shivered in whispers echoed when meant to be kept close. As Death stormed up the edge, the aliens parted. Like a boat breaking against the waves, Death left orange light in his wake. Nel'ul whispered apologies and gratitude to the crowd as they allowed her and the trio to pass without comment. Wide eyes trailed across each of the human women. Pigmented stones and rubble hung in the aliens' hands.

On the stage a black painted creature with two lines of gold trailing down from his entirely blue eyes stepped forward. In an open robe of burgundy, he paced the length. With each passing, the crowd's whispers fell further to silence until no one spoke at

231

all. Against the black paint, his blue eyes glowed. Like the rest of his species, the man had no nose, and when he blinked, three pairs of eyelids moved like falling dominos. Reaching back over his head, he pulled a white hood from the burgundy of his robes and cast it over his hairless head. Hunching his shoulders, the alien seemed to transform into a vulture. His long fingers twitched. He passed them over his face, stretching his thin white tongue over his brush-like teeth. Red beads lined his tongue down the center.

"We shouldn't be here," Marie murmured. Her words echoed through the previously still spheres, and all eyes shifted from the black-painted man to the trio.

Ngawang glared. "Stay together. We'll be fine."

Death snorted. Drawing within thirty feet of the platform, he was stopped due to the thickness of the crowd. "Stay close. We'll be fine."

Two aliens walked on stage. Burgundy robes flowed over their shoulders, and white hoods covered their bulbous heads. Painted shimmering bronze, one of the two stepped forward. White streaks marked the corners of his eyes. He tilted his head to the left at the crowd. In mirror, the second alien tilted his white painted face to the right. Red outlined his eyes and exaggerated the small circle of his mouth. Even as their eyes traced the crowd, a glaze covered them. No emotion passed across their faces.

The black painted alien pulled a length of rope from his sleeve. A low rumble broke out across the crowd. Like reeds, they waved back and forth. As if inflating from the attention, the gold-flecked alien waved his arms in the air. From the middle of the platform, a column of stone rose. The higher it grew, the lower an arm of it fell to the side. The noise of the crowd grew deeper and loud. Some of the painted people threw their fists into the air and wailed in piteous tones causing pebbles to skip across the ground. No words came while the crowd pushed from side to side in a tide of color.

"I don't know about you," Marie muttered as they stopped close to the front of the stage. "But I hadn't really imagined we'd be seeing a hanging today."

Holding his arms aloft, the bronze alien bowed his head. The crowd fell still. Stepping forward, the alien's hands fell to his sides. Two aliens pulled another figure on stage. They each held an arm of another being shrouded in black robes, so even his face was hidden from sight. The white painted and black painted aliens stepped backwards towards the column, and the black one looped the rope typing it into a hangman's noose.

"People of Sin!" the bronze-colored alien called over the crowd. "An injustice has been made known. Are we to simply sit back and permit its perpetrator to go unpunished?"

The loud rumbling began, and the orbs clicked above their heads, translating, "No!"

A cacophony of voices screamed, "Kill the traitor!"

"Burn him!" cried others.

"Let the birds feast upon his traitorous flesh!" someone bellowed.

Once again, the bronzed alien raised his hands and silenced the crowd. "He has been judged and found guilty. Today – justice shall prevail!"

"Is it just me? Or are the people not actually saying what those spheres suggest?" Kat asked, and when the spheres made no echo of her words, she threw up her hands. "This is all a huge hoax! Everyone remains silent because they feel they're alone in the crowd. Fucking hell, this is a huge oppressive socially manipulative plot!"

Death chuckled. "Don't tell me you're surprised."

Nel'ul didn't look at them as they spoke. Her eyes remained on the stage. The guards in black suits with their shining helmets threw the man forward pulling the black robes from his face leaving him bare save for a knee length skirt of black. While the rest of the aliens were painted one color or another in their metallic hues, the prisoner stood untouched with his light blue skin from head to toe. His eyes were entirely white. With his hands bound, he wavered on the stage. Crack split across his neon white lips. When he called out, his tongue was black.

Nothing came from the orbs. A teal-painted alien whispered something. An orange glow dimly grew, but when Death turned, the orange brightened, and the alien scurried away. In clear halls between the buildings, multitudes stared down in disinterest. The guards marched forward, pulling the man back by his upper arms and stood him carefully before the crowd in a ray of bright light. Though the prisoner trembled, his jaw clenched tight.

"See how he flaunts his skin in such a perverse display!" The black-painted one threw himself forward, pointing damningly with a single golden nail at the blue-skinned man who glowered with narrowed eyes. "See how he stands refusing to acknowledge his destructive deeds!"

"How many men have you killed?" The white-painted one leaned close in a reflection of the other speaker beside the prisoner.

When the chained alien spoke, the orbs shifted. "More than you will ever know!" At the words, the prisoner's face squeezed like a peeled orange. His eyes searched the crowd, but none of those in the front spoke. "A hundred and more! I'd do so a thousand times again!"

"Ha!" the white alien scoffed and crossed his arms. "This world was brought into alignment. Finally, we have peace! Finally, we have food and water enough to feed us all! Finally, we have brought this planet to kneel!"

"Ten bucks says the guy claimed innocence," Ngawang offered.

Raising a brow, Kat shrugged. "He's still speaking. Orbs aren't translating. Front row looks uncomfortable."

"They do realize this is all for show, right?" Marie asked, glancing around the crowd.

Dragging the man further back, the guards hefted him to stand. The rope rounded his neck. Further back, the crowd screamed. All the while, the prisoner kept his eyes locked on a single point. Kat frowned. Her eyes searched the horde of aliens. Dressed in rich purples, a hooded alien stood painted with metallic periwinkle. While the rest of the crowd stared up at the stage and roaring, the one figure in the crowd ducked low as if to remain invisible from view. Though the alien looked anywhere but the stage, the prisoner's eyes remained locked to the periwinkle-painted figure.

"He killed my child! Hang him!" the spheres projected from the roaring horde.

The alien bowed his blue head. Growling, he shimmered red. "You mindless fools, following whatever a voice in the sky tells you! You've abandoned our customs for your gluttonous feasts! Look – what pride you take in your painted skin! You've let our children adopt foreign ways, and yet you act shocked when they tear down what little is left of our traditions! You reap what you sow! You've abandoned our gods for a parasite!"

"Blasphemy!" Pointing a red painted finger at the prisoner, the white-painted alien crouched low toward the front of the stage.

"Do you even understand the meaning of the word?" the prisoner raged, but the guards stepped back, and the prisoner dropped.

His feet wriggled. Rolling back into his head, the prisoner cringed. Behind the swinging man, a new figure emerged in a suit of black and red. War moved across the stage. Kat's heart thundered in his chest. War took the man's legs and pulled. A loud snap echoed, and the people cheered. Swaggering forward to the edge of the stage, War raised a hand, pointing directly toward Death. The crowd shifted, following the Rider's gesture. A single thought echoed in Kat's head. Despite her better judgment, she stepped around Ngawang, pushing her friend further out of sight.

Large eyes turned on them. Silver spheres wove around their heads as War leapt from the stage. Marie rocked back and forth. Her eyes flicked between the red-haired alien and Nel'ul, who shook on her feet as if another aftershock occurred. War rounded them. His eyes held to another prize. Leaping from the stage, the two guards followed him. Kat's eyes traced War's path. The purple-robed alien stepped back. Though the periwinkle-painted alien attempted to escape, the mass closed in around the figure. Both guards wove around the trio, holding the other alien by the arms. They dragged him toward the platform.

"War?" Marie whispered, but the red and black suited alien ignored her.

Closing her eyes, Marie stepped back. Her hands fell uselessly by her side. The guards lifted the first prisoner, and disrobing the periwinkle alien, they lifted the next to the rope. Chanting and fear roiled through the crowd. Orange and red raged. Tears lined Marie's eyes. Shimmering like ice, they rolled down her skin to slide against black metal. War and the entirety of the crowd watched as the second prisoner hung. Unlike the first, there was no struggle. Instead, the periwinkle-painted alien folded beneath its own weight as if diving forward into death after the first.

The second hanging left the crowd in chaos. They swarmed and swelled like a storm. Orange and red blazed across their skin, and only as she stepped back did the lack of other species cross Kat's mind. Others had lined the roads. When the painted aliens moved with their pigmented stones, small fish children moved with them. Now, in front of the platform as the periwinkle body swung, there was only painted skin and Mah-Wærm's ilk, and for all who looked upon them, the trio of humans fell soundly into the latter category.

Rubbing the bridge of her nose, Kat sighed. "Either of you think you could find the way back to the shuttle?"

Ngawang shrugged. "If we can get back into the building with Nel'ul."

"Then let's go," Kat announced.

When neither moved, Kat left them. Dust kicked up around her feet as she trudged back through the crowd. Even in the panic, children tossed pigment. Colors splattered against the black of Kat's suit, but she never stopped moving. Pink and yellow chalk stained her sides, and at her lack of response, the children scurried away. From behind her, footsteps thundered. Ngawang and Marie raced to her side. Red splattered up Marie's hip. Green matted the dark brown of her hair. Encased in black, Marie's blue eyes stared down the horizon.

"He won't let us get off so easily," Marie warned.

Surrounded by glass, there were no limits to the reflections offered for backward glances. War stood on the platform. His helm stared out, and if his eyes fell where they seemed, his golden gaze trailed after Marie. Death, still facing War, gave no acknowledgement to having lost his trio. Eyes followed them. All around, the orange glow dimmed. When no ramification came for their assaults, those who followed grew bolder. Daring didn't exactly suit. There was nothing brave about what they were doing.

They reached the glass house when a group surrounded them. All seemed to be small children. None of them came up higher than Kat's waist. Their stones splattered, and when their hands reached out, the trio could get away easily enough. Then a piece of rumble slammed into the back of Marie's head. She stumbled two steps. One hand rose to the back of her head as she fell. Ngawang spun to face the responsible party. All of the children tensed, but nobody ran. Kat crouched by Marie. Searching for a pulse, she was unable to find one, but she passed a finger below Marie's nose, and the metal fogged.

"Ngawang, she's still breathing," Kat said, but buzzing covered her words.

The orbs loomed over them. Standing, Kat moved to grabbed Ngawang's arm, but as she stepped forward, electricity surged through her body. At the same time, a splatter of blue pigment hit the back of her head. Color powdered burst around her head. Falling to the side, Kat shook against the ground. Ngawang's eyes flicked back and forth to the children who surrounded her. When she growled, they ran in a circle like multicolored sharks. Her fingers elongated into claws. Stones flew, crossing over Marie and Kat. One of the children ran forward, pressing a hand against Kat's head before jumping over Marie to join the circle once more. Tears poured down Kat's face. Every time she tried to open her mouth, electricity surged from the white ring on her arm.

"Stay back!" Ngawang roared, towering over her fallen friends.

The children giggled. Another child ran across the circle, pressing a hand to both Marie and Kat. Gritting her teeth, Ngawang snarled. On her opposite side, a pink-painted hand slapped her hip. They dodged across as Ngawang lunged. While she focused on the children, a white mist clung to the ground. It rolled, spreading around Ngawang's feet. Another jolt passed through Kat's body. Sparks jumped beneath her tears, singing the skin of her face. Ngawang's hand wrapped around one of the children's arms. Throwing the child back into the rest, she roared, grabbing the next to throw them back. Both tumbled across the ground, and when the second stood, the alien child held its arm to its chest.

"Momma!" the spheres cried.

All the children stopped. Backing away, they all screamed. "Help! Help! She attacked us! Momma!"

From the plaza, the crowd of aliens came. They descended in neat lines. All eyes focused on Ngawang. Orange light glowed about the children. The parents, however, shimmered like black lights. Markings traveled across their faces. Clenching her fists, Ngawang readied, but they surrounded her. She dodged the first blow. When a taller figure wrapped long fingers around her wrist, Ngawang broke the hand which held her. More hands came. They stepped over Marie and Kat. Like corpses in the street, the aliens left them to rot.

Swarming Ngawang, they raised rubble and sharp wires over their heads. Everything a makeshift weapon as if they had none at the ready though a hangman's noose hung only a mile or so less away.

One alien, painted pale beige, wrapped the wire around Ngawang's neck. Kat's heart skipped a beat. Fear slowed the world even as lightning flew in sparks across her skin.

Ngawang was going to die. Like the best poisons, the thought slid down painlessly. One more dead. What was one more time when everyone died in the end? Pressing her lips together, Kat kept her eyes locked on the horizon. Those who wanted to live died. Space held no more cruelty in this than Earth. In his white-suit, Death stood in the center of Kat's sight. Mist stretched out, and he shimmered like a ghost. Ngawang screamed; blood sprayed across Kat like crimson rain. Closing her eyes, Kat stayed where Death placed her, praying to a god she didn't recognize for mercy.

By her side, Ngawang's body fell, and the crowd cheered. As blood dampened the ground, Kat opened her eyes as the painted monsters held Ngawang's severed head aloft. Blood poured out of the neck. Black metal retreated, and though the aliens had to see the movement, they patted one another on the back as if the wire had done the damage. Death had selected Ngawang to die. Though they cheered, the citizens of Sin only had the illusion of a hand in the affair. If Death had wanted, Kat had no doubt he could have struck the planet down, but this display gave them a sense of power as if they could select the monster that conquered them.

The roar of the crowd fell into the background as Death approached. Stepping over Ngawang's headless corpse, the humanoid crouched before Kat. His helm cleared to reveal his steel gray eyes. The mist gathering around him condensed. Humming, he ran a hand along Kat's arm. His fingers stopped at the white ring. Though the shocks had stopped a few seconds before Ngawang's death, the thrum ran in her cells. Exhaustion swallowed her where once self-righteousness roared.

"It gets easier," Death promised. "There are only five of you now. It'll be just like counting yourself to sleep."

Kat remained quiet. Speaking would've taken too much energy. Behind Death, War trudged through the crowds. As the people glowed a bright white and cheered as they passed the head between them, War kept his eyes forward. Dust brushed against the shine of his metal suit. Without a word, he scooped Marie into his arms and walked away. Tears poured down Kat's face. Salt water mixed with the blood below.

Death shook his head, lifting her into his arms. "If it comforts you at all, Marie will live to the final three with you."

Black spots danced in Kat's vision. Bile and poison pushed up against her tongue, but she swallowed back the hatred which crawled like parasites beneath her skin. If Death spoke the truth, she had time. Time enough to plan and destroy the reign of Mah-Wærm from within its core. Even if Death were wrong, watching his disappointment offered succor enough to quench the bitterness in her heart.

Chapter Thirteen

Five beds remained when Kat returned to their cell. Five beds sat in two rows with a clear gap where a sixth one might have been. A mocking reminder. Chelsea, Amondi, and Qamar hung together on a single bed, but as the Tweedles opened the door and pushed Kat inside, they leapt forward, running to embrace their comrade. Stuck in the center of the three, Kat wept though she had no more tears. Ngawang's blood no longer covered her. Death had shoved her through a sonic cleansing before leaving her to Bel'von's hive-minded guards. Now inside, the black metal retreated from her head.

"Where's Marie?" Chelsea whispered.

Though Amondi glowered at the blonde, Qamar stepped back, seeking Kat's gaze as if her eyes alone would tell her as she begged, "Tell me they didn't both die."

"Famine said Ngawang was going to die," Chelsea informed Kat.

"She did."

Pressing her lips together, Chelsea stepped back. "I can't help but feel guilty?"

"Because you won't have to end up like Rachel?" Amondi posited then shook her head. "Nobody wanted Ngawang to die, but she was definitely the biggest competition."

"She was scared," Qamar retorted.

Kat shook her head, sitting down on the nearest bed. "We were all scared. We all are."

"Nobody killed anybody else," Amondi retorted.

Chelsea reclined on the bed across from Kat. Her fingers knotted in the sheets. "It's rather exhausting, isn't it? They turn us against each other like we're dogs. Chained up and starving, so when we get a chance, we'll bite each other's throats out with barely a blink."

"So that's what Rachel did?" Kat whispered, pulling at the collar of her suit. "Blinked?"

Running a hand through her long golden hair, Chelsea pulled her knees against her chest. Amondi sat beside her. The bland gray of her clothes caught Kat by surprise. Glancing among the three women before her, Kat frowned at their casual wear. Though the suits offered only the illusion of protection, it gave a semblance of equality between captive and captor. They had chosen the safety versus the risk. Perhaps they were stronger for it. Kat couldn't. Decapitation or knife in the back, they were dying anyways.

"It doesn't matter," Amondi retorted.

Qamar nodded. "What's done is done. It's just us now."

"For how long?" Chelsea asked. "They're going to kill someone else next. Who will that be? One of us three?" She pointed in a circle at the three women who had gone down to the planet with Famine. "Or Marie? Is that why she didn't come back?"

"She got hit in the back of the head. It knocked her unconscious, so there's a chance she's in their med bay," Kat posited.

As if the consideration itself was good enough to bring them answers, the wall opened. Marie shuffled in, already in pajamas, but hers was a bright blue fluffy onesie. Someone, likely Marie herself, had separated and braided her hair into two loose pigtails revealing a sizeable bump on the back of her head. Blinking, she stumbled into the room. Tumbling off the back of the bed, Kat raced to her. Marie's eyes widened.

"Oh, hi," Marie smiled sleepily.

"Concussion?" Kat asked, studying her eyes. "Any other injuries?"

"No and none. Just the bump and some anti-inflammatory shots," Marie shrugged. There was no red lipstick when she smiled. "How 'bout you get me into bed? I'm super tired."

Wrapping an arm around Marie, Kat led her to a bed. Marie sunk beneath the covers. She wrapped her arms under the elongated pillow and rolled so her back faced Kat while her eyes faced the gap. The same gap where the empty sixth bed - Ngawang's bed - should've been..

"Things will be better soon," Marie whispered.

***

But they weren't. A cycle found them back in the arena. Standing up with her arms bound across her chest, Kat glared up at the observation room where Mah-Wærm stood with his loyal lap dogs at his sides. All four of them were up there. Famine shifted slightly behind War, who crossed his arms over his chest. Death stood on their master's left. He kept his eyes straight ahead, not even pretending to be watching the combat as if he knew already who would win. Perhaps he did. Between Marie and Qamar, the answer was as obvious as War's confident stance.

"Who wants to bet whoever survives this dies next?" Amondi grumbled. Her words carried over their heads through the silver spheres.

"I don't want to hurt you," Qamar announced, clasping her hands together.

Bel'von snorted. His mask was fully opaque. "And I don't want to be wasting my time here. You kill each other, or I kill one of you. I'm good with that decision."

"You mean you're good with that power," Kat retorted.

The insectoid shrugged. "If you think there's power in that decision, you haven't been paying attention."

"It's okay," Marie assured them all.

Walking over to the wall, Marie ran her hand along the hilts. They all seemed to be the same, but Marie studied each one carefully. She lifted one, holding the blade up the light. With a sigh, she placed it back. Her hand drifted once more. Kat's eyes jumped to War. No movement. Lifting a second over her head, Marie hummed softly, and two of War's fingers twitched. Marie smiled, handing Qamar the weapon she had picked up. Up in the observation room, War lurched forward, but Famine held him back. Frowning, Kat shifted her gaze to the blade and then back to War. Red bloomed across his suit. Something was wrong.

"They just want to see us try," Marie promised Qamar. "You don't need to try to kill me. I won't try to kill you. Here, just run it across my arm. You'll see. These blades aren't sharp enough to cut through the suits. It's all just a mind game."

"Marie…" Qamar whispered. Their voice trembled.

Shaking her head, Marie let her brown locks fly around like an earthly halo. "I promise. It's going to be okay, Qamar. See?" Marie ran her own blade lightly over Qamar's side. Nothing happened. "See?"

Bel'von crossed his arms. His mask remained in place. He hadn't bothered to show off even though he'd been scheduled for an eye replacement. Kat's blood ran cold. Her gaze jumped back to War. Red swelled and pulsed. His helm collapsed, and he pushed against Famine's grip, raising his arms as if to slam them against the transparent window in front of him.

"No…" Kat gasped. Amondi's brow furrowed, but Bel'von turned to face them.

"Keep quiet," he growled.

Kat's heart thundered against her bones. Qamar shifted their blade, mimicking Marie. When Kat lunged forward, Bel'von shoved her back again she wall. His mask shimmered, and two dark eyes silenced Kat as the blade slipped across Marie's leg, leaving a well of blood in its wake. Qamar cried out, dropping the blade as Marie smiled. Tears gathering on the edges of her eyelashes.

"No!" War bellowed. He phased through the wall, landing in the arena. His arms stretched out, catching Marie as she fell. "No," he whispered a second time. "Please, no…Marie…you can't…you lied to me."

"Had to. Weren't going to give me the poison to use on myself," Marie pointed out.

Qamar's hands flew to their mouth. "Oh, no. No! Marie!"

"Not how I planned on going out," Marie murmured. Each time she blinked, her eyes stayed closed longer. "Never got to answer the Star Wars versus Star Trek debate."

War's eyes jumped to Kat. His brows furrowed in confusion as his gaze returned to Marie. "I don't understand."

"Borg or Empire? Guess Lucas knew better…" Marie's eyes slipped shut.

The Tweedles jumped into motion. Two grabbed Qamar though they hardly needed any force to guide her from the arena. Amondi and Chelsea followed willingly, leaving Kat behind. She was stuck between Bel'von and the wall. Kat swallowed, holding back a scream that threatened to tear its way out of her. Jacobi's eyes stared back from Bel'von's golden face. Flecks of darker brown and gold - a pattern she could never forget.

"You fucking snake," Kat spat.

Bel'von tilted his head. "You know better than most what I am. I've never lied to you."

Her eyes lifted to the window. Death stood motionless. At his side, Mah-Wærm frowned. Soft grays covered him once more. Bel'von, for once, had

248

a point. For all the cruelty of deciding upon those eyes, he had never lied to her - not with hope.

Shoving Bel'von aside, Kat glared up at Death's opaque white mask. "She's going to survive to top three, eh?"

She spat at his feet. Her eyes blazed, and the fear in his eyes when they became visible did nothing to quench her thirst for blood. At her side, Kat's hands clenched into fists. War's screams reverberated in her mind, and as the Tweedles come to drag her out with the rest, Kat roared. Death's white ring spread down her arm. One shot sent the first Tweedle down with a hole in her chest. Each subsequent shot blew a head from the hive. With his new eyes - Jacobi's eyes - wide, Bel'von dove through the wall which opened and sealed it behind him too quickly for her to catch him. Plasma leapt until only she and War remained alive. Surrounded by corpses, Kat spun to face Death and his master. Famine backed away. His hands pressed against his chest.

His murmurs carried down by the spheres. "He will not be pleased. Oh, he will not be pleased."

"Quiet," Mah-Wærm commanded, lifting his hand as his eyes stayed on War's weeping form.

Slamming her fist into the walls, Kat burrowed her fingers into the metal. The walls would not open for her willingly, but she would give them no choice. Her rage swelled as she ascended. War held Marie's body tightly to his chest. Burrowing his face in her hair, he murmured untranslatable words.

"War?" Famine called in spite of his master's command. "They did not know, War. You cannot be angry with me - with them, War. They did not know."

Death turned, grabbing Famine by the throat. Shoving the taller alien into a wall, he growled, "You were ordered to be quiet."

"But…he will punish them for this. It was not their fault," Famine insisted. His hands trembled, but he did not press back against his elder.

Reaching the window overlooking the arena, Kat drew back her right hand. Her fingers curled into a fist. The first punch sent waves across the wall. Though translucent, the area and its surrounding black metal were the same material. Pulling back her fist, Kat rammed her hand back down. A point formed on the end of her fist. Third hit brought a crack. Fourth sent cracks crawling across the surface.

Mah-Wærm sighed. "War. Put down the body."

"Please," War begged even as he moved to follow his master's command. "Please, don't leave her this way."

"You interfered with the selection. Any deaths are on your conscience," Mah-Wærm informed him.

Laying Marie down, War clenched his teeth. Tears gathered along his eyelids. "Why didn't she love me, Mah-Wærm? Please, why didn't she love me enough to stay?"

Rearing back, Kat swung up to the edge of the transparent rectangle. She buried her suit's claws into the black and threw herself back. Her feet slammed into the window. Splinters flew back. Transparent sections of biosynthetic metal rained down. Diving forward, War covered Marie's body. Blood, red and warm, ran down his arms and face. Following her feet, Kat slid into the room. Black spread up her neck.

Before her shoulders passed the splintered hole, a helm covered her head. Not a single stretch of skin could be seen. White blended into blue and black like an abstract painting.

Lasers flew. Crashing against a shield, they scattered like light through a prism. Mah-Wærm stepped back, turning to face her. His quicksilver eyes honed in on Kat. Spikes slammed against the shield, shattering into dust around her feet. Death bowed his head, tossing Famine aside. He disappeared into the wall, leaving only Death and Mah-Wærm in her sight. Arms wrapped around her waist, and Kat screamed.

"They murdered her!" Kat shrieked. "Murderers! You killed her! You killed all of them!"

"No!" War cried, lifting her off her feet.

Metal elongated on her left arm into a knife. Stabbing blindly behind her, Kat buried her blade into War's thigh. Gritting his teeth, he shook her, bringing her feet further off the ground. Tears streamed down his tanned face. Crystals accented the blazing red of his lashes, but Kat only had eyes for the two monsters before her. On the edge of the room, War leaned back. Falling in his arms, Kat blasted the window around them, sending splinters of transparent biosynthetic material into the room in their wake.

Crashing against the black mats, Kat shoved War away from her. She grabbed the nearest Tweedle and tossed her through the glass. Peeling the chest plate off the next, she sent another insectoid flying. When War stood, she cast the next body his way. A beam of red light tore the corpse in half. In the light's wake, War stood in red. Helm to boot, his suit once again shimmered fully crimson.

"Stand down," War commanded.

Kat's eyes narrowed. Electricity pulsed around her arms. "You killed her."

"Yes," War agreed.

The air clicked, and fire flew forth. Kat leapt out of the way. Flames consumed everything, crawling up the walls. Thunder rolled. Plasma jumped from Kat's arms. Flipping, Kat dodged War's second rage of heat, landing beside Marie's body. Heart racing like a wild stampede in her chest, Kat tensed. Lightning cascaded across the floor. War fired a third time. Kat tumbled across the ground, leaving Marie to burn. At the very least, nobody would experiment on her body. Nobody would cut into her flesh, inspecting the invisible nature of her selflessness.

Surrounded by fire, Kat stayed on her knees. Four remained. Of the thousands on the Intrepid - there were only three humans left in less than a light year of her. Three left to be struck down. She'd failed to protect them. Watched helpless as Ngawang struck down Rachel and as Death struck down Ngawang. Promised Marie for at least a few deaths longer, she'd given up on wanting more. Stolen like pieces of her heart, they'd killed those she loved the most until only shadows of friendship remained. She hated her own thoughts. Her frustration at those who lived as much as those who died.

"Liars!" Kat roared. Around her, the room quivered. "You told me she'd live until there were only three of us! I can't believe I trusted you - any of you."

Mah-Wærm cleared his throat, crossing his arms over his chest. "War? Kill her."

"What?" Death murmured. Frozen, he shook. His pale face shifted to almost blue as War aimed another wave of fire at Kat. "Mah-Wærm...I do not understand."

"She's too unpredictable. War's too emotional already. A matter of balance, frankly," Mah-Wærm informed him.

Though he bowed his head, Death pressed further, "But she's adapted the quickest and most thoroughly to the Architect's equipment and neurotransmitters."

Kat crossed her arms, sending up a shield of connected electricity. Fire crashed against it like waves. Spikes shot down from her feet into the soft floor. Digging in, she pushed forward. Heat surrounded her, but the suit let out a rush of air. Cool liquid circulated above her skin. A chill ran across the new skin on her abdomen. Gritting her teeth, Kat took another step. Her heart and the lightning thrummed together. Long tendrils stretched from her back. Slamming into the floor, they fused together.

"She's adapted to the suit like another limb. None of the others can do that." Death insisted, pressing a hand to the wall.

Above their heads, the silver spheres stilled then rolled upward back into the ceiling as if on strings. War lunged. Black metal wove webs around him, entwining the red-haired alien in a metallic spider's web. Pressing her weight into the legs, Kat leapt, allowing the suit to send her backward and flying over War's head toward the transparent window. War bellowed, tearing the metal around him, and slammed into the closest leg, but they separated from Kat's back, sending her forward as the pillars of black metal fell down around War.

Crossing her arms before her, Kat smashed the already fractured window, tumbling across the floor at Death and Mah-Wærm's feet. Spines shot out as her back hit the floor. Rolling to her feet, Kat launched across the room, following the wave of sharp pieces with her fists. Death grabbed her first punch. He held it in his hand as she hooked a leg around his shoulders, slamming her opposite foot against his side. White mask in place, the alien's face couldn't be seen nor read. Mist stretched across his suit, leaving her grip to slide across his arm and body expanded and collapsed simultaneously. Sparks flickered across black metal, and though she could feel the shock burrowing into her muscles from the white ring on her arm, it didn't hurt.

"Stupid girl," Death growled.

His voice echoed, bouncing around the room like sonar. A hand came – grabbed her shoulder and dragged her back. Just like with Ngawang, the suit turned against her. Nothing clamped down on her neck. Her head remained attached, but Mah-Wærm dragged her off Death, and the suit fought against her limbs just enough to let her go with him. Throwing her against the wall, he studied her. His eyes dissected every inch, leaving her bones bare. In his soft gray clothes and socks without shoes, he shouldn't have been intimidating. From his black hair and pale face to the gray swallowing the rest of him, Mah-Wærm matched the rooms of his ship. He held her aloft, not blinking.

"Mercy?" Mah-Wærm hummed, glancing back at Death. "Do you honestly believe this will work?"

Death inclined his head. "Mercy will make vilifying you more difficult."

"But vilification doesn't prevent indoctrination," Mah-Wærm pointed out. The wall stretched out, wrapping around Kat. Folding his arms across his chest, the man clucked his tongue. "War's people never stopped vilifying me. I blew them up, and War's fine."

"Fine?" Death waved a hand at War.

War stood, all in red, trembling over the ashes of Marie's body. Mah-Wærm drummed his fingers against his arms. Tilting his head back and forth, he faced Death. "You have a point."

"Famine turned out far better, and your approach came across more savior than conqueror. If you want Conquest, mercy now matters," the white-suited alien insisted.

Mah-Wærm furrowed his brow. "These creatures are far more fragile psychologically than Famine. Rebellious and plastic, they'll take advantage of any sort of vulnerability."

"Then kill me," Kat growled, but her voice only echoed in the helm. Every sphere remained still.

White folded back, revealing Death's face. Running a hand through his hair, he sighed. "You stated these humans are the closest to your own species. Reasonable modifications could permit species replication. The natural way," Death pushed. "Mercy means sympathy. Sympathy creates the way for companionship, and that makes what you'll do next easier. You have galaxies of loyal people who need you. Children need watchful eyes. Mercy now means cooperation later – maybe even love."

Kat gritted her teeth, sneering at Death. Though he pled for her life, he painted a bleaker picture than she had believed for the survivor. The pressure left her skin crawling. Panic sent her heart racing. If they wanted reproduction, Amondi was on the chopping block. Chelsea, Qamar, and Kat remained. Her eyes traveled over the destruction. Every sparkling bit of translucent biosynthetic glimmered as fire raged on in the arena. Swallowing, she watched War. Burying his hand in the ash, the red-suited alien shrunk in on himself.

"I see," Mah-Wærm hummed.

Inhaling, Kat pulled against her helm. The metal shimmed but remained opaque as she growled, "You don't!" Her eyes ached. A tremble ran down her spine as her voice echoed only in the confines of the helm for the second time. "You wanted him to not be distracted. You wanted him to keep on ruling all alone. That's not going to happen. If he's merciful, Chelsea will humanize him. She already has. She'll think getting into his bed will save humanity – save him like he's someone who can be redeemed. Like Marie did with War, but worse – a thousand times worse."

If Death or his master could hear her, they gave no sign. Instead, Death forced a smile which didn't reach his eyes. "Conquest will come forward when called, as we all did, but this way…this way she's choosing you, not just the truth."

"Survival," Kat growled, struggling futilely against her bonds and the silence forced upon her.

"Not you, not truth, not power – survival. Life or death."

Mah-Wærm inclined his head. "I have been alone for some time."

"And wasn't that what all of this was about?" Death inquired. He sidled up to his master, gesturing toward the flames. "Recreating the greatest species to ever evolve in this universe?"

"I have time enough to wait," Mah-Wærm stated, and Kat frowned, uncertain if his words signified a rejection or acquiescence to Death's précis.

Stepping around the dictator to stand before Kat, Death pressed a hand against her bindings. "I will take this one back to the room, then?"

The bindings vanished, dropping Kat forward into Death's arms. Mah-Wærm shrugged, stepping down from the room and into the arena without a word. All around War, the flames died. Only ash and blood lingered. Kat growled, but the suit weighed her limbs down. Even as she struggled, she could not lift even one finger. Death carried her, skating through the strange halls. His hands trembled.

"Still muting me, jackass?" she grumbled.

Slamming her into the wall rather than forming a door, Death glared up at her. "Do you think I'm stupid?"

"Generally, yes."

Death narrowed his eyes. "I just saved your life. While I understand you would never thank me for such consideration, have the soundness of mind to recognize when I'm pleading with you to shut up!"

"I want to die. I want to mess up your little plan. If that undermines your position here, pick a different ringer," Kat retorted.

"I choose you. Nobody else will work."

Cocking an eyebrow, she scoffed. "Amondi would."

"He needs the illusion. She's cut that out of her rather successfully. There are modifications, and there's just turning someone into an incubator for clones. We've tried clones. They don't work," Death informed her. "You and I both know the countdown from here. Your species remains in control of their planet. Frankly, they've made strives to blockade the entire planetary system. Which of you do you think will distract him from that conquest? The one who spreads her legs for him? Or the one that fights against him?"

"Don't try that on me, Death," Kat spat. "I wouldn't be around if you thought the latter would do anything remotely distracting to your genocidal savior. He'd be distracted by family, and we both know I'm not a good enough liar to keep my species alive that way."

Death rolled his gray eyes, setting her back on the ground. His hand fell to his side. Exhaustion sat heavily around his eyes, and rubbing the bridge of his nose, he sighed. As his shoulders sagged, he stepped back and paced the width of the hall. All around him, white mist spread. His skin shimmered, turning almost pure white. When he rounded to face her, his eyes were like chips of slate. The color expanded and took over the whites of his eyes. Black lines spread down from the center and upward into his black hair.

Stray locks lifted into the air as if static held them. Lightning sparked between one corner of his eyes and the other.

"Your species will die. Today, tomorrow, in fifty of your years or a hundred, but Conquest will remain. We will remain. I will remain," he warned, walking back to stand in front of her. Lightning swelled in his eyes, brightening them like coiled wire. "Do you want more of him? An heir for the immortal? Heirs – frankly, he won't resign himself to a single child. If they are born before Earth's demise, do you think he would hesitate to select future mates for his children? Alter the whole of humanity for the good of his renewed species?"

Kat's lip curled into a sneer. "And you think someone's unwillingness will stop him? He's a genocidal maniac. You all are. What makes you think anyone saying no will make a difference?"

Death inclined his head. "It could."

"Could? That's not definite, so then why does it matter who survives? If he wants to breed someone to bring back his species, it sure as hell doesn't matter what that person thinks, considering everything else he's done. Even a monster can fool a child into loving them," Kat ranted, getting in his face. "He doesn't want love."

"And that's where you're wrong."

The words ricocheted like a bullet. Blinking, she stepped back. Along her jaw, the muscles tensed, and her head tilted as cold flooded her veins, sending a shiver along her limbs. Crossing her arms to unclench her hands from fists, Kat watched as the lightning faded from Death's eyes. They narrowed back to the gray rings she'd first seen in a human-pale face. As the color returned, his lips shifted from white to blue before settling on a light pink. Each pigment masked the alien beneath.

"Mad dictator wants love. Put out a personal ad," Kat drawled, turning away to face the wall between her and the surviving women. "Open the wall."

"Marie's death will speed up the clock. War will want Qamar to answer for it. Amondi already had her day set though it'll be pushed back further thanks to Marie's decision. In the end, it'll be just you and Chelsea. You've avoided killing your comrades. Can you die knowing what she'll be left to?" Death asked as the white mist condensed, melding back with his form.

Biting her lip, Kat shook her head. "You're an idiot. I'm not sacrificing myself to an eternity of rape and mental torture for someone I can barely stand."

"He won't," the white-suited alien insisted. "I underestimated how clever Marie was. She altered the order and accelerated our timetable. I should have realized the poison she had asked for wouldn't be for her own use. I knew War would give her the coated blade, but I thought it was a mercy for Qamar. That mistake is mine. However, I know Mah-Wærm. He'll torture you. Mentally, physically, he'll tear you apart to rebuild you. I understand that's terrifying, but he won't force you to breed with him. To achieve the renewal of his species, he needs a mate of his species. Nothing less could gestate one like him. To get you to that point, he'd have to make you his equal – and he doesn't project his will on those he considers his equals."

"How would you even know?" Kat demanded.

Death sighed. "I know because I was there through his earliest years. I have seen him faced with those who wanted him. Those who might have been – I've seen this situation before, and he never touched a single one in the way that terrifies you."

He had no idea what terrified her. A lifetime without another human's touch scared her for what it meant, not the absence itself. All of humanity separated from her. Whether by death or distance, the absence of humanity meant an absence of home. Meant being surrounded by a wondrous sonder. Almost ten billion minds worked and experienced life in ten billion unique ways. She couldn't understand. He skipped straight over the crux of the matter. Humanity destroyed outside of her; then, Mah-Wærm would tear the humanity out of her too.

"He'll make me a monster. Push me to Stockholm Syndrome, but don't worry, he'll only do what you don't want when you're so damaged you think you want it," Kat mocked.

Death rolled his eyes. With a wave of his hand, the wall opened. Without looking back, Kat stepped inside. As the room sealed behind her, Kat leaned back against the cool metallic coating. Weight pressed down on her. Her legs shook, and when she lifted her eyes, three pairs stared back from the far side of the room. While they'd huddled together after Ngawang's death, they each took a far corner. Cuddled up in the corner furthest from the door, Qamar held their knees tightly to their chest. Dried salt marred their cheeks.

Redness washed the white form their eyes. Amondi stood slightly toward the center of the room from the corner to the left of the door. Her arms wrapped around her body, squeezing her sides. Wrapped in blankets, Chelsea sat on her bed toward front right of the room. The blond was the closest to the door, but none of them moved.

"She's dead," Qamar murmured. Any last glisten of hope faded from their eyes.

Kat nodded. "She planned it."

Qamar pressed their lips together. Tugging at the edge of their suit, they vanished back into the depths of their mind. Amondi took two steps toward Kat, but something held her back. Her eyes widened. Backing up, the dark skinned woman clung to the wall. Chelsea slid from her bed. Holding the blankets wrapped around her, she glided over the floor to Kat's side.

"What do we do now?" Chelsea asked. Her blue eyes seemed to sink into her pale face, leaving her exhaustion on show in the light purple cradling her eyes.

"We fuck this up," Kat said.

Chelsea's brow furrowed. "What?"

"They've got the countdown played out. Marie messed it up. We mess it up further," Kat explained, pushing away from the door. "War will kill Qamar next. Amondi's planned for third. Me – then you," she informed the blond. "We screw that up. Amondi has to be the one to live through this. All the rest of us, he can use us the way he wants – get his big happy end day, but with Amondi, he can't. We end this right now."

"End this? By what? Killing each other?" Amondi asked.

Kat's lips twisted downward at the corners into a frown. "Exactly. Chelsea and I die first. If Qamar lives, War will make sure they die. He'll never let them last after they killed Marie, intentionally or not."

"And that's your grand plan?" Amondi demanded, storming away from the wall just to fall back as if the gravity of it was too great.

Tightening her hold on the blankets around her shoulders, Chelsea hummed. "I'm Conquest? I'm Conquest."

Her blue eyes glimmered. Acid rose in Kat's throat. A burning, bitterness crept up her tongue. Relief smoothed the lines of Chelsea's brow. Her lips smoothed from the nervous tension which Kat hadn't recognized until the information swept the fear away. She'd made a mistake. Chelsea shouldn't have known. Giving up life wasn't something everyone could do. Given the choice, Chelsea wanted to live as badly as Ngawang had. Greater good didn't measure into that kind of thinking.

"No, you're his fucking broodmare," Kat retorted.

The relief remained as Chelsea said, "Mah-Wærm brought you back. War split you in half, but he healed you. Even if we tried to kill each other, we can't be sure he wouldn't just do the same."

"We have to try," Kat insisted. Her eyes flicked to Amondi, who pressed her fingers against her lips. "I know it's horrible, but he's shown his hand. He doesn't want another soldier. He wants someone who can give birth to more in his species. Even with all their tech, they'd have to clone with you."

Chelsea scoffed. "Why? Because Death said so?"

A retort buzzed around Kat's mouth, but she swallowed it back. Chelsea showed her hand. There would be no point in revealing the rest of her cards. Shaking her head, Kat held up her hands. She didn't need Chelsea's permission to kill her. Nobody in the room needed permission to carve out their own womb and ovaries or do the same to another. They could hollow each other in a blink. Only Amondi was safe. The rest could be made useless, gutted like fish in seconds. None of that would change Chelsea's mind. Plans would loop around Kat's mind, but if Chelsea wasn't on their side anymore, she couldn't afford to have her involved.

"Maybe he's wrong. Maybe he lied. God, I hope he did, but if he didn't, are you really okay with that?" Kat asked, forcing her voice to be gentle and soft. Keeping her tone low, she bowed her head. "I couldn't live like that, Chelsea. The idea of him hurting you – any of you – like that. I'd rather be dead than know I failed you." Pushing her thoughts to Jacobi, Kat forced her eyes to weep, avoiding Chelsea's gaze as Kat sunk to the floor. "We're screwed, and if Death's right, you'll be raped and tortured for the rest of eternity. God, Chelsea, I don't know how to make that okay."

Kneeling before Kat, Chelsea laid a hand on Kat's shoulder. "And that's exactly why we're just going to leave it."

"What?" Amondi exclaimed.

"We're going to see how this goes. Ride it out," Chelsea replied. "If it ends with me, I'm okay with that. I'd rather be the one suffering anyways."

"Suffering?" Amondi spat. "You mean the only one alive. Don't fucking lie to us and pretend you don't want to act because you don't want to risk one of us being in your position. They pampered your skinny ass, and there's no one here who'll just beat sense into you, but that's just a part of the plan, isn't it? If Ngawang had learned what Kat just said, you'd be dead. But, no! They tell the suicidal woman with a martyr complex!"

Qamar shook, pressing their hands against their ears. Kat tore at the edges of her suit, feigning she was running away as she removed the armor, pulling on the gray pajamas as Chelsea faced Amondi. There was no telling how long they had. Death came in hours and then weeks. Whatever it took to break them down another step would be the length between Marie's undoing and whoever went next. Shedding the armor sent a chill across Kat's skin. Giving in offered no advantages. Lying hadn't been her first choice, but between better odds with manipulation and lower without, Kat hedged her bets. Qamar would be next, but Amondi wouldn't be. Not if Kat could ensure Chelsea died first.

Chapter Fourteen

The maze spanned before Kat. Above her head, the lights flickered. Walls stretched and pulled together, changing shape before her eyes. Blood oozed around her feet. Stepping over the latest mangled alien corpse, she ducked beneath the strange biosynthetic planet matter. A mix between cables and vines, they stretched along the walls in this region of the labyrinth. Electricity sparked along their lengths. Reaching up, she ran her hand along one, drawing the power into her suit. Around her arm, the ring glows. Machines ground their gears along the course, and somewhere in the damn center of the death machine lurked War.

All four remaining women recognized the threat in his presence. Qamar had shrunk beneath his name. Red engulfed his armor. Whatever uncertainty he had before had bled dry with Marie. Only Chelsea had smiled. Her bright eyes locked on Mah-Wærm, and the mercury of his own burned her back. They were poison. Madness passed between the two. If Chelsea were even in the maze, Kat doubted danger lurked anywhere near her. A trail of corpses marked Kat's route. Chelsea wouldn't have the same. Couldn't have the same. She knew the pacifist would only make it with intervention, and she had it in the end.

When the lights went out, Kat kept her pace. With her helm covering her head, she could see just as well in the dark. Pulses thundered ahead. They rounded bodies without a clear pump, but she'd torn enough Tweedles apart to know what their insides sounded like. Spines broke through the walls, throwing her into the sky. Though they tensed – having heard her coming, the three Tweedles failed, fumbling before their heads rolled across the sawdust covering the ground. The light brown ash clumped with red.

Gears whirled. Throwing her body to the ground, the saws missed Kat's head. They buzzed across and back into the walls. Rolling, she dodged those which lifted from the floor, tumbling into a corner and up the wall like a spider when the ceiling collapsed down upon where she'd once been. War had eyes on Qamar, but Mah-Wærm had no mercy for Kat. Best she could do was fight and find Amondi or Qamar. They had the best chance of survival together, and with Chelsea wandering on her own, her survival would only prove the issue.

To her left, through three walls, Kat's suit picked up a human heart. Four chambers worked to speed blood as the person ran. A horde of small, quadrupeds followed. Feline and carnivorous equines lurked in the shadows. Both hunted in packs. Based on size, whoever she'd found had felines in pursuit. Racing forward, Kat mirrored the other human's path, leaping over trap holes and scaling the walls. A field kept her from standing tall, but she was able to roll from one hall to the next on her stomach. Dropping down, she cut through an armored drone. Machines made up the bulk of their enemies. Stun guns threatened to leave anyone hit awake as the carnivores circled. Getting eaten alive wasn't on Kat's schedule.

"On your right!" Kat called, throwing herself over the next wall to slide down beside the human – Amondi. "Fuck! Duck!"

Amondi dropped to the ground, sliding around her. Bolts of plasma swirled then slammed forward like a net. The first row of the felines raced through, ending up crispy and dead on the opposite side. Those which followed were smart enough to slow and turn around. There were other meals in the maze. Swiveling, Kat raced to catch up to Amondi.

"You seen anybody else?" Amondi asked as they rounded a corner. Her arm shot out to stop Kat. "Saw a bug guy get his inners turned into outers in this hall."

"These walls are taller than the others, but there might be space to jump them," Kat suggested. Frowning as she studied the two halls, Kat shook her head. "Haven't seen Chelsea or Qamar. You?"

With a sigh, Amondi lamented, "Caught a glimpse of Blondie. Wall went up."

"Probably for the best. We get to Qamar. Stay alive, hunt War down," Kat announced, scaling the wall.

She separated a spike from her suit, holding the material in her hand. Exhaling as the yowling of cats returned, she lifted it. Electricity threw the spike from her hand. It bounced against the floor and into the hall ahead. Reaching the center, the spear collapsed in upon itself, crumpling on a single point.

268

Unleashing a long string of curses, Amondi backed toward the other hall. "Fucking cats have us cornered against a black hole."

"Well," Kat hummed, jumping back to the ground. "We'll just have to kill them."

"Five or six, sure. There were about fifty on my tail," Amondi retorted.

Kat stretched her neck. Listening in the helm for the cracking of her bones before she released her armor to slide guns into her hands. "What would you suggest?"

"Go through the wall."

Amondi spun, sending spear after spear of her suit through the wall. As soon as she withdrew one, the hole in its wake closed. Turning to the next wall, she tried the same. The wall healed itself just as the first had. Clawing at the metal, Amondi growled and slammed her fists down. Sparks spread down Kat's arms. Coming closer, the felines raced down the corridor. Some ran along the walls, gravity seeming to have no affect on them. Their double tongues licked the air like snakes. Red eyes glinted in the dark. Throwing herself back, Kat slammed her back into Amondi, sending them into the corner as she released the trigger.

A net of electricity wove in front of them. Amondi wrapped her arms around Kat, and their suits stretched out, forming a wall in front of them behind the plasma barrier. The felines sprung against the metal. As the first wave left to ash, those which followed steered away from the ash and into the second hall. One by one, they swirled into the singularity.

"Backtrack your way or mine?" Kat asked.

Amondi sighed. "Yours. There isn't much back my way."

Curling the metal of their suits, they closed off the hall behind the retreating felines. Kat clawed her way up the wall. Throwing herself over, she scanned the middle hall she'd hurdled over earlier. Overhead, the lights flicked back up. Mist rolled over the floor. Static popped along the walls, and something hummed in the distance, but there were no heartbeats in the distance. Nothing yowled or neighed. No footsteps thumped against the metal or scuffled through the sawdust around from the middle line of the hall.

Sparks flew through the vapors. Electricity caught within the fog. On either side, it rolled closer, pressing down to the grains of sawdust along the floor. Kat sidled toward the far wall. Amondi kept to the right. Serpents wove through the air. White coils with the fanned hoods of king cobras slithered closer. When the snakes opened their jaws, spits of fire fell to the ground. Cradled within the dust, they sparked. Each grain exploded like firecrackers. Leaping against opposite walls, Amondi and Kat climbed the rough metal. Red rust gathered on their fingertips. Climbing, they reached the top edge; the shield buzzed above their heads.

"So, we're screwed," Amondi lamented as the shield skimmed the edge of the wall.

With a sigh, Kat stretched, sending a spear of her suit into the mist. A serpent coiled and then lunged at the spike. Electricity traveled up the metal, spiraling around the blue spot on her back to the white

270

ring which absorbed the charge. Swinging around, the serpent spiraled in a death roll. Though the ground smolders and popped with flashes of light, Kat released her hold. Every snake slithered forward, abandoning the edges of the walls. Like eels, they whipped through the air. Their jaws unhinged. From the electrified tube of their throats, a secondary set of jaws launched.

Skimming her foot along the ground, Kat kicked up the smolders. Sawdust sparked, exploded, and scattered through the air. Some snakes recoiled. Other curled around the flashes. Their hoods billowed like sails. Slamming her fists against the ground, Kat spent spikes flying in all directions. Amondi shrieked. Throwing up a shield of metal, she pressed further against the wall. The snakes, however, weren't as lucky. They slammed into the walls and overhead shield.

"Yum," Kat murmured, brushing off the splatter of blue goop that splattered from their charged corpses. "Snake kabobs."

Amondi sighed as she slid down the wall. "I swear they've given you the super suit."

"Nah, just an upgrade," Kat retorted, tapping the ring.

"Why's Death fond of you? I get why psycho's got goo-goo eyes for Chelsea. Easy A and all that. You and Death? What the heck is the point of that?" Amondi asked as they headed further into the mist.

Slicing down an insectoid soldier, Kat shrugged. "Last choice? I was supposed to fight Ngawang, but I pissed off War. If I'd fought her,

Rachel would've lived, and she would've been his best choice."

"Why?"

"Well, War wanted Marie. Famine apparently has some connection with Qamar, and you don't have a reproductive system," Kat explained.

The hall ended in a straight upward climb. At the bottom of the metal cliff, both women tilted back their heads to view the path of their ascent. Like a waterfall, mist flowed down the dark side of the false cliff. Kat backed up, glancing over her shoulder. Blood and sawdust clumped on the ground. Running her feet through the mess, she trained her eyes on the precipice. Up was the only option. Sprinting, Kat leapt. A whip of metal flew when she stretched her arm. Slamming into the metal, the cord threw her higher. Her velocity rushed the air around her, and though her helmet blocked the breeze, the variance in the force of gravity versus her upward moment pounded through her body, sending a flood of adrenaline through her veins. Throwing a second cord forward, Kat spun backward to look down where Amondi climbed carefully up the wall's side.

The field around the adjoining halls shimmered below. Clouds rolled over them, pooling in the lower levels. A flash of gold caught Kat's eyes. Slamming her opposite hand into the sheer cliff, she stilled against the metal. Chelsea wasn't even wearing her helm. Tweedles stood on either side with their backs facing the human. She could have been testing the limits. Maybe the blonde didn't believe she had been named designated survivor. Perhaps she thought Kat lied. While her palpable relief suggested otherwise, the idea of any of her crewmates accepting survival selection without helping the others irked Kat. Her right arm bled white until the laser cannon threatened to weaken her grip. Shrugging the gun off, Kat refocused on the precipice. Killing Chelsea now wouldn't help. With the force field between them, she'd likely miss anyways.

"Hurry up, Amondi. Chelsea's already sitting on her tuffet. Don't want the three of us to get the boot before she's finished her curds and whey," Kat drawled though she doubted Amondi could hear her.

For once, there were no spheres. All the walls stood bare of them. Beams of green light streamed by her head. Pursing her lips, Kat pressed against the wall. Black expanded, smoothing her metal suit against the wall. She slid up the wall. Whoever or whatever lurked at the top stayed out of view. Her cocoon shifted in color as she rose, blending into the side of the tower. A shift of black metal caught her eye. A pulse jumped, but the heart was undeniably four quadrants. If someone had to die, she was more than willing to make herself an easy target. Throwing herself into the air, Kat glided through the air.

"Qamar!" Kat called.

"Stay back! Stay back! Stay back!" Qamar screamed, shooting all around Kat, and though they had been one of the better shots in their courses, Qamar missed every single one.

Landing on one knee, Kat stared up into a face contorted with absolute terror. Like Chelsea, Qamar's mask was down. Around their head, the smooth black scarf frayed in spots, revealing the dark curling hair which lay beneath. On their forehead, strands of baby hair and sharp, tight curls hung over each scrap and clung to every trail of blood. Brows peaked and eyes wide, Qamar released their gun. Their hands flew to claw against the edges and tuck every loose strand into place, but the obsessive motion only frayed the scarf further. Their hands and lips trembled.

"Go away," Qamar demanded. "I don't want your help!"

Standing, Kat surveyed the edges of the tower. Its flat top held no more than nine square feet of space. Barely two and a half or so feet by three and some, the peak had only rough spires and spark crevices. Shields saved two sides, but opposite from where Kat ascended, there was another sharp drop. At the bottom, a horde of felines clawed. Mutated corpses of Tweedles and the equine types littered the bottom. In the distance, however, War approached. His blood red suit pierced the fog. In one hand, he dragged a blade against the wall. Sparks flew, and the sawdust beneath his feet exploded, but the alien gave them no mind.

"War's coming. Come back our way, we'll find another way around," Kat suggested.

Qamar shook their head. "No. Get out of here. I don't want you here."

"He's going to kill you. We track back, get to that hall and jump to the one on the left…Chelsea's over there, but if we can jump the wall at the corner, we should be able to get to her. All of us together, we can get something done." Kat reached out, but Qamar dodged her hands.

"I don't want you here. You back track. This is my hill."

Kat frowned. Her mask cleared, folding back into the neckline of her suit. The first inhale of the maze's air tasted like smoke from the first fire in winter. Not one in the home, one somebody else set that lingered in the air and couldn't be placed. A strange comfort when faced with murder.

"This isn't Hell. This isn't some kind of penance. Marie made you kill her. Don't let him kill you because you feel you owe anybody anything," Kat informed her.

Shoulders sagging, Qamar half-wept and half-laughed. "War is worse than Hell."

"This isn't a war," Kat retorted. "This was a massacre. We're just survivors."

Clenching their fists, Qamar lifted their guns. "We're at war. Humanity versus Mah-Wærm. That's what Earth thinks. They're militarizing, unifying, hiding behind a shield, but we're at war. This is war. We're just caught behind enemy lines."

"If this is war, let me watch your six."

War turned down the hall. The felines charged, but they scattered in piles of bone, blood, and flesh when he skidded his sword over the wall. Covered in scraps of other creatures, the alien waded through the corpses. At the base of the tower, he waved the sword. Without her helm, Kat couldn't see why, but Qamar tensed. Their lasers shot down around their feet. The tension drained from their arms. As their guns retreated, they stepped up beside Kat.

"Okay," Qamar nodded.

Kat smiled; her helm rose. "We'll get through this."

Brown eyes lifted. They passed over the darkening mask of Kat's helm. Qamar forced a smile. The strain was starkly clear around their eyes as they said, "You will."

Qamar slammed into Kat. On the precarious peak, she stumbled back and fell over the edge. Air rushed around her, but this time in the wrong direction. Tumbling backward, Kat flipped, spinning as she tried to get her bearing. With the first turn, Qamar launched. Their lasers and helm rose. Green beams flew. As Kat spun around a second time, War's blood red suit came into view, and he lunged. When she turned for the third time, Kat threw her arm out, sending a wire into the tower. The fine metal wrapped around her waist, spinning her. Colliding with the metal, Kat clawed up. Her eyes rose, and Qamar fell. Through their stomach, the same sword they had been given by Marie.

"Qamar!" Kat shrieked, pushing off the wall, but Amondi scurried up the wall, grabbing Kat and pressing her back against the metal. "Qamar!"

Amondi shushed her. "Qamar's dead."

"We can't – I can't..." Kat protested, but each beginning died on her tongue.

Qamar collided with the ground. The sawdust scattered through the air as their body sprawled like a broken doll. Their left leg twisted almost parallel to their body at the thigh with the knee twisted the wrong way. Everything left of their right shoulder curved inward. Broken in segmented pieces, their spinal column erupted from their skin toward the edge where their right radius cut through her stomach as if they had tried to catch themselves in the fall. Though their suit had seemed as strong as the rest, it peeled back like satin, curling away from their wounds. In the midst of it all, the sword stood tall, having been pushed out for the most part by the fall.

Blood pooled around their head. Curls sprung out of their hijab. The black of their scarf blended into the metal of their suit and the floor below where their blood ran the sawdust bare. Through boot camp, Qamar kept at the front of the pack. Their eyes maintained a sort of peace in the face of physical exertion that few could emulate: strength in subtle gestures. All lights faded. A spotlight formed beneath them, and as their blood spread across the bright circle of light, they seemed more like an abstraction of death than a corpse. Life escaped seen yet unseen in its retreat.

"So much for this being armor," Amondi grumbled, lifting her eyes to War.

The red-suited alien jumped from the top of the tower. When he landed beside Qamar's body, the metal trembled, and Kat held her breath. He couldn't do anything more to Qamar. With the sword that had killed Marie, he had run them through, and it didn't matter that the fall had undoubtedly finished them. Qamar's chest wasn't rising. War couldn't hurt them, but that didn't stop him from trying. Dislodging the sword, he treated the weapon like an ax. Each chopping flail sent blood flying.

"No!" Kat screamed. Though Amondi held her tightly to the wall, her left arm shifted to a gun. Plasma raged through her system. Sparks crawled up the tower. "Back off, motherfucker, or I'll make you look worse than the casts of Pompeii."

Pausing, War tilted his head. He twirled the sword with a spin of his wrist. Blood sloshed around his feet as he shifted his stance. His left foot slid back through the gore. Raising the blade above his head, he swung down, decapitating Qamar's corpse. As their head rolled, a bolt of plasma slammed him into the far wall. Kat shoved Amondi back. Leaping down on top of War, she slammed her fist into his helm. Claws grew from the glove on her right hand. Electricity crackled across her suit. A hand grabbed her shoulder. Whirling around, she launched her claws into Death's side. He stood, unmasked and frowning.

"Stand down," Death commanded.

"Fuck you," Kat spat, pulling the trigger.

Nothing happened. Her arm clicked. A wave of electrified particles dispersed down her legs into the blood, guts, and sawdust at her feet. Growling, she withdrew her arm from the gun and twisted to punch his face. Her suit froze mid-motion, jamming her joints. Death sighed as she struggled uselessly. Behind her, War rose, drawing the sword up once more. Before he could bring it down, cords stretched from the wall, wrapping around the red-suited alien.

"You're done," Death informed him.

War scoffed. "What do you care?"

"I don't. Famine does."

As if his name summoned him, the black-suited alien came through the mist. All his limbs swung in humanoid proportions and angles. He stopped on the edge of the lit circle where Qamar's blood had yet to reach. His helm popped forward, hissing. Lifting it over his head, Famine revealed his reformed face. Dark brown skin covered the surface of his features. Black lashes outlined his pale blue eyes. Thick lips twisted, shifting up and down. As his black metal hood retracted into his color, he stepped forward. From the curls of his hair to dimple in his chin, he could've been Qamar's brother.

"Hypocrite," War scorned his fellow Rider. "You warned me repeatedly not to get attached. Despite my being in charge of the fight pairings, you told me that I couldn't predict what would happen, couldn't control how Death would interfere, how Mah-Wærm would decide. When Marie died, you called me emotional – hot-headed."

"And I was right," Famine said, cutting War off.

Famine's eyes rose from Qamar's corpse. They glimmered like ice chips in the dark of the maze. As they traced over War, Famine sighed, shaking his head. Turning back to Qamar, he knelt and took hold of their head. He pressed the tore flesh of their neck together. The black metal of his fingers raged red as he sealed them back together. Blood covered his legs, thickening and darkening around him as he worked. War trembled. Running from his shoulders to his fists which held tight to Marie's sword, the red-suited man fought against himself. Whirling around, he slammed the blade into the wall.

"You're still too emotional," Death warned him.

War screamed – animalistic in his wordless rage. He tore through the metal, throwing himself against the maze as if the ship itself were his enemy. Death scoffed. Throwing his hands up, the oldest of the three side-stepped and left Kat trapped as a statue.

Pressing and pushing, her suit wouldn't budge. The metal of the ship vibrated under War's onslaught, and the trembling traveled up her body, shaking her spine. Stuck within Death's makeshift prison, Kat raged. Her blood surged without anywhere to put the fury coursing in her system. Famine sealed Qamar's wounds. He shifted their leg as if he could fix them just like a broken doll. As if they would come alive if he put all the pieces back in the right place, but War raged with the inability to even touch what had been taken from him. That rage made sense. Marie was ash. She couldn't be brought back. Though the fall had smashed Qamar rather than burned them, it might as well have. They couldn't bring them back. Or, if they could, they wouldn't.

"Amondi?" Death called. "Come down. You've completed the trial."

Stuck to the towering metal wall, Amondi stayed in place. Her hands curled into the surface. "Why bother? Everyone's decided who they want to live, and nobody's on my team."

"True, but that should be encouragement to cooperate. I don't have much reason to keep you alive otherwise," Death retorted. Amondi slid down the tower. Sticking close to the far side of the corridor, she sidled around Death. He cocked a brow. "Your species is exhausting. They're dead. You aren't. Use that neural mess you call a brain."

"She did. Her neural mess informed her that you were a threat. Avoidance was her best defense," Famine defended as he straightened Qamar's legs.

War spun, throwing the sword. The blade skimmed by Amondi's helm and slammed into the wall from which she'd come. She tensed, and he charged shoving Kat forward as he sprinted at Amondi. Mid-fall, Kat's suit unlocked, and she reached out, catching herself before she fell. Her hands splashed in Qamar's blood. Famine frowned, shoving her backward as if her presence interrupted his mourning. If what he was doing could even be called that. He puttered around Qamar's body. There were no words with his motions. No prayers or verbalized grief, and even his eyes remained cold. Famine moved with obsession.

Pushing up, Kat sat back on her feet. War lunged at Amondi, but wires rose from the floor, wrapping around his legs, so he fell forward and slammed face first into the floor. Death leaned over him. Gray swirled into the white of his suit. Pale green blossomed like vines up his legs, and as War struggled to stand, to reach Amondi, to shoot her when he could do nothing else, Death laughed. His steel-colored eyes blazed molten.

"How many times will we go through this?" Death asked, but for the first time, he did not speak in English. The words slurred together in a rougher, unfamiliar tongue. Kat only heard their meaning in the echo from the spheres as they coalesced from the metal in the walls. "You rage; I stop you. Though you are young, you ought to have learned. You don't get to decide who lives and dies. That is the lesson here. You were chosen to be better. You made your decision. Live with it."

War stilled. His body slumped against the ground. He whispered in the same language so softly the words sounded only like the trickling of a distance stream, but the ship and the orbs heard him all the same. "I did not know the cost."

Kat's eyes closed. The world slowed as agonizing empathy curled up inside her chest. Anywhere had been better than home, but nowhere was acceptable without Jacobi. She had dragged him hundreds of miles across the country. When the Academy nominated them for the first flight outside the star system, she'd never considered how much further that would be. Away from his family, Jacobi died amongst the stars. A chill traveled down her spine. An ache settled low in the new skin across her abdomen. Standing, she stared down at her own reflection in the blood. A black mask with swirls of white and blue stared back. Back when the stars were all, Kat had never realized the cost. Now, looking down at a mask with no will to view the eyes which lay beneath, she looked upward once more. No stars in view, she kept her gaze on the fog and the shimmer of the shield.

Chapter Fifteen

Kat paced the length of their chamber. Everything had been changed. Three beds remained, but none were the ones that were left behind earlier that same cycle. Instead, large beds covered in plush blankets lined the back wall of the room. Fur rugs covered the floor, and every comfort Chelsea had originally been afforded filled the room. Toward one side, facing the wall which opened for the door, a large rectangular couch stretched. All furs and fabrics colored the room in shades of gray. No black remained, and white only painted the accents on the bedding. Folding her arms over her chest, Amondi jiggled her leg where she sat. She and Chelsea took opposite ends, and while Chelsea stripped her suit for a sweater dress, leggings, and thick socks, Amondi and Kat remained prepared for battle.

"I don't like it," Kat grumbled.

Her eyes jumped to the three Tweedles in the room. One stood behind Chelsea. Another hovered over Amondi. The third, her own, watched her from the wall of the door. While she had matched Kat's pace for some time, she found the human's movements too erratic. The alien hadn't said such. Her frustration hovered like neon letters in Kat's mind. A connection spanned between them – her and the Tweedles. When she invaded the first one's mind, she opened it, and now, Kat had no idea what to do with it. There was an advantage there, somewhere.

Chelsea huffed. "There are books. Read one." She ran a finger across the tablet in her hand.

Rolling her eyes, Amondi pushed her back harder against the couch. "Or we could discuss the elephant in the room?"

"They're insects," Chelsea retorted. Her eyes never left her text.

Jumping up from her seat, Amondi crossed the room to tower over the blond. "You know what I meant."

"I do," Chelsea affirmed, lifting her eyes. With a dull blink, she sighed. "There's nothing to discuss. I live. Humanity survives. That's it. There isn't anything to talk about."

"Not human. Modified from your flesh to your genes," Kat pointed out.

With a shrug, Chelsea rested the tablet on the back of the couch. "So?"

"So?" Amondi grumbled. "So humanity won't survive. Earth will be destroyed. You will give birth to monsters."

"And the same would be true of either of you," Chelsea retorted.

Pausing mid-step, Kat sighed, wavering where she stood. "Which do you care about less? The two of us? Or Earth?"

"Does it matter?" Chelsea crossed her arms over her chest. "It's really just a matter of logic. There's no point in sacrificing myself. The results will be the same. One of us will survive. Earth will die.

Whether it's one of you or me, nothing changes. Why shouldn't I live?"

Amondi's lips hung parted. Brows furrowed, she gestured with flailing hands at the other woman, who rolled her eyes and returned to her reading. "Because I don't have a womb, ovaries – I can't be used like you!" Amondi yelled back when she found her words.

The blonde snorted. "Sure."

"Really? You think I'm lying? You want to see my scars? Their pinpoints, but I think you'll get the idea," Amondi growled, pulled down her suit until it hung down below her hips. She stood proud and bare-chested. Two dark circles and a small line marked her skin. "I can't be used like you. That's why you shouldn't live."

Kat pressed the heels of her palms against her eyes. "That wasn't what she meant."

"Then what?" Amondi demanded as she rounded to glare at Kat.

"Why should I believe Death? He works for Mah-Wærm. He's probably lying. Anyway, why would he be dumb enough to state who he wanted to win? Mah-Wærm obviously kills whoever the Rider's favor. First with Marie, then with Qamar," Chelsea counted the two on her fingers. "He probably just wants Kat to die too."

"Or he's smarter than the others," Amondi retorted.

Chelsea's eyes narrowed. Squinting at Amondi, she pursed her lips. "I think not."

Neither and both made sense and none at all. Death had spoken to Mah-Wærm after Marie's death.

He had begged for her life. However, Chelsea was right. That hadn't been for Kat. Any purpose that Death had was his own. Unraveling that web took energy. Energy wasn't a commodity to waste.

"And if you're wrong?" Amondi asked. She, at least, still had energy. Underneath everything, she fought to live.

Another shrug came from the blond. "Unlikely. Forming relationships with potentials doesn't have a point unless it is to incite in-fighting and keep the three Riders divided. They scheme, betray one another, and that leaves them no time to do the same against Mah-Wærm. He, of course, never gave up his original plan."

Amondi scoffed. "What plan?"

"To recreate his species," Kat murmured. Her eyes drifted to the wall. Pale biosynthetic substance which shined like metal but chilled her fingers as reached out.

Chelsea nodded. A smile curled her lips. "We've seen him work. You should've died, but he knitted you back together like kintsugi."

Kat's brows furrowed. "What?"

"The use of gold to fix broken ceramic. Japanese tradition – gold and history beautify the item. You broke. He poured in gold," Chelsea explained.

Pressing a hand to her stomach, Kat forced her face to calm. A sneer lurked around the edges of her muscles, and this wasn't the time for goading. If Chelsea saw gold, Kat would give her the comfort. In the end, what Death wanted didn't matter. Chelsea's life or death wouldn't matter. Any desire to live on Amondi's behalf held the same intentions as Chelsea.

Neither one considered the future. They had already given up on humanity, and when presented with a life raft, both clamored to board. Kat's hand dropped away. Everything in the world left her cold. Walking away, Kat ignored the echo of footsteps following in her wake. She could no more escape the Tweedle than her thoughts. Chelsea returned to her reading, and Amondi stormed after Kat.

"Kat," Amondi hissed.

"What?"

"You know I'm right," Amondi accused. Still naked, she ransacked the racks, pulling a sweater over her head. Cream covered her from neck to mid-thigh. Her dark eyes blazed. Her suit hung about her from the waist. "Death wasn't lying. We have to do what he said."

"We don't have to do anything," Kat retorted.

The Tweedle stood back. By the couch, Amondi's Tweedle turned to face them. Both their hands twitched. Fingers crooked and straightened like a dance. Still facing Chelsea, the third twitched his hands behind his back. There were no orbs, and even if there were, Kat couldn't be certain they would be capable of translating whatever passed between the Tweedles.

"No. You don't get to pretend you weren't the one who told me I had to be the one to live. Qamar is dead. If you're right, I'm next, and then what? Chelsea folds? No. We aren't going to let that happen." Amondi's dark eyes narrowed. "I won't let that happen."

Along the wall, the metal rippled. The material peeled back, and Death stepped through. His eyes scanned the room. Dread pooled in Kat's soul. Drowning in its rush, Kat met his gaze. Nothing in his steel-colored star helped her. Liars rarely had such simple tells. Pressing her lips into a line, she glanced at Amondi, whose fingers curled into fists at her side.

"Mah-Wærm will meet with you each in order to better determine which one of you is Conquest," Death announced. "I would suggest you prepare for the end."

"Thank goodness," Chelsea exclaimed. She stretched her arms and legs before standing. "I'm first."

Death bowed his head. His eyes finally slipped to her. "That you are."

Her blue eyes shifted, and glancing over her shoulder at the other two women, Chelsea paused. For a moment, short as it was, she seemed to be preparing to speak, but she sighed and left without saying a thing. A Tweedle followed. Her fingers gave one last twitch. A movement followed by the other two. When the wall sealed behind them, Amondi sighed.

"We need to figure out how we're going to do this," Amondi murmured.

Kat cocked a brow. "We?"

"Don't flake on me now, Parker."

Holding out her hands with her palms facing Amondi, Kat shook her head. "I'm not participating in this."

"What? Why?"

"Chelsea's not entirely wrong," Kat replied. Amondi's eyes narrowed, and when she stayed silent, Kat sighed. "I'm not arguing to survive. You are. She

288

is. In the end, it's the same. You both want to live. I don't. Fight between the two of you."

Amondi pressed a hand to her forehead. "It's not about you or us. It's about the greater good."

"Is it? I don't really see any good anywhere 'round here," Kat informed her.

Setting her hands on her hips, Amondi sucked her teeth. "I don't care what Chelsea said. You were right. Doubt yourself all you want, I'm killing that blonde bitch, and I'm taking this empire down."

Kat nodded, sitting down on the bed. Her gaze flickered to the Tweedles as they shifted their fingers back and forth. "I want no part in this." Their fingers stilled. "If you want to kill her, do it on your own."

Amondi ground her teeth. "Fine."

She stormed away. Her hands in fists at her sides; she wouldn't forgive Kat before she died, and that was fine. They were both headed into oblivion anyway. Out there, Jacobi waited for her at best. At worst, there was nothing. Neither seemed a terrible option, and compared to what awaited her if she survived, either worked. With her feet hanging off the bed, Kat stared at the ceiling. Pulses ran like ripples across the surface. Like a lullaby, they sent her to sleep.

Chapter Sixteen

A sunrise woke her. Orange and gold painted the sky. Pink followed before bright blue swallowed the darkness. Though a star rose, it was not the sun. Smaller and more distant, the round yellow orb flew across a sky far larger than Earth. Gravity pulled her down until she could not stand. Illumination tore at the nerves in her eyes. Still, Kat kept her gaze on the path of the sphere. Wind whipped through her hair, and she woke, reaching for strands which weren't there. The short hair bristled as she ran her gloved hand over her scalp.

Opening her eyes, Kat blinked as a shadow obscured the bright light of the room. She bolted upright. Where the room had once been opened, there was a partially formed wall blocking off the center bed and the one to the far back left of the room where she had gone to sleep. Leaning against the far wall, the Tweedle assigned to guard her stood. Her hands flexed and shifted as if tying knots in the air. Frowning, Kat rubbed the skin behind her ear.

"I have no idea what you're saying," she confessed.

The Tweedle froze. Her hands fell back to her sides. Standing straight, she slid quickly back into his position, refusing to acknowledge that Kat had spoken at all beyond to correct her guard stance. Pressing her lips together, she tilted her head. Golden light and the near forgotten warmth of sun on her skin floated across her mind. Hope ached in her. Biting her lip, she glared about, wishing anything else could be used to excuse the shift in her emotions, but nobody else was there. Her shoulders slumped.

"I think I'm hooked into your matrix."

The Tweedle didn't respond.

Kat tapped her head. "You were thinking about the sunrise on your planet. Smaller star than Earth."

As she spoke, the sunrise continued to play and replay in her mind. With a sigh, she rested her face in her hands. Clearing her throat, she let her hands fall to her knees. Cold ice filled her mind. Gray clouds lumbered overhead in her memory. Slow flurries of thick white clumped flakes twirled to the ground across a blanket of snow. The itch of her grandmother's knitted scarf around her neck and the easy shift of a well-worn snowsuit tingled along her nerves. Across from her, the Tweedle stiffened. Gold and orange shifted to white and gray, and the sunset faded. Twinkling lights and the boom of fireworks. Cinnamon and ginger with the rough, rich underlying curl of almost burning caramel. Everything she would never know again. They clung to her mind and passed into the hive.

"See," Kat said though the Tweedle couldn't understand. "I'm hooked in, hacked the system."

When the flowers came, they were so pungent she nearly fell back against the mattress. Beneath the smog of floral, the clean, crisp cut of newly dampened earth flooded her senses. Long dry spells wove the scent into her soul. Petrichor drew all the children into yards and fields. After one long summer, rain came down first in late September. She had chased Jacobi through the woods behind his house. The drops tinkled like bells as they bounced down through the canopy. Drenched and smiling, they had held tightly to the trees, watching the water turn the light to rainbows.

With a twitch of her fingers, the Tweedle took a step closer. Mushrooms sprouted up a leaning tree. Curled ferns sparkled as dew slid down their furled leaves. All over the dark, moist earth, green sprung to life. Moss stretched. The light give of each step tingled up her legs and a second pair she didn't have as well. Across her ribs, the phantom limbs shifted. They ached. In a flash, the tranquility of the alien planet jumped to the war she'd seen before. Hez'i-bibs's dying thoughts flooded Kat's mind. Iron rained down. Gray coated the trees, and when the planet fought back alongside the Hive – the Vurtherar, Mah-Wærm crushed them. Bodies laid strewn across the forest. Golden spires which clung to the trunks of trees crumbled. The young children trapped inside. Their silhouettes cast against the bleeding iron.

Standing, Kat clenched her fists. Her lips pressed together as she wavered. A blimp on a screen crossed through her mind and passed to the Tweedle. The calm before the storm crept like shivers along her spine. Screams – her own at Jacobi – echoed in her ears. Racing across the deck to the protective gear, she refused to look back. Thomas's smile and the horror in his face as he flew into the vacuum of space tore at her. When she ran, she grabbed Jacobi's hand.

No one else had mattered. She had to save him. When the laser pierced his chest, the burn ached in her flesh. Every time she closed her eyes, she saw his, and now those same eyes, the eyes she loved, were in another's face.

Bel'von slunk through her memories. Silver lined him, flickering like a kinked neon line. The compound orbs shifted back and forth until only the rich, warm brown remained. Even in Bel'von, those eyes made her heart ache. They didn't hold love. Something cold and dark lurked beneath the insectoid's gaze. Want, self-loathing, loneliness – Mah-Wærm was blind. His truest companion joined him centuries ago. In a black ship, the immortal made landfall. Survivors cowered as he approached with their last dwarf mother at his side, but Bel'von, though that was not his name then, had no signs of the change. Before all, he tore his wings from his back with strange metal arms. The delicate membranes tore. Though Bel'von kept his head high, ignoring the tissue leaking before the metal of his suit sealed the gaps with fire, others wept. Hez'i-bibs hadn't. She'd frozen in terror, but this other Tweedle, Kat's guard, she collapsed to lie upon the ground, weeping.

An'el-taln

The name slipped through their connection as the Tweedle – as An'el-taln reached to knock their knuckles together. Her central limbs had been taken. Commands kept her feet still, but her fingers still could dance. Back home, on a planet of towering trees and flowers – a green world, An'el-taln watched the young Bel'von grow. The middle of five dwarf mothers, he had fought tooth and nail against his fate.

Screaming battles – fierce dances of refusal and denial passed between the young Vurtherar and the Mother. Whenever any spoke his given name, Bel'von spouted hatred and clawed at his wings. Every aspect of who he was, who he could one day be frustrated him. When the drones came, he rebuffed their customary courtship even knowing he was unlikely to be Mother. Two were in line before him, and peace lasted so long, the Vurtherar had no idea of what would fall down from the sky upon them.

Buzzing around from flower to flower, his younger siblings taunted him. Laughed and dripped dew upon him. They had no idea. Frolicking as the young things they were, they did not understand why Bel'von couldn't be friendly to the drones. Foreign stars with dances for names flickered through Kat's mind. An'el-taln stood beside her friend. His grief burrowed into her. Wings drooping, Bel'von wished to die, and when he tore off one of his central legs, the doctors reattached it regardless of his protests. When he successfully removed and burned both central appendages only to be found half-dead in his rooms by his eldest dwarf mother sister, Mother had listened.

"But it wasn't enough," Kat whispered. Her words echoed the emotions and pictures passed back to the Vurtherar. "He was still in line."

And in line meant the change could happen. No one understood why Bel'von wanted war. War led to casualties. Casualties opened up the possibility of the dwarf mothers dying, and while he was the last in his line, there were so few between him and the fate he dreaded. Of anybody, Bel'von should have avoided war, but he brought war to them. Mah-Wærm came. Humanoid – strange. So few limbs, so stout and squishy. Once more, An'el-taln and Bel'von stared at the sky. This time, Bel'von painted a picture of a new face, a new form. If he could not be removed entirely from the mother-line, he'd remove the Vurtherar from himself.

"Please," An'el-taln had begged. "I can't watch you tear yourself apart again. The alien leaves soon. Mother negotiated for peace. If you do something to jeopardize that…"

"I won't. I'll simply be going with him," Bel'von replied. An'el-taln shifted. Her movements became uncertain. Bel'von danced like he had never done before. His feet flew as he told her, "I am Bel'von now. I am a him too."

"A him?"

The pronoun had never been used like that before. Aliens were 'hims' and 'hers.' For Vurtherar, there were mothers, workers, and drones. For Bel'von to call himself a him, he removed the Vurtherar from his identity. Stripped himself of his family, his purpose, his people. An'el-taln betrayed him. She left with false well wishes and ran to the Mother. When the Mother forbid Bel'von's leaving and rejected his new name, Mah-Wærm shifted his mercurial eyes to An'el-taln. He could not fully replicate their dances despite his metal central limbs and wings, but he did better than any outsider had before. As if he had seen An'el-taln's actions, he politely acquiesced, and then he absconded with Bel'von and killed the Mother.

Bel'von's eldest sister wasn't prepared. A summer child without knowledge of war even between the hives, she underestimated Mah-Wærm at every turn. Death burned down the forests. Still newly formed, the first Rider slaughtered millions with an army of silver spheres. Volcanoes which had slept for centuries erupted. Rivers of magma cooled into shells, and the air filled with ash and smoke. Dark clouds blocked the sun. Fire rained down upon them. The worst, though, came in the miserable cold. Snow and metal froze the planet. When Bel'von mutilated himself – tearing the wings from his back before the survivors, those remaining few huddle together. No one danced. There were no wing songs. Only silence and Bel'von's fury.

"Do you forgive him?" Kat asked, watching An'el-taln's fingers dance like her missing legs once did. A question hummed in the air between them. "For what he did," Kat elaborated. "Do you forgive him?"

Emptiness rose in response. The vacuum of space unfolded. Nothingness in all its glory thundered through her mind, bringing a frown to Kat's face. While the cold trailed down her spine as if An'el-taln replied negatively, calm stretched like acceptance. Sending her confusion back at the Vurtherar, Kat waited. Long golden halls returned. Stretched out between the trees, the paper thin walls shimmered. Light projected through with dark edges as the seams. As her brows furrowed, Kat studied the compound eyes which watched her from the newly transparent helm.

"Nothing to forgive?" Kat guessed.

Warmth spread across her skin like sunlight. Affirmative. Running her tongue across her lip, the human glanced down at An'el-taln's fingers. Bel'von's face – his new one – swam through her thoughts. Frowning, Kat stepped back. A hand shot out, grabbing her wrist. Jacobi's eyes stared into her own through space and time. A corpse sat on a table with a gold hand on his shoulder. As Kat silently screamed, her spine arched, tossing her head back. Images flashed through her mind and an orb hovered over her head. Knives fell. Pieces cut away. One by one, cold hands pulled Bel'von apart and remade him.

"I have a tongue now," Bel'von said. The words vibrated in a way the spheres couldn't mimic. "His eyes, lips, throat, bits and pieces, but he's the one I want to become."

Fingers danced. Questions filtered through in memory. All An'el-taln had wanted to know was that her old friend was happy. All the survivors endured Bel'von's spite. Torn apart and remade, they looked down at bodies they hated and dreamed of a form no longer within their grasp. A cruel mimicry of Bel'von's agony, and one their leader had no pity for giving.

Bel'von watched those dancing fingers. An'el-taln could not read her friend's new eyes. The curve of his lips, duller and more beige than gold, shifted downward. "Not yet. My genetic material still needs working. I've mixed my traits with that one." Uncertainty and questioning followed. "Because he mattered. I want to be him."

"Why?" Kat gasped. Tears trailed into her hair as she struggled against the memories.

Cold gray melted into gold. Green sprouted through the volcanic ash. Floral filled the air. Deep in the warm earth, hundreds of sleeping eggs awoke. Regenerated central limbs and wings for only a couple dozen of the remaining Vurtherar lifted grubs. A new generation all genetically modified for parthenogenesis, if they so willed. No more Mothers, only mothers. No more drones. The technology of Mah-Wærm's empire at their fingertips to improve and alter their genome as each saw fit. The Vurtherar were dead. Long live the Vurtherar.

With a sigh, Kat whispered, "A better world."

"One day," Bel'von agreed.

Jumping back, Kat paled as Bel'von opened the wall hidden from view. With his arms folded behind his back, he stepped inside. An'el-taln's fingers danced, but Bel'von shook his head, and her hands fell back beside her. Pressing his lips together, Bel'von glanced up at Kat with Jacobi's dark brown eyes. Before he could speak, however, Amondi called from the other side of the wall.

"Who are you talking to?" she demanded, and her footsteps echoed through the room. The wall shifted, closing the area completely off from the rest of the room. "Kat? What the hell!? Parker!"

Giving her a tight smile, Bel'von trudged up to her. "We need to talk."

"If you wanted my help, you should've picked another cadaver's tongue," Kat retorted. With a heavy sigh, she tugged at the edges of her suit. "What do you want?"

"I don't like you. You don't like me. We both can acknowledge a certain madness between each of us," Bel'von drawled. He ran a hand against the wall as his lips curled around each word. His eyes slipped closed. A smile curled as if the taste of each word pleased him. Smiling with Jacobi's teeth, Bel'von sidled up close like a monster in the shadows. "I have particular goals in mind. Ones shared by certain parties, and they believe you are like-minded." His nose curled as a sneer shifted his features. "I'm not convinced."

"Pity. I have no intention of convincing you of anything."

Bobbing his head in the semblance of a nod, Bel'von ran his hand along the wall. "And if I told you the very ship we're in is alive, what would you say then?"

"That I'm sorry your species never learned the importance of mental health," Kat informed him dryly. "Beyond that, I'd simply tell you I don't care."

"I'll give you the first. The second..." His eyes grew bright.

Rubbing the bridge of her nose, Kat gathered an attempt at a retort, but nothing came to mind. For all her desire to deny his accusation, she cared. Not enough to do much good. In the end, life exhausted her, especially the idea of one spent enduring whatever psychotic torture Mah-Wærm would undoubtedly unfold on any who interfered with his own plans. Bel'von wanted a rebirth for his species. His desire for an improved Vurtherar matched Mah-Wærm's well enough, and if he worked with any of the Riders, it wasn't unreasonable to think the Rider, or even more than one of them, wanted the same. The sentience of the ship was another matter entirely.

"If I cared, it wouldn't change a thing," Kat said.

With a shrug, Bel'von let his hands fall to his side. The fingers of his left danced, and An'el-taln retreated, stepping backward until the wall consumed her entirely. With her Vurtherar guard out of sight, Bel'von pivoted to face her once more.

"You will be Conquest."

Sitting back on the bed, Kat rested her hands on her knees. "Now you're just being thick. He's already selected Chelsea. This meet-and-greet is just a run-around."

Bel'von shook his head. "Doesn't matter."

"Really? Desires of the supreme overlord – one you touted rather highly – that guy's end goal no longer matters? Do you think I'm stupid?" Kat held a hand. "Don't bother answering that. It's rhetorical." Pressing her lips together, she shook her head. Her eyes scanned the confined space. "Why don't you talk with Amondi?"

"Graduated change. Make it small at first. Bit by bit, the environment changes until the predator can no longer function," Bel'von explained.

"Like boiling a toad. I know how that goes."

Bel'von's golden brow shifted as if to furrow eyebrows he still didn't have. "Why would you...never mind. I'm right. You'll be Conquest. Nobody gets a block vote, and we're all a bit safer for it."

"Or it'll go down like a marshmallow in the microwave," Kat retorted. Another shift of gold skin caused her to sigh. "Exponential expansion then a rapid, sticky collapse."

Bel'von waved a hand. "I don't care."

"Then why are you here?"

He tapped the wall again. "Sentient. The second you start acting melancholy, the rest of us get an annoying redirection in the hallways to your location. You dismiss an opportunity to advance positions. Here I am. You burn wood which releases a low amount of toxic fumes which you allow to build up. Vents open to change your environment. War cuts you down, and Mah-Wærm – the only creature on the ship capable of fixing you – finds himself right outside the door. Do you honestly think you've survived this long by coincidence? Sheer luck?"

"Ah, so I do have a saboteur!" Kat exclaimed.

"I don't lie. I said you are Conquest, and you've fought me every step of the way. Death lies to get you to shape up, and he still has to put a shock collar on you to get anything done. Do you know how exhausting it is to keep someone alive when they have little to no desire to do so themselves?" Bel'von scoffed, crossing his arms. "Thankfully, you rarely are able to maintain these moods for long, but I don't have time for one now."

Kat narrowed her eyes. Studying the insectoid, she clucked her tongue. Whatever tells Bel'von had, she had no way of recognizing them without further conversation; however, nothing he said appeared, as of yet, to be a lie. After everything thrown at them since the destruction of the Intrepid, she had to be cautious. If this were a test, the wrong answer could very well mean death.

"Not in a mood. Waiting," Kat told him.

With a glare, Bel'von uncrossed his arms. "What?"

"I understand we're in a bit of a time crunch, but I've got two women with a particular keen survival instinct gunning for each other's heads. Have you noticed neither is after mine?" Kat pointed out, standing to mirror Bel'von.

A smirk twitched the corner of Bel'von's lips. "You're joking."

"It's called a bluff," Kat drawled, cocking a single brow.

Bel'von pressed his chin to chest. "Then you have a plan to finish them both off."

"I don't have to," she confessed. "I wait long enough, and Amondi will kill Chelsea or vice versa. I just have to have some idea what to do after that. And with this suit," she said, tapping the white ring around her arm. "There's not much I can't do."

If they took the suits, Bel'von was a liar. While she couldn't be certain she would survive the trick if Amondi succeeded in killing Chelsea, Kat hadn't ever fought Chelsea in close quarter combat, but she'd seen the other woman fight. Beyond basic, Chelsea maintained an athletic endurance at bare minimum. A few minutes would be enough, but Kat needed time alone with the other woman. Guards would interfere too quickly, and any suited interference wouldn't end well for the one Mah-Wærm didn't want alive. Though An'el-taln remained loyal to Bel'von, there was a chance the other Vurtherar wouldn't trust his old friend. Time didn't heal all wounds after all.

"I see. Then I suppose I've only made you a bit more threatening," Bel'von murmured.

Without another word, he turned his back on her and left the same way he came. As soon as the wall sealed behind him, An'el-taln returned and the two walls blockading them in dropped. The Vurtherar guard launched at Kat. Wrapping a hand around the human's neck, An'el-taln dragged her off the bed. On the other side of the falling walls, Amondi stood. Her suit was back in place. Amondi aimed her laser cannon at the Vurtherar.

"Put her down," Amondi demanded.

An'el-taln released her hold. An orb flew down from the ceiling. "Suicide is unacceptable." Kat blinked, rubbing at her throat. An'el-taln's fingers didn't dance. A buzzing echoed just like the Tweedles had done in the brig. "You will live and die by the will of the Mah-Wærm."

"I didn't try to kill myself," Kat protested.

A gurgle of laughter came from the Vurtherar. Clasping her hands behind her back, An'el-taln returned to her guarding position. Retracing her memories, Kat filtered through every interaction she had had with Bel'von's people. Before the final three, none of their fingers had danced. Invading Kat's recollection, a memory passed between the Hive and Kat. A golden room with the Mother higher up and guarded by an army of workers. Buzzing echoed in the hall as different species came. No one outside the Hive learned their dances. Mah-Wærm's acquiescence to the Mother about Bel'von hadn't just been a ploy in its phrasing. He should never have been taught the words, and even Bel'von hadn't taught him, or so

An'el-taln's memories claimed. Mah-Wærm watched. Mah-Wærm listened. Mah-Wærm learned. Given half a chance, any bit of suspicion would draw the dictator's keen eye, and if Bel'von had spoken the truth, whatever rebellion lurked in the halls and mind of the ship needed to be kept silent.

"Kat…" Amondi lowered her gun.

Pressing her lips together, Kat turned away. "It doesn't matter. If I want to die by my own hand, you can do me the dignity of respecting that."

"You call me selfish but won't let anyone suffer the guilt of killing you," Amondi muttered as she crossed her arms over her chest. "What am I gonna do with you?"

"Kill me, apparently, since I can't seem to manage it myself," Kat retorted. Standing, she brushed off her legs and stormed to the couch. She threw herself into the soft embrace of the cushions and pulled a blanket down over herself despite the heat of the suit. "Do me a favor, Amondi, kill Chelsea first?"

"Long as you promise not to struggle when it's your turn," Amondi retorted, and though laugher clung to the edges of her words, there was no humor in her eyes.

Chapter Seventeen

Metal shifted, and the walls parted, opening before Death and Chelsea. Dressed in leggings and a sweater dress, Chelsea pranced inside like a princess. With a dark glower, Amondi followed her movements, and Kat watched the two, keeping her eyes on the two. All along Amondi's arms, spikes protruded before smoothing back down. Death stepped inside the room. Folding his arms behind his back, he kept his eyes level. No contact made between his gaze and any other's.

"Amondi," he called. "Mah-Wærm will see you next."

Clenching her fists, Amondi swaggered around the couch to Death's side. He spun and left with her at his side. As the wall slid shut, Chelsea flounced down on the couch. Her pale pink lips spread into an easy smile. Tossing her blonde hair over her shoulder, Chelsea curled her legs up and faced Kat. Like a girl come to gossip, she waited. She wanted to speak. As strange and outlandish as the idea seemed, the way Chelsea paused recalled nothing else. Wrapping her arms around her legs, she burrowed her chin into her forearms. Spitefully, Kat held her tongue.

"Well?" Chelsea pushed when no one pushed her. "Aren't you going to ask?"

"I'm going to die anyway. Might as well not torture myself with genres I don't prefer," Kat retorted. "I'm not terribly fond of romances."

With a huff, Chelsea shook her head. "It's hardly a romance. We walked the halls. Ate a meal. A date, maybe, but not even hand holding." Her hands slid up and down her legs as if to warm herself. "I've never had someone look at me as if they could see every bit of my soul. He barely ever looked away, and he focused on me as if I was the only piece of the world worth seeing."

"Many children keep to a single toy for days, weeks, years…toys break. You will too," Kat assured the other woman.

Chelsea's blue eyes narrowed. "And yet, you're already broken."

"Hardly."

"Then why would you be willing to die?" Chelsea asked. Her voice remained soft.

Kat shrugged. "Why are you so willing to live?"

As her shoulders slumped, Chelsea reached out. Her fingers tumbled over the edges of the couch as if to peel the very fabric for answers. "Please, Katelyn. This could be the last conversation we ever have. We used to be friends. Weren't we?"

"I'm not sure what you want me to say," Kat lied. Chelsea pleaded for absolution, and Kat wasn't certain she could give it even as she planned the blonde's death. "I don't really want to die. At first, I did, but really, what remains is a lack of hope. I can't see the future becoming any better. You can. You're willing to selfishly toss aside your 'used to be friends.' Maybe you can see a better world, but all I see is a greed for life even if it's barely hospitable."

"It isn't selfish or greedy to want to live," Chelsea retorted, turning away from Kat.

With a shrug, Kat informed her, "It is when your life comes at the expense of others."

"I'm not deciding who lives or dies, and it's not like I could stop him from killing you or Amondi or anyone for that matter," Chelsea grumbled. She picked invisible lint from the hem of her sweater dress.

With her pursed pout, the younger woman made a pitiable show. Her bright eyes narrowed like sickles. She looked so young. The sight of her shook something loose inside Kat. While Chelsea would never admit it, she undeniably suffered some amount of guilt. Though no one had yet to be truly labeled a survivor, they endured nonetheless. She needed absolution. If all the plans and shadowy collusions succeeded, the only one who would require forgiveness from the dead was Kat. Pressing her lips together, she weighed the cost of words and silence in her mind.

"I forgive you," Kat whispered.

Chelsea's eyes jumped to Kat's face. Her eyes shimmered. Tears gathered along her lashes, and the small point of her chin trembled. In a voice as small as a grain of sand, she returned, "Thank you."

Shaking her head, she tossed the blanket aside. "I think you'll be happy. Not right away. Not really. The sort of relieved happy that this is over perhaps, but not actually happy for some time. You'll be happy. There will be children. Maybe you'll even convince yourself you love him," Kat posited though she didn't believe it. "But, it won't last. In the end, Mah-Wærm will grow bored. He'll have his children, and then what? Incest to solidify the new species? Hardly the best idea – to bottleneck the genome, but maybe he'll incorporate altered cloning, or most likely of all, he'll commit another genocide. Again and again to collect breeders and sires for his pet project."

Chelsea paled. "Stop it," she demanded though she seemed to shrink.

"Are you prepared to kill him? Or to give up your children? Watch them be used to recreate a species when you don't even know how his kind died in the first place. Maybe you'll wake up one day and some simple change in environment will have killed them. A cold will knock them all dead while your slightly more altered structure keeps you ticking," Kat ranted. "I can't possibly guess. Frankly, I don't want to, so when I tell you I don't want to live, take it as a suggestion. You can pack all the darkness away, but it will get out."

Chelsea's guard and An'el-taln loomed though they remained in position. Neither moved closer as Kat spoke. However, raging fire and raining metal echoed in the back of her mind. A memory pressed among the Hive. While the blood drained from Chelsea's face, she recovered as Kat finished. Shifting forward on the couch, she glared down at the floor. Chelsea kicked the pillows out of her way. Rounding on Kat, the blonde clenched her hands into fists.

"You have no idea what I think," Chelsea spat.

Kat blinked with a sigh. "No. No, I don't, and frankly, I don't care."

Grabbing her tablet, Chelsea stormed to the back of the room. She tossed herself on her bed and left Kat alone. Chelsea's guard followed her, leaving Kat alone with An'el-taln once more. Curling into the soft embrace of fabric, Kat burrowed her face into the back of the couch. A soft touch to her back sent electricity through her body. Tensed, she glanced up. An'el-taln remained a couple feet away. Shifting, Kat glanced behind her. No one was there. Her eyes trailed back to An'el-taln. Like a knock at her mental door, the touch returned. Every muscle in Kat's body tensed, but taking a breath, she pushed the panic aside.

Mah-Wærm appeared in her mind's eye. Tanned with shorter hair, the dictator sat beside Bel'von's old insectoid form. An'el-taln remained close even though an animalistic terror surged whenever she saw Mah-Wærm. Even then, she'd seen the monster within him. He preyed on self-loathing.

"Being alone is brave," Mah-Wærm murmured in the memory.

Bel'von chirped. His mandibles vibrated, but there were no orbs in the air. A glint of silver around Mah-Wærm's ears spoke of their beginning. Wings drooping, the Vurtherar informed him, "My species was not built to be alone. We are the Hive."

"They are a hive," Mah-Wærm corrected. "One of hundreds on this planet, thousands in this galaxy, and countless more in the whole universe."

When he spoke, a collar around his throat vibrated mimicking Bel'von's people's language. As if compounded into this instance, remembrances of other hives flooded into Kat's mind. Vibrations hummed through the air, but they weren't the same frequency. Some came like accents. Others as foreign to An'el-taln and her hive as Mandarin to a person who spoke only English. Swirling back to the conversation between Mah-Wærm and Bel'von, Kat blinked. Her body drifted away as if caught in a current. When she reached back to curl her fingers, a ripple passed through her mind. The rub of fabric mixing with metal curling through air, metal rushing against metal, and metal crushing a flower. Surprise jolted her back, but An'el-taln held tight.

"What if I regret leaving?" Bel'von asked.

Mah-Wærm laughed. "You won't."

"I could."

"Regret comes from actions not taken, or actions you were forced to take," Mah-Wærm offered, but Bel'von's wings remained low, and his forelimbs drummed against the ground. Reaching out, Mah-Wærm laid a hand on Bel'von's elbow. "Would you kill for what you need?"

"What?" Bel'von reared back. His wings thrummed, lifting him from the ground.

Mah-Wærm waved his hand. "The best question to ask yourself in these sorts of situations is whether what you want is a need, and if you think it is, ask yourself if you would kill to fulfill that need. If the answer is no, question whether what you're after is a need again. If it's not…" he trailed off, and Bel'von landed.

"I need to not be in line to be a Mother. I need to not be a dwarf mother," Bel'von proclaimed. Each word rushed, tumbling into the next. "I…I think I would."

"You think?" Mah-Wærm asked, raising a single brow. When Bel'von didn't immediately answer, the dictator nodded. "I thought for years before taking action. My people enslaved galaxies, slaughtered trillions without reason, rejected individuals who selected self-modification, believed in an elite deity who demanded sacrifices that the most elite enforced but never made. Our planet's resources went dry, and we didn't alter our course. We became the parasites of our galaxy, then the next, and next. Given the chance, I would have acted earlier. We were so prepared to live forever, we forget how quickly we could die."

Bel'von drummed his legs, hovering he looked to An'el-taln as he said, "My leaving shouldn't cause anything so dramatic, but…I will prepare if it does."

Pressing her lips together, Kat smiled when no one else within the collective could copy. With her own body in sight, she held tight to the feel of the couch's soft gray fabric against her cheek. She pulled back. Her eyes slid to An'el-taln. For a moment, the room spun. Kat inhaled. Against her sides, her fingers curled into fists. Spikes raised across the spine of her armor. A light orange glow pulsed in her mind. Kat took aim in her mind and drew a line in the sand, covered it in petrol, and set it on fire. An'el-taln stumbled; her head tipped back a minute amount before she corrected her stance.

"Don't," Kat hissed as her helm rose to cover her face.

Her hazel eyes slid to Chelsea. Reclining on one of the beds, the blonde remained oblivious. Few people knew the feeling of being drawn out of their own body like poison. It wasn't one Kat wanted to feel again. Shifting her jaw beneath the opaque swirling black and blue of her helm, she took stock of her thoughts. Whispers crept in through the dark. With a growl, she slammed up walls, wakening the image of her childhood home in her mind. Lucid dreaming taught her to build structure in the abstract. Without a defense, the voices crept in, but within the walls of her old bedroom, she could only hear the way they rattled the shutters like a rough breeze.

Opening her eyes, Kat glanced to An'el-taln. The Vurtherar guard stretched to her full height. Over six foot tall, the Vurtherar towered over the majority of the human women from the start, but the majority of those who remained after Marie were under five and a half feet. Chelsea barely reached five foot five inches, and Amondi was only five foot two inches. In between the two, Kat needed to tilt back her head to look at the guards' helmets regardless of whether she sat or stood. Turning her back on the insectoid, she kicked aside the pillows around her feet.

The wall shifted. Metal curled apart, folding against itself to form a doorway. Amondi trudged inside with Death a few feet behind. His helm covered his face. Misty vapors curled about his feet, and behind him, the hall darkened. Only the nodes lit the way in pale green.

"Parker," Death beckoned.

Amondi's hand shot out, wrapping around Kat's wrist. She dragged her close. "We have to kill

Chelsea," Amondi whispered. Her brown eyes darted to the back of the room. "If I don't, you have to do it. It can't be her, Kat." Kat shook her arm, brushing away the others fingers, but Amondi flung forward, hugging Kat tightly to her as she spoke in hushed tones, "She's psychotic. She told him who to kill and how. She's been in contact with him from the beginning!"

"He's lying," Kat retorted even as her mind filtered through the possibilities.

"He wasn't. He called me, told me, and sent me back. It's just a game to them. They're both psychopaths," Amondi insisted.

Death shifted his left arm to a gun. Aiming it at Amondi, he growled, "Parker, come."

"Don't do anything stupid," Kat commanded.

Even as Amondi released her, Kat recognized the set of her jaw. Amondi wasn't going to listen. She would attack Chelsea the second she could. When Kat returned, one or both of them would be dead. Bowing her head, Kat stepped into the hall. The wall sealed behind her.

"Would've saved me a lot of trouble if you'd let yourself get lost in the Hive," Death commented as the floor raised them through the ceiling.

Kat clucked her tongue. Behind the safety of her helm, her eyes darted in search of an escape. "Couldn't make things too easy for you."

Hands at his sides, Death hummed. The floor spun them through two levels, and when they stilled for an instant, the white-suited alien marched even as the floor shifted beneath their feet like a squared lava lamp. Like oil separating within water, the walls slipped and slumped as they passed. Rising further in the ship, they arrived at a long corridor. Like black marble woven with gold, the walls stretched up; however, the gold within them pulsed as if alive.

"Keep your head down," Death warned as he crossed to large archway of gold.

Kat scoffed. "Sure."

"You're a step away from winning," Death warned her. "I'm counting on you. Bel'von's counting on you. As little as you think of yourself, you are the lesser of two evils."

"That's rather insignificant consolation to me," she retorted.

He said nothing, and the doors opened. A window of space showed the bright stars twinkling in the distance. Pinpricks of light decorated a black interrupted only by a swirling rose nebula. Dressed in soft grays, Mah-Wærm faced the window. His eyes traced the stars. When Kat did not step inside, the floor lifted beneath her and chucked her into the room. Behind her, the doors slammed.

"Do you have any questions for me?" he asked. "I don't imagine there's anything unique enough about you to interest me."

Kat rolled her eyes beneath the guard of her helm. "Why did you kill your species?"

With a sigh, Mah-Wærm turned to face her. His mercurial eyes scanned her. "They were beyond saving. I tried to save a few, but no one agreed on the solution, or what we'd do after once we did."

"How?"

"With a virus," Mah-Wærm replied. "Simplest way to do such things."

"A virus? And you survived but no one else did? Sounds more like a toxin than a virus," Kat retorted as she trudged up beside him.

The man hummed softly. "I suppose it might help you to consider it a nuclear cancer. Radiation poisoning with additional toxicities, true, but virally transmitted nonetheless." Pressing his hands against the window, Mah-Wærm smiled. "They cheered when I did it. All the conquered planets – almost exhausted by my kind…they've thrived under my rule. A single moral rule makes sense, don't you think? Compared to the rest of the universe, I'm an immortal."

Crossing her arms, Kat looked into the vast emptiness of space. "But then you grew lonely."

"But then I grew lonely," he agreed with a nod. His hands fell away leaving foggy prints which faded against the pane. Shifting to face her, he leaned his back against the cold window. The glass behind him steamed. Like a smug cat, he stretched and preened beneath her attention as if there was anything else in the room to see. Compared to the backdrop of space, he was little more than a pale creature. "You understand the feeling, don't you? At first, you feel bereft of all life. I considered ending my species completely, but my people needed me."

"Illusions of grandeur."

"Practicality," he retorted. "I wanted to kill myself several times. Just like you, but like you, the universe just wouldn't listen."

Kat rolled her eyes, sliding her foot back to increase the distance between them. "No, I goaded War into fulfilling my want. You were the force that didn't listen."

"True, but I understand the way absolute loneliness feels."

Before she could stop herself, Kat snorted. Mah-Wærm smirked and cocked a brow. Holding up her hands, Kat corrected him, "I can't remember a single day in my life when I was alone. I had Jacobi." Her eyes narrowed into a glare though he could not see through her mask. "You were the force that took him too."

"You're welcome."

Gritting her teeth, Kat clenched her fists. "What?"

Mah-Wærm pushed away from the window. "I said, 'You're welcome.' Jacobi was a crutch. I've seen your records. You were so terrified of leaving your humble upbringing for a top slot at the Academy. Ha, the Academy! As if it were the only one. I do so love when people isolate terminology like that. It places all sorts of ridiculous importance on insignificant things."

"Mock away. You're only undermining your own argument," Kat pointed out.

"While not nearly as impressive as an isolated Academy, your acceptance was an achievement considering your district. You held the majority of your year's top scores. Your name popped up in all the noted records," Mah-Wærm commented. His lips curled up at the ends. "Did you know your registering officer warned your advisor about you? Told her you were likely to undermine your own success to assist others," he paused, and when she didn't reply, he smiled. "I saw your scores. Your registering officer was right."

"Or I had an off day," Kat retorted.

Mah-Wærm swaggered closer. "It's sad, isn't it? That we have to make ourselves smaller to make us acceptable to others," he lamented. "Sometimes, the darkness just isn't enough. Sometimes, you need to take the light. To make people work to catch up rather than altering yourself to be pulled back."

"I'm not some savant," Kat retorted. "My parents owned a house, land, and both had their degrees. I was an only child to financially stable parents. Not exactly humble. Rather privileged, really."

"The right teachers at the right time shouldn't be considered a privilege," Mah-Wærm commented.

Sighing, Kat nodded. "Fine."

"Fine?"

Kat backed away. "There's no point in further communication. Amondi had a shorter time, and there's no reason for us to have any longer."

Dark brow furrowing, Mah-Wærm reached out. When his hand wrapped around her wrist, the metal of her suit retracted. The helm dove back into her collar, leaving her face bare to him. His mercurial gaze scanned her face. All of his attention honed in on her, and the intensity might almost be mistaken for affection, but he was a scientist before anything else, and even his attention crossed over her skin like a dissection scalpel. His thumb traced the line of new skin on her face. Despite the tones becoming better matches, a clear variance between it and her original skin remained.

"I sent Amondi away immediately," he told her.

Biting her cheek to hold back a sneer, Kat murmured, "Death escorted her there and back again. Are you an idiot? Or just racist?"

"Racist? Rather ridiculous when your species has only a single non-subdivided species, but I'll answer your call on prejudice. No, it was not her skin color or physical features which make her unwanted by me and the rest. It's her strength," Mah-Wærm confessed. "Do you realize how determined someone has to be to self-mutilate as she did? Her mind must be dizzy with the cruelties she's imagined, and that sort of imagination stems from experience. I have no desire to deal with a trauma-hardened woman when a, what did you call yourself? Ah, a privileged domesticated breed will do." He smirked as he loomed over her. "No amount of tenderness would win her over. She'd see straight through the half-truths of any affection I could offer."

"And now, so would I," Kat affirmed. A smile curled her lips without reaching her eyes. "I'd ask if you ever had intentions on anyone but Chelsea, but you've just proved that question moot."

With a shrug, he dismissed the question without giving a straight answer one way or the other. "Do you want to leave?"

"I do."

Releasing his grip on her wrist, the dictator took a step back. The doors opened, and Death stood waiting on the other side. With one last glance at the universe through a monster's window, Kat headed toward the door. Every question in her mind passed like a panic. Each as useless to her situation as the next and easy enough to dismiss when Death waited

318

for her. One, however, stuck. Pausing, Kat looked over her shoulder at Mah-Wærm. He had already turned away. His eyes locked on the stars once more.

"Why did you give Bel'von Jacobi's eyes?"

Silence stretched for a moment. Long enough for Kat to believe he would not speak. However, when she moved to leave again, Mah-Wærm commanded, "Another moment, Death," and the doors slammed shut as Death jumped back with a cut-off exclamation. Rather than answer her, he remained silent.

Kat crossed her arms and stormed back to him. "Well?"

"I wanted to see how you would react to seeing a loved one in another's face. All the pieces together but in the wrong setting," he explained. "I wanted you to feel the same sense of unease I felt when I saw your kind on that ship. That sort of grief to see faces you thought long dead." Mah-Wærm eyes shifted to her. "You unease me," he confessed, and when her brow furrowed, he continued, "You are me. In the end, you would pick the same moves – greater good, self-sacrifice, make yourself miserable – small because if there are too many, too strong, you'd see the universe collapse, and which is worse? Being a bit lonely? Or watching everything else die? In the end, you're me. And that's why you could never be Conquest."

The first laugh bubbled up so quickly she had no way of realizing what was to come before the sound escaped her lips. Every one which followed after came freely with her permission. Nothing had ever been so absurd. No one had ever spoken with such self-indulgent narcissism to her before. Mah-Wærm's eyes narrowed. Frowning, he clenched his fists like a melodramatic fool.

Smirking vindictively, she mocked him, "You're a complete moron. No, that would be an insult to morons everywhere. I would never kill humanity for you, for me, for anyone. There's no way it would be even close to reasonable. Do you really think you're the only one capable of keeping the universe safe? Is your narcissism only overshadowed by your victim complex? Or are they just really one and the same? Too bad you had Rachel killed. She would've had a field day with you."

As if he were a bull and her words a matador's cape, Mah-Wærm charged forward, crowding her against the golden doors. Compared to entrance, the two were like dead pixels on a television screen. Everything in the room modeled around being too small or too big in a universe which loomed as a constant reminder to the looker's insignificance. Tilting her head back, she smirked up at him, half-hoping she had infuriated him enough to slit her throat himself. He disappointed her again. Pressing his lips to hers, he kissed her like a branding iron. A shiver of numb uncertainty traveled down her spine. Her legs froze beneath her.

As he pulled away, his quicksilver eyes searched her face. "If I'm a narcissist, a bit of self-love would fall rather nicely into your opinion of me."

"Opinion?" she sneered. "You hand me facts. What you see in me is indifference. You killed the man I love, but I'm going to die soon too. In life, in death – it's all the same to me. You're too weak to face an eternity looking at someone who hates you, but at least Amondi would feel something toward you. I can't even muster pity anymore. You are so small, so insignificant compared to someone like Jacobi, and if the universe could steal him from me...well, you'll be dead soon enough."

Kat tilted her head back against the cold gold. A soft laugh slipped through her lips, and with a growl, he shoved her away, storming back to his window with his hackles raised. Against her back, the door opened. Spinning, she smiled at Death and waltzed down the hall. He followed; his helm lowered as he came to walk beside her.

"How did you do that?" he demanded.

Pausing, Kat raised a brow. "What? Annoy him? It's a talent."

"No. The door. How did you open the door?"

Crossing her arms over her chest, she ran her tongue over the tops of her molars. "What?" She glanced back at the door. "I opened that? No. He got tired of me and opened it. I didn't do that."

"No, you did." His lips curled into a small smile. "Three of four - the Architect made his choice."

"Oh, great. The ship likes me," Kat grumbled.

Beneath their feet, the floor sunk, dropping them down a level. Another level dropped in a ramp, and Kat stepped forward. Death kept pace beside her. Even as his helm rose, his smile remained. Long narrow corridors rippled around them. Nothing about the ship made sense. Like a strange immeasurable multi-layered cube, each shift left them in another straight hallway. If some consciousness within it liked

Kat, she wasn't exactly relieved though maybe that meant she'd actually end up where she intended. When they arrived back on the correct level by Kat's count, the floor twirled, spinning her in the right direction. Behind her, Death chuckled. When her glared toward him, he looked straight ahead without making a sound.

The wall opened, and Chelsea glanced up from her tablet. Her hair was precariously balanced in a bun on the top of her head. Blood stained the rug in splattered marks. Kat's heart dropped. Amondi was nowhere to be found. Death stepped up beside her, frowning as his helm retreated into his collar.

"Amondi's dead," Chelsea informed them.

Kat's gun dropped, and Death offered a hand. Bel'von trudged up behind them with two Vurtherar at his side. He glanced down at the plasma skipping around the veining stretches of pale blue on her black suit. With a sigh, the golden faced alien held out a hand.

"Amondi is dead," he confirmed. "She has been incinerated. Additionally, the Potentials are no longer permitted their suits."

Death's eyes narrowed. "I see."

Bel'von refocused on Kat. "I need your suit."

Inhaling, Kat released the tension in her shoulders. The plasma cannon retracted into the arm of the suit. Pulling at the collar of the suit, Kat traced her fingers around the edges. As she did so, the gloves retracted and, like a molting snake, she slipped out of the softening fabric as it deflated back to its original form. She stepped back, kicking the suit at Bel'von and sauntered into the room naked. Her eyes remained on Chelsea as she stepped through the drying blood, smearing it deeper into the carpet. One of the walls shifted. A tendril wrapped around one of the oversized sweaters and tossed the clothing at Kat. Catching them, she slipped the sweater over her head.

"I am now unarmed," Kat said. She spun to curtsey, nearly tripping over her own feet.

Bel'von scoffed, rolling Jacobi's eyes as he led the Vurtherar away. Death glanced between Chelsea and Kat. The blonde had already returned to her reading, but Kat watched Death. Their eyes met, and a smirk quirked the corner of the alien's lips before his helm rose and obscured his face once again. As the wall slid shut, Kat's eyes drifted to Chelsea. They were alone.

Chapter Eighteen

Killing weighed on the soul. Books told her that though common sense taught the lesson first. Kat never used a magnifying glass to set ants on fire. She also hadn't flinched when her mother taught her how to kill a chicken. Sometimes, death was necessary, but her mother assured her cruelty never was. Though warning bells rang in her mind, she pushed aside the adrenaline sending her heart to race. Perhaps there was a chance. Optimism reared its deadly head. If only she could reason with Chelsea, they could fight back together.

Chelsea reclined on the couch. Her eyes remained on the tablet in her lap, scanning whatever it said with such concentration that even as Kat approached her, the blonde didn't bother to look up. The confidence tore at Kat's conscience. Though the other woman trusted her, the misguided faith had nothing to do with their relationship and everything to do with overconfidence. Amondi had come for Chelsea, and someone had stopped her, but the guards had been removed. No one was here to save her. Kat's eyes shifted to the ship. This had to be a trap. They had said Conquest would pick being a Rider, and if she killed Chelsea, the warped minds of those involved could readily see her actions as acceptance.

"How are you going to kill me?" Kat asked.

Chelsea didn't bother glancing up from her reading. "There're scarves. Feel free to hang yourself."

"I'd prefer something more immediate."

"Then you should have convinced Amondi not to attack me," the blonde retorted, sliding a finger across the tablet.

Kat stepped closer. "How did you kill her?"

"I didn't. The insect thingy did it," Chelsea informed her. When Kat opened her mouth, Chelsea held up a single finger. "Don't care how you do it. Don't care when. It'll happen, so...leave me alone, kay?"

Standing in front of the last human left alive beside herself, Kat called, "Chelsea."

Chelsea's blue eyes jumped as she tilted her chin up to growl only to have her voice stolen as Kat slammed her fist into the other woman's throat. Gasping for breath, the blonde flailed as Kat's hands wrapped around her head, dragging her off the table. Kat slammed Chelsea's head against the corner of the table. With the first blow, Kat drew blood. By the second, Chelsea went still. Each blow after sent blood flying across the gray. Crimson drops splattered onto Kat's face.

Kat's pulse raced in her ears. Drumming thundered in her head, so she didn't hear the door on the wall open. Troops marched into the room. Bel'von grabbed one shoulder, pulling Kat back, but she swept his legs out from under him. Brain leaked through the gaps in Chelsea's skull. But it wasn't enough. As long as there was even a speck of her left, there remained a minute chance she could be brought back. That this would all be for nothing. Slamming her elbow against cartilage between Chelsea's ribs and sternum, Kat struggled to tear her apart with her bare hands.

The Vurtherar circled, enclosing around her. Spikes dropped from the ceiling. Tearing one from the ground, Kat sliced through the flesh, spreading the gore. Sound slowly returned with each slash. Someone screamed, and the blood and tears blurred the world into a swirl of gray. The cry echoed. Tearing at her eardrums, the scream rattled the frayed edges of Kat's nerves. All the walls dropped. Lanky creatures - like Thin-Limb - trudged forward. Their too long limbs shortened and lengthened with each stride. Through the mass of black suits, Death wove in a pale mist. His suit shimmered green as the light shifted. Beneath Chelsea, the floor glowed like it had with Qamar. A red arm wrapped around Kat's waist. Lifting her over the spikes, War dragged her back. His other arm stretched, and with a single spark, Chelsea's body burned. In the rush of the fire, the scream softened to a hoarse whisper, but the sound remained as War half-carried her through the crowd. Their eyes watched the black smoke rise.

"You are safe," Famine told her when War brought her to him.

Death crackled into being beside War. He held out his hands and took her from him. Shushing her, he ran a white gloved hand through her short hair. "Hush, you'll be okay."

"Let her scream. He'll correct her volume control first, and she'll be mute for ages before he realizes he overcorrected," War predicted. His hands twitched at his sides with every rise and fall of the agony-laden call.

All helms raised and opaque, they gathered round her like specters. In each shining surface, she could only see the dead. Marie painted in red. Qamar buried in the black. A thousand more in every speck of Death's vapors. His white became a shroud to the thousands she could never count or confirm with her own eyes or hands. Pulses ceased in space. Voiceless crying to an expanse of darkness.

The scream slowed. Kat closed her lips, furrowing her brow as she realized her part in the sound. Hatred boiled beneath her skin. Nothing in the killing had been kind. Cruelty laced the first blow. Rage tore through her with each subsequent until desperation and self-loathing took up the reins. Bile rose in her throat, and Kat fell limp against Death's chest. Covered in blood, brains and ash, Kat closed her eyes. Nothing mattered. She had won. Victory had never left a gaping hole in her chest.

Death pulled her close. His chin rested on the top of her head. Like a white sheet spread over furniture in an abandoned home, liquid metal rose through the floor. It swirled, mixing with bits and pieces from the Riders gathered tight around her. Pale and white and a swirl of black - small and veined. It ate away her clothes as it spread. As she leaned against Death's hold, her suit's helm rose. The metallic synthetics clicked into place. A shimmer at the edge of her eye before the suit locked around her. All around them, the Vurtherar gathered. Thin-Limb's gaseous based species lumbered into the gaps, but the insectoid guards shouted, gestured them back.

Bel'von stepped through the dust. Standing between War and Death, he lowered his helm. Golden skin and Jacobi's brown eyes stung. They were not his. Beyond everything else, the intent in them differed from the soft warmth she had always seen in them before his death.

"He'll need to be informed," Bel'von announced.

War snorted. "What makes you think he doesn't already know?"

"This wasn't planned. He didn't intend her to survive," Bel'von retorted.

Crossing his arms, War glimmered. The red of his suit swirled like Jupiter's storm in lighter hues across his chest. "What do you mean? He's been gunning for her from the start."

"No. He wanted Chelsea," Famine corrected.

"If he wanted the other one, the other one would be alive," War argued, and through the ground, Thin-Limb forced his way to the front. "Tsundroxini, he gave you the scores. Who was supposed to win?"

Kat tensed. Her breath paused in her lungs. Their words drifted around her, and though she heard them, they made no sense. "What?"

Orbs flew down from the ceiling as Thin-Limb squeaked, "Three contingencies."

Slamming his hand into the wall, War demanded, "Are you certain, Tsundroxini?"

"Yes. Three," the gas-based life form affirmed.

"Contingencies are not usual," Famine stated. Tilting his head, he shifted his weight back and forth between his legs. "There were no contingencies with War."

"Reptiles are predictable," Bel'von groused.

War grabbed the sharp lines of Bel'von's suit. Lifting him up off the ground, War growled, "Watch your tongue."

"I do, daily. It's new. Do you like it?" Bel'von drawled. His lip spread into a sly grin.

Tossing him aside, War crouched down beside Death and whispered in the other Rider's ear, "This was his plan. Wasn't it?"

Death squeezed Kat. His arms curled around her, pulling her further into his chest as he shifted to place himself cleanly between War and her. "Of course."

Famine hummed. "Death has lied."

"Death wouldn't lie to me," War claimed, but his voice wavered toward the end.

Kat pressed a hand against Death's chest. She pushed, but he did not move. Bel'von rubbed the bridge of his nose between his new eyes. The gestured moved in measured increments as if he had spent hours in a mirror practicing the expression. Tsundroxini leaned. His arms unrolled like fire hoses. They hung down by his sides, swinging back and forth as he inched closer. Bel'von slammed an arm into Tsundroxini's chest.

"Arms up," he commanded. While the other grumbled and did as commanded, the insectoid sauntered over to kneel beside Death. "Phase One: Complete. Knock the new recruit out."

"What?" Kat exclaimed, struggling against Death's hold.

Death held her tightly in place. "Bel'von, explain yourself."

A smirk twisted his lips, and with his new tongue and teeth, the quirk remained even as he spoke, "You didn't think he'd be surprised, did you? Three contingencies - Chelsea survives - damaged, that one survives, and all are dead. That one survived. Phase Two: Modification Underway. Well, once she's unconscious."

Electricity gathered along her arms, but when she shot her plasma cannon against Death's chest, the charge traveled along the fanning particles of mist around his edges. Pressing her lips together, she shoved him, clawed at his armor, screamed, and slammed her helmet against his. Nothing she did moved the white-suited alien. Spines grew from her suit. They slipped right through him as if he were intangible to everything save to contain her. Emotionally and physically exhausted, Kat sagged against him. They would destroy her. Like the dead, she would be taken apart and scattered. Pieces of her would remain. Maybe she'd have the same eyes, or perhaps she would wake to a face she didn't know, and her body would become just as frayed as her mind.

Death's fingers slid beneath her armor. The metal pierced her skin as he whispered, "You have survived. Keep surviving."

Cold flooded her skin. Gritting her teeth, she fought the shivers which traveled the length of her spine. Goosebumps rose along her arms beneath the swirling black, white, and blue of her armor. Her eyelids drooped. As her head fell forward to press her forehead against his shoulder, she cursed him and herself. Space - the final frontier. A joke made with slow cruelty. With this ridiculous finality, Kat gave into the cold. Her eyes shut, and darkness consumed her.

Chapter Nineteen

Frank Sinatra crooned. His voice stretched through the air like sweet syrup. Eyes closed, Kat struggled to lift her eyelids. Light shimmered in the distance. A glow on the edge of the darkness wrapped around her brain. Stretching her spine, she turned her head. Her right cheek rubbed against cool, smooth fabric. Through her eyelashes, the light filtered, and white consumed her view. Drab white walls - duller than those she recalled - stared back. Curved, vertical plastic curtains blocked the sunlight which peaked through the bottom of the window. Square lines crisped the corners of the room. Frowning, Kat glanced to the ceiling. Slightly off white, the squared panels were dented and spotted with holes.

Her brows furrowed. Chairs lined the right. Two near the bed and one further off - all were plastic with hard cushions on their seat and back. Leaning toward the side of the bed, Kat gritted her teeth. Agony tore down her abdomen. Pressing a hand against the new skin, she continued on. Slightly pink-white tiles covered the floor. All hues of white clashed. The tones mixed with fluorescent lights and streaked with sterile cleanings. Still, Sinatra sang.

Over his voice, a beep echoed. Turning her head, she glared up at the heart monitor. A tangle of wires stretched down beneath the gown they had dressed her in, but the intravenous line in her left hand stunned her. White medical tape held it in place. Her door was open, and other doors were visible through the hall. On her left, another bed sat. On a curved metal rail, a curtain sat, but someone had pushed it back to reveal the door. Two people walked by the room. Blue scrubs covered them, and they murmured back and forth, pointing at a clipboard in one of their hands.

A flush roared over Sinatra. Kat's eyes jumped to the end of her bed. A door stood with a false wood finish. Opening the door, Jacobi stepped out. He was dead. There was no way he should be standing. Blinking, she pressed up against the mattress.

"Kat?" Jacobi called. His voice was the same. In his brown eyes, she saw the warmth she had always seen before. "Thank god you're awake!"

Kat shook her head. "You're dead," she told him. "This isn't real."

His dark brows furrowed. Sitting on the edge of the bed, he reached for her hand. When she pulled away, he froze. Jacobi lifted his hand to run her fingers against her cheek. They trailed over her jaw to cup her neck. Running his thumb along her cheek, he bit his lip. A chill ran through her bones. Every move he made reminded her of him, but she had watched him die. Standing here before her as a ghost, Jacobi couldn't be real. From Bel'von's antennae to some shifting illusion by Famine in her head, anything on the alien ship could have created the false image before her.

"You aren't real," she repeated.

Jacobi shook his head. "The Intrepid blew up when it exited the atmosphere. You got me to the pod in time, but we crash landed when some debris hit us. You've been unconscious for three days."

"We were exiting the solar system. We left the atmosphere months ago." Or longer. Without anything to keep track of time, the weight and possibility of years crashed down on her. "Stop this. I know you aren't him."

Shifting back to stand, the false Jacobi sighed. "Your parents are here."

"No, they aren't."

"I'll go get them. Kat…" his lips moved, but no words came out. "Just…"

Cold stretched through her fingertips. In the back of her mind, metal shifted on metal. Fingers curled and flexed. Whispers of flowers stung her nose though there were none in the room. Closing her eyes, Kat stretched her consciousness into the Hive. Just outside the door of this room, Bel'von paced. When her mind slipped into the otherness of the Hive's connection, she stilled. A world stretched before her. Golden and bright green with edges of summer warming the thin forelimbs of the insectoid. Opening her eyes, she met Mah-Wærm's questioning gaze. Though she couldn't see the quicksilver behind the mask of Jacobi's brown, she glared at him with a sneer.

"Today, tomorrow, the next…I won't be Conquest here."

Furrowed brows and then a smirk. The illusion faded. Dressed in black, the dictator stepped forward, and the room fell to pieces. A starker white subsumed the walls. They were in the infirmary on the ship.

"Today, tomorrow? You think small. I have the rest of eternity to learn your mind. To learn how to unmake you," he told her.

A laugh bubbled out her lips. "Same."

Nodding, he grinned. Something feral shined through the white of his teeth and the darkness shadowing his eyes. "You do. I'll be excited to see it." The bed beneath her stood, shoving her forward. Around her, the floor rose. "Don't be afraid, little conqueror. I will wake you up when we arrive. You need to see your *Earth* burn, after all. Nothing quite like it."

Chapter Twenty

Gold shimmered. A veil spread across the void of space, separating the Earth and its orbit in its entirety. When one of their ships approached, the gold spiraled and reached out. Tendrils drew the ship closer, dissolving every inch until the undulating surface stilled for a breath before shifting like an ocean's tide. Another ship followed. Then another traveled in its wake. Nobody breached. Nothing reached the other side or managed to escape once the nanites took hold.

"What is it?" Mah-Wærm asked.

Crouched on the floor amongst blankets and pillows, he rested his chin on his knee as he studied the shield. War paced in the corner. His eyes avoided Kat. Whatever Famine had done failed to dilute his rage. If only she could catch his gaze, a glance – a smirk – anything could press against the wound of Marie's death, and maybe – just maybe that would be enough to send him over the edge. Cuffs bound her arms behind her back. On her own, death wasn't an option, but War's weapons twitched with each tightening of his fists.

Fingers grabbed her chin, wrenching her gaze forward. Death clucked his tongue. "You were asked a question."

336

"I don't know."

"Lies," War spat.

"Unimportant." Mah-Wærm stretched, uncurling to press a hand against the view screen. "How do we get through it?"

"You can't," Kat said.

Running his tongue along his teeth, the dictator sighed. "This is where you tell me that one of the others would know more than you."

"This is a combined global effort. Even if one of us had known about part of it, nobody would've been able to tell you how to get through it. We weren't that kind of ship." But the dread which rolled in her stomach calmed. Amondi had been right. Earth was safe. "Have you tried your biggest explosive?"

War snorted, slamming his fist into the wall. Beneath his feet, the floor shifted, and he vanished from view. Mah-Wærm traced the edges of Earth's silhouette. "He's too emotional, Death."

"You're just upset you won't get to make me a collector's item." Kat shrugged, smirking at the hope which glowed brighter with each second she held Earth - safe and out of the mad man's reach - within her sight. "Big bad emperor wasted all this time. You tortured and killed everybody else on that ship, and now – now your little ritual can't happen. Might as well kill me."

Hand dropping to his side, the man faced her. "I am immortal. The universe is endless." His lips peeled into a joyless smile. "Perhaps when I have conquered more, this little cage will have suffocated your pathetic species. Perhaps they will grow bold.

337

Think they have outlasted me. One way or another, this ends the same. Earth dies. I live. I rule. I win."

"But not today," said Kat.

The muscles in his jaw twitched. Shifting to stare out at his battalions as they failed again and again to pierce Earth's golden shield, Mah-Wærm crossed his arms over his chest. "Put Conquest back to sleep."

A wall rose, and the floor rippled, sending them through the ship's shifting interior. Guiding Kat by her bound arms, Death remained silent, which was perfectly fine with the human. Tears gathered in her eyes as her lips strained in a smile she couldn't and didn't want to will away. Earth was safe. Even as the ship built a stasis tube around her – hiding Kat away in a make-shift coffin, joy thrummed in her blood.